I0607187

PRAISE FOR THE DIGITAL NOW

Silver Medal, Science Fiction, 2016 Feathered Quill Book Awards

Finalist, Science Fiction, 2016 Pacific Book Review Book Awards

"A well written dystopian novel that fits perfectly into the genre and tells an excellent story." Ryan Jordan, Readers' Favorite

"Carly (Westing) is a very interesting, well developed character who is not the typical heroine...I found her honesty refreshing and this made her character very likeable and authentic."
Janelle Fila, Readers' Favorite

"Very interesting and complex: This is a dark vision of the future with many of the themes characteristic of classic dystopian literature but with a modern spin...completely enthralling, terrifying and unique."
Pacific Book Review

"The complexity of the world, particularly in terms of cyber tech, reminds me of Masamune Shirow's 'Ghost in the Shell'...'The Digital Now' is an intriguing read with an imaginative premise and plot."
Lit Amri, Readers' Favorite

"This is an author who has given his dystopian world real legs to stand on. His characters are attractive, the pace is all action, and the City itself is a riveting place to spend some time...one read of an Allnach title and you'll be a fan for life!"
Amy Lignor, Feathered Quill Reviews

THE DIGITAL

ROLAND ALLNACH

Copyright ©2015 by Roland Allnach

All rights reserved. This book or any portion thereof may not be reproduced or used in any manner whatsoever without the express written permission of the publisher except for the use of brief quotations in a book review.

Published by Tabalt Press, Kings Park, New York
ISBN 978-0-9967854-0-2

Original cover artwork by Alicia Hollinger, whose creative talent has summoned a striking vision of Ms. Carly Westing.
View her artwork at: www.wonderlandart.biz

Editorial and layout services provided by Nancy Barnes, whose indispensable skills and support helped bring this book to light.
www.storiestotellbooks.com

To those who believe in me...
for helping me believe in myself

CONTENTS

FICTION by ROLAND ALLNACH

Prism

Prism collects seventeen stories into one volume and follows a trail of diverse genres and narrative forms. From literary fiction to speculative fiction, from humor to horror, from tragedy to mythical poetry, **Prism** presents a wide-ranging journey of contemplations on the human condition.

*Silver Medal, Short Stories, 2015 Feathered Quill Book Awards; Winner - Short Stories, 2015 Pacific Book Review Book Awards

"Allnach delivers a wonderful collection of stories in Prism." **Lisa Jones, Readers' Favorite**

"A timeless, exquisite collection of short stories that's bound to leave you mesmerized and awestruck. The collection is a masterpiece." **Rattan Whig, Readers' Favorite**

"Allnach has a voice that speaks so loud readers lose themselves in the stories ... A dazzling collection." **Amy Lignor, Feathered Quill Reviews**

"Prism is a book of stories written with precision ... it chisels out what is needed with laser description, true to the ear dialogue, characters built into believability, and stories that capture the attention. This collection is to be savored, read again and again." **F.T. Donereau, Rebecca's Reads**

Oddities & Entities

Oddities & Entities is a surreal, provocative anthology of six tales within the supernatural, paranormal, and horror genres, exploring a definition of life beyond the fragile vessel of the human body.

Oddities & Entities has been recognized with seven national book awards, with multiple awards from Readers' Favorite Book of the Year Awards and USA Book News Best Book Awards. Single awards include National Indie Excellence Awards, Foreword Reviews Book of the Year Awards, and Pacific Book Reviews Book Awards.

"If you only read one book this year, make it this one. Be prepared to have your comfort zone challenged." **Lee Ashford, Readers' Favorite**

"Allnach is a master storyteller with a powerful pen. The stories are gritty, gruesome, bewitching, and beautiful." **Cynthia Brian, NY Times Bestselling author and host of "Starstyle"**

"This is a great book. Nothing you expect to happen happens. The author keeps you thinking and turning the page over and over." **Jason Lulos, Pacific Book Review**

Remnant

Remnant is a stirring, thought-provoking anthology of three novellas within the speculative and science fiction genres. Following a path from the shores of a doomed paradise, through an illusory reality, and ending in a devastated future, *Remnant* is both the sum of these tales and the element that binds them together.

Remnant has been recognized with four national book awards from National Indie Excellence Awards, Readers' Favorite Book of the Year Awards, USA Book News Best Book Awards, and Feathered Quill Book of the Year Awards.

"Each of the three novellas is a beautifully crafted gem of a story." **Douglas R. Cobb, Bestsellersworld.com**

"Allnach's writing style can be described as smart, elegant, and addicting." **San Francisco Book Review**

"Roland Allnach is destined to become recognized for his contributions in whatever genre of writing he may choose." **Richard R. Blake, Reader Views**

"With Remnant, *Roland Allnach presents three novellas that promise to haunt the readers long after the cover has been closed. A nearly perfect gem of sci-fi."* **Peter Dabbene, Foreword, *Clarion Review***

ILL THE CONTINENTALS, THEIR ROCKETS make me mental...
Carly hummed along with the riotous song bouncing in her head. She'd heard the tune countless times, but even so she lost the words beneath its pounding rhythm. It was good just to feel it in her bones and let its infectious energy buoy her mood.

She popped a fresh clip into her repeater and chambered the first round, her blood simmering with the anticipation of violence. Her palm slapped home the weapon's bolt before she cradled the repeater to her chest plate. It felt right to hold it close. It would feel even better when she pulled the trigger and the stock pounded her shoulder.

Hungry for that moment, she pulled at the chinstrap of her helmet as she looked out from the windshield of her armored Patrol car. Crouched between the front seats, she could still make out the chaos of a riot through the rainy night. Burning tires littered the street, their heavy smoke skating over the teased surface of puddles. The neon glow of storefronts went dark as bricks and public sanitation pails were thrown through windows.

Her patrolmate held a steady stare through the windshield. "Come on, Chap," she said, encouraging him with a poke of her elbow. "Chiggers to this. We go in hot, now."

He looked to her and returned her nudge. There was no mistaking the humor in his eyes. "Easy does it. Already looking for another good aim?"

"Why not?" Carly raised an eyebrow. "I already made it on *Killshot*. I even got a move to a new domicile out of it."

He looked back to the net screen on the car's console to watch their communication bands. "We'll see what tonight brings. No word about coverage yet."

Carly kept her gaze out the windshield. "Just another day, right?"

He was about to answer when he pressed his headset to his ear and held up a hand. "Copy, this is Chapel," he said before wrapping his hand over the microphone and mouthing *Beak-nose* to Carly. He pointed to the net screen and let go of the mike. "We copy your orders, Patrolmaster Bayard."

Carly shifted back toward the sliding door of the crew area. "Are we going hot?"

He took off his headset and tossed it beside the net screen. "Drive Control passed word to Bayard. Non-lethal intervention only. Suppression protocol. No firearms."

Carly admired her repeater before stowing it with a muttered curse. She came by Graham and rested against the side of his seat. "So, I guess we do it up close and personal." She leaned over with a smile as she put her lips by his ear. "Patrolman Chapel, are you ready to crack some heads?"

He reached up to caress her cheek. "Right proper, Patrolman Westing."

Carly opened the crew door and hopped out. Rain dripped from her helmet. Graham came around the front of the car as a second vehicle rolled to a stop. Two patrolmen from their detachment hopped out to join them. Oboe was a stocky brute of a man, while Gwen had a lean build similar to Carly. Unlike Carly, who kept her dark hair short, Gwen had a knot of strawberry blond hair poking from the back of her helmet. Carly glanced at Oboe before looking back at Graham. He was a little taller than her, and his body was a solid wall of Patrol-honed musculature.

Gwen hooked a thumb toward the turreted machine cannons of her car. "You mates are on your own. Bayard wants me on the turret. The cars stay here."

Oboe pointed to his side. "We're to move down the alley, through a building, and come out at the tail of the mob."

Graham looked up. "Keep those roofs clear, Gwen."

"Drive Control says there's no vertical threat," Gwen said as she walked to her car. "You should be good. Street level engagement only."

Oboe came over to Carly and Graham and punched their shoulders. "Are we ready?"

Carly slapped Oboe's chest plate. "Crack a few heads and then crack a few bottles of Heavy, right?" she said as she pulled free the length of her civi-stick.

Graham and Oboe clacked their sticks with Carly's. Graham nodded. "Heavy, domicile, bulls on the rise. We're Patrol."

"Nobody better," Oboe said.

Carly nodded. "And we never back down."

They jogged down the alley, found the rear entrance Patrolmaster Bayard had described to Oboe, and made their way into an apartment building. An unlucky resident came down the stairs and received a prompt greeting from Graham's civi-stick. The man collapsed and tumbled down the last two steps to the floor. Carly ignored the resident's slumped shadow as she stepped over his prone form and advanced through the darkened lobby to the front doors. She sank to a crouch, waving Graham and Oboe forward until she signaled them to duck and cover.

She was anxious to charge out and swing away, except they wouldn't stand a chance if the mob made a determined turn. They'd be overwhelmed, regardless of armor, weapons, and training, and she had no intention of getting meat-farmed before she could move to her new domicile. Besides, whether people in the mob were citizens or just dissident cones wasn't important. It wasn't just a riot; it was an unendorsed riot. There wouldn't be any media coverage. Even if she blew someone's head off, no waiting camera would make a record of the shot.

The tail end of the mob passed by. She turned to Oboe and Graham. The look in their eyes changed, just as she knew the look in her eyes changed. Predatory thrill and its wild excess hardened their stares even as it lit their gazes. They waited for the signal, hands wrapped tight about their civi-sticks.

It came soon enough in the metallic grate of a bullhorn.

"Disperse immediately. You are ordered to disperse."

Screams sounded out from the far end of the street. Carly looked over her shoulder. Graham pointed out their directions. Carly had the middle. He put out his hand and counted off his fingers.

One, two, three—

Carly threw open the doors of the building, startling the people already panicked by the sudden onslaught of Patrol ahead of them. Graham and Oboe came out to either side of her, cracking their sticks into the heads of two people. Carly already had her target in sight, a lumbering mountain of a laborer standing straight in front of her with a pipe clenched in his hand. She planted her feet and swung with everything she had, the end of the stick whipping in a vicious upward arc that smashed into the laborer's cheekbone. Blood and skin took flight from the man's face. Carly swore she almost took off the top of his head before he toppled back and flattened a woman beneath his weight.

His fall was already forgotten as Carly bulled her way forward with Graham and Oboe. They smashed anyone in their path, taking no care as to male or female, young or old. When Carly had no space to swing she drove the stick out to crack ribs; when someone tried to fend her off she struck with the stick before driving her heel into the person's gut. She swung low to collapse the knees of those taller than her, swung across her chest to shatter the elbows of people with weapons, swung over her shoulder to bring the merciless end of the stick straight down on the foreheads of those shorter than her.

Screams and blood filled the air as the panicked rioters rushed about in a futile effort to escape. A few of them fought back, crazed with the delusion of resistance, only to discover that resistance tripled the beating they received. A window shattered when Graham threw someone, and Oboe let out a shout when he slammed his stick so hard across a defiant rioter's nose that the man's face collapsed into his skull.

Carly lowered her arms, her chest heaving, as the mob fled. She unclipped her helmet's chinstrap and surveyed the street. What was once a swarm of rioters had been reduced to a squirming mass of broken flesh crying for help. Several bands of strays ran about, but they didn't get far. Cornered on the sealed street, they were chased down by other members of Patrol and received savage group beatings. Trucks from Drive Control were already rolling toward the scene. Their little blue marker lights swirled across the heights of the buildings and reflected on long sheets of polarized glass.

The metallic voice of the bullhorn continued to shout the order to disperse.

Graham and Oboe returned to Carly, shaking their fists in the air. Oboe paused to stomp someone who grabbed at his leg, drawing a laugh from Graham. Carly slid her stick into its belt loop and opened her hands to the mess of humanity around her. "Got them all; got them good!"

Graham looked to her. His eyes bulged.

Before Carly understood his alarm a brick crashed to the street beside her. She whipped her stick free. Her gaze darted upward, too late.

The brick was just a shadow in the dark. Shadows, she thought, weren't supposed to hurt anyone. Shadows were supposed to bring peace.

The brick crashed into her helmet. It was more a white flash than a bolt of pain that plowed through her awareness, but she had no time to consider that distinction. Unstrung, unconscious, she dropped to the street like a pile of uncooked dough.

| 0 | 0 | 0 |

"SHE'LL BE FINE," SHE HEARD a man's voice say. A bright, tight cone of light swung from one of her eyes to the other. Someone flicked her forehead to summon a reflexive jolt. "See? She took a good shot, but her brains didn't get scrambled. Not much in there to damage anyway," the man said before tapping a finger on the bridge of her nose. A pill was shoved into her mouth. "Swallow that, Patrolman."

The pill slithered down her throat as she swung at the light in her face. Her eyes came to focus on the interior of her Patrol car, where she was laid out on her back in the crew area. She propped herself up on her elbows and realized she was still at the riot scene. "Time for some Heavy?" she said, her voice hoarse.

Graham was sitting sideways in the driver's seat to watch her. His eyes were narrowed with concern. "Hey, you alright?"

She was about to give him a defiant *right proper* when a long nose zoomed into her sight, its protrusion flanked by a set of pale irises. Her blue eyes widened as she blinked to focus. Recognition dawned through her muddy vision. "Beak—" she started to say, but then caught herself. "Patrolmaster Bayard." She coughed. "I'm, I'm still good to go—where's my stick?"

Bayard grabbed her neck cowl and pulled her upright. He patted her cheek with the back of his bony hand while he looked into her eyes. "No, Patrolman Westing, I think you're done for the night." He turned to Graham. "Take us back to her domicile, Patrolman Chapel. I'll see she gets inside."

Graham hesitated a moment before nodding. "Sir," he said and started the car.

Bayard stared at Carly with a smile, the corners of his mouth looking like they would split open the sides of his narrow face. He waved to her before letting her flop on the floor of the car.

| 0 | 0 | 0 |

HER EYES OPENED AT THE hiss of elevator doors. She staggered along, her arm draped over Bayard's shoulders as he led her toward her domicile. He stopped before her door and she waited while he dug through the pockets of her bodysuit to find her security card. When the lock clicked open he led her in. Her arm slid away from him as she stepped into the cramped space of her living quarters. She stared out her windows, her arms hanging at her sides, her head swimming between the impact of the brick and the pill that was stuffed down her throat.

Bayard lingered behind her. She could see his reflection in the window. "You're off duty, Patrolman," he said.

She replied with a nod. Her fingers found the buckles of her body armor and dropped it piece by piece to the floor. She shrugged off her armor vest, pushed off her cracked helmet, pulled off her boots, and unzipped her bodysuit. The suit slipped down as she rolled her shoulders free and sank to a crumpled mass around her ankles. She stood there, naked except for a black sleeveless shirt, as she shook her feet free of the suit.

Bayard shoved aside her equipment with his foot. He took the bottom of her shirt and lifted it, watching as reflex summoned her to pull the shirt over her head and drop it on her bunk. He looked at the shirt, still able to pick out the letters across the front. Large and blue, they spelled out the name ENDO.

The color matched her eyes.

"Patrolmaster?"

He stared at her naked back. "Call me Alden, please."

Her vacant gaze lingered on her windows. "Why did my city hurt me?"

"The city belongs to Drive Control and Central. It's not yours."

Her head sank. "Okay."

He looked her over, his gaze darting to the windows. They were polarized, so no one could see in, but he wasn't concerned with privacy. He wanted to see the rest of her, the tight, aerobic tone of her combat trained physique, the alluring taper of her waist, the small globes of her breasts, the graceful length of her neck, her parted lips beneath the smooth curve of her cheeks. He stared into the vacant reflection of her bottomless blue eyes before resting his gaze on her neck.

He licked a finger and traced it down the length of her back.

She turned to stare over her shoulder.

"Such a lovely specimen," he whispered to himself. He met her gaze. "Okay?"

Her empty, dilated eyes held to his before she looked away. "Okay."

He rested his hand between her shoulders. Her body was loose, devoid of the taught energy that fueled her aggression during the riot, but he knew the explosive savagery that lurked within her. It thrilled him as if he held a grenade with the pin pulled. His heart pounded with the risk of imminent annihilation.

The excitement was too much for him to resist. He slid his hand up her neck to grab her short locks as he nibbled on her shoulder. It only took a quick tug of her hair to shove her against the wall, given the confines of her single room domicile. He grinned as he thought of her nipples pressed against the damp concrete. Two little kicks against the inside of her ankles moved her feet apart. He unzipped his bodysuit with one hand as he kept a tight hold on her hair. Nostrils flared, teeth clenched, he grabbed her hip and pushed into her.

He whispered into her ear. Her eyes did not open.

| 0 | 0 | 0 |

"WESTING, CARLY. ACTIVE STATUS. CALLBACK DELAY INITIATED."

Carly groaned in the wake of the synthetic voice, the small sphere from which it came covered by the drooping edge of her blanket. She had no interest in moving, but her eyelids crept open to find the ceiling and its idle fan. Her net screen mumbled away, folded flat against the wall over her head to keep the never-ending programs out of her waking gaze. She heard the patter of raindrops against the slanted outer sills of her windows.

Just another day.

She ran her hands through the disheveled mass of her short, black hair. She pulled at the chaotic locks between her tingling fingers until she heard the low echo of a memory, a little gray thing that nagged the raw edge of her awareness as a single whispered word.

Nimbus.

She shook her head and dismissed the memory with a silent curse. She rolled on her side and sat up after grabbing the beeping black sphere of the reporter orb. With two angry shakes it went silent, and she stole enough time to look over the haphazard pile of gear on the floor of her domicile.

The beep returned with a lower, angry tone. "WESTING, CARLY, ACTIVE—"

"Confirm! Westing, Carly, five-four-six, two-three-two, five-one-ten."

The sphere went silent.

Her instilled sense of duty caused her to stir, tightening her legs to drive her from bed. It only took three shaky steps to cross her single room domicile to her sink. She grabbed the metal basin, ran the cold water, and dunked her head. The chill pressed through her skull, and she held still to let the water pierce her temples like two spikes. When her lungs ached for air she lifted her head to stare at herself in the little mirror over her sink. A deep purple bruise poked out from the wet tangle of her hair. Her eyes narrowed as she probed the welt with a cautious finger.

The void within her mind began to fill with shadows. She remembered the sprawled bodies of the mob. She remembered being laid out from the brick. It explained the dull ache in her head.

Just a shadow.

Her eyes widened as her stare lingered on the bruise. She blinked and leaned toward the mirror, her focus dwelling on the bruise as she neared her reflection. It wasn't so much knowing the bruise was a bruise that disturbed her, but knowing *how* the bruise became a bruise was something quite different. Her skin crawled as her stomach knotted with trepidation. It was dangerous to wonder the how or why of things. Not only was she aware of that standard, enforcing it was her duty.

"Cones," she said with disdain as she grabbed the towel hanging on the wall beside the mirror. She dried her hair and hung the towel, only for it to slip off the hook and fall on the floor. Her lips fell in a frown before she waved and turned away to pull on her bodysuit.

A single step put her before the large rectangular locker of her dispensary. From the top she took out a box of Shaky Flakes, poured them into the metered bowl on the dispensary's weigh plate, and returned the gray cereal box. From the bottom of the dispensary she opened her cold storage and pulled out a waxed carton of Moo-ju to pour the white liquid on her flakes.

Shaky Flakes and Moo-ju, breakfast for good drive.

With her bowl in hand she opened a shallow drawer beneath her sink to produce a metal spoon. She devoured the cereal at once, the flakes crackling in her mouth as she locked out the windows that formed the exterior wall of her domicile. A sprawling urban landscape met her gaze. Obscured in the hazy drizzle, she still knew it as a scattered collection of gray buildings beneath a gray sky, matching the gray of her Patrol bodysuit.

She ate with the City of Seven Hills—her city—reflected on her eyes.

|0|0|0|

SHE SAT ON THE FRONT steps of her building, once again probing the lump on her temple. Her helmet hung off the back of her neck cowl. Its padded interior was soft but still antagonized the bruise. It would probably annoy her all day, the stupid little thing. At least the headache had eased up.

She dropped her hand from her temple and frowned. She couldn't wait to get her hands on the first cone that stepped out of line.

A mischievous grin crept across her lips as she looked down the street. A small knot of children stood beneath the corner streetlight and the mumbling programs of its net screen. The children were laughing as they took turns splashing their booted feet in a puddle beside the curb. They looked like little dolls beneath the bright colors of their slickers, a splash of red, yellow, two blues, a violet; joyful splashes of color in a world of gray.

They were part of Rainbow Go, reminding Carly of her own time in the youth training program. Rainbow Go had fun with little games and splashing in puddles.

Patrol had fun with drunken riots and smashing heads.

She took her repeater off her shoulder and leaned her cheek on its muzzle guard. One of the children looked to her. Carly waved, but the child turned away in haste. The local kids knew she was part of Patrol and what she did as part of Central. They might shy from her intimidating presence in their youth but, in the end, she knew some of them would be part of Patrol—at least the ones that didn't get drafted into the ranks of Central's bureaucrats. It was the way of things, and that was that.

She savored the thought, the elegant simplicity of Central's way. Yet, as the moments passed and the idea grew of those happy little children being part of the life Carly knew under Central, so too her heart grew heavy. She dropped her hand and let it dangle over her knee.

Little cones, some of them, I bet. No difference.

Her hand returned to her temple.

One way or the other, we get them all in the end. It's just easier to catch them early.

She looked away before closing her eyes.

| 0 | 0 | 0 |

GRAHAM GLANCED FROM THE ROAD to watch Carly as she went through the vehicle's maintenance list. Their armored car rumbled around them as Graham drove down the street. Carly felt his stare as she imagined him visualizing the bruise on the side of her head. She turned to him. "I'm fine, Chap."

He nodded before looking back to the road. The traffic grew in volume as they drove across the city, leaving Carly's Danfield apartment quadrant behind them. "Kilby quad's a mess," Graham said, his gaze darting to Carly at every opportunity. "Riot was bad. You're the only one that got hurt."

"Did we get the chigger that hit me with that brick?"

Graham shook his head. "No. Roof was empty when I got up there. Don't worry. We'll get the prick, and then we'll have our fun."

"Right proper to that," Carly said with a sigh. "What's the word from Patrol?"

"Bayard called on the line when I was driving over. Old Beak-nose is all crabby."

Carly's eyes narrowed for a moment before she shook her head at Graham's mention of Bayard. "Crabby about me getting hurt, or crabby about the coverage?"

Graham tipped his head as he came to a stop. A bright yellow bus filled with children clad in colored slickers passed before the sloped hood of the car. The drizzle became a downpour. "Coverage," he said at last.

Carly tucked away the checklist. "It wasn't an endorsed riot. You know how it goes. Local envens have coverage rights. Patrol only gets the riots when we sponsor them."

"No matter to that, the Beak is crabby," Graham said with a sigh.

"No matter to that," Carly echoed, keying the display screen on the dashboard to cycle the car's ammo counts. "Hey, you know, I'll be changing envens when I move."

Graham's eyebrows rose. "You don't say?"

"I—" She rapped a fist on the dashboard. "Shit. Stop the car."

Graham grunted and swerved, the car bucking as the large front tires rolled over the curb and onto the sidewalk. Pedestrian traffic scattered at the intrusion of the menacing car and its armored mass. Only one man remained, a cowering figure that sank to the concrete beneath a poster covered in graffiti. Carly was out the door, her civi-stick raised high and threatening, before Graham could even engage the car's foot brake. Her helmet dangled from her neck cowl by its retaining strap. Graham stepped from the car and propped the butt of his repeater on his hip. He surveyed the street traffic as she shouted at the cringing man.

Carly jammed the end of her civi-stick under the man's chin. She pushed in and up, giving the man no option to breathe except by rising to his feet. It was a prod-and-lift, one of Patrol's favorite methods of intimidation. She kept some inward pressure on the man's throat just to be sure he didn't get any ideas more stupid than the one that caught her attention from the car.

She rested a hand on her thigh mount and popped the buckle on her sidearm as she stared into the man's eyes. It was tempting to pull her gun and meat-farm him right there on the street. No one would say anything. She was Patrol. The anticipation of venting her morning's frustration for the welt on her head tightened her arm. She pushed harder on the civi-stick.

The man gasped and raised his hands in surrender.

She bared her clenched teeth before backing off. It was a routine defacement intervention, nothing more. She pointed at the poster beside the man, the graffiti laden poster that was the source of the man's violation. It was a large placard of a silver-haired, hawkish military officer, face uplifted, eyes determined. The words beneath, though, were the problem. "That's not Standard," she said as she looked back to the cowering man. "Don't disgrace General Asper by putting some silly-speak over his recruitment call. No silly-speak allowed. Rip it down."

The man nodded amid his trembling. He sprang into action, hoping to avoid what loomed ahead of him. It was pathetic. His meek obedience betrayed the very guilt of his crime in defacing the poster.

Carly watched as the man clawed at the paper. As much as she wanted to put a hole in his head she couldn't shoot someone for a simple silly-speak offense. He wasn't the one that had hit her with the brick, but he could be a target for her anger. It would be bad drive to let it go to waste.

She planted her feet and rolled her shoulders. "Turn around, fucker."

The man trembled as he glanced at her.

She put her civi-stick to work with a three-swing punishment. The first swing went to the back of his knees. He staggered before going down with a shriek. The second swing was to the back of his head, a vicious strike that drove his face straight into the wall before him. It brought a thankful end to his annoying cry. He flopped over, senseless. Carly planted her boot on his elbow before the third swing smashed the fingers of his limp right hand.

Graham's head bobbed with each strike. "That's three."

Carly stepped back, her chin held high. "Right proper."

Graham looked about. He lingered by the driver's door, rain dripping from the rim of his helmet as he surveyed the street with a predatory glare. Satisfied, he nodded and settled in the driver's seat.

Carly hesitated a moment, letting the rain soak her hair as she stared at her handiwork. She glanced at her civi-stick before shaking the water from her head and strolling back to the car, her frustration somewhat satiated. After settling in her seat she typed at the dash screen, mocking the perpetrator as she imitated him with a diminutive yelp. Graham laughed. She eased, giving him a wink as she hit the enter key to send her report. "Okay, the file's logged with Drive Control. Pickup crew is on the way."

"Right," Graham replied and released the brake. He pulled off the sidewalk and continued their drive to Patrol headquarters. He remembered their conversation after watching another yellow bus pass by their gray car. "So, tell me about this new enven."

She relaxed in her seat and rested an elbow on the door. "Well, I'm looking at either StarNet or BlueNet, depending what quad I get. I'm hoping for StarNet. Then we can watch *Riot* and *Killshot* right after shift."

"Outstanding," Graham said. "Maybe we'll down a little Heavy while we get naked and let our bulls rise. Sound proper?"

Her eyelids drooped over a wide smile. "Sounds *right* proper, Patrolman Chapel."

| 0 | 0 | 0 |

CARLY SAT IN BAYARD'S OFFICE and watched him pace behind his desk as he lectured her. Her gaze wandered over the office as his words went in one ear and out the other. There were two file cabinets, a black desk of stamped sheet metal with a black resin surface, a black reporter globe to the right side, a black armchair with four coaster wheels—she could've been in any office in the city. The chair was the only testament to Bayard's authority, evidenced by its high back and cushioned armrests.

A map of the city hung to her left where the desk met the wall. She knew it well. The city sat with its seven hills curved around one edge of the distant Downlow, the massive, sunken concrete dome that entombed the waste pile of the old city. Blue lines denoted the city's quads; red lines the different enven zones.

She licked her lips as she pondered the nature of her sudden curiosity regarding the details of Bayard's office. She'd sat there before—how many times, she couldn't tell, and didn't care to know. Something was different, though, and she couldn't put her finger on it except to know that something was different. It was unsettling for the linear clarity of

Patrol thinking.

Her hand rose to touch her bruise.

She took a breath and looked past Bayard to the window wall of his office. The wall consisted of the same long, polarized panels that could be seen on building after building, allowing occupants to look upon the concrete sprawl of the city.

She dropped her hand.

Bayard passed before her and cleared his throat. He gave her a side-long gaze that oozed disapproval, as if he knew she was paying him little attention. "And need I remind you, Patrolman Westing, that your service helmet will only provide full protection when properly strapped? Yes? The helmet you currently hold shall be tested for integrity. In the meantime, you will requisition a certified piece of equipment."

He turned on his heel to make another course behind his desk. "I've already spoken with your mate, Patrolmen Chapel, and I shall now inform you as I have informed him. We are returning to Kilby quad this evening to search for illegal hard line access. It appears last night's riot was a cover for activity of a more sinister nature. Both Drive Control and Sector Control have detected uncertified line usage within the quad and have ordered—demanded—that we put an end to it. Both Mondial Killswitch and MG42 are coming to the city to provide entertainment for the next cycle of endorsed riots, and the aforementioned authorities wish for no civic violence until then. It would detract from the authenticity of the planned events, you understand."

Carly perked up as she absorbed the news. "Wait, MG42? Endo Stutts! Will we be on his security detachment?"

Bayard walked around his desk to stand before her. He looked down at her and seemed annoyed by the question. "Yes, that is the plan." He cleared his throat once more before leaning over her to examine her bruised temple. Avoiding the gaze of her large blue eyes, he drew a deep breath and traced the periphery of discolored skin with a finger. "Ah, fair Westing. How they hurt you, my lovely Nimbus," he whispered, exhaling his words on her.

She closed her eyes as he kissed her temple. Her memory flashed.

Bayard lingered over her. "Did you already forget?"

Her gaze rested on the windows to see her reflection. "No."

His jaw clenched before he licked his lips. "Do you mind?"

Her lips parted. It took a moment for her voice to come low and slow in a simple mechanical response. "No." It was part of good drive, of good citizenship, after all. *Sex, it's free, and it's right proper. Like Shaky Flakes and Moo-ju, essential for good drive.*

The sky darkened over the City of Seven Hills.

She blinked. The moment vanished from her mind. "Hey, I think it's raining."

| 0 | 0 | 0 |

Patrol's motor pool was in the building's basement. Between thick concrete support columns it housed the intimidating hulks of the detachment's cars in a neat row. Carly and Graham sat on the roof of their car with the open turret between them. They each worked on one of the twin ten-millimeter machine cannons housed in the turret, removing piece after piece for inspection and cleaning.

The silence broke when Bayard emerged from the stairwell entrance to the motor pool and made his way from crew to crew to check their preparations. "Big operation, important operation," he said to each, nodding as he went. "Drive Control will be paying extra attention," he added, enunciating each syllable to stress the 'extra attention.'

Carly rubbed her forehead with the side of her wrist, wondering why he stressed those words. No one of right mind and good drive would tangle with Drive Control. Central made no secret that there were fates worse than the wrong end of a civi-stick.

Right. That's what they tell us.

She sat up straight, her eyes going wide in the wake of the thought that whispered through her. Her stomach knotted. The grease on her fingers failed to register with her as she touched the bruise on her temple.

What kind of think was that? Where did that come from?

"Carly?" she heard from both sides.

She looked around. Graham's gaze darted from her to Bayard before sinking to the cannons. She looked to her side to see Bayard holding a steady stare on her, his eyes locked on hers, as she realized her hand was still by her bruised temple. Her throat went dry at the undue attention.

Graham glanced at Bayard and waved his wrench at Carly. "She's fine."

"Right, right, I'm right fine," she said and turned back to her work.

Bayard kept his stare on her for several heartbeats before continuing on his way.

Carly let out a deep sigh of relief.

Graham slid his hand across the cannon to grab her wrist. "Hey, I need you sharp tonight. We're on the line detachment. If you're not good to go you can rotate out with Gwen and pull perimeter with Oboe."

Carly blinked. She was unsure of herself. It was a horrible feeling, even though the day was no different than any other. They had a good workout in the gym pushing their bodies while Endo Stutts and MG42 blasted from the room's raspy speakers. Just another day. They practiced club fighting with their civi-sticks. Just another day. They went through close-quarter combat drills, working on their handgun draws and proper arm bracing for recoil in the cramped confines of domiciles.

After lunch break they had their usual quick-draw competition. She won. She always won. She was by far the fastest draw in their Patrol detachment. It was easy for her. There was a little tingle in her head that told her someone was going to draw and, just like that, her gun was out and ready. Graham was the only one close to matching her, but she figured that was his familiarity with her as patrolmate. Just like always, and just another day.

Despite all those assurances she knew something was off. It was a feeling of uncertainty, a feeling that she was being watched. It reminded her of the tingle she knew from quick-draw. At the same time she knew it was different, although she couldn't decide how it was different. It left her wondering if the brick did more damage than just a bruise.

She closed her eyes and turned her hand in Graham's grasp to close her fingers on his forearm. The musculature beneath his skin was as solid as she remembered. Good old Graham. She opened her eyes and forced a hollow smile. "Hey, Patrolman Chapel. Patrol, enven, some Heavy, and then bulls on the rise, right?"

Graham stared at her for a moment before mirroring her smile. "Right proper, Patrolman Westing. Let's get these cannons back together."

"Hey, Chap?"

"What?"

"I think I had a dream that I scored a headshot on a cone in the middle of a riot."

He cocked a finger at her and closed one eye as he took aim. "That wasn't a dream. You did it for real. It got you a feature on *Killshot*, remember?"

"Yeah, I remember." She rubbed her forehead with her wrist. "When was that?"

Graham kept his gaze on his work. "Who cares? Some other day. Doesn't matter."

"Maybe it does."

He looked up at her. "What are you talking about?"

"I don't know," she said with a shrug. "It feels like a dream. Actually, it feels good either way when I think about it. If I did it for real or if I dreamed it, I mean."

He tipped his head as he worked. "Dreams are bullshit. You know that. Tell you what. Next time you take a brick go ahead and take your shot. Who knows, maybe you'll earn a move to an even better quad."

She looked at her hands. "I guess that's the thing about dreams." She caught Graham's gaze as he looked back to her. "Because you can make things the way you want, right? You know, I want that, I want that right proper."

He stared at her for a moment before shaking his head. "Whatever. Get back to work."

She patted her hands on the length of the cannon barrel and nodded. Looking back on her day she decided she should've meat-farmed the asshole she caught on the street during the ride in. A few demerits wouldn't hurt. Bayard might even give her a pass for payback on a cone after the brick. It was a simple line, after all. Get hurt, hurt back. She could hand out all sorts of hurt in Kilby, and Drive Control would be just fine with her. Compared to the uncertainty of doubt the visceral anticipation of retribution felt wonderful.

Graham was right, she decided.

Just another day.

Dreams were thoughts. That's why dreams were bullshit.

Her mind skipped to thoughts of Endo Stutts. The bad-ass of MG42, coming to Seven Hills! That, she decided, was something out of dreams and right into reality, double right proper.

Thinking of him lifted her mood and abolished her misguided abstraction. She whispered the words of the song she knew so well, her imagination letting them burst from Endo's mouth.

Kill the Continentals...

| 0 | 0 | 0

LATER, WHEN THE COOLING AFTERNOON air thickened with dampness from the morning rain, she found herself walking a foot duty through Kilby quad's day market. It was a sprawling open-air exchange of businesses run by a mix of cones and citizens. They set up the market by whim from one day to the next with tables, merchants, and a motley assortment of residents from various quads gathering on the green outside the outer edge of Kilby. It was a mess of odors from open food stands and shouts between haggling consumers and merchants accompanied by the inescapable mumble of net screens atop portable power stands. Drive Control made sure the screens were positioned at regular intervals. It was Patrol's job to make sure they stayed that way.

Day markets were considered forums for infiltration teams from the Continent. They consisted of cones that snuck across the rough waters of the Narrows, the cratered Wasteland, the swampy Mudwash River, and then north around the Downlow to reach Seven Hills. They brought in modular weapons and espionage equipment to the scattered insurgents among the city's quads. Likewise, day markets served as an easy access for Patrol to manifest itself as the strong arm of Drive Control and to make Central's presence known in whatever way was deemed necessary at the moment. It gave Carly and everyone else within Patrol open license to put some notches on their civi-sticks, if for nothing else than their own personal entertainment.

Carly walked through the crowd. People made a point of parting to let her through. Her civi-stick rested on her shoulder, ready to go. Market tour was tedious duty. She didn't care for it, a consideration she was willing to entertain despite its flirtation with bad drive.

She shook her head as she watched the cones. As far as she was concerned they were all for the chiggers. Despite rubbing shoulders with them as she made her way through the market, they might as well have been on another planet. Their ways, their habits, their disgusting living conditions and, worse, their unerring tendency to reduce any quad in which they lived to squalor made her resolute in Central's belief that the cones needed to be kept in line. Their ways, their habits, and their annoying silly-speaks could then be pounded into oblivion.

Her thoughts wandered as she gazed over the crowd. She blew out a breath at the notion of the desperate assholes that crossed the Narrows and the Wasteland just to deliver a few rounds of ammo, maybe a hard line splicer, or even a small rocket or firearm. It seemed so pointless, the effort of those cones, when they always wound up under the heel of Patrol. For all the violence of Patrol and her own life she was ingrained with Central's goal from her earliest days in Rainbow Go. While the cones were bent on dragging things down, Central wanted to get humanity on one track to both secure its future and end the war. Why—how—could anyone resist that noble goal?

She stopped before a stand displaying some apples and found herself all too willing to ignore the question and its aimless demands. Instead, she looked at the apples. They were red, a rich, vivid color in the midst of a gray day and the green shadow-laden trees that stood at the edge of the day market opposite the city's edge. With a quick glance at the merchant and a drum of her fingers on her stick she picked an apple and walked away.

Despite the apple, her mood turned for the worse. Sure, it seemed an innocent thing, selling apples at a market under a cloudy sky in the open light of day. For all she knew the apple vendor or some other clod walking beside her could've been the very cone that dropped the brick on her head.

One bad apple spoils the whole damn bunch. Have to meat-farm them all, I guess.

She came to a halt with the apple in her hand. Looking into the faces of the people around her, she realized they were ignoring her as much as she ignored them. If they could all be done away with, if the lot of them were just gone, she would be alone in the market, and then—

Well, then there wouldn't be much point to Patrol, or Central, or me.

Her gaze fell to the apple. She turned it over in her hand to study its rounded form. It was a nice apple, free of blemish. She could've gone through a hundred apples and not found one quite as nice as that particular apple, yet there it was in her hand, just by stupid, careless chance, a consequence of the careless blunders that were known together as Chance. And what, she asked herself, was the meaning of that?

Nothing.

It was just another apple, and it was just another day. It had to be. After all, how couldn't it be?

She cursed under her breath, tossed the apple over the crowd, and watched it fly away into some distant part of the market. When it vanished from sight she lowered her helmet microphone. "Graham?" She turned from the market toward the car. "Chap, you copy? I'm coming out."

"We haven't scratched the surface here."

Carly glanced over her shoulder and slid her civi-stick into its belt loop. She shook her head. "There's nothing here. They won't show. Not now."

"Bayard won't like this," Graham replied, his voice crackling over her headset.

"Yeah? I don't like it either."

She faltered, surprised by her answer. She had her orders.

"We have our orders," Graham said.

"I said, it's clear." She clenched her fists. "That's all there is to it."

She walked back to the car in silence, her only company the random pops and squeaks of interference over her headset.

| 0 | 0 | 0 |

THE MOOD IN KILBY CHANGED with the waning gray day as the quad settled for the night. Streetlights faded and air raid sirens let off their whining wail to signal the night curfew. Kilby, furthest south of the seven hills, sat within range of the latest generation of rockets leveled against the city from the Continent. In response Central had abandoned the cratered Wasteland and moved its phased arrays back from the coast. For Kilby and the adjacent Cheshire quad the incidence of rocket fatalities was a recurrent aggravation. Advertisements for newer arrays had hit the envens, and conventional wisdom dictated that if the envens said it, it had to be true.

Carly sat in the driver seat of the Patrol car, the door swung up to form a rain shelter. She was alone on an empty street. Rain poured off the hull of the car and dripped from the cannon barrels in the turret above her. She held her repeater, loaded with safety off, across her lap. A portable net screen sat atop the dashboard, spooling the feed from Patrol's own NetPrime enven.

She liked the little portable units Drive Control loaned to Patrol. Unlike every other net screen around her the portables from Drive Control had a volume wheel. With the Kilby operation in progress she kept the volume down so she could hear the scratchy recon transmissions coming through her headset. A hardwire line evaluator sat beside the net screen, its feed wire plugged to a drum spool sitting on the street. It let out an intermittent squeak as it played out its length, following Graham and the recon detachment down the main sewer of Kilby as they checked for line access violations.

The screen hosted a replay of a Patrol detachment pounding two perpetrators to pulp. The 'interact' panel scrolling across the bottom of the display caught her attention. Ads blinked for the sale of imitation civi-sticks, Drive Control posted rewards for citizen reports of silly-speakers or signs of poor drive in neighbors, Central flashed sales positions for premium tickets to the upcoming shows of Mondial Killswitch and MG42, news queries offered access to an interview with the Madman of MG42, Endo Stutts, while another enven sold copies of clothing Stutts had worn in recent appearances.

She touched the interact panel's pause icon when a blinking 'Order now!' button scrolled across for a black shirt emblazoned with ENDO in large yellow print. Interested as she was, after counting off her inventory of shirts on her fingers she decided against the purchase. A tap of her finger let the scroll continue.

The display of the line evaluator was boring compared to the net screen. After the mess of the riot she was eager for something to happen. Nothing would satisfy her more than getting the order to mobilize, go hot, and get clearance to meat-farm some cones. Sitting idle and waiting for something—anything—was insufferable.

She let her breath go in a long sigh.

Come on, come on already!

The clean signal lines rolling across the evaluator popped up in a little wave.

Fuck yeah!

Her radio crackled to life. "Drive Control. An anomaly trace has been initiated. All detachments to live fire pursuit status."

"Patrol confirmation," Bayard's voice chimed after the click of a frequency change. "Awaiting anomaly location fix. Prepare to move on Drive Control's order."

Carly tapped her headset. "Westing, copy that." The screens beeped as she powered them down and lowered her visor. She hopped out of the car, grabbed the two handguns holstered beside the seat, and slid them into her thigh mounts.

She looked to either end of the street. "Come on," she said under her breath, her impatience getting the best of her. "Where's the fix? Let it be here, let it—"

The streetlights blinked, popped, and blew.

Her lips parted. *Shit, it's here.*

Her heart bucked. *It's here!*

She sank to a crouch, snapping her repeater to the ready. Her cheek settled against the weapon as she peered down its length to study the darkness with a slow sweep. An infiltration party had to be near, she knew. They always shorted the lights before they moved. All she had to do was get a bead and she could blow the chiggers away.

Static scratched across her radio. She activated her infrared scope. Several silhouettes came into view, lit with pale red signatures. There were six, nearing her with every step.

"Perimeter, this is Westing. Are you advancing on me?"

Silence.

She kept her gaze in her repeater scope as she reached back to key on the line evaluator. Her blood steamed for the coming firefight. Her gaze darted to the evaluator. The shaky waveforms that met her sight were a clear sign of a violation in progress.

The infrared shadows neared. A little closer, clear of the old trees lining the street, and she'd have the bunch of them free of any cover. It took everything within her to be patient.

The even grate of a Drive Controller's voice hid the urgency of a simple transmission.

"Patrol, we have a suspect rogue."

Gunfire erupted from a window above her. A hail of bullets smashed and scattered across the car's armored hull. She hopped into the car and kicked the door release to let it slam shut behind her. Ignoring the rattle of bullets on the hull, she ditched her repeater, pulled herself up to the turret, and shouted into her headset for Graham. She ground her teeth, grabbed the trigger mounts for the cannons and opened fire. The car echoed with deafening blasts as she let heavy ten-millimeter shells obliterate the windows above her.

"Forward, hold position," Bayard's voice called through the headset. "Recon, evacuate priority one. Perimeter advance. Move!"

Cannon recoil rippled through Carly's arms. "Chap, get out of that sewer!"

A flash caught her eye. A small rocket tore from a window above her turret to explode against the car, the shock heaving her shoulders against the cannon grips. She shook her head as the car dropped down on one side. A wheel had been blown loose and the armor perhaps compromised. She grabbed her repeater, pulled open the car's crew door, and hopped out to the wet pavement.

To her relief a pair of cars greeted her as they roared down the street with their turrets blazing into the abandoned buildings to either side. Shattered glass glittered in the air amid plumes of gray masonry fragments. Rage usurped her better sense, her heart pounding as she dodged away from the car and scurried to the corner of a building. With a quick breath she emerged from the corner to charge down the street, letting off short bursts into the windows above her. Two crumpled bodies caught her eye on the side of the road. The cars ahead of her picked up speed and parted at the end of the street to lead in opposite directions. Still running, she glanced in her scope and picked out a lone shadow as it ran down the street ahead of her.

Voices erupted on the headset.

She slowed and leveled her repeater to fire until she noticed a sewer cover lift from the street. Her gaze darted between the sewer cover and the fleeing shadow. When she saw the armored outline of a patrolman emerge from the sewer she lowered her repeater and shouted an acknowledgment. The moment she heard the reply she ran into the street to grab the shoulder cowl of the patrolman. There was only one thing she wanted to know as she helped him from the sewer.

"Chapel! Where's Chapel?"

The man wiped some grime from his face and pointed down the street. Carly ran until she splashed to a halt beside a rising manhole. Her repeater dangled on its sling as she shoved the rising cover aside to find another grime soaked patrolman. She grabbed his neck cowl and couldn't restrain a smile when she found Graham's waiting face.

A bullet smashed into her right shoulder cowl and threw her to the pavement. Graham whipped his repeater to the ready and fired blind to provide cover. Carly shook off the tingling in her arm and grabbed Graham's neck cowl. She gave him another heave to get him off his stomach and shouted for him to follow her. Graham slipped with the sewer slime on his boots and splashed on the street, almost dragging Carly down with him. Her fingers popped free as she took off at a full run.

"Westing, Chapel, hold position," Bayard ordered through their headsets.

The Drive Controller's disinterested voice returned. "The Kilby array is down. Repeat, the Kilby array is down. Everybody out. We have incoming."

Bayard's voice assaulted their ears. "Westing, Chapel—out, now!"

Graham yelled to Carly but she tore ahead of him with her pursuit of the fugitive. Her legs burned, her lungs burned, and her blood burned even hotter. She rounded a corner and looked down a dark street to see the city give way to one of the wooded expanses along its border. Kilby Copse was one of the largest of those tracts, reaching southward from the city until it gave way to fallow fields and the cratered wastes of the coast. Between the copse and the city lay a set of phased arrays, with their spindly, black metallic shapes parked on the green field where only hours before the open day market had been in full swing.

It was nothing short of suicide for the cone to go there and get trapped among the discharges of an active array. As the thought crossed her mind she spotted the cone's shadow in the light of a rocket trail.

Graham came up next to her, panting, as the rocket buzzed overhead and sank into Cheshire. He pushed his helmet back to wipe his forehead as he spat on the ground. He looked to her when her armored vest dropped to his feet. "What are you doing?"

Carly shook her head. "I'm too heavy." She hit the release for her equipment belt and let it fall. "This cone dies," she said, her wild gaze darting from the shadows as the rocket's explosion lit the cityscape.

Graham looked around the abandoned buildings before giving her a nod. "Right. This place is dead, and so is that cone when the array comes back up."

"Chiggers to that. We get him now!"

Graham looked at the array before grabbing Carly's shoulder and jerking her around to get her full attention. "No! Orders were to get out, so we get out."

Carly grunted in frustration at the voices crackling over her headset. In one quick motion she unsnapped her helmet and threw it at Graham, distracting him enough for her to shrug off his hold. Her legs sprang to life and propelled her down the street. Graham called after her but her nimble speed left him in the dark.

Carly shouted at the cone as she passed from the last buildings of Kilby to clamber up a berm of broken concrete blocks. She still felt light on her feet, despite the run to the berm. Without her armor vest, rain soaked through her bodysuit and mingled with her sweat to keep her body cool even as her temper boiled. She wanted the killshot, wanted it so bad she could taste it, but there was no sight of the cone. Her scope offered no help, the arrays throwing off enough heat to mask the cone's signature. Her gaze swept around her as she began to wonder if the cone even ran into the array.

She sank to a crouch atop the mounded rubble, contemplating, when the uneasy sensation that she was being watched chilled her nerves. She spun toward the buildings at the edge of Kilby to look for a target. A rocket buzzed by, disintegrating over Kilby's copse under fire from Cheshire's array. The explosion lit the sky for a moment but it was all she needed. She caught the outline of a figure standing atop one of the buildings, a silhouette of a slender figure covered in a hooded overcoat.

She remembered the brick.

Vertical threat.

Her finger tensed over the trigger, yet she found herself incapable of giving the final squeeze as she stared at the figure through her scope. The unknown man stuck out his left hand to still her, holding a moment before extending his right hand to point to the array.

Another rocket detonated over Kilby's copse. She blinked. When she looked back to the roof the stranger was gone. Her anger got the better of her, and she scampered down the back of the berm toward the array.

When she drew near she hunched over and wound her way between the dishes, her repeater following her gaze.

At the sound of a footfall she spun to see the cone run off behind her. She let off a quick burst, but her bullets found nothing as they clanged off the frames of the trailer mounts. Annoyed, she pressed the chase, her blue eyes gleaming with intent.

The array hummed as it powered to life. The nerve-wracking hiss of an incoming rocket grew in volume. Graham's disembodied voice carried through the night as he called her name.

She rounded the dish of a trailer mount and emerged from behind the cupped black mesh to find the cone staring skyward.

"Cone!"

The man spun.

She let off her burst. Repeater rounds tore ragged holes through the man's torso. He staggered back in a mist of blood before dropping to the muddy earth.

Carly stood straight and looked over the length of her repeater, the stock still tight to her shoulder. She wiped the rain from her face as her gaze lingered on the dead man. Her fingers froze over the bruise on her temple. Her head began to pound. Only then did she hear the incoming rocket and the hum of the array's generators; only then did she understand that whatever the bruise did to her head yesterday, it was going to kill her now.

The cone had led her into the middle of the array. There wasn't enough time to run clear.

She looked back to the cone.

A red apple sat in the grass beside him.

The array crackled with electrostatic discharge.

Her world exploded.

I T WAS A CLOUDY MORNING, with only a few shafts of sunlight making their way through as a reminder of the new day. It caught the gaze of a slender man sitting in a small eatery, drawing his gaze up from the tea and biscuit he was about to enjoy. He pushed back the hood of his long overcoat, unconcerned by the prospect of revealing himself. It was still early. The locals would be groggy after a night of their net screens mumbling over their heads.

He hummed to himself as he looked at his breakfast. He had some time to eat despite the timetable that loomed over him. The biscuit drew a sigh of satisfaction as he bit into it and let its flavor mingle with the aroma of his tea. Common belief held that cones made the best food, and he wasn't one to disagree with that notion. In his opinion, the only disposable commodities at which Central excelled were people and concrete.

He relaxed in his chair as he ate. Like any man with a complicated past behind him and a delicate future before him, he weighed his thoughts. He had used several names in his life, but he knew he had to pick a new one and follow its lead. Given his situation and his meticulous plans it wasn't a difficult decision. So, with a blink, he honed his perceptions and settled on the name Victor Mortas.

"Yes, indeed," he whispered to himself as he reached for his tea. "Now the game begins in earnest. I hope you're ready, my dear."

| 0 | 0 | 0 |

"WESTING, CARLY. ACTIVE STATUS. CALLBACK DELAY INITIATED."

Just another day.

The thought lingered in Carly's mind until her eyelids rose. She looked to her ceiling, the still blades of her ceiling fan, and knew it wasn't just another day. Even in those first waking moments it seemed she was keeping track of those moments, that her conscious mind was making a record of moment after moment, breath after breath—

She shot up and gasped at the pain that lanced her body. Her eyes rolled in her head before she flopped on her pillow.

It seemed a long way back before she regained enough of herself to ease up in her bunk. She rubbed her face in dismay over her aching body. She dropped her hand and looked down at her shoulder, studying the blue-purple bruise that stared back at her. Her gaze continued its descent, noting the sleeveless black shirt she wore, before ending in her lap to reveal the lean length of her thighs.

Right, so that's my body.

She sucked in a breath as her heart raced. *Of course it's my body, right proper it's my body. Get a hold of yourself, Westing. Clear your head!*

Her gaze rose and scanned to her left in an attempt to comfort herself with the familiarity of her domicile. Beside her bed was her door, across from the door her tiny corner curtain stall with shower and toilet. Beside the stall were her sink and mirror and hanging towel, next to them her warm/cold dispensary, and last her window wall with its narrow table and chair, both of which could be folded flat to give more space. The view ended where it began, on her bunk and, over it, the swivel mount of her net screen with its endless babble.

Her world, she realized, was very small.

Her head shook in a nervous denial of her domicile. It was something she failed to understand and she tried to force the thought away by putting her face in her hands. Sitting there, she began to realize something else, that her concrete floor was damp and cold. It reminded her of the rain outside.

The reporter orb resumed its stubborn beep.

She snatched it from the floor and shook it until her head began to pound. "Confirm, confirm," she said between clenched teeth. "Westing, Carly—"

Her memory was blank where her identification number used to reside. A dry rasp came from her throat as she struggled with herself. In desperation she repeated her name and stuffed the orb under her pillow.

Thunder rumbled outside.

Across a green field, a stand of trees.

She winced and ground her palms against her temples. Memories burst from the shadows in her mind and shocked her with vivid detail. They were clear in sound, shape, and color in a way she had never known. They pounded her mind as her memories spooled that last sight of the cone unraveling beneath her repeater blast, his blood spraying to mix with the rain—blood that was red like an apple, the apple in the grass.

Her eyes popped open. "Apples, apples! What's with the fucking apples?"

A knock on her door startled her. "Sup-side."

"Fuck off," she said at once, her words returning to her with a slap. She forced herself up from her bunk and threw her door open to find a box at her feet. In a heartbeat of staring at the box her confusion flashed to annoyance. Before she knew it she was out of her domicile and into the hall, looking either way before calling out. At the end of the hall she caught a glimpse of the supply side deliveryman as the elevator doors shut him from sight.

A few moments passed as she stood there, fuming, until she had the uneasy sensation of eyes on her back. She looked over her shoulder and glared at an older man at the other end of the hall. He stood in his doorway, his sup-side delivery in hand, his eyes resting on her bare bottom. Self-conscious at once, she stepped into her domicile and almost tripped over her delivery box.

Rage overwhelmed her, and she let herself ride its stormy tide as it drove away her otherwise confused and fearful perception of the morning. She pulled off her shirt and tossed it aside, then grabbed her bodysuit and pulled it over her legs. Reaching under her bed she pulled out a fresh

T-shirt, slipped it over her head, and pulled the quick strap of her suit to tighten the waist, leaving the top half dangling over her legs.

She leaned on her sink and paused as she caught her disheveled reflection. There was nothing proper in that sight from the red burn of her cheeks, to the large red letters that spelled ENDO on the front of her shirt, to the crazed look in her bloodshot eyes. With a shake of her head she grabbed the civi-stick she kept behind her sink.

Spinning it around her hand with practiced ease she stepped barefoot from her domicile and paced with rapid steps down the hall to the domicile of the man that was staring at her. She swung the stick behind her and pounded the door with her open hand.

The door opened wide. The man gave her a curious look. He was middle-aged, pale, with small eyes and a mass of close shaved, salt-and-pepper hair. What drove her rage, she realized, was another memory, erupting from some time ago, of this man, *this* man, naked, with his head between her breasts, his—

He tipped his head in greeting. "Patrolman Westing."

She blinked.

Her hand whipped out, the civi-stick whistling through an arc that shot up between his legs to bury in his crotch. A sickening, high-pitched yelp burst from his throat as he crumpled forward. Disgusted with him, she pulled her stick back, took it in both hands, and drove her arms out to catch his body and throw him away. He crashed against his dispensary and flopped to the floor in a fetal ball.

With a grunt she spun away and walked back to her domicile. A door opened beside her, the woman there startled when Carly turned on her with the civi-stick snapped for the strike. The woman bowed her head and closed the door.

Carly kicked her sup-side box into her domicile and slammed the door shut. Her civi-stick clattered to the floor as she once again ground her palms against her temples. The pain in her head pounded against the inside of her skull.

She sank to her knees as the pain erupted. Her eyes squeezed so hard tears fell to the floor.

Across a green field, a stand of trees.

"What, what is that memory? That's not mine. That's, that's—shit! My head—"

Her eyelids fluttered. The domicile spun about her. She looked down in an effort not to vomit, only to see the floor fade beneath her. She felt weightless, and then she was falling, falling far down through nothingness toward a sea of red, red apples.

A gasp broke her lips. She sank to the floor in a ragged heap.

|0|0|0|

"CARLY."

She woke with a start. Her arms flailed in confusion. Graham seized her, pinning her against his chest as he lifted her clear of the floor. She grunted and struggled, pulling at his gloved hands until her strength failed to leave her body limp in his arms.

He dumped her on her bunk. "Carly, come on."

She lay there for a moment before rubbing her forehead to feel the bruise on her temple. Her eyelids drooped, her memories once again spooling to remind her of her morning, the sup-side delivery, the beating, and the pain in her head.

"Graham?" she said, grabbing his arm.

He pulled her up and steadied her as she sat on her bunk. She looked down at her hands, turning them over before running them up her arms, her lips parting as she saw the same redness on her skin that she remembered on her face. Her breath quickened as she looked up at Graham with plaintive eyes. "I'm all burned," she said under her breath. "Chap, what happened to me?"

He stared at her for a moment before looking out her window. His jaw clenched. After several moments he eased, his gaze sinking to the floor. "You're late. Get your shit together."

He left, closing the door as he went.

Her heart began to pound. She looked down. Her hands were balled to fists, blanched white-knuckle tight.

| 0 | 0 | 0 |

SHE MET GRAHAM ON THE street after dressing and devouring her Shaky Flakes. He was standing through the open roof hatch of their Patrol car, arms crossed on his chest as he watched the sparse morning traffic on Carly's quiet Danfield apartment row. He looked to her and frowned when he noticed her befuddled expression.

"What?"

She stood transfixed on the bottom step of her building as she stared at the car. Her face fell as her head resumed its nervous shake. There wasn't a trace of damage on the car, yet she struggled with the renewed spooling of her memory that told her a wheel had been blown free from the car the night before. Doubt bit at her, her certainty fading when she recalled her inability to recite her identification number to her reporter orb.

The wheel was gone, but it was back, plain in her sight. Her Shaky Flakes were empty, but she got a new box without asking, just got it out of thin air—how did the supply side deliveryman know to supply her? She knew she left her towel on the floor, but she found it hanging on the hook.

They were meaningless things, yet she nevertheless knew them, knew them as distinct events, regardless of the mundane oblivion to which they should belong. Worse, she realized she couldn't drive the memory of those things from her mind, couldn't deny their place in her life, and failed to understand why she couldn't dismiss them with the casual carelessness she knew so well.

She tried to swallow as a new thought whispered through her. She couldn't blunder through her morning, because everything was wrong.

Graham opened his hands. "Hey, Westing, you with me?"

She stepped to the car and put her hands on its wet hull to believe it was real. Her fingers traced the length of the car as she walked from the rear wheel to her passenger side door, her forehead wrinkled in hopeless confusion.

Graham slipped down and pulled the roof hatch closed behind him. He keyed her door open and met her gaze when the door hissed up. "Let's go."

With a nod she settled in her seat and pulled her door shut. She sat there, numb, until Graham pulled her repeater from her grasp to secure it beside her. He stuffed the maintenance checklist in her hands and stared at her with open expectation.

Her thoughts were far away as she gazed at the checklist. She had a desperate desire to ask him if they were in the same car. Such a question would mean comparing one day to another day, and to do that was to fly in the face of Central.

Her eyes slid shut as her innards constricted with fear. She knew what was waiting for her. There was no way around it, and knowing that only made it worse. It was Drive Control, and there was no escape from what they'd do to her.

She was going to be reformatted.

|0|0|0|

THE RIDE TO PATROL HEADQUARTERS was a torture of its own as her confidence eroded with every turn of the car's wheels. Graham said nothing, his gaze resting on her only when he looked out her window for traffic. Her throat was dry and tight, her stomach knotted as her fear solidified around the fibrous block of her Shaky Flakes. The fear became a new eye within her, summoning a paranoid glimpse of Graham reporting her to Bayard for drive failure. She knew Bayard would report her to Drive Control, even though he had sex with her only two nights ago.

She squeezed her eyes shut, understanding why she beat the man in her apartment building. How many men had been with her?

Graham, Bayard, Oboe, her neighbor down the hall, the man living by the elevator—

She clamped her hands over her face as the nervous shake of her head returned. It was a reflex that gained a voice within her and spoke a single word timed to the beat of her heart.

No, no, no—

Everything's wrong!

Graham stopped at an intersection. She looked out her window. A man walked by, slender, wearing an overcoat. His hooded head turned toward her, but she failed to see his face. Her lips parted. Graham took off and the moment dissolved in her confusion.

She drew in a shaky breath. The car rolled beneath her but she felt as if she was floating in her seat, perhaps even floating in her body. Her hands fell in her lap in what seemed slow motion. She sank into a stupor, her surroundings lost to her. Her head rolled to her left to see Graham leaning toward her, his lips moving, his voice lost. Only then did she realize she heard nothing, nothing but a low buzz in her head.

Her gaze rolled to her right across the view of their motor pool to look out her open door at Graham. Her eyes closed as she wondered how he had moved there so fast, but then she sighed, wondering why she should care about such a thing. Fast, slow—it was just time, and what was time? Time meant nothing; time was a criminal because it stole her carelessness, time was the enemy of good drive, because only in timelessness lay salvation from the monotony of the world, from worries of what was and what would be, from the war with the Continentals, from the endless beating of the inexhaustible cones—and who were the cones, the Continentals, and what was the monotony of the world, what was it all but a load of silly-speak next to a hearty bowl of Shaky Flakes, a glass of Heavy, and a good enven?

Her grin couldn't be contained. "It's all a load of crap."

She blinked and looked at Graham. She watched her hand as if it belonged to someone else, watched it reach out slow and clumsy to pat Graham's chest plate.

"Good old Chap."

She slumped into his arms.

| 0 | 0 | 0 |

SHE WOKE ON HER BACK in a stark white room.

"Patrolman."

Her eyelids fluttered before she gained focus. Her gaze wandered around the featureless white ceiling.

"Patrolman," a voice repeated. A hand reached into view before snapping its fingers twice. She turned her head to the side. A young man entered her sight, a slender, clean-shaven fellow wearing a crisp, gray bodysuit. His eyes unnerved her with their endless, reflective blue beneath his short, slick mass of black hair. He attempted a smile, yet it did little to change his dissecting glare. "Patrolman," he said once more, his voice a soothing, childish singsong.

She licked her lips, but she couldn't move. Her body felt both numb and heavy, as if someone had filled it with concrete.

The man seated beside her seemed to notice her alarm and patted her shoulder. "No, Patrolman, you are not paralyzed, merely held in the grasp of one of our little medications. It's for our protection, and yours as well. Your body is far too precious to us to waste in such a way. We are here to help you."

Her eyes welled up, her chin quivering as she fought for her voice. "Yes, please, help—help me? It's not my fault. I didn't do anything wrong. I don't want to be reformatted. The array, the array did this to me. I was after some stupid cone, I was doing my job, please—"

"Easy," the man said, his hand settling on her forehead. "Whatever it is, we will know, Patrolman. We will know everything about it."

She sucked in a breath as her fear mounted. "Is this Drive Control?"

The man nodded.

She squeezed her eyes shut and tried not to weep. "Why—" she began, but then let out a sob. "Why can't it be just another day?"

His smile returned, her question seeming to satisfy him. "You see, Patrolman? You still embrace Central. You don't challenge it like a cone. Do you know why we call them cones, we citizens of Central?"

She stared at him, the question meaningless to her.

"Traffic cones," he replied with a shrug. "No feeling, no meaning, no consequence. We roll them over like so many traffic cones." He smiled again as he looked past her. "I say, let's have it now," he ordered, reaching out to take a slim tablet from someone standing out of her sight. "Well, well, Patrolman, let's have a look at who you are, so we can see just what we'll do with you. Sounds fair, yes? You don't need to fear Drive Control, Patrolman. No, as long as you stay faithful to us, to Central, we are your best friends," he went on, saying words that he'd obviously said many times before.

He looked down at the tablet to study the information on its display. His easy demeanor fled him then, his blue eyes bulging before he regained his composure and handed the tablet off to the unseen person in the room.

Carly trembled. "What? What's wrong?"

The man swallowed before licking his lips. He stood and cupped his hands behind his back. "Fear not, Patrolman," he said with an encouraging tone. "In short order it will be just another day. You must learn to trust in Central. Yes, you must learn to trust in Central and all the intricacies of what Central knows," he added, raising an eyebrow as he heard his own words. "Good day, Patrolman Westing."

Her eyes locked on his. A needle pierced her arm before she could utter another word.

He waved a hand over her head. "Dream," he said and walked away.

Dreams are bullshit…

Blackness took her.

A thought whispered to her from the midst of her medicinal sensory deprivation.

Across a green field, a stand of trees.

The words evoked a memory within her, and the memory evoked a vision. The past loomed forward to overwhelm the present until there was only the *now*, a timeless, immortal, immutable, and everlasting moment. Images came to her perception, things she saw from the windows of the domicile she knew as a young girl.

There were things in that timeless vision any citizen of Central would know: the breakfast of Shaky Flakes, the cold glass of pure white Moo-ju, the endless babble of a net screen fixed to a wall. She had her mother—a patrolman—her brother Noel, and a father, one she always remembered as a pair of long, strong arms. He went to fight the Continentals with General Asper and never came back.

They enjoyed the comfort of a single/double, a single level, two-room domicile at the end of an apartment row in Cheshire quad. The copse was near and its wooded depths were very dark, black dark, at night.

It was a common scene, a common memory, but what followed was a singular moment.

Carly looked up from her breakfast bowl to see her bright red slicker from Rainbow Go hanging on the wall. One of the sleeves had a tear at the shoulder. She trembled, her gaze darting away to see her brother, Noel, at the window with his face and hands pressed to the glass. Her mother sat waiting on a bunk, a bottle of Heavy clamped in one hand, her repeater in the other. Her eyes were fixed on Carly with a hypnotic stare.

Two hazy ovals of condensation clouded the glass beneath Noel's nostrils. He glanced over his shoulder to his mother. "Are you going to do it?"

Carly looked out the window to see the neighborhood boys playing dodge-the-rocket with an empty can, its dented cylinder clattering across the street. Their carefree laughter reached up from the street to pierce her ears. Her blood congealed and her fear boiled until she tore her gaze from the window. In desperation she looked to Noel before focusing on her mother.

The bottle tipped up at her mother's lips to empty the intoxicating liquid.

Noel failed to hold his impatience. "Rebecca, will you?"

"Don't call me that," their mother said, her voice hoarse from the Heavy.

Noel swallowed, his eyes widening at her tone, but anticipation got the better of him. "Mum, come on. Will you?"

Their mother grunted, dropped the bottle on the bunk, and pulled back the bolt of her repeater. Her drunken eyes fell on Carly and lingered on her for too long—far too long—for intoxication to excuse, a length of time that withered Carly where she sat. Her mother stood, the woman's eyes narrowed with the intensity of some hidden, burning thought. She was wearing her bodysuit and a pair of untied boots. It was sloppy attire for an active duty patrolman.

She opened the door and left the domicile.

Noel's eager whisper came to Carly. "Mum will see to it. She'll do it." He walked around the table and cradled Carly's head to his stomach. "Nobody will bother our Carly, not at all. We won't have it, will we?"

Quick to agree with him, she bobbed her head as she wrapped her arms around her chest. Her mother's muffled shout came up from the street and through the glass. Carly plugged her ears with her fingers. Noel rocked her as he tried to soothe her by humming along with the raucous, bouncy tune on the net screen. After a few moments he started to sing along.

"Kill the Continentals, their rockets make me mental—"

MG42. Endo Stutts.

The boys below screamed. Their terror reverberated past Carly's fingers and into her ears.

Her childhood ended in the rattle of her mother's repeater.

| 0 | 0 | 0 |

TIME PASSED. LIFE CHANGED. THE moment revealed itself to be anything but immutable and eternal. Despite the lingering depth of a subjective impression the moment was buried in the mute avalanche of time. Carly's childhood ended in the rattle of a repeater. Her youth ended in the orchestrated violence of Teen-stomp. She discovered an unknown penchant for brutality and soon excelled at the roughest edge of Teen-stomp, a duty known as Neighborhood Awareness.

The work required a broad measure of apathy to the suffering of others. She fit the need like a hand in a black glove.

She never thought twice about the beatings she handed out. Repetition made them all the same. There was the moment of confrontation, the moment of threat, and then she would explode, the violence scorching her with a reckless sense of liberation. She knew what waited for her as her reputation grew. Neighborhood Awareness was Central's training program for Patrol.

Once again, life changed color. She had traded her bright red slicker of Rainbow Go for the black jumpsuit of Teen-stomp only to graduate to the even gray of Patrol. Neighborhood Awareness was forgotten. Teen-stomp faded from her until it held nothing more than the same idealized memories she watched on envens after joining Patrol.

She learned to sing along whenever she heard Endo Stutts. He filled her dreams, covering something dark and horrible that stirred within her when she tried to sleep. Endo Stutts was the embodiment of Central's roaring fury and the fantasy of any woman with good drive. Her imagination took him, her fantasies ravished him, and he came to dwell within her as her beautiful bad-ass.

Life, as she knew it, felt good.

| 0 | 0 | 0 |

SHE WOKE WITH A COUGH, passing from one vision to another with the same ease as changing enven channels on a portable net screen. Awareness returned to her and she found herself not in the familiarity of her domicile but in the familiarity of her Patrol car.

She blinked, her gaze racing around to take in the car and Graham before turning out to the depths of night beyond the car's windshield. The ghosts of a copse's trees lingered in the darkness before fading with a blink of her eyes. She forgot her unease, and the world—her world—her city, her life, they all seemed right, right proper.

The night flashed. Fog diffused the light before the deep rumble of an explosion shook the car. Graham cursed as he pressed his thumb against the steering column. The car's powerful engine came to life with a rumble to rival that of the explosion. Carly leaned forward to peer up through the windshield, her face bathed in the blinking yellow system lights of the dashboard until a brighter yellow trail crossed the night sky and illuminated the fog. "There goes another," she said, turning to Graham.

"Better make our quits and get behind the exclusion line."

They rolled along the streets of the city and passed from the quads as they made their way north along the perimeter highway, the Greenway, which ran just inside the borders of the quads and their greens. Not quite a highway like the stretch of uninterrupted concrete they knew between the city and the manufactories to the north, it was more a local twist and turn, a serpentine channel through the localities of the quads. The heart of the city was enclosed by the length of the Greenway, containing the regular blocks of apartment rows with their little domiciles, the street shops with their enven supplied goods, the dim glow of sex dens for citizens to meet and vent their rising bulls, the little bars and pubs serving their own distinct variations of Heavy, and the well-regarded eateries of the cones, with their interesting blends of tastes and textures.

The road rose and fell along the humps of the land. They went through the little valleys between the quads and their respective hills until the city was almost behind them.

Separated from rockets by the exclusion line, separated from the screams, explosions, and hapless sirens by the car's armor, separated from themselves by the mental dissociation of Central's ingrained way, Carly felt herself sink with Graham into an ideal of her life. It was a vision that Central condoned, that afforded her a new detachment to see reality in a new way, not just the way Central wanted her to see it, but the way she needed to see it to keep her good drive intact. It was a perception that spilled from her to encompass Graham, and perception it was, for there was nothing solid, nothing definite; nothing to touch, to feel, to prove this reality was *the* reality. They each became an ironic symbol within their existence, a something of nothing, a nothing residing in a something. They were hollow spirits gliding through an undead neon nightmare they knew as the City of Seven Hills, the endless void above marred and punctuated by the white fires of rocket impacts.

That was their world; that was their way; that was the reality they created for themselves by an unknown conscious effort under Central's dictates: to see and not to see, to know and not to know, to understand and forget. Yet for Carly the process was apparent—perhaps transparent—as it crept through her like a spidery crack in glass. Awareness whispered to her, and the nothing that was her mind in the something of her body began to wake, to race, to engulf everything around her with the infinite detail of each second.

It was a sensory eruption that left her dazed and wide-eyed in the undulating reflections on her window. The blue oceans of her eyes drank it all in—the sudden blooms of fire, the shadows of flying debris and bodies—and yet, the nothing within her refused to go without protest. It was an empty whisper that came to her, one she recognized, one that she knew was always there, lurking silent within her. With it came the nauseating, dizzying sensation she knew in some other time, the stupefying and befuddling sensation that she was a witness to herself, at once herself and not herself, no longer a something and a nothing, but a something and a *something*.

She thought of the city as it passed in all its convulsions of the night attack. The seven hills, the distant Downlow and its radiation, the copses and their dark depths, the greens and the shadows of their day markets— they existed to her outside of reason, a place she occupied in the life she lived where there was no yesterday in the timelessness of Central, a place where tomorrow had no meaning, where there was only the present, the moment, the *now*, always the now, only the now, erasing any standard of compassion or care. It gave her and Graham the fearless, remorseless, amoral and apathetic ease of their lives.

Just another day.

Rocket attacks, patrols, Drive Control.

Just another day.

Claustrophobic domiciles, cones, day markets, envens.

Just another day.

There was no meaning to anything. It was the only way, the only way to make sense of things. It was impossible for her to understand. She had never known anything else, any other way and, in that, she knew nothing but what Central told her. Yet Central told her that any day was just another day, just another patrol, just another domicile to search, just another resident to harass. Mundane and meaningless, marginalized and trivialized, there was nothing left but the moment and the sense of the moment. The only way to prove to herself that she existed, to confirm her presence in the world and silence the hollow voice whispering within her, to quiet that *something* that nagged her, that always nagged her, was to follow the excessive way of Central.

Central was her reality and only through Central could she survive in that reality, because in the absence of a future and a past the current moment was every moment. If that was lost—*when you begin to think, that becomes a new moment, the moment Drive Control trashes your life, and this is my life, the now I know.*

The now!

She returned to herself from abstraction and recognized some familiarity to her world. She knew the moment. Patrol. Rocket attack. Explosions. Graham laughing in defiance as rockets dropped on the city. All a game, just a game—just another day. In the riot of fear and fire, of screams and sirens, there was only one way not to be lost, to embrace it all and revel in the madness of everything—the excess of Central, of envens, of senseless violence and excessive drinking, of orders without logic, of reasons not questioned, of her endless capacity to beat and kill and destroy and let her bull rise, to clutch Graham and vanish within each other, to obliterate themselves in the very moment they were most aware of each other.

She knew the moment, the sweat between her and Graham as she straddled him behind the driver seat of the car. Their bulls had come and gone and, with the passing of their beasts, the frenzy of Central passed as well. In the empty wake of that elation they separated enough to rest their foreheads together and let their breaths tingle on their sweat-dappled skin. They sat there, neither wanting to move as they savored the raw sensation of their way. Without a word between them the mutual thought summoned the return of their beasts, their lust, and set their bulls back on the rise.

It began with the opening of their eyes, a silent, intense stare before he found her lips and she clamped her fingers into his shoulders. Then it had little to do with either of them, their eyes closed as they retreated within themselves, only their grasp and sway reminding them they weren't alone. Sensory overload, sensory collapse, selfish implosion—it was so very good, to feel so good.

It was the way in Patrol, for a citizen. Sex, it's free, and it's right proper.

She knew what came next as well, the clumsy fumbling as they pulled on their bodysuits and showed up in their sloppy dress to the meeting place of off-duty patrolmen, the Underworld. An abandoned manufactory from the old times of the city, the Underworld had been overwhelmed as the city spread across its hills and the quads were rezoned for either commercial or residential use. The more important industrial base of the city was moved to the north, out of reach of the Continentals and their annoying rockets.

Among the rusting machinery, away from their domiciles, Patrol made their home, their place to both create and vent their anxieties. Strobe lights flashed down on them, leaving their movements rough and stuttered to their eyes, their voices and ears drowned in a deafening wall of noise so loud it was hard to recognize as the sonic assault of MG42, except for the occasional break of Endo Stutts' voice from the acoustic melee. Large net screens hung at angles from the distant ceiling to bombard them with a constant visual barrage of Patrol violence. There were the usual civi-stick beatings, the mass brawls of a Patrol endorsed riot, the cone interceptions in the Wasteland, even bloody street firefights.

Her gaze shot upward as an image of Endo filled a monitor, his outline painted with strobe lights, his bare torso wrapped in bands of black tape, fists clenched in the beautiful brutality of his bad-ass rage. She shook a fist and howled to him, shouting curses until the image flashed away to more mundane propaganda.

Bottles of Heavy flowed through the crowd, passed from hand to hand as bodies jostled against each other. Carly and Graham were drawn into that befuddling depth and joined their fellow patrolmen at a large table off to one side of the Underworld. Gwen and Oboe were pawing each other as Bayard sat next to them with legs and arms crossed, an amused smile on his face as he watched them. There were other members of Carly's detachment that she and Graham saw on a regular basis, and they all slapped shoulders in greeting.

Hands grabbed and pressed in the cluster of bodies as bottles were raised high. Without care of where the bottles originated they called for more, always more, there had to be more. They staggered to the music's pounding rhythm, shoving and shouting in the push and sway of the tangled crowd. They spilled their Heavy as they drank, careless that they stomped on broken glass.

At some point Carly found herself riding on Graham's shoulders, pouring Heavy into both their mouths from her uplifted arm as Graham tilted his head back. They bumped into walls and knocked people over but Carly ignored it all, shaking her fists in the air and howling for more to drink. From some hand a bottle emerged, the drinking continued, and the feeling of it all, the rush of it all was so right, so *good*, so good to be alive and careless and not to care about having those very thoughts, so reckless that they had no need of the word reckless.

They were unleashed, wild in a way that led to more than good-natured rough-housing as they spotted other women of Patrol finding their way onto the shoulders of their patrolmates. Arms were held high, bottles were raised, and the call came out. Ragged, drunken voices screamed over the music until one word was audible.

"Joust!"

The crowd swarmed over itself as civi-sticks were tossed into the air. The women riding high on their mates' shoulders caught some of the sticks. Others fell into the crowd, stunning the patrolmen they struck. Carly grabbed a stick but, in her delirium, she dropped the stick instead of her bottle of Heavy. The crowd surged around the jousters. The mounted women seemed to float over the party while the men they rode were lost to view in the tangle of bodies. Sticks flashed and blurred in the strobe lights, teeth were bared, and screams sounded as the jousters made their charge.

Graham lost his footing between spilled Heavy, broken glass, and his own drunkenness. Carly felt weightless until the abrupt jab of a stick impacted her chest and knocked her off Graham's shoulders. She landed flat on her back on a table, her laugh booming from her the moment she caught her breath. Graham piled into a knot of patrolmen, all but plowing them over until they shoved back and sent him stumbling. He struggled for footing until he fell on top of Carly, stunning her. His laughter filled her ears as his head struck her chest, but then the table gave out beneath them. They fell to the floor, knocking over several other patrolmen who wound up sprawled beside them.

The world dissolved in raucous merriment. Carly bounced through the crowd, clueless as to where her feet carried her until she caught a glimpse of Bayard from the corner of her eye. She pushed her way to him and watched him stand as she neared. He pulled her into a tight embrace and gave her a rough kiss before resting his lips by her ear. His voice came to her, something about her move to a new quad, about getting a new enven, something about her being on *Killshot* as a featured patrolman for shooting a cone in the head during a riot. She laughed at the news and leaned back from him to wrap the fingers of one hand about his nose. He glared at her, but eased when she submitted to his lips once more.

She lingered there, disinterested in his gropes, his presence long forgotten in her delirium, until some other hand clamped her shoulder. The moment she saw Graham she shoved Bayard away. Graham took her hand, and she almost fell with his sudden pull, but then she was up, up in the air. Her head spun before she realized Graham had her over his shoulder as he headed for the door. The Underworld sank away behind her, the patrolmen devolving into a good-natured riot of their own as bottles and helmets took flight.

Just another day.

The night chill hit her like a wet slap when Graham brought her outside. Her ears were useless, the aftermath of the Underworld's sonic assault leaving a loud buzz in her skull that the alcohol did little to control. She lifted her head and let out a yelp as Graham slid her off his shoulder onto the hood of their car. She looked up at the turreted cannon barrels, laughing until Graham's arms closed about her. In turn her legs wrapped around him, and she held his head so that their kiss couldn't end. Too soon, Graham stumbled back from the car. She slid off the hood to flop on the ground, laughter bursting from her as Graham steadied himself against another vehicle.

He stood up straight before unzipping his bodysuit to urinate on a tire. He looked over his shoulder, laughing with Carly as she struggled to stand. "Hey, Westing," he said and pulled a bottle of Heavy from his thigh pocket. He waited until Carly looked to him, then raised the bottle to his lips and let his urine go. "Through filtration," he said, coughing at his own amusement until he dropped the bottle.

She was still giggling with Graham as they stumbled through the door of her domicile after leaving the car half on the sidewalk. Her head rolled back and her eyes slid shut with the relief of returning to her familiar seclusion. She shook off her bodysuit and let it drop around her ankles to leave her standing with nothing but her thin ENDO shirt. Graham slammed the door behind her in the clumsiness of his drink before spinning her around to take her in his arms. They swayed together, hands and lips at play, until they flopped onto her bunk. She wheezed under the impact of Graham's weight on top of her, but a sudden sense of urgency gave her the strength to push free of him, roll off the bunk, and vomit in the toilet.

There was no sense of disgust, only delirious laughter. She lingered beside the toilet, resting her head on the seat as the room spun around her and the toilet water spun beside her. Too drunk to be bothered by it, she turned her head as the need came and groped for the flush with a numb hand.

When her stomach was empty she looked to Graham. "Is this real?"

He rolled onto his back and shrugged. "Real enough, right?"

She giggled as she looked into the palm of her hand before draping her arm over her head. "I feel like I'm dreaming, you know?"

"Okay." He burped. "Dreams are bullshit, you know."

"Does this feel like bullshit?"

"Feels double right fucking proper, is what it feels like." He rubbed his face. "Look, if you're the one doing the dreaming, tell me what I'm thinking."

Her eyes bulged for a moment. "Whatever," she said and spat in the toilet before pulling the lid down to rest her cheek on the cold plastic.

"No. You tell me what you're thinking."

He put his feet up on her bed and closed his eyes. "I think I like it here. You like it here, like this?" He closed his eyes and chuckled as he rested a hand on her leg. "Yeah, I like it here," he said and gave her leg a squeeze. "I like it here, with you."

She smiled as she stared at him. "I like it here with me, too," she echoed, her voice hoarse over her sore throat. She watched his chest rise from his opened bodysuit as he took a deep breath. His hand grew loose on her leg as sleep overtook him.

Alone, her eyes drooped. Her eternal moment developed a crack.

It was the temporal crack to remind her that her ideal moment wasn't eternal after all. There was a past, there would be a future, and somewhere between them lingered the ever-changing present—her present, the present that summoned her return.

| 0 | 0 | 0 |

HER EYES WERE CLOSED AS a smile seized her in the warmth of her life, the warmth of all her memories, recalled and assembled to one idealized night of her life as she knew it, as she perceived it to be, as she came to know it in its own perfection.

She coughed, and her eyes opened. The white ceiling of Drive Control hung over her. There was no Graham, no drunken craze of the Underworld, only herself. Nevertheless, she felt drunk, drunk with the dislocation of all those realities sent careening through her head. It felt good to be drunk, to be mindless. No thought, no concern, no worry. Her smile returned as she heard the babble of a net screen over her head.

Central was still there for her. She decided that was a good thing.

A voice came to her. "Do you understand?"

"I understand." She sobbed. "I understand!"

Her arm was pierced again. There was time for one last thought.

Yes, life is good.

And, with that, she returned to the delirious world of her dreams.

| 0 | 0 | 0 |

SEVERAL FLOORS BENEATH CARLY, IN the depths of Drive Control, the man who had stood over her sat in his office staring at Carly's file as it glowed from the screen of a personnel tablet. A net screen was to his left, not one that babbled with the envens but one he could control, one with a keyboard. His reporter orb sat off to his right. It was silent, now that his shift was over. After several moments he slumped back in his chair and rubbed his eyes as he tapped the foot switch to darken his desk lamp.

His name was Noel Westing.

"I don't like this," he said at last.

"You must have known," a woman's voice replied.

He dropped his hands and gazed at the ceiling. "Sonya, you don't understand. We were separated after our mother was taken away. I thought it was just a dictate of Central. I was sent on my way up the ranks of Drive Control and I figured Carly was sent her way up some other channel. When we were in Rainbow Go we were both screened and accepted for Drive Control. How could I have known? You just can't go poking around the personnel file of another controller, even if it happens to be a sibling. You know that."

"Yes, it's most improper."

Noel rubbed his chin, his gaze distant and lost in the depths of his own thoughts. In a way he felt as if his life had been on autopilot until a few hours ago, when everything seemed to have changed. "I couldn't believe that was her on that table in front of me this morning. I almost fell off the chair when I saw her file on the personnel tablet. I didn't even recognize her," he said, not believing the truth of that moment.

"It's a long time since you last saw her."

"Too long, I think."

"Nonsense."

He pointed to her. "Did you grow up in one of Rainbow Go's child dormitories, or did you have charter parents?"

"Why do you ask?"

He closed his eyes. "I have some memories of my childhood. My father went off to the war, and I never saw him again. My mother was part of Patrol."

"That's impossible. Patrol members don't sponsor children. You know that."

He shook his head. "No, no, she was part of Patrol. I can still see her gray bodysuit, her repeater, the bottles of Heavy she chugged down. One day Drive Control took her away, and then I went to a dormitory. That's all I remember. I never saw Carly after that." He opened his eyes on Sonya. "Does that mean anything?"

Sonya opened a hand. "I think your memories are confused. Tell me this. If I were to ask you now whether those memories are accurate or if you indeed grew up in a dormitory and what you remember is some strange dream, would it have any effect on who you are in this moment?"

He frowned. "No."

Sonya tipped her head. "Then let me ask you this. What's more important, the reality of some old memories, or what you do as a drive controller within Central?"

He thought for a moment. "What I do now, of course." She nodded. "Exactly. We do what's expected of us. Nothing more and nothing less. That's our equilibrium as individuals under Central."

He looked to her. "So you have no memory of your childhood?"

She took a breath as her face went blank. "I am who I am in this moment, and I'm defined by what I do in this moment. Those two allow me the luxury of knowing a future moment."

"You didn't answer the question."

"The question is irrelevant. What I said negates the need for the question."

So they sat, staring at each other, as her stark sentiment lingered between them.

He leaned forward in his chair, resting his elbows on his desk as he stared at Sonya, seated across from him. She wore a simple, tailored bodysuit, burgundy in color. It was a two-piece suit that lacked the utilitarian appearance of a standard bodysuit. Instead of a zipped collar, her suit jacket zippered to an open v-neck. Beneath the jacket she wore a white shirt with a high, closed collar. There was one small pocket over her left breast, probably more for show than function. She even had painted fingernails, burgundy to match her suit. Her long, dark hair was pulled back in a bun, highlighting the alloy-rimmed glasses framing her brown eyes.

She held little semblance to what Noel knew of women around the City of Seven Hills, but she claimed she came from across the ocean, from Central itself. She was a power broker within the division of Central in which he worked. The first time he saw her he was struck by her, by the fact that everything about her differed from anything he knew of the people in his life and the anonymous women he met in the sex dens. It compelled him to pursue her. She entertained his puppy-dog interest even though he was yet to experience all the wonderful charms he was sure lurked beneath her suit. Nevertheless, their relationship possessed hints of emotion, transcending their professional boundaries and allowing them to exchange information that people of their varying ranks wouldn't share under typical conditions.

"Sonya," he said, "I never thought my sister would end up in Patrol. She's become one of those mutton-headed drunken thugs who can't remember one day from the next."

"You know there's a very good reason for Patrol to be like that."

He ground his teeth in stubbornness, but soon relented. "I know, but I just don't understand this. I wasn't supposed to be there, in that room, this morning. I was only there because Henshaw called in sick. It doesn't make sense. If Central knows what's going on in every moment, and if I wasn't supposed to see her, how does it happen that I do see her? Is it some stupid, random thing that Henshaw called in?"

Sonya shrugged as she stared at him. She crossed her arms on her chest. "Tell me, Noel, what is it that upsets you? Finding out your sister is a mutton-headed drunken thug, as you say, or that you think there was some aberration in the course of Central?"

He opened his mouth, ready to reply, but found he had no reply. He gave her an angry glare, forgetting for a moment that authority rested by far in her favor. She was a scriptor and he was just a controller. He might make things happen, but she was from Central, and she was one of the people who decided what things would happen. He sank back in his chair, his eyebrows falling to conceal his gaze in shadow.

She stood and looked down at him with her large, brown eyes. "She was set to be reformatted, and you stopped that. You can feel as you wish about the situation you discovered, but now it is what you made it to be, and she is now what you left her to be, and both those realities are now part of Central. Perhaps that was intended, yet again, perhaps not. It keeps you guessing, yes?"

She paused a moment before smiling. "There are things within Central that scriptors don't know, that not even the predilectors know." She tapped a hand on his desk before she took off her glasses. She held them to the light and blew off a speck of dust before putting them back on. "Think about it, but don't take too long, yes?" She glanced at her watch, a delicate alloy piece alien to the city. "It's late. I can stay hidden only for so long."

He looked up at her, at the clean symmetrical curves of her face. His gaze sank to the floor. "Do you think I can keep her from reformat? I put in orders for her to be immersed in a dream construct. I even wrote the orders to repeat for five days. It should be enough, shouldn't it?"

"We shall see," Sonya replied with the vague tone typical of a scriptor. "Either way, you shouldn't let this go any further. If Gadwick gets hold of it you know where it will end. City elders aren't known for their patience. In the meantime, don't worry about Henshaw. I'll have it seen to."

He sat up straight in his chair, blurting her name as she walked to the door. She turned to him with a quizzical gaze, causing him to fidget for a moment. He cleared his throat. "Can I see you tonight?"

Her lips parted and her face went blank.

"Sonya?"

She blinked, her eyes returning to their usual cast. "No, I don't think that's possible." She stepped into the doorway. "Goodnight, Noel."

Alone, he sat in the silence of his office and brooded. He sighed as he thought of his sister. Things should've been different, but they weren't. Something, somewhere, must've gone wrong. There was nothing else to conclude because he knew the fickle hand of Chance held no sway in the meticulous plans of Central. For Central everything happened in a proper time and a proper place. Circumstance always seemed a mysterious thing, a suspicious thing. He never thought he would find himself in the middle of such a dilemma, the dilemma of uncertainty.

He knew the wise course was to do nothing. He should put his faith in the wisdom of Central and convince himself that there was an agenda at work beyond his understanding and so beyond his realm of action. But those were rational conclusions, and the dim memories that served as the last clinging remnants of his childhood summoned a compulsion that was far from rational. It was the compulsion to help Carly in some way, in some form.

In a heartbeat his perception of Central's will spun around to a new conclusion.

It wasn't some failure of Central that put Carly before him by circumstance, but rather some hidden agenda of Central that summoned such an improbable moment.

"That's it," he said to himself. "I can't abandon her. I was supposed to find her."

He shook his head. *Time.* If he waited too long to act, the moment of opportunity would fade. On the other hand, if he acted too soon, he might disrupt the intended maturation of Central's unseen plan. Either way, he would disappoint Central, and he knew that wouldn't bode well for him.

So, how long do I wait to do something?

He looked to his net screen. The display was blank.

|0|0|0|

VICTOR MORTAS STROLLED DOWN THE hall of a comfortable apartment building until he came to one particular door. He looked down at the card lock and stared at it for a moment before tapping his finger on its metal housing. The door clicked open.

He walked into the domicile, leaving the lights off and ignoring the furnishings until he found a comfortable chair. He turned it toward the door and sat down. With nothing else to do, he closed his eyes, twiddled his thumbs, and put his mind to work.

Before long the door clicked. His eyes snapped open to reveal Sonya Mortas standing in the doorway. He stood and shrugged off his long overcoat. "Good evening, my love." He opened a hand. "Won't you come in?"

She lingered in the doorway. "I live here."

He smiled as his head throbbed with the exertion of his mind. "Yes, with your husband."

"I have a husband."

He eased somewhat. "Yes, you have a husband, and he has returned to you. I am your husband, and I have returned to you. Surely you know this to be true, yes?"

"I have a husband named Victor." She closed her eyes for a moment. "Yes, I do." Her eyes opened as she looked to him, and her face soon lit with warmth. She closed the door and came to him to take his face in her hands. "Where have you been?"

He put his arms around her. "I've always been with you, in your dreams," he said, kissing her forehead. He could smell her, the wonderful scent he had imagined and craved for so long. He found her lips and held her close. She fit in his arms the way he imagined she would in all his obsessive projections. He pulled her coat from her shoulders and let it drop to the floor, unable to check his desire any longer. Overwhelmed, he let his guard down, knowing it would overwhelm Sonya as well.

He wasn't concerned. It seemed a lifetime since he last knew the touch of a woman, since he last reveled in the delicious delirium of sensuality. The vitality of youth bloomed through his limbs, silencing any memory of the many years his life encompassed. He kissed her neck as he unzipped her suit. The supple rebound of her pulse, the warm blood flowing under her skin, quickened the beat of his heart. When she let her hair loose from its bun to sweep over his face and fill him with its scent he quaked, his fingers trembling under her shirt until he grabbed her hand and led her toward the bedroom.

For all his doubts and concerns the thrill of the moment both obliterated his careful reservations and solidified his convictions. There was nothing to fear, nothing to concern him. All his actions, all his plans, they had to be in the right, they had to be of proper focus, or else he wouldn't know the thrill searing his every nerve as he reveled in her embrace.

Ends and means.

Means and ends.

He wondered if there was any difference, or if it was a matter of mutual exclusion.

But that was a distant thought, lost as he let the moment, and his Sonya, devour him.

SONYA'S EYES OPENED TO THE ceiling above her. She stretched where she lay in bed, only then conscious that she was naked beneath her sheets. Her mind sparked in confusion until she sat up. She reached out to find her glasses and set them on her nose.

Her gaze wandered over her bedroom.

She flipped the sheets away, walked to her closet, and opened the door. She looked down at her body before looking back in the closet.

All the clothes were hers.

Of course they were, because she knew no other way.

Moments passed before she found her breath. When it came it raced in her lungs, and her mind cleared.

"Yes," she said, comforted by the sound of her voice. "My name is Sonya Mortas, and I live alone."

|0|0|0

"WESTING, CARLY. ACT-"

Carly woke with a start and snatched the reporter orb from the floor as she sat up. Her quick response, identification and all, satisfied the reporter. She tossed the orb on her bunk, stood, and stretched her arms high with a yawn, enjoying the pull of her lithe musculature. She dropped her hands to her sides and looked about her domicile, not understanding, and not caring, why she nodded with satisfaction. It was one of those wonderful mornings, she realized, one of those wonderful days when the moment shone through the rain, the ever elusive beautiful moment, the guiltless, shameless *now* of a single moment that told her every following moment would be as perfect and exciting because they too would exist alone, sparkle, and cede to others without care.

After all, it was just another day.

The industrial growl of MG42 caught her attention, her gaze rolling over her shoulder to watch a video feed of Endo Stutts on stage, hands clenched on his microphone, veins bulging on his neck in one of his bestial howls. He was flanked by a pair of the antique tripod-mounted machineguns that gave MG42 its name, their menacing muzzles tipped down toward the people before the stage. Endo wore his usual black pants and black army boots, his bare torso wrapped in chaotic bands of narrow black tape to highlight his sinewy build.

She stared at him before throwing her head back and closing her eyes. Her body tightened in a splendid isometric contraction, her head throbbing as her blood pressure soared. With the constriction of her body every nerve in her skin tingled to life, and she imagined those fleeting impulses stemming from the clutch of Endo's hands upon her, the wanton fury of his body closing around her in an electric, erotic eruption.

A gasp burst from her lips as her eyes popped open, her irises dilating to two black pools adrift in the gentle blue sea of her gaze. She fell back a step, only to shake her head and look at her net screen. "My beautiful bad-ass," she said with a greedy grin, kissing her fingers before slapping them to the screen.

She pulled off her sleeping shirt, reached beneath her bunk, and frowned when she failed to find her red lettered ENDO shirt. Frustrated, she settled on a blue lettered replacement, pulling it on before slipping into her patrol suit. Armor plates came next, then her bowl of Shaky Flakes, which she slurped down before chugging a few mouthfuls of Moo-ju from the container.

She grabbed her repeater off the rack over the head of her bunk, put her boot up on the bunk's foot rail, and settled the repeater's butt on her knee cowl. The clip popped free in her hand and she glanced at the ammo window as she sang along with her net screen.

"Kill the Continentals, their rockets make me mental—"

Her face fell, her gaze rising from the clip to rest on the bare wall over her bunk. The moments passed. She slapped the clip home and left her domicile.

Outside her door she watched Milston, her neighbor from down the hall, hobble past her, one hand clutching the inside of his thigh. She glared at him as she realized he was in fact cupping himself. "Hey," she said, walking with him as she slung her repeater over her shoulder. "Milk your bull in private, citizen."

He glared at her from beneath the stubble of his salt and pepper hair and gave her a nod. "Patrolman Westing," he said between clenched teeth.

She patted his shoulder and paced ahead of him, skipping the elevator to take the stairs two steps at a time down to the street. The Patrol car was rolling toward her building as she came out the door. She hopped on the railing of the building's front steps, lifted her feet to slide down the wet rail, and landed on the street. The bright slickers of the school children on the corner caught her eye. She ignored them and hopped in the car.

She turned to Graham with a smile and slammed the door shut. "Morning, Chap."

Graham watched as she stowed her repeater and pulled out the maintenance checklist, his expression darkening with each moment. "Morning, Carly."

She looked up from the checklist to the street, then to Graham. "We're not moving," she said, pointing down the street with her pen.

He looked away with a grunt and dropped the car in gear.

"Problem, Patrolman Chapel?" Carly said as she continued her checklist.

"No. Just another day, right?"

"Right proper it is." She glanced at him with her bright smile. "You know I'll be changing envens when I move."

"You don't say," he said with disinterest.

"Right I will. I'm looking at either StarNet or BlueNet, depending what quad I get. I—"

"Right, right," Graham interrupted, seeming annoyed. "And we can watch *Riot* and *Killshot* after shift if you get StarNet."

She tried to ignore his tone, giving him a quick glare before putting away the checklist. "I see it as quite outstanding. We can do shift, maybe drink some Heavy while we get naked and let the bulls rise, eh?" she added with a mischievous grin.

He rolled to a stop at an intersection and turned to give her a troubled look she failed to understand. He studied her for a moment, then looked back to the road and rubbed his forehead. "Whatever," he said before stomping the accelerator to get them moving.

She ran a hand through her hair, pushing it back in a failed attempt to bring some order to her disheveled locks. She had the growing suspicion that Graham didn't start the day with the same clarity of drive as she. No matter, she decided. The moments would tell their tale. She knew what Central expected of her.

| 0 | 0 | 0 |

NOEL STARTED THE DAY IN his domicile at the outskirts of Rooking quad with an early rise ahead of the reporter orb's call. The aroma of fresh tea wafted through his spacious single/triple, all three rooms letting in the first light of dawn through their polarized windows to fall on his oak floors. He had strolled with a yawn as he absent-mindedly made his way from his bedroom, through his living room, and into his kitchen. The auto-dispensary had already dropped his rationed portions of smoked ham, Shaky Flakes, and toasted bread. The brew machine sat waiting with a steaming pot of tea.

It was then, standing there in his sleeping trunks before the little digital timer of his brew machine, that it hit him. Even though his sister lived only a few quads away from the sealed area of Rooking she might as well be on another planet. Something as simple as a brew machine with a timer would never be allowed outside Rooking, for a machine with a timer would admit the conscious measure of time and, for most of humanity, that was forbidden by Central.

In fact, as part of Patrol, she wasn't entitled to the same ration package as he, so he was certain that she never had the experience of a cup of tea. Chances were almost absolute, he knew, that she didn't even understand the remote monitoring of her consumption of Shaky Flakes and milk by her dispensary's weigh plate to trigger the deliveries of supply side. No, she wouldn't understand that at all, even though she would crack the head of someone stealing from a supply side truck without understanding what purpose a supply side truck served.

With a shake of his head he drank the tea and ate his breakfast as he listened to the news on his net screen, the little unit molded into the wall over the table in his kitchen. He heard the regular reports of cones and Patrol activity and the continued hype concerning the pending arrival of MG42 and Mondial Killswitch. It made his ears perk up, for the coming of MG42 meant that Endo Stutts would be around. Noel, as well as everyone else in Rooking, knew that meant much work ahead. Sonya had hinted to him they would have to part ways while Stutts was in town to avoid any undue suspicion.

Both thoughts made him frown and drop the spoon of his Shaky Flakes, because both thoughts returned him to the reason he rose early that morning and the awkward timing of circumstances in his life. The irony of it struck him, how he, as a controller, spent his professional life without giving thought to the means employed to make people forget the very thing that now seemed to hang upon him with such weight: *time*. Time for Stutts to poke his nose into the business of Noel's chapter of Central, time for Sonya to retreat from him when he could use her, time wasting for him to track Carly as she returned to her life.

With a silent curse he pushed away his Shaky Flakes and walked back to his bedroom to take a shower. He didn't miss the fibrous cereal, knowing the name was one of those winking jokes within Central, the 'Shaky' coming from the cereal being loaded with caffeine and sugar to get both cones and citizens up and moving in the morning. It was loaded with nutrients as well, but Central made no fuss about promoting that, because there was nothing exciting about nutrition in the world Central had fashioned.

After slipping into one of his dozen gray bodysuits he clipped his identification badge to his pocket and left his domicile. His building was a low structure, only four stories, as opposed to the typical ten story concrete stacks in the rest of the city. There were gardens by his front door, little manicured gardens with partitions of wood lattice laced with ivy. The practice lingered from the days when the expansive island on which the city sat went by a different name, when the cones were the native people and the sprawl of Central was yet to become the sprawl of Central, even in its homeland across the ocean.

While taking his morning walk to his subway link he wondered about the time before Central, when the world was different, before the sky was ripped by flashing sun bombs that had turned cities into waste, like the Downlow that lay off from Seven Hills. It made him wonder how long ago that time was, so far back that Central could obscure enough of it to refashion the current war with the Continentals to suit Central's various outward objectives.

There was one occasion, one of those wonderful, nervous moments when Sonya joined him for dinner at his domicile, that he remembered sitting with her in his living room before his windows. They were sharing a bottle of red wine when she began to tell him a tale, a fantastic tale of what she knew of that other time. To his surprise she told him that she heard it from none other than the Madman of MG42, Endo Stutts.

"He's much more than you know," she had replied to Noel's open consternation.

Riding the short distance on the subway link to his office in the basements of Drive Control, he realized why he'd thought so little of his sister. His life had been one of cryptic tales and half stories; which kept him guessing as to what he knew of Central and how it came to be Central. In that fashion, Central had managed to befuddle him with its nature, as well as it had managed to befuddle Carly by an entirely different method.

The orders of the various chapters of Central—the controller order to which he belonged, the scriptor order, and the reclusive members of the elite predilector order—existed by theory in a rigid hierarchy. They nevertheless mingled and sometimes spoke of the various fragments of what they knew. There was at once so much that one could claim to be known, but no one could say what was *true*, or what in any event it created, in the final analysis. At the same time there were those, himself included, who guessed that little bits of stories were started from Central itself, planted to map informal information channels. It would allow Central to obscure reality in the blurred margin between fact and fantasy that defined a thing known as gossip.

It was that specific margin he hoped to work to track Carly. Following a specific individual—worse, a blood relation—was forbidden, unless the order came down from Central itself. There were many allowances for him as a working member of Drive Control, but he knew full well from the very things he'd done in the past that Drive Control had no hesitation to treat one of its own as it would the lowest cone or citizen. Life was conducted upon a thin sheet of ice, and the dark waters beneath offered nothing but the chill of Sector Control, the shadowy arm of Drive Control. It was Sector Control that handled the horrifying process embodied by the heartless, clinical word known as *reformat*.

Despite that possibility, he was haunted by his childhood memories from the moment he realized it was Carly laying before him that one morning in the evaluation chambers of Drive Control. Unlike her, he was allowed to keep his memories, to keep track of his days, and thereby retain some semblance of his childhood recollections, devoid as they were of sentimental attachments. They existed as a context to his adulthood and nothing more. He was whom he was because of what had happened to him in his past. A redux, clean and efficient, a sanitized way for Central to keep those it needed to function with temporal awareness within the needs of Central's societal way, its Process.

The concept was embodied in the sculpture of a single, massive gear before the entrance to Drive Control from the subway link. He presented his identification to the guards, which he thought silly, as they were members of Patrol. In light of his thoughts that morning it brought little humor to him. He had the sickening suspicion that if his sister was one of those guards he would've walked past her and never noticed her and, in turn, she wouldn't recognize him.

Siblings, yet sundered.

He shook his head as he thought about it when he entered his little office. For all his thoughts, he still had his duties, so he keyed on his screen and initiated his traces, looking through his official orders while he waited to locate Carly. He settled in his chair, his reporter orb giving a single beep. On cue he responded by keying in an operator code and received a single beep in reply.

His gaze rested on the screen, his anxiety rising as he watched the timer in the corner tick away.

A knock on his door startled him. He looked to Sonya as she stepped into his office and gave a quick nod. "So far, so good," she said with a sigh, "but I must tell you, I still don't agree with this course of action. I don't see where you wish to take this, or what you hope to achieve by watching her for a day. If she doesn't end up here again, then you would know all was well for her. We could do that—*you* could do that—without causing any undo attention."

He looked to his net screen.

Sonya fell silent and stared at him for a moment, her face expression-less. They had argued for the last several days in just such a way as to whether or not he should trace Carly after her release from Drive Control. In the end, despite Sonya's concerns and objections, Noel won her over.

She lifted her glasses from her nose and set them back down, her lips drawing to an even line as she relented. "I'll notify Bayard," she said before leaving him.

Noel's jaw clenched. It was common practice not to trust anyone in Patrol, given the lives they led under Central. The same went for patrol-masters, who often took advantage of their position. Bayard's behavior was typical of his kind.

Noel stared at his screen, sickened. Tracing his sister might force him to accept things he didn't care to know on a personal level. Perhaps, a thought whispered, running the trace wasn't such a good idea after all. On the other hand, it was too late, because the trace was already running, so maybe it was something Central wanted him to see.

He settled back in his chair, his dismay shifting to satisfaction the more he considered his thoughts. They seemed to him more in tune with the way a scriptor would think, and so his pride glowed. Deep down he always believed his intellect was greater than that allowed by his position as a controller.

He wondered if that would put Sonya at ease.

| 0 | 0 | 0 |

CARLY STOOD IN THE MOTOR pool of Patrol headquarters, arms crossed on her chest as she stared at a map of the city. Her gaze was focused on the outline of Cheshire quad and the dotted black line that ran through the middle of the quadrant and then down along Kilby. It was the exclusion line, showing the area of the city that was under risk of rocket landings.

"Poor Cheshire, yes?"

She turned, her blue eyes widening as she noticed Master Bayard lurking behind her. Her gaze darted to the beak of his nose before returning to the map. "I grew up in Cheshire," she said under her breath.

"Did you?" he said with little interest. He didn't flinch when she looked over her shoulder to see his eyes trace down the side of her neck. "Perhaps we can discuss this later, just the two of us, and your blue Endo shirt? I prefer it to your others. The color compliments your eyes. Or perhaps no shirt, Patrolman?"

She stared at him, something in his question creating a sickening feeling in the pit of her stomach. It grew and gained voice, muttering a thought that puzzled her on such a wonderful morning.

No, no, no!

Her attention darted away when she noticed Graham walking toward them.

Bayard followed her gaze and gave Graham a polite smile. "Patrolman Chapel," he said, ignoring Graham's greeting to look back to Carly. "So, perhaps later?"

She opened her mouth, but then closed it. "Perhaps."

Bayard nodded and turned away when he spotted Gwen and Oboe perched beside their half assembled cannon turret. "Patrolmen Dunston and Oboe, back to work," he said, pointing to their turret as he walked off.

Graham waited until Bayard was out of hearing range before looking to Carly, her gaze on the map once again. "I thought you went for an ammo spool," he said. He followed her stare to the city map. "Carly?"

She blinked, her lips parting as she traced a finger along the exclusion line, across the border of Kilby, and into Cheshire. Shadows crept from her memory as vague images of violence. Her sight blurred to reveal a group of boys shuddering under a heavy stream of repeater fire, but the vision transformed to reveal the memory of a lone man collapsing in the rain under a burst of repeater rounds. Before she could figure the link between those dreamy illusions a gray mist rolled across her sight, brightening until it erupted in blinding white brilliance.

"Kilby," Graham said, his gaze darting back to her. "Come on, Carly," he hissed in her ear. "Kilby!"

She dropped her hand, her dilated eyes turning on him.

He met her stare.

Her chin sank before she shook her head. "Let's go," she said over her shoulder as she walked off to their car.

|0|0|0|

NOEL'S FACE FELL AS HE studied his screen. Sonya walked around his desk and leaned over his shoulder to have a look. "Bayard," they said in unison, but then took a new interest as the data continued to flow. Noel pointed. "What was that?" He turned to Sonya to see a trace of dismay in her eyes. "What—"

"Kill the trace," she said at once.

He stared at her in disbelief. "It's already a matter of record. We agreed the best way to do this was to run it as we would any other trace, to draw as little attention as possible. If I put in stop codes it'll send red

flags right through Drive Control. Somebody's sure to look at it then."
He studied her, seeing the unease in her eyes that went beyond the risk
of tracing Carly. "What's bothering you?"

She straightened and crossed her arms over her chest. "I think we've
been tracing the wrong person," she said as she turned from him. "I'm
going to have a look in the scripting code for this man, Chapel. I'll
be back."

Confused, Noel looked to his screen and scrolled through the data
thread. His lips parted in shock when he reviewed the conversation.

Chapel had control of his memory.

| 0 | 0 | 0 |

"Now that's a sunset," Graham said with a sigh. He glanced at Carly
as he waved a sandwich at the pink and red hues that washed over the rich
evergreen canopy of Danfield Copse. Heavy gray clouds lurked to either
side of the sunset. The departing day rains were drifting southward, away
from the field where Graham had parked the Patrol car, but to the right
lurked the incoming night rains. The break in the clouds wasn't unusual,
but to have it happen so, to frame the sunset to amplify its beauty, it was
a moment uncommon enough that Central deemed it good drive for
citizens to pause and enjoy the view.

Carly narrowed her eyes against the light before looking down to
the strong aroma from a mug of street soup she had procured. Procured,
she knew, was the drive-proper term used for taking things from cones
without reparation. Despite her inbred disdain for the cones as both a
citizen and a patrolman, she couldn't deny that the cones had a particular
skill for making tasty food. Compared to the sandwich that served as
her daily meal ration from Patrol the soup was packed with flavor. On
the contrary, the sandwich consisted of a large, dry, heavy biscuit cut and
stuffed with a smoked, compressed product of meat, soy and vegetables
that had the varicolored appearance of dried vomit and a consistency not
much different. It was known as compress. The biscuit, at least, helped

hold it together.

She sipped from the metal cup the cones used at their soup stands. Some of the cups were shaped scraps of alloy collected from fallen rockets. The cones claimed to wash the metal before stamping it to make the cups. Among citizens there was the common belief that residues of fuel and explosives were left behind to add extra flavor.

She looked into the cup, frowned, and glared at her sandwich. Her teeth crunched through the biscuit's crust and her eyes narrowed at the unsavory squish of the compress. They combined for a salty, salty taste. The corners of her mouth pulled down as her jaw worked on the sandwich, her eyes narrowing more when she forced herself to swallow.

Her gaze rose to the sunset before she looked across the barrels of the turreted cannons toward Graham. He was chewing as he reached through the open roof hatch between them to find their water bottle. She watched his steady gaze on the fading sunset. The moments of its beauty were fleeting.

A crabby mood seized her. "This is for the chiggers," she said, raising her sandwich when Graham turned to her.

"It's safer than that street slop," he said, tipping his head to the tin cup.

"Street soup," she corrected.

"Right. Eat and watch the sunset, Patrolman," he said before taking a long gulp from the water bottle. He wiped his mouth on the back of his hand and offered her the bottle without looking at her.

She took the bottle and drank, wiping her mouth on her hand afterward, just as he had. It was something she had never noticed before, that they had the same routine of drinking. It was another moment that added to the inexhaustible trail of moments that marked her day since staring at the city map in the motor pool. Those mounting moments had eroded her blissful, carefree morning cheer to leave her with her current melancholy distemper.

Just another day. The thought reverberated throughout the afternoon but, in the recesses of her suspicions, she knew it was a stark fallacy. Every moment since that moment with Graham and Bayard by the city map had stuck with her, and every facet of her Patrol rounds with Graham were stuck in her head. She had gained a view of her duty she suspected she never knew in the past, for she was aware of the long waits between orders and, more so, the tedious, pointless drives around the city quads until either Patrol or Drive Control would mutter new orders.

Despite her stubbornness to will herself to believe it was just another day she nevertheless found herself forced to accept that this day was quite different. The silence in the car between her and Graham made her growing sense of isolation—of dissociation—only more intense than she was willing to believe. It was, she knew, the source of her increasing crabbiness through the day, something she perceived in Graham's growing discomfort as the creases of his forehead multiplied.

Her behavior didn't help the situation. On two separate drives through Kilby they caught cones in acts of disobedience. Both perpetrators were tearing down recruitment posters of General Asper in plain daylight. Both times she hopped from the car only to find herself frozen where she stood, her hand clenched tight on the civi-stick she couldn't bring herself to bear. Both times Graham took it to task, both times glaring at her with annoyance when he turned back to the car.

If those calls were awkward, the call they answered in the early afternoon was a disaster. It was a domestic disturbance at a single/double domicile. It was the residence of a charter family, a paired couple who were deemed worthy of housing a child from Rainbow Go. Only those deemed most worthy among the citizens of Central were afforded the privilege of hosting a child from Rainbow Go, whereas among the cones it was common practice. For citizens, though, there was an expectation. Charter family units were expected to foster the best and brightest of Central's bureaucrats, the future high-ranking members of Drive Control. Disturbances in such families were taken as grave trespasses.

What Graham and Carly found when they arrived was a nightmare. There was an argument between the charter parents, to the point where the neighbors notified Patrol. The charter wife opened the door, only for the husband to slap her in open view of Graham and Carly. Graham was on the husband in an instant, pummeling him into submission with a civi-stick. Carly grabbed the wife and shoved her into the hallway before pulling her handgun and moving to the domicile's second room. She found a girl sitting on a bunk, hands clamped over her ears, the hood of her bright red slicker drooping over her face.

Carly pushed the hood back. "Hey, are you alright?"

The girl looked to her. Carly guessed her age at twelve, going on thirteen. Teen-stomp was right around the corner. Charter families were dissolved at that point. She was a pretty girl.

"He said it was time," the girl whispered.

Carly clenched her fists.

"He said it was free and right proper. He said I'd learn to like it."

Things just seemed to happen after that. Carly felt as if she was watching herself as she turned from the girl and walked out of the bedroom. Graham was on his radio, calling for Drive Control, keeping the husband at bay with a prod-and-lift. She waited until the man turned to her. His lip was bleeding from Graham's work, but she ignored it, and looked into his eyes.

Before Graham knew what was happening she grabbed the husband by the hair and threw him into the hallway. He hit the wall with his head but managed to catch himself before falling to the floor. It served her well as she ripped her boot up into his gut. He went down with a wheeze. No sooner had he hit the floor than she whipped her civi-stick free and went to work, smashing him relentlessly, pounding him with swing after swing as he groveled at her feet. The wife ran down the hall, screaming. The neighbors disappeared behind their doors. Graham charged out of the domicile and wrestled with Carly, but her limbs were supercharged with rage. She shook him off twice to rejoin the symphony of trauma at her feet. Graham at last managed to pin her to the wall, stilling her writhing mass of fury only by shouting into her face that Drive Control would take her too if she didn't stop.

Drive Control dragged the husband away, a bloody mess of swollen purple flesh and broken bones. They took the wife as well, and the daughter. They ignored Carly and Graham.

Just another day.

It was the only thing Carly could say when Graham dragged her back to their car.

She decided that he knew something wasn't right with her, something that went beyond considerations of good or bad drive. She was seized with the fear that he would report her, that Drive Control would grab her. Even her instilled paranoia of Drive Control had changed—it wasn't just the terror of being sent for reformat but the prospect of losing her new awareness, an awareness circling back to let her recognize the fact that her fear had changed.

Her varying moods and emotions came to her like waves, waves that crested several times, and each time she would sink further down to confront a single conclusion: *Graham doesn't know.* The moment the thought whispered through her suspicions her moods would stir once more, her world would turn on its head once more, and her growing anxiety would mix and meld with the flow of her thoughts.

Why doesn't he know?

Shouldn't he know?

Should I tell him?

Tell him what?

In the end, at the deepest trough of her emotional wave, there was only hollow frustration. She could see that her life, crafted in the hands of Central from Rainbow Go to Patrol, had failed to equip her with any mental capacity to wrap her mind around what was happening to her. Then again, hadn't that been the intent of Central? She knew it was paranoid, but it was what she knew of life, and everything she knew of life she knew from Central. It was a maddening spiral, a paradox she was powerless to unravel.

So ran her thoughts, down into that trough. She doubted her sanity and feared the loss of her drive. Central had left her with no way to express herself—not just to others, but to herself as well—even as she became certain that what was happening to her on this day had started on some other day, a day that had, in some way, been much more than just another day. With her memory in shambles she had no way to tell.

It was all nonsense. It had to be. If not, Central would've made sense of it for her.

Right proper.

And so the wave would crest again.

By the time she and Graham stopped for their ration and sunset the waves had passed in such number and the moments had tallied in such number that only her crabbiness seemed to remind her of some shadow of herself.

She looked to Graham as he hopped from the car, walked off on the green grass, and drank from their bottle as he urinated in the open before the copse. *Through filtration.* It brought a brief, small smile to her. He was the only person who knew anything about her, but even he didn't seem quite himself. Whatever choice she thought she had, she felt it was being made for her.

She frowned. *Well, today's in the crapper.* She looked to the sunset. The colors had faded and the nearing sky rumbled.

Shit.

It was such a simple thought, yet it spoke volumes to her, even as it covered the very lapses in her mind she yearned to fill. She was Patrol, after all. Patrol never backed down.

She let her breath go, despondent in her aimless frustration.

"There has to be more than this," she said to herself. Her gaze drifted up to the sky, its dome deepening in color as the day waned. Her mind filled in the void. *There is something more.* She pointed up and looked to Graham. "Hey, Chap, you ever think about up-top?"

He glanced up as he walked back to the car. "What about it?"

She opened her hands. "Do you think it's different up there than it is down here?"

He shrugged. "I guess it's harder to do through filtration without gravity."

"What do you think they do up there?"

He clambered up the side of the car to join her on the roof. He avoided her gaze. "What do you think they do across the ocean, in Central?"

"I, I don't know."

He pointed to her as he sipped some water. "Exactly. None of our business."

"But—"

He rolled his eyes as he shook his head. "Carly, you know we're not supposed to talk about that stuff. Central sends people into space. We live with rations to support that effort. Sending people up is supposed to make our future safe, whatever that means. Accept it. The sky is blue. Two and two is four. Whatever. Just another day." He looked to her. "Let me ask you something. All you have to say for today is to wonder about up-top?"

She blew out a breath and turned away. "I filed the report. It's done with."

"Did you add 'What the fuck?' to the file tag? You were two seconds from meat-farming that prick."

"He deserved it."

"That's for Drive Control to decide. You know he's bought a ticket to reformat for what he did. The wife too, for that matter." He shook his head. "Maybe the girl, too, and she's probably going to be better for it, having that perverted shit flushed out of her head."

Carly threw her soup cup away. "And that's it?"

"For us, at least." He grabbed her neck cowl and gave her a gentle shake. "Talk to me. What's bothering you?"

"I have to tell you?"

He shook her again. "Besides what that prick did to that girl. Come on. It's me, Chap. Talk to me."

She pushed away his hand, glanced at the sky, and debated with herself before looking back to him. "Do you remember growing up?"

"I guess." He shrugged. "Why?"

She pointed at him. "Were you in a charter family or the dormitories?"

"Dormitories. I didn't place out to charter status on my aptitudes." He closed his eyes for a moment. "Not much to tell. What about you?"

"Family." She waited until he looked to her. "I think it was more than just a charter family."

"What makes you say that?"

She rubbed her face, leaving her hands over her eyes to peer between her fingers into the blurred visions of her memories. "There was a day, when I was little. Something happened, something bad. I think some

kids in the neighborhood roughed me up. My mother meat-farmed them."
She took a breath and dropped her hands. "And then Patrol meat-farmed
her. So that was it. I went to a dormitory for Teen-stomp. I never saw
my brother again."

Graham studied her for a moment before waving it off. "Fuck it. You're
Patrol. Nobody pushes us around. Forget that other stuff."

She pulled at her lips as her eyes narrowed in thought. "My mother
was in Patrol."

"Patrol doesn't get family charter. Period. You know that." He tapped
a finger to his head. "I think that brick hit you harder than you think.
What about your father?"

She hooked a thumb over her shoulder. "Off to the war—"

Graham opened his hands as she realized what she was saying.
"Charter fathers are exempt from draft," Graham said. "See? That brick
hit you too hard."

"Then what happened to me when I was a kid?"

He put a hand on her back. "Carly, it doesn't mean anything.
Something happened. So what. You are what you are right now, and
you are what you do in this time. I think you saw something in that girl
that maybe reminded you of yourself and your charter family going to
the chiggers. You took it out on that prick. Whatever."

"You make it sound so simple."

"Simple is easy." He tipped his head. "Besides, easy works, works
right proper."

She thumped a fist on his chest. "Good old Chap. Just another day?"

He nodded. "Just another day."

"Right."

He capped the water bottle and tossed it to her before slipping through
the roof hatch.

She closed her eyes. It was her only way to make the world disappear.

| 0 | 0 | 0 |

NOEL PUT HIS HANDS TOGETHER as he watched the data flow on his screen. He looked down at his steaming teapot and the biscuit on his plate with its slab of seasoned compress sticking out one side.

Sonya came into his office and closed the door before leaning against the wall.

Noel looked up to her. "I'm losing her. Even through Bayard—"

"No," Sonya interrupted, her lips drawn. "*We* are losing *them*."

Noel blinked. "I don't understand."

"Chapel has been labeled a suspect rogue." Sonya let that sink in for a moment. "The belief is that he's the one who started the trouble in Kilby, the trouble that led your sister to a review table in front of you. He dropped off the scripting codes. It has to be reported."

Noel's face went slack as fears of Sector Control filled his mind.

"Not quite yet," she said, guessing his thoughts. "I think if we can find something on this Chapel, perhaps link him some other way to your sister for something that of itself would've prompted an investigation, I might be able to salvage both of us."

Noel rubbed his forehead before opening his hands. "The array discharge! They were both exposed, he less—"

She nodded and reached for the door. "Exactly. I'll try to do some work with the order coding and the times. I'll put a formal trace order through for your sister. That at least will explain why we were tracing her and hopefully separate us from suspicion of drive tampering. Unless someone looks close enough to see the timing of the order coding on the trace, we should be in the clear."

He looked to her.

She silenced him with a raised finger. "Don't thank me. If this is breached, you'll be joining me in a dark place."

|0|0|0|

FATIGUE SNUCK UP ON CARLY. Before she knew it her eyelids drooped, her head sank back against her seat, and she was off to sleep. From the darkness of her memories a voice welled up in her dreams, and she found herself in the surreal perspective of witnessing her childhood. She became an unseen witness sitting in her gray Patrol bodysuit, the way her mother often did in those forgotten days.

The bedroom she shared with her brother was dark. She watched herself sit up as a shadow loomed in the doorway. Carly looked, and then she remembered, and heard her youthful voice.

"Daddy, I don't want you to go."

Her father looked down at her. He sat on her bunk, pulled her into his lap, and rocked her as her arms circled his neck. "Ah, sweet Carly, the apple of my eye," he whispered to her. "I have to go. I—"

"Dad's going to kill Continentals," Noel said with enthusiasm from the bunk above.

"To sleep, boy," her father ordered over his shoulder. He looked back to Carly with a smile. "Don't worry. Central needs me. And don't be sad. Mother will say you're being weak, a cone, like your father," he said without losing his smile, but the outline of her mother slid across the doorway. He tipped his head to stay in Carly's gaze. "Carly, don't cry. I want you to listen to me. Look out your window, across the green field to the stand of trees. There, in the copse, the angels will wait for you."

"What's an angel?"

He raised an eyebrow. "Angels are the voices in our dreams. They whisper the secrets we try to remember under the daylight. If you find an angel, they'll make your dreams real."

"Does anybody else know about them?"

He pressed his forehead to hers. "No," he whispered. "It's our secret."

She buried her face in his neck as she squeezed him. "Take me with you."

"Maybe one day," he whispered. "Nothing would make me happier."

She sucked back her tears. "I love you, Daddy."

When she woke the next morning, he was gone. That afternoon, after Rainbow Go, she asked her mother where he went. Her mother slapped her senseless.

Carly sucked in a breath and opened her eyes.

Charter family? Chiggers to that.

Graham shook her shoulder and waited until she turned to him. "Come on," he said, looking to the building across the street from them. "Naptime's over. Last orders for shift. Let's get this done."

"Right, right." Her hands dropped from her legs to grab the handguns holstered on either side of her seat. She stepped from the car as she slid them into her thigh mounts. A dark, rainy night hung overhead as she studied the building before her. It was concrete, with long polarized windows.

She could be anywhere. She could be nowhere.

The day felt long behind her. Her head swam as if she'd downed half a bottle of Heavy.

She had the strange feeling she was still dreaming.

|0|0|0|

NOEL SAT BEFORE HIS SCREEN, his tea and compress biscuit long forgotten. His gaze was locked on the display, his hands frozen over the keyboard as if stung. Thoughts mumbled through his head in a mix of recriminations and regrets. The data flow had eluded him, its thread lost, despite his tools and resources to track the monitor inputs of Chapel and Carly. He had lost her before he could decide whether or not he even found something of her, before he could be certain whether she remembered that one morning that had put their mother out on the street, killing the neighborhood boys.

The beep of his reporter orb startled him. He sucked in a breath and keyed the orb's relay. "Controller Westing."

"Noel—"

His hand constricted on the orb. "Sonya! I lost her, I lost the thread."

"I need to see you, Noel."

"I'm in my—" he began, but fell silent. She was summoning him down to the scriptors. His hand trembled, no longer for Carly, but for himself and Sonya. Central had taken notice, he decided. Sonya's code deception had failed and now they all faced reformat if things went wrong.

"Noel," Sonya's voice came again. "I need to see you now. We can't track them either. We confirmed an unregistered predilector thread. It's diagnostic of a rogue."

Noel stood. He fell back a step from his desk.

I'll never see tomorrow.

|0|0|0|

AN ELEVATOR.

Carly felt as if she was watching herself.

Her gaze rolled to Graham.

He stared back at her, expressionless.

|0|0|0|

NOEL WAS BROUGHT TO THE utilitarian functionality of Sonya's office by an attendant and told to sit. No sooner had he ignored the empty man and started pacing between the black chairs, black desk, and white walls than Sonya came and waved him out. They walked down a long hall of stark cement blocks, past several closed offices, to a large white room with banks of screens and their operators. It was a scripting locus, a room Noel had never seen before, and one that he wasn't allowed to see as a controller. Sonya gestured for him to relax. It did little to alleviate his anxiety.

She pointed to a corner and waited until he stood there. Only then did she come beside him, yet her focus remained on the room as she spoke. "We're doing what we can to re-establish a trace on your sister's thread. It's not going well."

He leaned toward her. "What's happening?"

She licked her lips, debating with herself. In the end, she turned to him and shook her head. "Perhaps later I can explain. For now, we wait."

"Wait for what?"

"Well, we wait to see what happens, of course," she said with her vague scriptor's tone.

|0|0|0|

CARLY FOUND HERSELF STANDING IN a domicile. She heard herself spouting the usual threatening statements a patrolman spewed when searching a cone. At least, she assumed it was a cone. Most often it was cones on the receiving end of search orders. Somehow she knew that, but she wasn't sure how. Either Graham hadn't told her, or she had already forgotten.

There was a small shelf beside the resident's mirror. The shelf didn't seize her attention, but what sat there shocked her. It was a book, a bound hardcopy. She picked it up, stared at it in disbelief, and then fanned through the pages until she came to a sudden stop. Eyes wide, she turned back several pages and froze as she read the passage that caught her attention.

Across a starlit field, a stand of trees and, above them, only the quiet night, home to the whispering angels and their impenetrable mysteries. Is this solitude the domain of my madness, or is this the last refuge I shall know? In the end, it matters not. The world, it seems, is only that which I choose to believe, and that which I choose to believe is whispered in the breeze of this starlit field.

"Westing!"

Carly blinked, her lids fluttering as her mind was jarred to the present. She blinked again, her eyes focusing on the old faded book she held in her gloved hand. Then she remembered herself, closing the book before turning to look over the small room in which she stood. It was a typical domicile; a single/single much like her own, except the details of the room assaulted her. There was a smell, the odd smell of dilute detergent and stale urine that seemed to permeate many of the single/single dwelling blocks. She frowned in disgust, shaking the book in her hand as her gaze rested on the threatening, body-armored outline of Graham and the impassive stare of the aged resident they were investigating.

"This shit's on the censor list," she said and tossed the book to the floor. "You need clearance for hardcopy, you forget that?"

The resident stared at her, his eyes dark and blank as if he were on another planet. "May I speak, Patrolman?"

Something about his gaze at once soothed and disturbed her. "Say what you want."

"The book is empty," the resident said, his voice calm. "The pages are blank."

Carly ignored Graham's quick glance. "You're lying. I saw words."

The man smiled. "That book only shows you the words you want to see."

"What?" Her eyes narrowed. She looked to Graham. "Chap?"

Graham responded with a quick tightening of his lips. He looked to the resident, pushed him against a wall, and waited until Carly pulled her handgun before turning away. There was a small desk before the domicile's polarized windows. He looked at it, waiting.

Carly tipped her chin. "Give it the rip."

He hesitated, his gaze darting from the desk, to the resident, and back to the desk. He ground his teeth. "Right," he said and went to work on the top drawer.

Carly looked to the resident as the man stood silent, expressionless, while the empty drawers of his desk were tossed to the floor. "Name," Carly said. Her old detachment returned to her like a warm blanket, but in a different way, in a way that told her what she was doing wasn't so important, wasn't so necessary, that she should give a second look to that bound hardcopy—

"Patrolman," the resident whispered. "Tell me, what did you see in the book?"

She shifted on her feet.

Graham held the last empty drawer in his hand before tossing it on the unmade bunk. "Empty," he said with a wave at the desk. "There's nothing here."

The resident took a long, patient breath as his gaze settled on Carly.

Her eyes fell in confusion. She kept her weapon on the resident as she reached down to pick up the book. When she turned to the shelf she stopped short.

A red, red apple sat on the shelf.

Dreams are bullshit.

|0|0|0|

SONYA LOOKED AROUND THE ROOM of the scripting locus.

Noel noted the obvious worry in the clench of her jaw. In contrast, there was no difference in the attitude of the room's operators.

He whispered Sonya's name.

She looked to him before tipping her head back toward her office.

He followed her as she paced down the hall, her arms wrapped about her chest. She opened the door and waited for him to enter, then closed the door behind him. He watched as she paced before him, making several passes before her well-ordered desk. She stopped without warning, took off her glasses, and set them on her desk. Keeping her back to him, she reached up and ran her hands over her hair before loosening her bun to let her hair fall past her shoulders. She crossed her arms again, refusing to face him.

He cleared his throat. "Drive Control?"

She shook her head. "The thread is gone. Not just lost—gone, all of it. The trace on your sister, the trace on Chapel, even our global positioning track on their car, it all disappeared. I don't know what we stumbled into, but alarm flags are racing through Central as we speak. My order codes are going to be under all those flags. It's over." She drew in a breath. "Go back to your office, Noel."

He hesitated, unsure what to say or think.

She turned and took his face in her hands to give him a gentle kiss. She lingered for a moment until she drew in another breath, her fingers trembling. He opened his eyes to see tears on her cheeks.

"Sonya?"

"Go," she said, wiping her eyes as she turned from him and walked behind her desk. "Go while you remember me as you've known me. Let me have that dignity."

He fell back a step, horrified as he began to understand. "I—I'm sorry—"

She opened a hand and swept it back to him. "Go! They're coming for me. I can feel it, I can feel their every footfall."

He opened the door as his head hung in shame. He looked to her one last time.

"Remember me, Noel Westing."

He turned and closed her black door.

|0|0|0|

Carly looked from the apple to the resident.

The resident smiled. "My name, you ask? Ian Gadwick."

"Name."

"Ian Gadwick."

"Name."

Graham glanced at her.

The resident's smile faded. He opened his mouth, but then closed it without uttering a sound. His gaze locked on her eyes.

It took a moment, and then she felt an involuntary tip of her head in the sudden silence. She was whispering the man's name when she realized the desk search had ended.

She blinked. "What?"

Graham took the book from her and fanned through the pages. He folded the book back on itself to reveal a hollowed chamber containing two small black cubes. With a shake of his head he dumped the cubes into his hand and tossed the book on the bed.

Carly blinked. "I searched that book."

"You didn't look closely enough," Graham said and held out his hand.

She looked at his palm before turning to the resident. "Concentration cubes. You've been reformatted." She holstered her handgun as Graham tossed the cubes into one of the empty drawers.

He stared at Carly for a long time before exchanging a glance with the resident. He looked back to Carly. "Let's go," he said with a sigh. "No story here. Waste of effort." He went by her and pushed open the domicile's door. The smell of the hallway met them at once, stronger than the odor of the domicile.

Carly remained. She breathed.

The resident took a step toward her. The hard light of his one ceiling bulb cast a bright sheen on his balding head. "What are you waiting for? Do you want another apple, Carly Westing?"

Graham called to her from the end of the hallway.

Her lips parted, but her voice was lost.

"Tell me, why did you come here?"

The resident's voice filled her senses. "Central. . ."

He shook his head. "And what is this nameless thing, this anonymous authority that sent you here?" He waited for an answer until he shook his head once more. "Nobody sent you here, because I summoned you here. Ask your patrolmate. You see, I am the City of Seven Hills, and I'm looking for my successor, Patrolman Westing. I'm looking for you."

She stared at him, not believing her ears.

Graham shouted to her.

"This city will be yours," the resident continued. "You want it, yes?"

She blinked, back-stepping from the domicile to stand in the hallway. She felt nauseous, not from the odor, but from something else, an unnerving imbalance that left her feeling as if she wasn't quite standing within herself. The waves of emotions and doubt she had felt during the day crashed over her in a singular torrent that left her senses spinning.

The door to the domicile closed.

Graham grabbed her neck cowl, dragged her along, and pushed her into the elevator at the end of the hall. He waited until the doors cycled before shoving her shoulder. "Come on, Carly. Think! Kilby—"

He jumped back when he saw the pallor of her face. Overcome by the nausea of the hall and the plummet of the elevator, she tipped her head down, heaved, and vomited on the floor between her feet. Only the quick reach of her hand to grab Graham's shoulder saved her from collapsing. He bolstered her, pushing her shoulders to the back of the elevator to support her. With a glance at her vomit he hissed a quiet curse and looked back at her sweaty face. "I told you not to eat that street soup. You know those people. They cook the same pot for months; just keep throwing more shit in there to keep it full. Look at that," he said, tipping his chin to the vomit. "Probably rat meat."

She pulled down her visor. "Let's get back to the car."

The elevator doors opened to the main lobby of the domicile block. Her senses assailed her once again. The smell wasn't quite as bad, though. The frequent coming and going of residents over the course of the day allowed a wash of outside air to dilute the odors.

They walked out to the cold night and put the lobby behind them. Fog gathered on the street. The menacing armored hull of their Patrol car was almost lost, its gray armor plate blending with the gray mist. Only the reflective light housings on the roof and the oily sheen of the turreted cannons caught any glint of the distant flickering streetlights. They walked around the car, Graham pointing to the passenger side when she lingered by the curb. They stared at each other across the hood for a moment before she conceded. Her gaze fell to the chipped, faded paint of the car's registry, a set of weary letters that spelled out the name GRENDEL. After all her Patrol shifts, she had never noticed the name of their car. It amazed her in a disquieting way.

She looked down either end of the street before glancing across the car to Graham.

He was ready to slide into his seat. "What?"

She struggled to find her voice. "Just another day?"

"Right," he said after a pause and then slammed his door shut.

Carly sat in the car. She took a swig of water to wash out her mouth and spat on the street before closing her door. She unsnapped her helmet and pushed it off to the side. It fell to the floor between them, drawing Graham's attention.

He pointed to her lips. "Are you going to spew again? You can walk back to Danfield if you're going to stink up the car."

She frowned as she looked to Graham. It seemed that time was spooling out, that she was growing numb. Despite her confusion she suspected she knew the answer to her own desperate question. Her choice was being made for her, and it would happen in no other moment but that one moment. She trembled, meshing her hands together to hide the slow tightening of her body. "I, I was just thinking—that resident, he had concentration cubes. You only get concentration cubes if Drive Control reformatted you. That's a one-way street. Why would Central have us check on someone who already went through Drive Control?"

Graham looked across the car's hood to watch the muted reflection of a distant streetlight flickering in the night. "Rockets. Power winks when there's a lot coming in." He looked to Carly and rested his hand on her shoulder cowl to draw her close. "Listen to me. You know how it goes. Drive Control does the background work. They give the orders to Central's Patrol detachments. We search. We report. Next order, next search. Simple." He studied her, his gaze boring into her. "You still know that, right?"

"I know that," she echoed. The authority of Central was in his voice, but she heard something else as well, something she wasn't sure of, something that she felt was calling to her in the guise of the resident, in the hardcopy and its passage, in her stupor, in Graham's hand tightening on her shoulder cowl. Yet—

She folded her arm to close her hand over his.

"I know."

The moments passed. The corrosive process of forgetfulness clawed at her consciousness. It failed to escape her perception, her nerves bucking and resisting the mental invasion. The stupor of Central was an addictive bliss, but she wanted none of it. The resident's words were blurring in her mind, yet the concept they held and the terrifying implication of what he said entrenched itself within her.

A terrible thought glimmered within her.

The concentration cubes. They weren't for the resident.

They were for me.

They rolled through the streets and put the resident behind them.

The throbbing trails of rockets glowed overhead, some of them ending in bright balls of light as they were caught by an array.

The beep of the car's reporter broke the silence.

"WESTING, CARLY. CHAPEL, GRAHAM. STANDBY STATUS."

Graham's arm shot out to silence the orb as they rolled to a stop beneath an overpass. His hand pulled back to the steering wheel, his jaw muscles bulging as he ground his teeth.

Carly turned to him. The fading glow of a rocket lit his tension-laden face.

He gave her a sidelong glance as he leaned back in his seat to hide in shadow.

She had her answer then, the answer she sought. "Kilby," she said under her breath, her memories spooling without control. "That resident," she added, staring into Graham's eyes as she decided to take the step she knew she couldn't take back. "That resident, Gadwick, he said he summoned us, that you knew about it." She fell silent as something within clamped down on the last thing Gadwick said to her, something she felt was only for her ears. Her nerves tightened as the moments passed in silence.

Graham sat stone still. The streetlights went out, plunging them in darkness. There was a rustle as he turned in his seat to stroke her cheek. Her face fell, her hand rising to hold his as she felt his fingers tremble.

"Carly," he said as if her name was ripped from his throat, but then he pulled his hand away. He dropped the car into drive, stomped the accelerator, and sped across the city behind the exclusion line. He raced through her Danfield quad and out to the open darkness of the green between her apartment row and Danfield Copse. When the car's rumbling motor went silent he turned to her, his jaw clenched. Without a word he crawled from his seat and squeezed past her. He hit the stow release for the turret seat. It rose on its storage mount to fold flat into the turret and leave the crew area open.

She followed to sit on the deck across from him. He looked to her again and raised a finger before taking off his armor. She followed suit and piled their gear behind his seat before resuming her place before him. He reached out and pulled her into his lap. She straddled him, resting her hands on his shoulders as she stared at him with a mixture of curiosity and satisfaction. It was their usual way, she knew. Although there was nothing usual about the moment it gave her the sense of security she craved. He wrapped his arms around her and pulled her close, resting his face on her neck as he held her. She tightened for a moment, her hands hovering over his shoulders, but then she closed her eyes. A new feeling welled up within her, one she found herself incapable of describing. She submitted to that feeling and, before she realized, found her cheek resting on his head as she rubbed his back.

Their breaths came slow and deep, coming into rhythm until they rocked in the shadowy solitude of the car.

He lifted his head, the short stubble of his hair tickling her. He whispered her name and waited until she hummed a reply. "You haven't felt the same since Kilby, have you?"

She shook her head, too comfortable to bother with talk.

"It was the array discharge," he whispered, laying his hands on her shoulders to ease her back. He studied her as he rallied his nerve. "We should've died that night, but we didn't. It changed us, Carly, you more than me, being right next to one of the projectors. I thought you were dead," he said, his face tightening. "The array knocked us both out, but you were in the middle of it. I remember looking up to see them take you away. Drive Control and Bayard, that skinny chigger.

"I couldn't sleep that night. Every time I closed my eyes I thought I heard this voice—my voice, but not my voice—mumbling in the back of my head, telling me there was no incident at the array, that you weren't hurt, that all these things I knew happened didn't happen. Then I heard another voice mumbling away, and I knew it was my voice, and it kept saying the same thing."

"No," she said, understanding him, her anxiety soothed as she listened to him. "Over and over, no."

He nodded and lowered his head. "The next day—I still can't get used to saying that—I had to force myself out of my bunk. I couldn't remember my identification code. Weird thing was the orb didn't care. I couldn't figure that out. I got in the car and started driving and then it hit me that it couldn't be our car. Our car had a wheel blown off, but there it was waiting for me, parked where I always park. Then the order came for me to get Gwen instead of you.

"That's when I knew, when I had this feeling, that I was sure," he said, his hands tightening. "Something was far from proper. I rode with Gwen that day but every moment I kept wondering what happened to you. I thought of Drive Control, I—Carly, I thought it was quits for me. Five days later, when I was just getting used to living with all the memories of each moment, I got the order to pick you up instead of Gwen. It was like nothing ever happened, like you'd never been hurt, like those five days never existed. I wanted to talk to you that morning, but then I saw you, and you were a priority one mess."

She stared at him, her face slack. "So those things I remember, my hands and face all red, that's true?"

"All of it." He took her face in his hands. "I was hiding like some animal so nobody would notice I wasn't like anyone else because I could remember. I didn't want Gwen in my car, I wanted you, and the more I thought of you, the more it seemed those voices at night tried to work on me. That's when I knew it, I knew they were trying to take you away from me, not just in body, but here," he said, pointing to his head. "I knew it then, I finally got a hold of it, and as un-proper as it was, it was right proper to me. Carly, they make us forget," he said, his jaw clamping as he heard the madness of his own words.

She rested her hands on his chest. She wasn't sure what to say.

He grabbed her wrists. "The night before I got you back I dropped off Gwen and I was driving to my domicile when a dispatch came through. I was going to call Patrol because I was off duty, but the dispatch came to me anyway. Before I reached for the dashboard I heard a new thought, and it wasn't mine, silly-speak as that might sound. It was Gadwick, summoning me. We talked. He told me he covered me with the reporter orb. If he knew about that, it seemed it wouldn't make any sense not to believe what he said to me. He knew about you, told me where you were, what to do today to get you out of the daze Drive Control put on you."

"Graham," she said.

"He's above Drive Control," Graham said with a shake of his head. "He's over everything. He runs the whole city! He wants us to work for him."

"Did he tell you why?"

"He set us free," Graham said, speaking over her question in his stubbornness. "He set us free, Carly, we never have to lose each other and those chiggers can never take us away from each other. That's what Central wants! All along, they've been keeping us stupid, keeping us from remembering anything—but no more."

She pulled his head to her chest to hold him tight. She whispered his name as his arms circled her, his long strong arms—

Graham's elation was lost to her as a large burden settled on her shoulders and blotted his optimism in shadows of uncertainty.

Her eyes popped open to the hull of their car. It was solid armor, but she felt defenseless.

She closed her eyes and buried her face against him.

| 0 | 0 | 0

FAR BEHIND, WHERE GRAHAM AND Carly had parked to meet Gadwick, a lone figure walked down the street with his hood pulled up. Victor hummed a little tune as he strolled into the same building and took the elevator. His nose bunched at the lumpy, odorous puddle of Carly's vomit. When the doors opened he found an empty hallway in front of him. He hesitated a moment, letting his sensitivities feel out his surroundings to be sure he was in fact alone before he cupped his hands behind his back and walked to the domicile where Gadwick lingered.

He opened the door. "Hello, Elder Gadwick."

Gadwick turned, his jaw dropping. He shook his head. "Excuse me. Sir, I, I had no idea a person of your rank was in the city. I received no notice to expect a high predilector."

Victor tipped his head. "That was my intention."

Gadwick looked to the window wall before blinking and looking back to Victor. "How did you get here?"

Victor bobbed his head from side to side. "My position has its privileges, and anonymity has its advantages. A surface ship here, an airship there, and now I stand before you."

Gadwick's eyebrows drew low over his gaze as his thoughts churned. "So I see."

Victor walked into the domicile and closed the door. He held up a finger as he looked around at the mess Carly and Graham left behind. "Taking an austere path, Elder?"

Gadwick tipped his chin up. "A setting of choice, you could say."

"And what business are you up to?" Victor asked, gazing at the bookshelf.

Gadwick's eyes narrowed. "I'm tending to my charges." He studied Victor for a moment. "How would you prefer I address you?"

"Ah, the business of names," Victor said under his breath. He turned to Gadwick. "You can call me Victor Mortas."

"Mortas?" Gadwick pulled at his chin. "I know that name. I have a scriptor by the name of Sonya Mortas."

"Made an impression, did she? She's a lovely specimen."

"And much younger than you."

"I don't look a day over sixty," Victor said with pride as he held his head high. "Taking care of my body is one thing Central got right, I have to say." He grinned. "In any event, regarding Sonya, there's no business like new business. She's wiser than you might think, perhaps wiser than her age might suggest, but I still wouldn't call her old. Not by any normal standard, I'd say, and certainly not by any chronological measure." He opened his hand. "She's not the only reason I came to your city."

Gadwick held his composure. "I see."

Victor smiled. "I know what you're doing here. I know it's within your authority as elder. However, I must warn you to be careful."

Gadwick's eyes narrowed. "The process is tried and true."

"I'm appealing to you as a courtesy," Victor said as he opened the door.

"I'm just an old man seeking his retirement, hoping to pass on some of his hard learned wisdom. I suggest you consider that when you close your eyes tonight. Sleep well," he said with a wave and walked away.

Gadwick stepped out in the hall. "Is it only Sonya Mortas you seek?"

Victor turned. "Be careful, Elder."

"Is it only her you seek?"

Victor hesitated. "Yes," he said at last. "I only seek Sonya."

"Good." Gadwick crossed his arms on his chest. "Well, as you know, it's a messy business, dealing with rogues. No one can take their safety for granted in such situations."

Victor wagged a finger at the veiled threat. "Perhaps it's best if you forget me." He retreated toward the elevator. "Forget you ever saw me. Forget I was ever here. Forget everything but the precious business you seek. I am nothing, I am a dream—a harmless shadow—and you stand alone in the might of your authority, yes?"

Gadwick blinked. His hands dropped to his sides.

"Yes indeed," Victor said as the elevator doors closed. He ran a hand over his head, debating with himself. Gadwick could be a problem, a dire problem, and Victor hadn't calculated the proper parameters of risk. Even so, the elder seemed content with addressing Victor under his Mortas name.

But then, why should he be a problem? Gadwick was an elder and so a predilector of some capability, but he was nothing compared to Victor. The name Victor had used during his last visit was buried under years of mundane oblivion, a name that ceased to exist when his aspirations for its use went awry. He sighed with the bitter loss of those plans and the time he had invested in them.

"Ah, yes, those days are long gone," he whispered to himself. "I was once John Westing. I had a family of my own, the way it was in times before Central."

He blew out his breath. "The way it should be." Almost fifteen years had passed, but it might as well be fifteen seconds.

Central still wanted John Westing dead.

FAR NORTH OF SEVEN HILLS sat the massive port complex of Inward, the link to Central's home across the ocean. Unlike the concrete slabs of Seven Hills, Inward was a gleaming, glittering collection of glass towers piercing the night sky, its districts protected by rings of projector arrays and reflective alloy masses of air spheres that hung motionless over the city's perimeter. From the air spheres stemmed the ports of entry for the intercontinental air shuttles, their heft held aloft by the same mysterious technology as the spheres. Beneath their masses sat the city and, along the city's western edge, the ocean shore, studded with long fingers of industrial docks and the insectile sprawl of cranes, hoists, rail systems and tramways. Together they worked to speed the unloading of the huge surface ships constituting supply side's lifeline to Central.

At night the city of Inward defied visual comprehension, its lights and beacons reaching through the darkness from above, below, and all sides. Anyone in its midst felt engulfed by an eternity of urbanity embodied by an inescapable multiplicity of girders, concrete, and polarized glass.

Through this dazzling and dizzying array a small airship pressed its course, ignoring the sparse traffic of the city's night lanes. The bulbous craft's marker beacons were lost in the countless lights reflected from the glass-paned buildings towering about its hull, creating the surreal impression that it was diving into a kaleidoscope. It continued on, leaving the sea behind and making its way across the city until it found an outlying air sphere.

Radio frequencies stirred with the precarious operation of docking the airship to the sphere. Wind direction, air speed, electrostatic dampers and ion bleeders, they all came into play to harmonize the ship with the sphere to prevent any disastrous mechanical or electrical clashes. A small chorus of voices, garbled and static-laden on their respective frequency bands, referenced their checks and crosschecks in the smooth mechanical fashion that delighted Central. All who dwelled within the towers of Inward were members of Central. They were intolerant of carelessness, the very thing that Central bred into its subject populations.

At the ship's stern the quadruple propeller screws went to neutral pitch and slowed to a halt in the lazy night breeze. A hatch opened near the bow as the final securing measures were verified. Five men emerged from the hatch, with one last man trailing alone behind them. He looked about the star rich sky, then down to the ground far below with its hidden arrays, and then behind him to the glimmering city. A nod of satisfaction tipped his chin, a nod that work at Inward had gone well.

He hastened across the dock extension to join the rest of his party and enter the quiet comfort of the sphere's docking bay. The external lock cycled shut behind him, his eyes adjusting to the light to see past his party where a man and woman waited for him. The man, a controller of Drive Control, stepped forward and bowed his head in greeting. "Watcher—" the man began, but fell silent as the visitor laid a hand on his shoulder and gave him a gentle push away, instead taking the woman's hand and pulling her forward.

The visitor smiled.

The woman returned the smile with a proprietary tip of her head, and then lifted her eyeglasses to reset them on her nose. "Welcome to Inward, Watcher Stutts."

"Scriptor Sonya Mortas," Endo Stutts said through his smile. He put his arm around her waist and led her from the lock as his party bulled a clear path through the narrow corridors of the sphere. "So, tell me, Sonya," he said, his voice smooth and relaxed, "what brings you all the way from the City of Seven Sewers to meet me here at Inward?"

She cupped her hands before her and swallowed to keep calm. Endo knew why. Beneath his short, black hair resided a dark, penetrating gaze.

Everything about him was dark and linear, indicative of a calculating, cunning intellect.

It was an appearance he took care to maintain.

"I was sent to receive you, Endo. You seem, oh, a little different, I should say, than I last remember."

"Change is the hallmark of life, Sonya, but I'm still as you know me." He looked to her. "Who ordered you to receive me?"

Sonya blinked. "The order came from Central itself. I was surprised, I must say."

"I imagine you would be. Quite a mess you found yourself in with this whole Chapel-Westing business." He felt her tighten at the mention of it, and he could imagine why. No reprimand was issued, no criticism logged against her, not a word filed that the incident had occurred. He knew the only logical conclusion for her was the one Central wanted her to deduce, that she had stumbled into something that went deeper into Central than she guessed. It was just as well, because it required great care to wake the memories that haunted the Westing name. He shook his head. "Sticky business indeed, this Chapel-Westing thing."

She swallowed. "Oh, yes, quite sticky. Ah, here are your quarters for the night," she said, opening her hand before a sealed door.

Endo stopped and looked over his shoulder to the five men behind him. They were tall men, the clean lines of their long coats making them seem taller than they were and their solemn expressions giving them a threatening air. They were known to society as Mondial Killswitch, but to Endo Stutts they were known as One, Two, Three, Four and Five, their original identities and personalities long ago wiped away by the workings of Sector Control in one of its many darker hours. "Back to the ship," he said to them, "and requisition some suitable ground transport. Goodnight."

The five men nodded and left.

Sonya pulled a pass card from her hip pocket to cycle the door to Endo's quarters. He kept his arm around her, leading her in before cycling the door shut behind them. He made a quick tour of the quarters, a large flat that would pass as a single/quadruple in Seven Hills, but served as

VIP lodging in an Inward air sphere. Wherever he found net screens he touched them to darken their screens and silence their chatter.

"That's better," he said at last, turning to find Sonya by the door with her hands still cupped before her. He smiled, reaching over to dim the lights so they could see the glow of the city through the curved outer windows of the lodging. "Relax, Sonya," he said, taking her hand as his eyes filled with concern. "I think you've been too long at the periphery of Central. Have they completely mired you?"

"I would like to be closer, one day." She swallowed again and fought to find her voice. "It's a long way across the ocean, though."

"Yes, yes it is." His eyebrows rose, softening the scrutinizing cast of his gaze. "Please, come sit with me. I haven't seen you in such a long time."

Her jaw clenched, but her feet moved beneath her. For all her abilities and faculties as a scriptor, there was no denying the will of Endo Stutts. He took her hand, noting but saying nothing about her clammy palm as he led her to a couch by the window wall. He let her go and walked to the lodge's bar to search for some wine. She stood still, wringing her hands.

"Relax, Sonya. I only wish to have a pleasant glass of red wine with you and enjoy your company. I've always found your nervous demeanor rather endearing, but it's not necessary with me." He looked up to scan the well-stocked shelves before spotting a row of bottles resting on their sides, the tops angled down. "Ah, there we are," he said with relief, turning to glance back at her. He picked out two wine glasses and located the corkscrew. He studied her as he threaded the cork. "It's a peaceful view, the lights in the night. I've always found such a view very relaxing. Perhaps it's what makes me at ease on stage."

"Perhaps," she said with a sigh, her eyes closing.

He studied her, watching her shoulders settle beneath the angular lines of her tailored bodysuit. "Why not let your hair down, and put yourself at ease?"

She reached up and released her hair from its characteristic bun. She tipped her head back as she ran her hands through its dark length to leave it hanging straight and lustrous in the dim light. She opened her eyes to find him before her. Without a word she put her arms around him, ready to welcome him with parted lips.

"No," he said and rested a finger on her chin. Her hands slid down his back to rest on his hips, her eyes wide and dilated on his. He separated from her. She clenched her fists.

"Forgive me, Sonya."

She blinked. He understood her disorientation. He was no longer before her but at the bar, at the bar where he'd been all along while he worked his predilection upon her.

She put her hands to her temples and squeezed her eyes shut. "You promised not to do that," she hissed as she checked her hair. It was, of course, still in a bun.

He avoided her gaze. "I know. Forgive me."

She was silent for several moments before he heard her reply. "If that fantasy lives so brightly within you, why do you hold it away from yourself?" Her voice drifted across the room like a whisper nestled in a dream. "I won't lie to you, Endo. The desires of Central live in me, too. I've dreamed of you, dreamed of being with you sometimes, when I see you on stage. It might be a wonderful thing, if you'd let it happen. All I would need from you is a word, just a word, a low whisper of my name in my ear, and that dream would open around us. Besides, I live alone."

His pulse quickened. For all that he desired her in that moment, he once again found himself stilled in her presence. He was Endo Stutts. He could have anyone, yet he was powerless to take her, despite how easily he could have her. No, there was something about her, an indescribable, simple purity that suffused her, dispelling and debilitating the facile charms he knew he embodied under Central.

He took a breath. The quickening of his pulse changed. Temptation shed its veil to reveal the ugliness of its hidden nature, and what he found himself incapable of enjoying by natural progression he knew he was ready to take by force. Disgusted with himself, he shook his head. "You should go. Self-control is not at its best with me tonight. The road I follow is long and difficult."

She walked to him to lay a hand on his arm.

Sympathy. He knew it drew her to him the first time they met.

She let her breath go. "They're going to destroy you, the way they push you."

He looked to her hand. His lips parted, but he decided ignorance would keep her safe. He met her gaze. "You have a gentle heart, Sonya. For your sake, it's better that you leave me." He waited until she cycled the lock before he walked around the bar to stand by the window wall. Determined to discern what was bothering him, he dissected his thoughts and inclinations. In the end, it was a pointless game of self-deception. He knew with exacting precision what it was that bothered him. He had anticipated it when he was dispatched to Seven Hills, he felt it awaken on the airship, he knew it the entire time he talked with Sonya, and knew it haunted his stunted temptation for Sonya.

The Chapel-Westing business.

Carly Westing. I've watched you for so long that you've become one with my dreams.

"Dreams are images, and images are illusions." He blew out a breath. "Illusions aren't real." He knew people in Patrol had a different perspective.

Dreams are bullshit.

Frustrated, annoyed, he lifted the bottle and drank the wine. He wiped his mouth on the back of his wrist. He put a hand on his hip, swirling the bottle as he looked down on the city. In the quiet, in the growing numbness the alcohol brought to his outer senses, he felt a stirring, a tingle within his mind.

He closed his eyes, and the million-fold data threads opened themselves to his gaze.

| 0 | 0 | 0 |

CARLY STOOD BEFORE HER WINDOW wall, toweling herself dry as she watched a heavy morning rain drench the city. "So we just walk into Patrol like nothing happened, like we haven't been gone for two days listening to Gadwick?"

The shower fell silent as Graham finished washing. Gadwick had instructed them to sleep in their car, the one place that lacked a net screen for Central to purge their memories. After a night slumped in the crew compartment they felt rather grungy. The plastic shower curtain rattled open as Graham reached for Carly's towel. "Right. We walk in like it's just another day. That's the plan."

"Sounds like a short road to the meat-farm," she said with a sigh.

Graham tossed the towel over her shoulder and pulled on his bodysuit. "Gadwick says he would cover our tracks with Drive Control."

"Right," she said, turning to him. "But for all he said to us, he didn't tell us what he wants us to do, did he?" She never told Graham of Gadwick's plans for her. She figured it was for the best, that in some way it would protect Graham if the whole escapade went to the chiggers. Despite the assurances Gadwick gave them concerning his resources and abilities, she still had her suspicions that they would roll into Patrol and find a gang of Drive Control agents waiting for them.

"Don't tell me you're going lame," Graham said in disbelief. "We're Patrol, Carly. We don't back down."

"That was before. Things are different." She tossed the towel over her net screen. She took a black shirt that Graham handed her from beneath her bunk. It was a purple lettered ENDO shirt, and she stared at the letters before pulling the towel from her net screen. The shifting displays and the endless banner ads across the bottom of the screen were the same as before. Everything was the same as before, but her perception was different. She had learned too much, even without Gadwick. In the creeping paranoia of their isolation her attachment to Graham solidified, its roots deeper than she could've guessed. She could conceive a day, a moment, when something might jeopardize all she knew. It gutted her resolve—her drive—despite how much she despised Central for the way it had manipulated her. She was jarred to the reality of herself even as the forgetfulness of sleep still held its allure.

"Well, think what you want of Gadwick's plans, but you have to admit they're better than what you wanted to do," Graham said as he clipped on his armor vest. "Opening fire on your neighbors because their bulls rose with you wasn't the most level plan. I knew that, and some of the women in my building I never would've touched if it was up to me."

She pulled on a boot and looked up to him as she shook her head. "But that's what I'm talking about. Gadwick was long in the words telling me what a bad idea it was to open fire; long in the talk that it was Central that drove our bulls around our buildings, that it was Central driving us to do all the things we do in Patrol. Two days he spent explaining that, how Central made us forget so we could work through the things we do, but he never explained why. Why does Central have us putting our bulls on the rise with everyone around us? Why make us forget everything, and not just the crazy things? Why take away this whole shit-stinking sense of moment to moment to let us sit in *this?*" she said as she opened her hands to the claustrophobic confinement of her domicile. She turned to Graham. "That doesn't bother you? You can keep all this straight in your head?"

"No," Graham said with a shrug. He handed Carly her armor vest and waited until she was done with its clips to hand over her repeater. "What I know is this. If we live through tonight Drive Control won't be able to touch us. That's Gadwick's promise. He said he's covering us from Central until we do what he wants. After that he said he wouldn't have to cover for us, and if he doesn't have to cover for us we can say chiggers to him if we want, because we'll be free."

"Free?" Carly blew out a breath. "I don't know. We thought we were free all along, and now we know that was a lie. What is free? Living in fear of Drive Control, even if we always lived in a different kind of fear of Drive Control?" She reached out to grab Graham's neck cowl. "What is Gadwick's idea of free? He said we might have to pay for it. Our freedom or his freedom—freedom like we had with Central?"

Graham laid his hand over hers. "I don't care. I'm not going to think that far. I don't know if I can think that far. But whatever way we get free there's only one thing I do think of. You know what that is?" He rested his hand on the back of her neck and pulled her close. "Whether it's hiding in a copse, running away to the Continent, or riding a rocket up-top, I don't care, because we'll be there together. That's all that matters."

| 0 | 0 | 0 |

"So, TELL ME," ENDO SAID as he stared at the passing landscape outside his limousine, "is there anything else we know about Chapel and Westing that isn't in the reports?"

Sonya picked up the tablet on the seat beside her, set it in her lap, and tapped at the file interface before shaking her head. The screen shone as a bright reflection on her glasses. "I was on short notice," she began, but then cleared her throat. She decided there was no need to make excuses or be defensive. She closed the files and looked up at Endo, his gaze still fixed out the windows of their limousine. Beyond the back window she could see the convoy of three trucks following them toward the City of Seven Hills.

The Mondial group had awakened her before dawn and ordered her to go to Endo's quarters to summon him. They were an intimidating lot, the Mondial group, when she found them outside her door. She dressed in haste, met Endo, and gathered with the Mondial at the air sphere's ground elevator to descend to the surface and board the convoy. The five men of Mondial, despite having worked the night to secure the convoy vehicles, showed no sign of fatigue. Chances were, Sonya decided, they slept in one of the trucks.

"Don't worry about them," Endo said, shifting his gaze to Sonya. "The Mondial. They get their rest. If something should happen to them I can draw replacements wherever I go. Sector Control is always accommodating."

The suggestion of pending violence unnerved her. "I just—"

Endo's eyes narrowed. "What? There's something you haven't told me, yes?"

"Is there some other way?" she said, surprised she found the will to voice the thought over her reservations.

Endo shook his head and leaned forward, staring at her as his elbows settled on his knees. "These two, Chapel and Westing, what are they to you, Scriptor Mortas?"

Her face fell as she realized he knew she had tampered with the scripting codes that morning when she and Noel traced Carly. It was possible Endo knew about Noel, something that afforded her little comfort. She decided to offset any suspicion of her involvement with Noel against the missteps of her tampering with the scripting codes. "So you already know," she said, her fingers clutching the seat cushion as he nodded. "You just asked the question now to open a lane in me, didn't you?"

He said nothing.

"And that's why there was no punishment for me, no bad business with Drive Control," she finished, following the lead of her logic. "There were predilectors involved from the start of this, weren't there?"

He continued to hold his silence.

She set her teeth and leaned her elbows on her knees to meet his gaze, their faces close together. She took off her glasses and held his stare as she summoned her will. "Tell me what I've stepped into, Endo."

He tipped his head as he probed her resolve.

"You wanted to relate to someone freely, no manipulation, and I agreed, agreed to you in your capacity as a predilector." She paused as she let her reminder sit unveiled between them. "You can't have that and play games with me at the same time. It can't work that way, for either of us."

He settled back in his seat, folded his hands in his lap, and crossed his legs. She held still before him, waiting for his response. After several moments he grinned and opened his hands. "Very well, Sonya, we'll do it your way. You can breathe your sigh of relief now," he said, not missing the strain that spilled from her. "You've grown bold since the last time I saw you. The Sonya I knew would never come at me like that, promise or no between us."

"Things change." She settled her glasses before her eyes. "That realization is what sets us apart from the rest of Central's subjects, yes?"

"Yes, that, and the knowledge of what people do to conceal things, such as using the best defense for a good offense. I am well aware that you know Westing's brother, this Noel Westing. I know that you were acting on his behalf regarding his sister." He nodded once when her jaw dropped in shock. "Did you think you could conceal such a thing from Central, from me? I was hoping you would tell me; I was hoping that 'you would admit it to me on your own. That was part of the promise, wasn't it, my dear Sonya? Next time you raise your ire with me, consult your better judgment, or you won't be dealing with the Endo who makes intimate little promises, but the Watcher Stutts who justifies all means by their ends. We can play our games but in the end we have our places. Those paths must not and cannot conflict. Do you understand?"

She forced herself to swallow, her resolve only a memory. "Yes."

"Good," Endo said lightly, as if nothing had happened.

She stared at her hands. "I live alone, Endo. I always have."

He gave her a quick, curious glance. "Tell me about this Noel Westing, and how he got you so involved with this Chapel business."

Her stomach knotted. "If you know I've been associating with him, then you must have accessed his records through Central."

His jaw clenched. "Sonya, I will warn you for the last time. Don't make me do this the hard way. I'm protecting you from Drive Control. That can change in a heartbeat. Promise or no promise, the wheels of Central must go on, and little affections will not get in the way. I—"

She raised a hand to silence him. "Enough, Endo, please. I understand. I met him after I last saw you. I missed you," she said, finding it hard to recall that sentiment as she stared at the Endo sitting before her. She took a deep breath before speaking again. "I was lonely. There was something about Noel, his neediness, his vulnerability, and it went from there. I haven't slept with him. He's not an unattractive man, but he spends too much time in the sex dens."

Endo shrugged. "That only makes him a typical citizen. I'm sure he met some other ordinary woman under those dim lights."

There was no mistaking the disdain in his voice.

Sonya shifted in her seat. "I wasn't passing judgment. I only wanted you to know the extent of our relationship." She took a breath as she pushed an unsavory image out of her mind. "He thought his sister was following the same course in life as he until she turned up at Drive

Control. He was covering for another controller who called in sick. It was dumb chance that he wound up evaluating his own sister for possible reformat. That's when he came to me for help. He was concerned. She's part of Patrol. He was upset. You understand, yes? I agreed to help him. I had no idea about Chapel. I thought it was a simple trace, but it turned out to be much more."

"You stumbled across a rogue predilector."

Her eyebrows rose. "We didn't know. The whole thing, it, it ran away from us. Before I knew what was happening it was too late, too late to pull back, too many flags already in the flow."

"Yes, it was a mess." Endo took a deep breath before raising a finger. "There are two types of rogues, Sonya. The first type—the most common type—is, to our good fortune, the easier to deal with. Such subjects are those who wake to the realization that they possess predilectory skills without yet understanding what that means. They are ignorant, but pure, and thereby easy to discern among the data threads, because they lack the subtlety and guile of a trained predilector. When confronted they respond in one of two ways. They either embrace their potential within Central or they rebel. The vast majority of subjects default to the rational pursuit of embracing Central. The remaining few insist on rebellion and, without fail, end up in Sector Control for reformat.

"The second type of rogue is far more difficult to handle. This type of rogue is one who has resided within the folds of Central but has decided to turn against Central. These traitors can move unseen among the data threads, deceiving and manipulating anyone they choose until the lies crumble and expose their schemes. All the skills such subjects possess, all the intimate understanding they hold of Central and the Process, they employ against Central in service to their own agenda."

Sonya considered what Endo said. "You don't believe Chapel is the rogue, do you?"

Endo opened his hands. "It's not up to me to disagree with the convictions of Central."

"But if not Chapel, then who? If the rogue is an established predilector, wouldn't the rogue have known the risk of detection?" She shook her head. "That would be a contradictory action. An established predilector would be wary of such a thing."

Endo opened his hands. "And yet this predilector insisted on playing the game out, at least for the night in question. Any predilector would have been aware of the traces. Any predilector would know what repercussions such antics would bring. And yet—and yet," he added with a gleam in his eyes, "this predilector went about its way, knowing I was coming to the city for an endorsed cycle of riots, that I was in fact within forty-eight hours of arriving."

Sonya debated between Endo's allusion and the audacity of the entire idea. "A predilector challenging you? Challenging Central, in essence?"

"And doing it through a clever shell game, starting with cone misbehavior in one little area known as Kilby Quad." He smiled. "The Intricacies, Sonya, the Intricacies, they make fools of us all. It is the irony of any rogue that for all the cunning of predilectors who step away from Central they all forget that their very divergence is at once part of Central, that there is in fact no divergence at all because, in the end, they all realize the futility of resistance."

"Westing, Chapel—all of that, it's just a game?"

Endo nodded, gazing at the rolling green landscape that sped by the limousine. "You see, if there is anything to what a predilector comes to know, a predilector who lives completely in the understanding of Central, it's knowing that there's no such thing as freedom as it was thought to be, 'freedom' in the way of making decisions independent of Central. Freedom is nothing more than the opportunity for ill-informed individuals to make bad choices, because we must believe Central makes all the right choices, or there really is no point to all of this, yes?" he said as he waved a hand to the countryside beyond the limousine windows.

Sonya swallowed, no longer sure if Endo was aware of her presence.

He lowered his hand, his face settling. "Yes," he answered himself. "Yes indeed."

She followed his gaze out the window of the limousine. In the distance a herd of cattle chomped at the green turf of the rolling hills. She turned back to Endo to catch the little grin tugging at his lips.

"Do you understand, Sonya? Come sun, come rain, come howling tempest winds, the herds will graze, complacent and serene in the wisdom of their humility."

| 0 | 0 | 0 |

GRAHAM PUT HIS HAND ON the hatch release of the Patrol car as his gaze fixed on the expanse of Patrol's garage. Like Carly, he was frozen in his seat. "Ready?"

"I guess," Carly said under her breath, peering out the windshield with Graham. "I guess we'll find out just how many of those moments we keep talking about we'll have."

Graham glanced at her. "That's not funny."

"I know," she whispered. Her face fell. "Shit. Beak-nose. This is it."

Graham swallowed over a dry throat.

She heard him, but didn't move. "Not so easy now as it seemed before, is it, to trust Gadwick?"

Graham closed his eyes and said nothing before he hit the hatch release to swing up the car's door. He hopped out, Carly following on the other side of the car. They looked about the garage, nodded to Gwen and Oboe, and then to Bayard as the thin man neared them.

"Patrolmen," Bayard said in greeting, his face bunching up as he looked over their car. "Those barrels are filthy," he said, waving a hand at their turret. "Such sloppiness cannot be condoned. Endo Stutts arrives today. The riots start tonight. *Riot* and *Killshot* will be monitoring us for possible presentation on the nets. Everything is to be polished. See to it Patrolman Chapel. See to it *now*," he said, the order crisp with irritation.

His gaze fell to Carly, his forehead knotting and relaxing, knotting and relaxing, as if a switch in his head was being flipped to and fro. "Patrolman Westing," he said, tipping his head back to scrutinize her down the length of his nose. "Come here."

"Sir." Her nerves raced within her as she neared him, detecting a threat from him that she had never felt before. It was Central, she decided, the reach of Central through him to manifest before her.

Bayard continued to study her, his gaze sinking from the smooth curve of her cheeks to her lips before returning to her eyes. "I missed you the other night, but I understand that Drive Control had other priorities for you. I was quite disappointed, my Nimbus." He held his threatening air, but it soon dissipated in the wake of a gloating smile. "Tonight? Tonight indeed," he said with confidence, despite the absence of her reply. "Yes, tonight."

It was difficult for Carly to keep her composure. She saw him then as she failed to see him before, in all his intimate detail, leering at her naked from her memories. Revulsion swept through her. In its wake, she felt a violent surge of anger that this man had used the wiles of Central to—*to stick himself in me.* Her rage boiled, and the temptation to beat him senseless with her civi-stick was almost irresistible. *You piece of shit! One day, one day soon, you're getting a bullet between the balls—*

Bayard blinked. "Patrolman? Are you listening to me?"

She let out a little cough. "Sir."

I'm sending you out on a mirror route of two other patrolmen.

The thought that whispered through her wasn't her voice. It took a moment to recognize it as Gadwick, and her confusion formed a silent question in her mind.

It will keep you from having to interact with Central. Follow the lead of your patrolmates. It should keep you two out of trouble, for today.

"I'm sending you and Chapel on a mirror route with Dunston and Oboe," Bayard said, nodding with clear satisfaction. "I think that should keep you two out of trouble for today, yes?"

"Sir," she said and forced a smile as she lowered her gaze to put him off her lack of attention. She looked up to see if he was nodding, only then realizing it sold the deception with more conviction than anything else she could've done at that point. Bayard turned and walked away, barking orders at another pair of patrolmen across the garage from her. She began to turn but stopped, looking over her shoulder across the various cars. Only then did she realize that of all the Patrol groups in the garage she knew only Gwen and Oboe by name. It was one of those little perceptions

Gadwick had warned of, that she would begin to notice certain things that were part of Central's former way upon her.

Her head spun with everything Gadwick had told her. All silly-speak, she decided in an effort to allay her anxiety. It wasn't her way to be patient, not the way of Patrol to be patient, but patience was the very thing Gadwick asked. How could she question his plans if she didn't know what to ask, or what the questions—not to mention the answers—would mean? All she knew, all she clung to, was Gadwick's simple statement that he intervened in her life because it was required of him. Where was freedom, if even that choice hadn't been a choice? It was a thin line, a very thin line, she decided, between choice and manipulation, chance and contrivance, options and foregone conclusions.

She pulled herself atop the car and sat across the turret from Graham as he wiped down the turret's barrels. A deep sigh escaped her, one that caught Graham's attention.

"What?" he whispered, his gaze darting about the garage as he worked.

"Freedom," she whispered back to him. "I just don't get it."

|0|0|0|

NOEL SAT IN HIS OFFICE with a vacant gaze on his screen, tapping his fingers together before his creased forehead. His stomach was bloated with acid and growled in protest at the anxiety that filled him. It was a burning sensation, matched by the burning, festering certainty that somebody, somewhere, had manipulated him, had orchestrated his entire life in the last few days.

It all seemed so sickening, so suspicious in its convenience, the way things had worked out. A sick call: a common, yet random thing. His reassignment on a particular day for a particular sick call: part of the coverage rotation list, a common, yet random thing. Meeting his sister, having her judgment within Central dropped into his hands: not common, yet at once maddening in its randomness and glaring in its contrivance. And Carly, what of her? Who in their right mind would run into a defense array when it was about to fire?

He shook his head. In retrospect, the only thing disturbing him more than the origin of events was their conclusion. The emergence of a rogue predilector, Sonya being whisked away to Inward, the total absence of any response from the higher ranks of Central, of Drive Control; each of them were singular events that left him dizzy. Central had obliterated their very existence by omitting any note or reference.

The entire flag trail was deleted from the data threads. His own meeting and evaluation of his sister wasn't just removed from Central's records but was erased with such thoroughness that not even the erasure left any evidence of its action. If a thing had no record of it ever existing, who could argue against the record that it did exist? It became a thing that would linger only in the minds of those who knew of it, and Central could argue the frailty and subjective illusory nature of individual or even group memories. It would be easy to discredit any credible argument that the thing had ever existed. The only solution for those who were witness was to forget, knowing that if, some day, that memory were to be hinted or spoken outright, then Drive Control would be on the way. In the lonesome darkness of night there would be a swarm of black-gloved hands, and never again would one know the light of day the way it was known before.

Noel knew this. He knew it as a certainty, for it was part of his function in Drive Control. He had, after all, arranged for such actions based on his interrogations and evaluations of people brought to him, people like his sister. It was maintenance, maintenance for the Process. Society must go on; Central must go on. The data threads must not be disturbed.

He swallowed and dropped his hands on his desk. He gazed over his office and memorized the details one by one. Beige walls, brown chairs, brown metal desk, black floor; the place exuded mental lassitude, whereas Sonya's office was sharp with contrast. It buoyed his awareness to a stark thought. Time was working against him. Time was running out for him. It might not be today, might not be tomorrow, but one night it was coming as sure as night itself was coming—the black-gloved hands, the grab in the lonesome darkness. Central was cleaning up after the rogue, and that would include all the loose ends.

He was just another loose end.

Sonya couldn't help him. It was possible, quite possible, that he'd already doomed her by involving her in the mess. He couldn't help her. She would have to fend for herself. For Drive Control to send a scriptor to Sector Control was a delicate thing, but he'd seen it happen, twice. The ripples and repercussions were long and far, the result of unfinished scripting codes in the data flow, threads without ends—*uncertainty*. How Central hated uncertainty.

He frowned as he reached for his tea and took a sip. It was long cold, bitter and beyond drinking, but he drank it anyway. He would need the caffeine. Central may not have realized it, but Central had made his decision for him.

Just as it always has.

His hand shook. He put down the cup, worried that he might drop it. His desperation—his paranoia—drove the flight into his legs. In a heartbeat, he knew what he had to do. He had to run, flee, and he had to do it soon.

It has to be tonight. They're coming to get me. It has to be tonight!

| 0 | 0 | 0 |

A SMALL CONVOY OF BLACK vehicles rolled to a halt before the wall of shrubbery that separated Drive Control from the apartment rows of Rooking quad. The truck at the rear opened first, and the five intimidating figures of the Mondial Killswitch hopped out onto the quiet street. It was noontime, with a somewhat warm sun weighing down the damp, cool air until it felt like a close, heavy blanket. The Mondial made no note of it, splitting to peer down the street before they walked along the line of vehicles and knocked on the windows of each. One by one the vehicles discharged their occupants, with Endo and Sonya emerging last.

Endo looked about and turned to Sonya. "Not bad. I see things have improved."

"Efforts are made."

"Good. I find that encouraging, considering Elder Gadwick's reputation."

Sonya swallowed over a dry throat. "Seven Hills is on the edge of Central's reach. We have to deal with significant numbers of cones that get brought into the population. I don't need to tell you that assimilation isn't always a smooth process."

Endo gave her a glance. "Your loyalty is to be admired, but you don't need to make excuses for the elder."

She fidgeted with her glasses in a weak attempt to hide her nerves. "It's just—I know things here can be rough. I don't want to see things get rougher, for anyone."

"Nor do I, Sonya. But I know how men like the elder think. They insist on having a doily under their teacup while they sign execution orders."

Sonya stiffened with fear.

Endo noted the change in her demeanor. "An expression, not a fact. Don't forget, your safety is secured as long as you're with me. I am the Watcher, after all." He opened a hand. "Well then, let's see to it, shall we?"

Sonya blinked. "See to it?"

"It's not like you haven't seen two predilectors chat before."

"But this is no afternoon tea chat. Approaching a city elder concerning a rogue in his city's midst, that's not an easy talk."

"Let's not dwell on such unpleasantness," Endo said with a sigh. "There may be time enough for that."

Sonya lowered her head and opened a hand to the long brick building of Drive Control. It wasn't a distinct structure by any means. Built with a low, two-story height, it appeared somewhat quaint with its white lattice windows and their flower boxes poking out between the rich green ivy creeping up the building. Like most things with Drive Control the substance lay hidden. Though the building reached only two stories above ground, beneath the ground it delved more stories than she knew, as the lower levels were the hold of Sector Control, and their secrets were their own. The heart of the building was at the subway nexus linking it with the rest of Rooking quad and the many members of Central who dwelled there, like Sonya and Noel, in their comfortable domiciles.

She led Endo into the building's front double doors. The marble annex within echoed with the rap of their heels. From the annex they entered a large lobby, also floored with marble, containing many dark-stained, wooden doors leading off to different areas of the building. The Mondial group passed between Sonya and Endo and took a stance in the middle of the lobby, turning their backs to each other to form a circle of watchful eyes. Sonya glanced at Endo, but he showed no notice of their behavior.

"I don't have clearance," Sonya said, reminding him of her lesser stature.

Endo hummed. "You're with me. I serve as clearance to everything."

Sonya stared at him, considering that little statement. She led him to a door to the left of the lobby and opened it to reveal a small office with two secretaries, a man and a woman, their black hair cropped close to their scalps. They looked up from their screens to Endo and rose from their chairs without a word.

Endo's gaze was elsewhere, though. Oak paneling lined the room, but the warmth of the paneling was lost in the sterility of the room's functionality. Nothing was out of place. The desks of the two secretaries were ordered to a degree that bordered compulsive. Each supported two piles of hardcopy reports, one to process and one processed, in even stacks at right angles to the desk edge. The desks, to either side of the doorway beyond them, were perfect mirror images of each other. If not for the difference in gender of the secretaries, one could be fooled into thinking there was one secretary next to a mirror.

Endo seemed unfazed. "Elder Gadwick lives up to his reputation after all," he said under his breath. He stepped forward, reaching out to cup the chin of the female secretary. "Would you be so kind as to tell me your name?"

The secretary stared through him, her eyes as empty as those of a doll.

Endo dropped his hand. "The door, please."

"Yes, Watcher Stutts," the woman said at once, though her face held no detectable change in expression. She reached behind her and turned the knob to open the door ajar.

Endo glanced back at Sonya. "Sector Control has been hard at work here." He indicated the wood paneling with a tip of his chin before rolling his gaze between the secretaries. "Doilies and orders," he whispered to Sonya and pushed open the door to enter the elder's office.

Sonya followed, dropping her gaze as she passed before the blank eyes of the secretaries. There was something beyond their vacant presence, beyond their obvious reformat, that disturbed her. It was one thing to be reformatted and another thing to be a wipe. People sent to reformat were at least returned to society as some pale semblance of their former selves. Those who became wipes underwent full reformat and never again knew who they were or what offense they had committed to forfeit the right to their awareness. They were as thoughtless as a weigh plate on a dispensary, responding only when pressure was applied.

It was something to consider as she stood outside Elder Gadwick's office. She hesitated in the doorway, unsure of herself. She had never entered the elder's office, nor seen him, for that matter.

"The door as you enter, please, Scriptor Mortas," a gentle voice said to her.

She stepped to the side to close the door behind her and put her back to the wall. "Sir," she said, her gaze rising to meet the aged, dark-eyed face of Ian Gadwick, the Elder of Seven Hills, as he sat behind his large oak desk. He ignored Endo, studying her for several moments, too many moments, before pointing to a green leather chair in a corner.

Endo took note of the long gaze. He glanced over his shoulder, a curious gleam in his eyes as he looked at her.

Her nerves raced under the scrutiny of two predilectors. She fidgeted with her glasses before settling into a chair. Her feet were close together, her knees pressed against each other to hide her anxiety yet ready to propel her from the room at a moment's excuse.

"I've been looking forward to seeing you again, Predilector Stutts," the elder said, opening his hand to another leather chair before his desk. "It's been quite some time since the Watcher visited Seven Hills."

Endo bowed and sat. "Noted and likewise, Elder Gadwick. If only the circumstances could be more pleasant."

"Oh, yes. So Central knows of the rogue," Gadwick said with a sigh.

Endo waited several moments for Gadwick to continue. "I—"

"It's being handled."

Endo shook his head. "Elder," he said in a low voice, "we speak pre-dilector to predilector. As predilectors we have our degrees of individual action, do we not? Yet those actions are still in the focus of Central. I wouldn't come to your city and advise you how to handle a rogue predi-lector, something with which you know I have experience. Nevertheless, you have taken no actions within the awareness of Central. Patrolmen Westing and Chapel are back on patrol. As a matter of fact, you know that your own people, people within this very building, have supplied to the data flow that Chapel is indeed the suspect rogue."

Gadwick held his silence, contemplating before he spoke. "You have your experience, Endo, and I have mine. We are both old men, far older than men should be. I know well enough my responsibilities to Central, so you need not remind me. Yes, Westing and Chapel are on patrol. Did you care to notice that they're on a mirror patrol? That if either of them makes a move, they are immediately confronted—scrutinized—by two other patrolmen?"

"And what end does that serve?"

Gadwick gave Endo a patronizing nod. "We elders have our priorities with Central, Endo."

Endo stared at the elder. He stood.

"Scriptor Mortas," the elder prompted, keeping his gaze on Endo, "return to your office if you would, please."

Sonya rose and bowed her head. She forced a swallow before bolting from the room.

The elder grinned, but the gesture faded as he looked back to Endo. He put his hands on his desk and stood from his chair. "You're a welcome guest in my city, Endo," he said with officious courtesy, "but this is a matter for an elder to consider."

Endo refused to relent. "Rogues are my matter. Regardless of their nature they are to be handled a certain way. You know this. Need I continue?"

"And I would remind you that there are things between elders and Central to which even Endo Stutts is not privy." Gadwick opened a hand. "Or need I remind you of my authority, of our respective places in the scheme of things, and turn this into a most unpleasant meeting?"

"It is what you make of it," Endo said, his patience growing short. He licked his lips, drawing a blink from the elder. He smiled then, his confidence returning. "We have our domains, we predilectors. Don't force me to take care of yours, because if I must, I will, and that is an exercise of *my* authority. Do you understand me, Elder?"

Gadwick tipped his head. "Please, let's not take this course. No need to argue. Such a wasteful thing, when we both serve the same cause, wouldn't you agree? I don't desire it, and I know as well that you don't desire it, as we both know it's a horrible inefficiency, yes? Let us start this again, shall we?"

Endo held a wary gaze on the elder. "There is another perspective to consider. Carly Westing."

Gadwick nodded. "I'm well aware of her proximity to this matter."

Endo studied the elder for a moment. "Carly and Noel Westing are the children of Rebecca and John Westing. John Westing remains an outlaw high predilector of unknown identity. A death warrant remains open on him for defying all established breeding and charter laws by having children with Rebecca Westing and attempting to raise them himself. Carly Westing was assaulted, Rebecca Westing was shot dead, and Noel Westing became a mediocre bureaucrat in Drive Control." Endo pointed at the elder. "All these things happened under your watch, Elder."

Gadwick gave Endo a tired roll of his eyes. "I'm well aware of the failures ascribed to me in the Westing matter. For your sake I will once again repeat my claim: I knew nothing of Westing's activities in this city. I was cleared of any suspicion in the assault on Carly Westing. Nothing has changed in the years since John Westing's disappearance."

"Carly Westing is part of the rogue activity. She remains a subject of concern for Central." Endo tipped his chin up. There was no sense in avoiding the unspoken question rising up around them. "Has John Westing resurfaced in Seven Hills?"

Gadwick shook his head. "Watcher, please. No one knows who Westing was—not even Central. John Westing is a ghost."

"John Westing is a criminal."

Gadwick held up his hands in deference. "Do you really think the rogue is the same predilector who operated under the proxy identity of John Westing?"

"That remains to be seen, but one thing is clear. Carly Westing held great promise as a potential predilector. Central believes this potential persists within her, despite the appearance that it was lost after her assault. After Westing's disappearance I was charged to monitor her. I've watched her ever since."

Gadwick's eyes narrowed. "Do you think she's the rogue?"

"No," Endo said at once, but then caught himself. He ground his teeth. "Her disposition in this matter is yet to be determined."

"And how long do you expect it will take to make that determination?"

Endo closed his eyes for a moment. "As long as necessary."

Gadwick grinned. "Well, at least in the meantime she's a most pleasant specimen to observe, isn't she?" He chuckled, holding his humor despite Endo's stolid expression. "Only an observation, Watcher. We all have our tastes, don't we? I imagine you do as well. Is there some taste Seven Hills may service for you?" He opened a hand to the cabinet behind Endo. "A drink, perhaps? I see you lick your lips. You thirst from the drive. Red wine is your preference, is it not? I picked up the request in the data flow from your stay at Inward."

Endo blinked.

"Yes, I can scrutinize the data threads with such ease," the elder said, to Endo's surprise. "Did you think you were the only predilector of such power?" He waved off the notion. "No, you need not answer such a foolish question. To challenge you would be folly on my part. You could, without a doubt, have found such inconsequential information without as much effort as it required of me. After all, I'm an old man and you, in the relative youth of that body you use, quite the superior in your faculties, yes?

"Yes, indeed. So, please, drink. Just behind you, you will find some fresh red wine I have for you, for you alone. A carafe to slake your thirst; and it is one of many thirsts you have denied yourself since arriving at Inward, yes? I know how difficult it must be. Scriptor Mortas, she is a tempting, lovely specimen—though not nearly as lovely as our dear Carly, is she?" Gadwick waited several moments before waving a hand. "Never mind. We digress, for it is rich wine of which we speak, as red in its luster as a fresh picked apple. Now, would you like some, just a taste, perhaps?"

Endo walked around his chair and reached for the carafe the elder indicated. "You understand, I will be watching."

Gadwick tipped his head. "Central watches us all, does it not?"

Endo blinked. He was on the sidewalk before Drive Control, walking with his hands out as if he was pouring a glass of wine. The Mondial trailed behind him, dutiful in their stupidity. He stopped short and turned to the building.

Three armed patrolmen occupied the annex.

He lowered his hands and clenched his fists.

| 0 | 0 | 0 |

CARLY STOOD BY THE FRONT of the Patrol car on a street in Kilby quad. She looked across the car's hood to Graham, certain she possessed the same bewildered expression she saw on his face.

The street echoed with shouts and screams as Gwen and Oboe dragged two cones from their building. It was a domestic disturbance call, another mess of claustrophobic rage, but it was always worse with the cones. Charter families at least went through a rigorous screening before they were mated and given children from Rainbow Go, but cone families were different. Shipped in from the scattered settlements outside the city, they came as a messy mix of parents and children. They never failed to serve as stark testament to the rightness of Central's way.

Carly shook her head in frustration as Oboe ignored the couple's son, a boy no more than five years old, and left him by the curb. Other cone residents from the building were filing out on the street, complaining as Oboe slammed the father face down on the hood of a Patrol car and Gwen pinned the mother with a prod-and-lift by the hood of Carly's car. Graham moved past them, waving at the cone residents and ordering them back into the building.

"When do we get a better array?" an old woman said, pointing toward the Continent.

A man with a limping gait opened his hands. "When do we get power back? It's dark at night. We were promised things would be better if we came here."

Graham glared at the man. "It's dark for everyone. You'll get your lights when Central says it's safe to take the quad off power curfew. Now, back inside."

The father struggled against Oboe. "Bitch was humping around," he said between his grunts. "She was sneaking out behind my back!"

The mother jabbed a finger at her husband. "Lazy shit! What do you know? All you do is drink and snore!"

The father blurted several curses until Oboe lost his patience. He grabbed the man's hair, jerked his head back, and slammed it against the armored hood of the car. A sickening, wet thud sounded out as the man's nose collapsed in a spurt of blood.

The boy started to cry. Several of the neighbors pushed him back as they shouted out in protest. Gwen turned, distracted for a moment, even as Graham and Carly pulled free their civi-sticks. The mother took advantage as Gwen looked away, slapping the civi-stick from under her neck to charge at her husband.

Gwen barked for the woman to halt.

Graham spun toward Gwen. He missed Carly's warning as a rock flew from the neighbors and rebounded off his helmet, sending him off in a stagger. Carly cursed and swung with her civi-stick, taking out several neighbors with quick strikes to leave them sprawled senseless on the street.

Oboe looked up in surprise. All he saw was the mother charging toward him, and all he heard was the eruption of violence behind him. He rammed his elbow into the father's back and whipped his sidearm free with his other hand.

The woman couldn't stop her charge.

Oboe fired.

The bullet smashed through her forehead and popped out the back of her skull, her hair puffing as it absorbed the red spray of gore from her cranium. Momentum carried her one more step before her legs gave out. She dropped in a motionless pile.

Carly went numb.

The neighbors went quiet.

Gwen walked over to the dead woman and poked the corpse with her civi-stick. "Shit. Stupid cone." She spat on the ground and looked up. "I'll notify Drive Control."

Oboe pointed to the curb. "Hey, Westing, wake up," he said, looking back to Carly to get her attention. "Secure the kid."

Carly blinked as she looked to the boy.

Gwen laughed, misunderstanding. "Think you can handle the little pecker?" she said before waving to Graham. "Come on Chapel, let's get the rest of these chiggers in line."

Carly and Graham looked at each other to rally the nerve to move. Graham shouted at the neighbors, ordering them back into the building. Carly shoved some of them with her civi-stick as she made her way over to the boy. He stood, frozen, staring at his mother's body. Carly stepped in front of him to block his sight.

The father writhed, but Oboe whipped him with the handgun to silence him. The man slid off the hood and fell on the street.

Carly's gaze darted up as Graham and Gwen herded the last neighbors into the building. She slipped her civi-stick back in its loop. "Look at me," she said and waited until the boy's swollen, dazed eyes rose to meet her gaze. "Forget this. Rainbow Go will take care of you. If you behave, you'll even get to live with a charter family until you enter Teen-stomp. It's for the best. Central is here for you. Understand?"

The boy stared at her.

It was a rehearsed speech. Carly wondered how many times she said those words after a cone domestic call. Standing there, she wondered if she understood them any better than the boy.

The squeal of truck brakes caught her attention. She looked over her shoulder to see two black vans from Drive Control. The body of the boy's mother was already off the street. Two men of Drive Control were lugging the father's limp form into the back of the open van. From the other van a woman in a bright yellow coat walked over to Carly. She was young, pretty, with her light brown hair pulled up in a perky tail, her lips curved in a welcoming smile beneath her bright eyes.

Carly looked from the boy to the agent from Rainbow Go, to the bloodstain on the street, and back to the agent.

"Patrolman?" The woman nodded to her. "Thank you for your service. We'll take it from here."

Carly fell back a step, lingering until Graham grabbed her neck cowl and pulled her along.

The agent crouched in front of the boy to fill his sight. "You poor thing. All this will go away. You'll see. You're going to know a good life with Central. Doesn't that sound nice?"

He was a little boy standing alone on the curb, surrounded by trucks, Patrol cars, violence, and a pretty woman in a bright yellow coat with a lovely smile. He looked at her open palm.

It wasn't a choice; it was an empty question.

The boy sniffled and took the woman's hand.

Carly couldn't help but stare as she settled in the Patrol car. It was a scene, she realized, that she knew well, not from Patrol, but from having lived it herself. She rubbed her face as she slammed the door shut and waited until the engine roared to look at Graham between her fingers. "Did this just happen?"

Graham shrugged as he put the car in gear and followed Oboe's vehicle. "Yes, it just happened. Cones," he said with disdain before blowing out his breath. "Animals. They squirm, screw, and stink like rats."

Carly turned to him. "You believe that?"

Graham shook his head. "How many times have we done domestics on cones? You don't see this with charters. Central might steal our memories, but it got some things right."

"What about that fucker that went after his daughter?"

Graham shrugged. "Every system has its failures. That's what we're here for."

"Right, to break what's already broken." Carly sighed. "Do you think the dormitories of Rainbow Go are better than families?"

"Hey, I was a dormitory boy." Graham opened his hand on the steering wheel. "You're the one questioning things, not me."

Carly shoved his shoulder. "What's that supposed to mean?"

"It means you don't have to question everything. I guess it means you shouldn't question everything. Yes, I grew up in a dormitory. You grew up in some kind of charter and you've got something, something messed up, knocking around in your head from that. I don't. I mean, I grew up, and that was that. I ate, I went to school, I slept. So what." He waved a hand at her. "You're thinking too much. Gadwick said we might get confused. I think you're confused."

She tipped her chin up, too stubborn to surrender the mist of her memories. "I didn't grow up in a charter. I told you that." She crossed her arms on her chest. "I grew up in a family, like the ones the cones have. I'm sure of it."

"And it went to the chiggers," Graham said, wagging a finger at her. "You're in Patrol, right next to me, so whatever happened then, it didn't make a difference, did it? That should tell you all you need to know."

"No, it doesn't tell me anything, except that maybe Central doesn't want me to remember anything because of what happened." She clenched a fist. "There's something about the way I grew up that has to be important, even now. Why else would I remember it?"

"Are you listening to yourself? Central doesn't care about any one person."

She rested her head back. "Well, I have one more question."

"Carly—"

"Why can't people in Patrol charter?"

Graham's eyes bulged. "Look at the way we live! Us, with kids?

That's crazy."

She looked over the buildings as they passed by. "Fine. Then answer this one. If all the families under Central are charters, then where do all the kids come from?"

Graham opened his mouth, only to press his lips together as his jaw clenched. He shifted in his seat several times before glancing at her, his discomfort clear in his eyes. "Like I said, you think too much."

| 0 | 0 | 0 |

SONYA PACED THE HALLS OF Drive Control toward her office, obedient to the elder's order. She kept her arms crossed over her chest, one hand rising to push her glasses up when they slid down her nose. She fought to control the knots in her stomach as her fears gained hold of her. She was certain that the meeting between Endo and Gadwick wasn't going well and that she'd be caught between them, an unfortunate pawn in a power struggle of predilectors. The data threads held faint traces of such confrontations, and she learned how to find them through her association with Endo and his business of routing out rogues. Despite the promise she shared with him she regretted having associated with him. The promise was a frail link, a frailty exposed as she sensed the cold malevolence brewing beneath Endo's calmer moments.

She was left staring at the raw reality of her vulnerability. Tenuous as her security was, though, she feared for Noel, because he wouldn't see the threat coming for him until it was too late.

Where to run, when Central comes for you?

To me, Gadwick's voice whispered through her.

Sonya trembled, faltering as she paced the last steps to her office.

The elder's thoughts pushed into her consciousness. *You feel for this man, Westing's brother. You can't hide it, and you can't hide from it. It drives your concerns, even now as you fear for yourself. I can show you a way. You want to know how, yes?*

Her eyes welled up. *Yes!*

Then lead him. I'll show him where to go, but he won't run without you.

She opened the door to her office and found Noel waiting for her—*imagine that.* He ceased his anxious pacing when he noticed her. She closed the door behind her.

He opened his hands. "Sonya? I was told you called for me. We agreed—"

She stared at him, in that moment feeling very far from herself, from the things that troubled her, and at once very near to herself, to the things she treasured. It was the work of the elder, but that was a forgotten concern as she gazed at Noel. His boyish looks, from his soft cheeks to his large eyes, had always charmed her with their air of innocence. His lesser habits weren't important. The sex dens were just a way to blow off steam. He blushed whenever they were mentioned. It would be easy to take him, and the ease only quickened the temptation. No games, no sharing, no waiting; no, he would curl up within her affection in every way imaginable.

Control could be a potent aphrodisiac. Endo had told her as much.

She let her hair down and took off her glasses. She paced to Noel, slipped a hand around the back of his head and drew him to her, to her lips. Confused, he laid his hands on her shoulders to stop her, but she continued, kissing his cheek and letting her lips trace along his skin until she kissed him again just under his ear, her other hand sliding across his hip to press against the small of his back.

"Sonya, wait, I don't understand, I—"

"Quiet now," she said, resting her lips by his ear, "now is the time to listen. Time is drawing short for us. You have to leave. I know that you're considering this very thing, planning it tonight, perhaps?"

He pulled back, his eyes narrowing on her. "How do you know that?"

"Easy," she said and kissed him. "You must go to the market, our market, the Rooking day market, this evening." She kissed him again, and felt his hands press against her back to pull her close.

He drew in a stuttered breath and ran his fingers through her hair to cradle her head to his shoulder. "I won't leave you behind, Sonya. I can't. I got you involved in all this. I have to get you out. It's too dangerous to stay here."

She turned her face into his neck as she held him tight. "Oh Noel, you have such a kind heart," she lamented. "First you want to save your sister, and now you want to save me."

He took her face in his hands. "Forget about Carly. I hardly remember her. That time is no more real to me than a dream. You're real, you're here, and I won't let you go. Why wait until this evening? Let's run right now."

"We can't just run away. If we abandon our desks Central will know. Let's finish our day here, okay?"

His jaw clenched as he considered her wisdom. "Okay," he said at last. "I don't like it, but we'll do our day and leave like normal."

She tipped her head to give him a sidelong gaze. "Do you trust me?" Before he could answer she laid a finger on his lips and looked straight into his eyes. "There's something so familiar in you, something that feels so near to me. I don't understand it, but I feel deep inside me that we share something, and it seems that it's whispering in me all the time now." She laid her hands over his. "Do you love me?"

"Yes," he said at once, closing his eyes at the creak of his voice before looking at her again. His thoughts were as plain as monochrome text across his forehead. She knew the warm welcome of her scriptor's sensitivities drew him to her, where before he only knew rejection and the vacant, anonymous exercise of the city's sex dens. He led an empty, lonesome life.

His jaw clenched with conviction. "You're the only one I've ever loved, Sonya."

She grinned as she raised an eyebrow. "Am I more than the sex dens?"

He blushed. "I don't want to do that anymore. I go to the dens to hide from myself. It's the only way I know to deal with myself." He gave her a quick look. "I, I haven't gone to the dens for a long time. I don't want that anymore. I want you, and that's all I want."

She put a finger on his chin, found his gaze, and gave him a smile before kissing him. His arms constricted around her as his lips parted and she felt his breath. He trembled with anticipation. She rolled her head back and stilled him with nothing more than a finger on his lips. Obedient and submissive in her control of his lust, his arms slid from her to let her go as she leaned away from him. "I know what you want," she whispered. "I want it too. I'm tired of living alone."

He closed his eyes and clutched her hand as he pressed his lips to her finger.

"Wait for me at Rooking market, and you'll have everything you've desired."

He pulled her close and gave her a rough kiss. Then he forced himself away, clamping his hands on her shoulders and locking his arms straight to create some distance. "At Rooking market," he said with a nod. His hands snapped open. He stared into her eyes for a moment longer and then left her office.

She didn't move. Her lips parted as her eyes dulled. She blinked once, twice, before she shuddered and was startled to her senses. She turned on her feet several times to look over her office until she looked at her desk and its empty chair.

"I, I live alone," she said under her breath. "Yes, yes—I always have. Yes, I believe so."

| 0 | 0 | 0 |

"I'M A CONTROLLER! CONTROLLER HENSHAW!"

Carly planted her feet and swung her civi-stick. The suspect Graham had shoved against the wall caught the blow of the stick full in his gut, doubling him over before his knees gave out to dump him headlong to the floor. The lobby of the Rooking apartment building they occupied emptied in a hurry. The residents, even as members of Central, wanted no part of a Patrol beating. Gwen and Oboe shouted at the residents to hasten their retreat before turning to the now crumpled man on the floor.

Carly stepped back and lowered her civi-stick as she turned to Gwen. "He had a box of hardcopy. Nothing else."

Oboe shook his head. "Not so easy. He was stuffing books of silly-speak propaganda into sup-side deliveries. He's up to something."

Graham waved a hand to the floors above them. "Up to what? All he had to do was see who had a box in front of their door."

Gwen poked Graham's shoulder with her civi-stick. "Going soft, eh Chap?" Her green eyes were full of good humor above her pleasant smile. She stepped by Carly and grabbed Henshaw's hair to jerk his face toward her. "Where'd you get the hardcopy, asshole?" When the suspect failed to answer she swung at him with her other hand, her gloved fist pounding into his face. She drew back, ready for another strike as her civi-stick dangled from its wrist strap.

Her expression lost its disarming demeanor.

Carly closed her eyes and opened them to find the same sickened look on Graham's face. It wasn't the violence that bothered her in that moment but the mindless demand of the moment itself. It was pointless, and it made no sense except to strike fear in everyone around her. She had dim memories of recounting similar beatings at the Underworld, reveling in their excess as she laughed in drunken delirium. No, she had to find some reason for the ruin of one Controller Henshaw.

"Enough," she said with a shake of her head. She shoved by Gwen to grab Henshaw's shoulders and drag him to his feet. She slapped him to get his attention before slamming him against the wall. "Hey! Where did the hardcopy come from?"

Henshaw sucked in a breath and looked from Carly to Oboe as Oboe pulled out his civi-stick. "I, I don't know," Henshaw said between quivering lips. He wrapped his arms around his belly. "I'm a controller, Controller Henshaw. Check with Drive Control! All I did was report in sick a few days ago, that's it!"

Oboe laid a hand on Carly's shoulder.

Graham's glare shot toward him.

Desperation drove tears from Henshaw. "They were just there, those hardcopies, I swear. I woke up, and there they were. I swear! I don't know where they came from—"

Graham's eyes narrowed with interest. "Are you saying sup-side left the hardcopy?"

Oboe swung back his civi-stick. "That's right proper sil-ly-speak bullshit!"

Henshaw grabbed Graham's wrist in desperation. "No, it's the truth! Sup-side, they left it. They were waiting for me, and there was a woman from Drive Control—glasses, hair pulled up, wearing a tailored suit—I could point her out if I saw her again. She told me to give out the books to anyone who had a sup-side delivery."

Carly blew out a breath. "Set you up for making citizens look like cones? What is that?"

"Chiggers to that," Gwen said. "Hit him."

Henshaw's hands shot up in defense. "No, they did this to me, Drive Control did this!"

Gwen bared her teeth. "Hit him."

Carly raised her hand to Oboe. Graham blocked her. He gave her a quick shake of his head when she turned on him.

A wet snap sounded out. Blood sprayed across Carly's cheek. Oboe and Gwen began to laugh as Oboe swung his stick back. Henshaw slipped down the wall, his nose a bloody ruin of smashed flesh.

Oboe nudged Graham with an elbow. "Come on, Chap. This little bitch thinks he's funny. Might run before Drive Control gets here. Drive Control giving out hardcopy. Drive Control making him look like a cone. Chiggers to that."

Gwen thumped a fist on Oboe's shoulder. "Right proper."

Henshaw coughed from where he sat on the floor, his hands cradling his nose. Graham stepped beside him, civi-stick in hand as he looked down to Henshaw's desperate eyes.

It has to be done, Gadwick whispered to Carly. *He would've sent you for reformat if he'd been the one to review you.*

Carly's gaze darted to Graham. By the widening of his eyes and the snap of his civi-stick to attention she knew he too had heard Gadwick's voice.

Gwen misunderstood their reaction and took hold of her stick. "It's a foursome, it's a foursome!"

Graham ground his teeth. He whipped his stick down on one of Henshaw's knees, shattering it. The man screamed as he reached for his knee, his voice silenced when Oboe's stick came down to shatter the other knee and several reaching fingers at the same time. Gwen's stick whistled by, cracking into Henshaw's elbow. He writhed, screaming until Carly's stick smashed into his other elbow.

They backed away then, Gwen and Oboe laughing as they walked off to the Patrol cars. Graham and Carly fell back another step, their focus locked on the sight of Henshaw. The ruined man had urinated on himself in the midst of his agony. Blood ran around his gaping mouth as he slumped on his side, the only sound a wet click as his diaphragm tried to suck in a breath to drive another scream from his tortured throat. And this, they knew, was before Drive Control got their hands on him.

"Fucker," Carly said under her breath. "Now we'll see who gets reformatted."

Graham kicked Henshaw in the stomach. "Right proper."

Carly swung, bashing Henshaw across the side of his head. Senseless, his hands twitched as vomit dribbled from his open mouth. She stomped her boot into his gut and raised her stick in both hands as he curled into a breathless ball.

Gwen came back in the lobby and leaned on the door to keep it open. "Hey, let's go! Don't meat-farm that chigger. He's for Drive Control. We just got orders to patrol Rooking's market."

| 0 | 0 | 0 |

GADWICK SAT IN HIS OFFICE, eyes closed as he massaged his temples. He could feel Endo pressing through the data threads, pursuing Gadwick's deceptions to find any little mistake that could unravel his game. Despite his confidence his nerves were on edge. The game balanced on the edge of a knife.

Focus and remember the goal, remember the goal!

The pieces were in place. The stage was set. The sacrifice, the price, had to be paid.

He took a breath and severed Noel's presence from the data threads. For all intents and purposes, Noel ceased to exist.

"And who would do such a thing?" he whispered to himself. "Only a rogue."

It was a charming deception because no one would expect it.

He chuckled. "You have my sympathies, Sonya."

|0|0|0|

Sonya blinked. She came to her senses to find herself sitting at her desk, her hands to either side of her keyboard, her vacant gaze on her door. After several blinks she moved with a start, her hands snapping up to the loose trail of her hair. Her heart raced with stumbling panic, but then her befuddlement collided headlong with her returning memory. In that surreal vision she perceived the subversion—perversion, perhaps—of her sensibilities, to manipulate the will of her weaker self.

"Noel," she said under her breath as she struggled to remember what she had said to him. It waited unmasked in the data threads, had been left exposed as she sat in a stupor through the afternoon. She clapped her hands over her head, pulling at her hair until she deduced the only person who could—or would—predilect such a long period of inaction.

"Gadwick," she said to herself, her hands shaking as she realized the elder had used her. She rose from her chair, but then returned to look at her screen. Her fingers tapped at the keys as she checked her scripting code routines. The threads of her charge were progressing without alteration. She was about to stand when she caught herself, noticing a small deviation in the thread she had initiated for a particular Controller Henshaw, whose sick call had started all her worries. Her head shook as her gaze picked up the Patrol detachment sent to carry out her plan for the controller's carelessness.

Chapel and Westing. She put her hands over her face. *What to do, what to do?*

Gadwick might not be aware of it, but she was sure Endo had his sensitivities bent around her. If he did, he would guess what she realized Gadwick wanted him to guess. Endo would know all the things Gadwick had spurred her to say to Noel.

Run away—with Noel?

It was insane, but she had said it, said it aloud, for it to become part of the data threads. The elder was using her as bait to draw Endo's jealous attention to her and, through her, onto Noel. She was the only connection from Noel back to Noel's sister and Chapel, and Gadwick had cast a specter of collusion about her by having her conspire to flee with Noel.

Gadwick had left her dangling between himself and Endo.

She bolted from her chair and all but ran out of the building to the underground subway nexus. Her plan took shape with the reckless urgency of desperation. Endo would be waiting for her. She would make it back to her domicile and divulge what she knew to him—if she could give him enough information to point the way back to Gadwick she might put him off well enough to save herself. If she was convincing, she might even afford Noel enough time to escape.

But escape to where? There is no escape from Central!

Riding the subway, she fought to hide the tears that seeped from her eyes. She was fond of Noel, and she knew that he wasn't a threat to Endo, Gadwick, or anyone else for that matter. Like her, he was a pawn caught in a dangerous game.

Something welled up within her as she considered his plight. In the desperation of the moment she couldn't be sure if it was pity or love. In the end, she decided it didn't matter. He was innocent. Even if she was doomed, she felt she owed him a chance to escape.

She came off the subway and walked toward the stairs to reach street level. Halfway up she felt her gaze drawn forward, and she came to a sudden stop. She stared at the man coming down the stairs across the railing from her.

Her lips parted.

Victor smiled. *You've been busy, busy betraying me.*

She blinked.

He came down another step, almost even with her. *No matter. I see how the choice was made in you. Gadwick has betrayed you. Forget him. I will join you soon, my love. Until then, I will watch over you. No one will hurt you.*

She turned on the step.

He glanced over his shoulder as he passed her. *Pity, that Noel is in such a predicament.*

"I know," she whispered.

And still you make this choice for him, he who is but a shadow of me.

The noise of the station rose up around her. Someone bumped into her. She looked about, confused, unsure as to why she had stopped on the steps. Then she remembered, remembered her urgency, all the more desperate as she remembered that she lived alone.

She paced with hurried steps to her apartment building and ignored the elevator to charge up the stairs to her third story domicile. When she pushed open the hallway door she heard the sound of footsteps echoing in the stairwell. Her pace slowed as she glanced over her shoulder to see one of the Mondial emerge from the stairwell behind her. Her head snapped forward to see a second Mondial emerge from the stairwell at the far end of the hall. The door to her domicile opened, and a third Mondial stepped into the hall to stare at her.

Her lips quivered as a chill ran up her spine. She was too late. The long stupor Gadwick had put her into had served its end. Endo had reached his own conclusion in the time after her talk with Noel. There was nowhere to run, nowhere to hide. Her heart pounded, but soon enough her anxiety subsided as she accepted the horrible reality collapsing around her.

There is no escape from Central.

The futility of her hopeless plans disemboweled her and left her broken and obedient. Her shoulders sagged; her hands dangled at her sides. The Mondial following her grabbed the shoulder of her coat and gave her a shove. Without looking at him she let her breath go and shuffled into her domicile.

There was no light in her dwelling except the gray glow of the cloudy afternoon, dim and diffuse with shadow. Her net screen was dark and silent. Endo sat in a chair, staring out her window wall. He said nothing and waited until the Mondial in the hall closed the door of the domicile before looking to her.

She fell back a step and forced herself to swallow. "Endo?"

"Sonya," he said in greeting and rose from the chair. He walked to her and took her hand, leading her to stand with him by the window wall. He let go of her and stared out the window for some time before he spoke. "You wish to tell me something?"

She spoke his name again, a plaintive look in her eyes. She laid her hand on his arm. "Please, listen to me. I didn't know what was going on. Gadwick, he, he—"

"Stop," he said, silencing her with his stern tone. "I'm going to ask you this once, and I would ask you to remember our promise before you answer, and forget—" His voice fell off, his eyes squeezing shut before he opened them. "Forget the promises you made to this Westing spawn."

Fear drove a short breath from Sonya's chest, desperation seeping from her eyes. "Endo, I beg you! Gadwick made me."

Endo turned to face her. He glanced at her grasp of his arm.

Sonya froze under the fire in his stare.

His hands moved in a flash to seize her wrists. He shoved her, her back slamming against the wall by the entrance to her bedroom. She wheezed, clutching her chest until Endo seized her wrists again and pinned them to the wall by her ears. He squeezed so hard she thought her wrists would shatter in his clutch. She turned her head away as Endo leaned into her, only to see another Mondial step from the shadows of her bedroom. The man stared at her until he held her gaze in his possession, then he lowered his eyes to force her gaze down. She watched as he pulled a band of leather from a pocket of his long coat and wound it about one hand. When he was done he clenched his fist, the leather tightening over his knuckles.

She struggled until Endo shushed her and rested his forehead against hers. He held her up as her knees went soft, her hands going numb with the strength of his grip.

Endo's jaw muscles bulged. "I know what Gadwick did with you. He thinks my sensitivity for you will dissuade me. He used the Chapel-Westing business to distract me from Noel Westing. The only conclusion left for me is that Noel is the rogue. Tell me where he is."

"I don't know!"

He squeezed her wrists once more, drawing a wince from her. "Listen to me, Sonya. Gadwick is locking me out. He's concealing things from me. I don't like that. I have traces on Westing's sister, on Chapel, on you, my dear Sonya, but my trace on Noel has been broken. I traced him to your office and then I lost him. He's off the data flow. He has to be the rogue. Gadwick is in league with him and has plotted your ruin to protect himself and the rogue. You can't hide him from me. I know you were the last one to see him. All promises are empty before the call of Central. Do not make me ruin you. I know the Rooking market rendezvous is a ruse of Gadwick's making. Where is Noel going?"

Sonya looked from Endo to the Mondial staring at her. She closed her eyes and turned her face up. Her memories flashed as she saw the majestic horror of Gadwick's game, though she failed to understand the reason of it beyond her own destruction. It was inevitable, whether it be quick, there in her domicile, or slow and terrible, in Sector Control. Betraying Noel—or not—wouldn't make a difference to her fate; that, she knew, had been decided in Gadwick's game with Endo.

She saw the hidden subtlety of Gadwick's manipulation, using his predilector's skill to coax the words from Noel that would seal her decision, and yet make her give Gadwick what he wanted at the cost of her life—time for Noel to evade Endo. And yet, Noel—harmless, needy, meek Noel—a rogue?

Endo clenched his teeth. "I'm waiting!"

Sonya went limp in Endo's grasp. "I don't know!" Tears flowed down her cheeks. "How would I know? Can't you see I live alone?"

There was a pause, and then Endo's grip snapped open to release her. She could feel his glare, could sense him pressing into her mind. She dropped her hands when she heard him fall back a step.

Endo drew in a deep breath. "I see the choice Elder Gadwick put in you. You feel for this man, this Noel Westing, while to Endo Stutts you give only a promise. Gadwick gave you a choice, but he gave you no choice. He believes he has won this round." Endo frowned. "He misjudges me."

Sonya opened her eyes. A leather-wrapped fist struck her square in the forehead. Her head snapped back against the wall behind her, doubling the breach of her senses. She watched the reflection of her face sliding down the glass of her window wall as she sank to the floor.

"You will tell me where to find Noel Westing," Endo said, his voice even.

Sonya blinked. Her head was swimming with the impact of the Mondial's fist. Her vision began to fade as she lay on the floor. Endo seemed a ghost as he sat in a chair. The Mondial stepped beside her. A rough hand rolled her over. The Mondial grabbed her shoulders and hoisted her to her feet before shoving her against the wall. The man's intimidating shadow retreated from her sight, only for Endo to return.

"Endo, please," she said, whimpering as he neared.

Endo tipped his chin up. He steadied her and stared into her, his gaze narrowing until his face seemed to dissolve around the glittering brilliance of his black-eyed scrutiny. He let it bore into her, bore into her with all his awareness of the data threads, tearing through all the folds of her character, ripping her convictions open to seek the secret of Noel's location, buried somewhere within her in a place that was denied to him.

She closed her eyes, but the barrier of her lids served no refuge.

The air seemed to crackle between them. Her whimpering faded, and she heard the whispering trace of Endo's curiosity.

So simple. So pure. How could someone be so?

She wondered herself where to find the secret place within her, the hidden residence of the secret Endo sought.

Such intent. It was pointless, she realized. After all, she lived alone. She always had.

And what was there, in an empty home, other than silence?

Nothing, nothing at all.

Her hands dropped to her sides. Her mind went blank. She forgot her name.

Endo gasped. He fell back a step, his knees shaking. One of the Mondial grabbed his arm to steady him, but Endo shook his head before pushing off the Mondial. He went to Sonya to take her face in his hands. "Look at me," he said, his voice coming in a rush. "Look at me!"

Her eyelids slid open over her dilated gaze.

He jumped back from her, letting her sink comatose to the floor. "No," he said, his face paling. "No, not all this time, it—it can't, it can't be!"

His heart froze, but there was no denying what he had seen within her. He ran about her domicile in a panic, tearing through her cabinets and drawers. He found a set of concentration cubes taped to the back of a kitchen drawer. Two more sets were taped to the back of the nightstands flanking her bed. He clutched them in his hands, beating his fists to his head as his perceptions imploded. With a determined step he flushed the cubes down her toilet and stormed back to loom over her.

He knew her as Sonya Mortas, but there was no such person as Sonya Mortas. Everything she was, every thought in her head, every emotion that stirred her heart, was the creation of someone else.

She wasn't real.

She was a wipe.

Horrified, he looked into her eyes. He saw nothing but his own emptiness.

| 0 | 0 | 0 |

CARLY PACED THE CROWDED DAY market outside Rooking quad, her gaze tracing past the pleasant apartment buildings that formed the quad's skyline. The difference in the quality of buildings from one quad to another struck her, but it was one more thing she filed away as something plain before her that she had never appreciated. Rooking was filled with people who worked with Drive Control. It was off limits to the rest of the city, almost a city unto itself. Patrol rarely went there, at least in what memories she could summon, and it was her memories that troubled her.

It wasn't that she lacked memories from her time under Central's ignorance, but more that she came to take a silent inventory of her recollections. Her recent memories held a definitive aspect of detail, a gritty texture rich with subtle and sublime impressions of the reality they mirrored. They mocked the stark simplicity of her older memories, memories under Central, which were like empty statements on a checklist. She had a cracked helmet, so she needed a new one. Kilby quad was a troublesome quad because it was always a troublesome quad.

There was nothing definitive, no *why*, things just were what they were. Her whole life, it could be scribbled out on one piece of paper, if she had the nerve to create hardcopy. Even that sparked her curiosity, but she could answer that for herself—if she, or anyone else, had the impulse to create hardcopy, she could create a record of events independent of Central's record, and Central's way of forgetfulness would fail.

She looked across the crowded masses of the market with a sudden sense of contempt. If she was Central she could meat-farm everyone at the market, pretend it never happened and, for all purposes, it wouldn't have happened. She could make up any story she wanted. The fat clod selling street soup beside her, he wasn't shot, he got hit by a truck, a truck driven by the toothless pig selling whatever garbage was on her table—and on and on it would go.

I could remake the world however I wanted.

A shout pierced the air. It was Oboe.

Is that it? Is that the point of sending people up-top?

She stood still, stupefied by the thought as her gaze rose to the sky above her.

Vertical threat. Was it another one of Central's inside jokes?

There was a commotion in the next aisle over, punctuated by the curses of angry voices. Still lost in her thoughts, Carly was slow to react until Gwen and Oboe called her name over her headset, her ears buzzing with their volume. She snapped to attention, whipping her civi-stick high in the air as she turned and bulled her way between the fat clod and the toothless pig. Soup cans clattered and spilled, the clod throwing his hands up in annoyance. Ignoring him, Carly burst into the next aisle and looked down the length of the crowd to see Oboe laboring as he chased someone through the market.

She took off at once, her civi-stick high as her unspoken threat. Her handgun was snapped secure at her thigh. Graham and Gwen were driving in a wide circle about the market. There was no escape for the sap Oboe was chasing. She could hear Oboe on her headset calling for Gwen and Graham between his heavy breaths. It woke another disgusting memory that almost sent her stumbling, one that joined Bayard and Milston, her neighbor down the hall, on the list of men who'd spent their lust in her under the permission of Central.

She ground her teeth and focused her rage. She'd take it out on the sap.

A broad shouldered laborer blundered in front of her. It was too late to sidestep, and she slammed into the laborer's back. She bounced off the man and stumbled before crashing into a table of rain slickers, her civi-stick slipping from her hand to dangle from its wrist strap. The laborer turned with a curse, reaching out with angry hands to grab the fool who ran into him until he realized it was a member of Patrol.

He checked his disposition.

Carly missed it, only seeing another set of hands looking to grab her. In an instant she seized her stick and lashed out to crack the laborer in the temple. He staggered as his skin split with a puff of blood, but she wasted no time on mercy, letting her arm swing with its momentum as she rolled to her feet. The second she was up she swung her arm back, cracked the stick across his other temple, and broke into a run.

Oboe called for the sap to halt. Carly spotted Oboe ahead of her, but then her eyes bulged as his body crumpled. A hoarse scream sounded across her headset as he threw his hands up to his face.

A single thought burst from her lips. "Gun!"

Still charging through the crowd, she glanced at the small hills that surrounded the market to see Gwen and Graham closing in from opposite directions with their Patrol cars. Without breaking pace she whipped her handgun free, the safety off with a flick of her thumb as the civi-stick dangled from her wrist.

At the sight of the open weapon the crowd around her ducked down, flat as if they'd been shot, and revealed the fleeing man. Oboe was crouched on the ground with his hands pressed to his face. Carly's gaze darted by Oboe to pick out the steaming cauldron of another street soup vendor and a nest of overturned cups. Cones kept the cauldrons at extreme temperatures to make the soup edible despite all the flies that joined the mysterious mix. She realized from the mess of cups that Oboe had taken a dousing of soup in the face.

She shouted for the sap to halt; the fleeing man was a mere twenty paces ahead of her. She was catching him, and fast. He was running out of what little cover the market could offer as he neared the end of the aisle. Gwen and Graham were pinching his escape from the market, but still the man charged ahead. There was nothing before him except the waiting shadows of Rooking Copse. Beyond that there was only a long expanse of uninhabited land.

The man was a cone running from Central, she decided as she sprinted after him. In the wake of those thoughts she found herself losing a pace, then two.

Shit, I'm running from Central!

The man glanced over his shoulder, a frantic eye catching her behind him before he picked up his pace. She cursed, forgetting about him to save herself. There were too many watching. There was too much attention from Gwen and, through her, the unseen eye of Central.

Despite the selfishness of it, the sap had to go down.

She came to a halt, leveled her gun to aim between the man's shoulders, and steadied herself against her heaving breaths. "Hold up!"

The sap didn't break his step as he cleared the market and ran up the slope between the market and the copse. Carly fired over his head. He ducked, only to trip over his slicker and tumble to the ground in a disheveled pile. Gwen and Graham rolled up from either side in their Patrol cars and popped from their roof hatches with their repeaters trained. Carly raced toward them, keeping her gun locked on the man as he rose to his knees.

The three of them spoke in unison. "Hands, now!"

The sap stuck his arms up, hands trembling.

Gwen rose from her hatch to stand on top of her car. "Oboe?"

A grunt sounded over the headset.

The cone shook his hands. "I don't have a gun!"

Carly blinked. *I know that voice—*

Of course you do, Gadwick whispered to her.

The cone turned, the hood of his slicker sliding from his head. He looked back at his sister with open desperation.

Carly blinked again, her mind flashing like a bad display that she wanted to kick. Her jaw dropped when her memory cooperated.

Noel?

Oboe cried out in pain, loud enough for them to hear over the growl of the idling cars. "My face! That bastard fried my face!"

Gwen bared her teeth as she peered down the length of her repeater.

Graham and Carly exchanged a quick glance.

Carly's arms tightened. *Gadwick, what about this? What do I do now?*

He had a simple reply. *Shoot her.*

Carly forced herself to swallow. Her gaze darted between her brother and Gwen. Her heart pounded. Gadwick already had them on a difficult course, but this, there was no turning back, *ever*, from this—

"Let's plug this pig," Gwen said.

Oboe cursed. "Shoot that chigger! Meat-farm his ass!"

Carly's heart seized. She snapped her aim up and fired square into Gwen's chest. Gwen's gasp came clear over the headset as she flopped back on her turret, her repeater dropping from her hands.

Noel took off at once.

Gwen rose up, firing wild with her handgun. A scream sounded out from the market as her bullets flew unchecked, her hand wobbling from the daze of Carly's bullet.

Carly opened fire, squeezing the trigger as fast as she could until her clip was empty. Gwen gasped as bullet after bullet pounded her chest plate. The second to last round tore through her neck and blew out a hole beneath the base of her skull. Blood spurted from the cratered flesh under her chin, her muscles losing their rigor to dump her from the car.

Carly ducked, ditched her spent clip, and slapped a fresh one home. Graham shouted but she ignored him, grinding her teeth as she set to finish what she started. No sooner did she spin than she caught the aim of Oboe's handgun, his good eye burning at her between the fingers of the hand clutched over his cheek.

Before she could fire a barrage of repeater fire tore into Oboe's face. His helmet popped free, tumbling away atop the ragged eruption of his skull. Carly turned to find Graham perched on the roof of the car, staring down the length of his smoking repeater. Spent shells rolled off the car's roof to land in the soft grass.

People in the market, pressed to the ground, looked about, uncertain.

The late afternoon breeze whispered under the cloudy sky.

Gadwick's voice returned. *You have to kill them all. They're watching. Central will know. You have to do it.*

Graham shook his head.

"Carly," Noel said, scrambling toward her. He tugged her arm. "Central, they'll know. We have to run!"

"Shut up," Graham barked at Noel, leveling his repeater on Noel to drive him to the ground in fear.

Do it now! I've already made one sacrifice to make this moment.

Noel rose to his feet. Carly shoved him toward her car. Graham looked to her over the sights of his repeater. She spun and trained her handgun over the market's crowd as they began to rise. She backpedaled in a hurry until her shoulders slapped against the car. Her gaze snapped toward Graham.

They didn't have to talk it out. They knew they had no choice.

Graham dropped into the hatch. Carly ran to Gwen's car and scrambled onto the roof. She slipped on the spatters of blood and fell into the car, but gained herself and grabbed hold of the turreted cannons' sights. A harsh roar sounded out as Graham opened fire. She forced herself to look through the sights into the crowd. People were running in all directions, but Graham had used the height of the slope to their advantage and had slaughtered a line of people far back to form a tripping ground for the rest. Hemmed by that line of appalling gore, the crowd sought to scatter. Carly found her resolve and squeezed her triggers, firing down the right side of the crowd to form another trip line as Graham followed her lead and mowed down the left. They had the crowd hemmed in on three sides with the only opening the devouring barrels of their cannons.

Fountains of spent shells rained about their feet.

Carly, beaten to deafness by the roaring fire, never noticed when the cannons fell silent. Only when she realized the cannon bolts were idle in their mounts did she know it was over, just as by sight she knew that what lay beyond the turret wasn't grass but a lumpy field of flesh, crumpled tables, broken soup cauldrons, and shredded slickers. Everything out there was obliterated in a red wash of fresh, free flowing blood.

Numb, she dropped her hands from the trigger grips and slumped against the hull of the car to catch her breath. The steady, horror-laden scream of her brother filled her headset until she heard Graham order him to shut up.

She remembered how she had thought about meat-farming the whole market.

She wondered what Central would think of them meat-farming the whole market.

Shit.

Desperation propelled her with newfound momentum as she scrambled over the driver's seat to get out of the car. She forgot about Gwen until she tripped and fell to the cool grass. With a curse she rolled over, staring at Gwen's lifeless face before sprinting for her car. Graham popped from the roof hatch, his repeater held ready in one arm as he waved for her to hurry. She hopped into the car to find her brother huddled in a back corner of the crew area with his hands clutched over his ears.

Graham dropped into the driver's seat and dumped his repeater onto the floor to start the car. The engine fired with a roar.

Noel wept.

Carly grabbed Graham's shoulder. "Go!"

Graham's hand hesitated on the shifter. "Where—"

"Fucking anywhere but here!"

I told you there would be a price, Gadwick's voice whispered to them.

"The copse." Carly jabbed a finger away from the market. "Head for the copse!"

Yes, into the copse before Central comes for you.

Carly slapped the dashboard. Graham dropped the car in gear and floored the accelerator.

Clumps of grass flew from the tires as the car raced from the market.

| 0 | 0 | 0 |

IN A ROOKING APARTMENT MONDIAL Three sat in a chair and looked to the floor. There was no expression on his face as he unwound the band of leather from his fist and threw it in frustration. "She doesn't even know we're here," he said under his breath, looking down at the vacant gaze of the Scriptor Sonya Mortas.

"Wipe-lock." He shook his head. "She doesn't even know *she's* here."

| 0 | 0 | 0 |

ACROSS THE CITY ENDO SAT on the edge of a bunk, rubbing his temples. His initial horror at discovering Sonya was a wipe had transformed to a violent, brooding rage. He'd been duped. It was hard for him to fathom, no matter how he looked at the situation. It was bad enough that someone, some predilector of cunning skill, had created Sonya's personality, scripting her personality into the mind of a wipe to deceive him. Worse, though, was that he had let himself be deceived, that he let some unknown part of him sink into the delirious delusion of her simple purity and the allure it held for him. Her presence had nestled within a hidden fantasy to know something free of Central's presence, even as he should've known such a creature was an impossible thing. He had ignored his intuition and created his own folly.

There was a phrase for that in Central—*self-predilection*—but he refused to utter its label in conjunction with himself. Even the thought of it left his blood boiling.

Someone would have to pay. Someone had played him for a fool, but it would be the last game that person would ever know.

For the time being he was well aware his leads were scarce. Whoever had created Sonya had left a brain lock embedded in her consciousness as a last defense. The moment she realized she was a wipe her thoughts went into shut down, like pulling the plug from a net screen. It was known as wipe-lock, and only the person who scripted it in a wipe could undo its effect.

He wouldn't be able to get any information from her, so he had left her domicile behind to take his only other viable course of action. He heard the whispers of the data threads, he heard the resignation of Mondial Three, he heard the first reports of a massacre at Rooking's day market, and he heard the futility of his traces, all of them lost.

He opened his eyes to stare at Carly's red lettered ENDO shirt before looking out the window wall of her domicile. It felt surreal to find himself in the very location she called home and then have nothing of her other than the ethereal knowledge that the domicile was indeed hers. The irony was also inescapable that he had held one woman and found her presence to be an illusion, only to cross the city in search of a real woman to find nothing but the illusion of her presence.

It was a frustrating situation. He couldn't deduce the identity of the rogue, yet he could very well sense the rogue's plans around Carly. Years ago, in Carly's youth, she would have had no idea that her father was a predilector, one who had snuck away from Central to pursue the madness of raising a family on his own. The plan failed, as it had to, and he had abandoned his daughter to her own devices. Her ignorance of her potential led to a brutal attack, one which had silenced her mind. Central sustained hope for her potential, even as the fruitless search for John Westing ground forward through the years.

The responsibility to monitor Carly was handed over to Endo. Although he failed to understand the reason for this curious assignment, he also understood it was not his place to question the wisdom of Central or the wisdom in watching Carly devolve through Teen-stomp to Patrol.

Nevertheless, as time passed, she formed a singular presence within his mind, her image just out of reach of his dreams, and her thoughts—as he imagined them—spoken in a voice he couldn't hear. He wanted to believe in her potential. Why, he wasn't sure, but he recognized that desire within him just as he now recognized his foolish temptation to

Sonya's allure.

Illusions, images, and dreams. Is this what I've become?

"Don't be so hard on yourself."

Endo spun as he noticed the reflection of a tall man from the domicile windows. In the fog of Endo's surprise the man's words penetrated his mind but gained little purchase. He was ready to strike, but he stilled when he realized who stood before him. "What are you doing here?"

The visitor looked over the domicile. "I just thought I'd say hello to the Madman of MG42."

Endo held his stance. "I wasn't notified a high predilector was coming to Seven Hills. Why are you here?"

The man shrugged. "Passing through, on my way to retirement."

"How should I address you?"

"Call me Victor." He shook his head. "You disappoint me, Endo."

"Victor?" Endo pressed his lips together. "What's the rest of the name?"

"Mortas." Victor's eyes narrowed. "Yes, as in Sonya Mortas."

Endo's fists clenched.

Victor held up a hand. "Easy, old fellow. I'm not the one who used her. Yes, it was me that scripted her personality, but someone else got into her head. Someone else is responsible for the wipe-lock." He tapped a finger to his temple. "I can imagine your rage, but understand that I created her for company in my retirement. You're not alone in your anger, because someone—someone very crafty—has also betrayed *me*." He shrugged. "Be that as it may, I don't want any misunderstanding between us. You do see that I'm blameless in her deception upon you, yes?"

Endo ground his teeth. "You should've informed me."

"How was I to know you would desire the product of *my* imagination?" Victor held up a hand once more when Endo took a step. "I forget how well I did my work. I wanted to create the likeness of a desirable woman beyond Central's vision of humanity, something more than those candy-coated starlets paraded on the envens. I failed to appreciate the lure of my vision and how it might entice the inner desires of other men."

Endo waved off the subject. "You picked a bad time to come here.

There's a rogue."

"So I've sensed. That's why I came to see you, to offer my assistance, should you need it. Have you deduced the identity of this rogue?"

Endo rapped a fist into his palm and walked to the window wall. He hesitated a moment before turning back to Victor. "I suspect Elder Gadwick. I also suspect he used Sonya to deceive not just me but Central as well. I don't see who else it could be at this point other than Gadwick."

"As do I, Endo, as do I."

Endo rapped his fist again. "But I can't make a definitive link without Noel Westing in custody, and not with Sonya's mind silenced in wipe-lock. The pall of suspicion on Gadwick might be part of a greater scheme. It's something a rogue would do to shift blame. Either way, I can't remove a sitting city elder on suspicion alone."

Victor tipped his head. "Well, in that case, you'll just have to live with the fact that you incited Sonya's wipe-lock with nothing to show for it."

"How was I to know? Do you think I wanted that?" Endo took a breath. "This is the business of rogues. It gets messy. You should understand that, as a high predilector. You should understand that better than anyone."

"Mister Stutts, that was uncalled for."

Endo frowned but refused to apologize. He rolled his shoulders and eased somewhat. "You came here for Sonya?"

Victor opened his hands. "To Seven Hills, yes. But here, now, I came to talk some sense to you. I came to offer you some sound advice, a gift of my hard-earned wisdom. You've seen what I accomplished by creating Sonya's personality. What better way to fulfill an aging man's fantasy than with the very figment of his desires? I plan to retire, Endo, and take her with me." He crossed his arms on his chest. "Or so I had hoped."

"Is Gadwick's mess involved in your retirement?"

"No." Victor shook his head. "An unfortunate circumstance, nothing more."

"That's it?"

"That's it." Victor shrugged. "I have nothing to do with the Chapel-Westing rogue incident. I hoped for a quiet retirement, but now my Sonya is involved. Should you wish, I can offer my assistance in dealing with Gadwick. Otherwise, consider me nothing more than a shadow. So, now that you know my intentions, I will leave you. Goodnight, Mister Stutts."

Endo hesitated. "Wait."

Victor stopped in the doorway and gazed over his shoulder.

Endo's lips parted, yet he found himself struggling for words. "Sonya." He ground his teeth in humiliation. "You did your work too well with her."

Victor studied him. "Interesting. The great, powerful, and wise Endo Stutts is fooled by a wipe construct, and all he offers is to flatter the man responsible for the scripting." He leaned against the doorframe. "Tell me, did you ever suspect her nature?"

Endo's face fell. "Never," he said under his breath. "Never, in any moment."

"I know what you fear, Endo. I must confess I feared it myself when I scripted her. You felt the allure of her nature, only now you know her nature isn't real. The troubling question—the golden question—is what that might say about you, isn't that right?"

Endo pressed his lips together and stared at Victor.

"What does it say about any of us under Central, when the illusion of a person feels just as genuine as an independent intellect? Are we nothing but a society of simulacra, cheap images of some idealized form of ourselves that are nothing but fantasies nestled within those images, driving them in some eternal paradox? Is this what we've become under Central? Is this all we have to show for all the sacrifice, all the brutality, that we have cheapened ourselves to mass produced mannequins of flesh?"

Endo felt his face redden. "You threaten the borders of propriety."

Victor laughed. "Of course I do." He leaned toward Endo. "That's why I'm retiring, my old fellow, because my vision for humanity has diverged from Central's vision. I've lost my focus, in Central's view, and that's a view I know better than to challenge. Time to go away. Time to settle across the ocean. Time for quiet; time to sleep. What better way to subscribe to my mortality than with an illusion of my own creation, my dear Sonya, at my side?"

Endo shook his head. "Vanity is a dangerous temptation."

Victor jabbed a finger at Endo. "Again, all the more reason I want to retire. I won't predilect myself. We both know I've made mistakes long ago, but I won't make the same mistake as John Westing, that bastard pariah that haunts Central's nightmares—and this city. I've learned I'm just a man, a mortal man. For all I've done for Central I only want the favor to find my end as I see fit. I'll go my way and Central can go its way. Is that such a selfish thing?"

Endo stared at him. "Why did you mention John Westing?"

Victor opened his hands to the domicile. "Well, here we are in the city of his infamous crimes, no less in the domicile of his daughter. I'd say the same if we were in his son's domicile, but no one is interested in that dolt. Tell me, do you think John Westing has resurfaced after all these years?"

"His stink lingers in this city." Endo looked to the window wall. "If he's here, I will kill him."

Victor put a hand on Endo's shoulder. "Do you know what I think, as a man of similar rank? I think John Westing died long ago. You're chasing a ghost."

Endo looked back to Victor. "Interesting. Elder Gadwick has the same opinion."

"Perhaps the hunt for John Westing is a self-predilection of Central itself." Victor opened a hand when Endo tensed. "I know, I know, it sounds like sacrilege, but consider it. Westing committed his crimes and vanished. Central has been obsessed with killing him ever since. He earned himself a special place of infamy in the awareness of Central. The very system that built its power on forgetfulness can't forget this one man. Doesn't that seem more like Westing's last laugh rather than a legitimate pursuit?"

"His crimes are beyond excuse."

"Beyond excuse—and beyond answer," Victor said. He opened his hands when Endo's face reddened with righteous rage. "Think about it with all the intellectual power you possess. The one best chance Central had to identify Westing was by comparing the known gene bases of high predilectors with the identified bases of the Westing siblings. No match was ever found."

Endo shook his head. "Westing altered his records."

"Without Central's knowledge? Was he also able to hide his time in Seven Hills, altering the time stamps on his stay to conceal his very obvious absence from other high predilectors? Did he also sprout wings and fly to Mars?"

"Don't mock me," Endo hissed in warning.

Victor took a breath. "Forgive me. The absurd extension was only to illustrate a very practical point. There are only two realities to accept. Either Westing was—or remains—the most talented and cunning high predilector ever to exist, or he has long died and Central employs his ghost to haunt the remaining high predilectors. Both conclusions are troubling in their own unique way. Nevertheless, only one can exist. Which do you embrace, Watcher Stutts?"

"That's a pointless tangent." Endo waved off the question. "I don't have time for exercises in philosophy. I came here to deal with a rogue. My gut tells me Gadwick is involved, even though the evidence seems to indicate otherwise."

"Then perhaps the elder is indeed innocent. You'll have to look further for this rogue. After all, at the time of Westing's crimes not a single suspicion or accusation stuck to Gadwick. Not only was he cleared, he was allowed to retain his post as elder."

Endo frowned.

Victor patted Endo's shoulder. "Think about it, old boy. Think about it." He smiled, his fingers trailing off Endo's shoulder as he walked away.

Alone, Endo frowned. He looked to Carly's windows. The data threads were silent.

He sniffed. It took a few moments, but the feeling within him gained momentum until his suspicion became certainty.

Somehow, in some way, something in Central had gone wrong.

EARLY OPENED HER EYES TO darkness. Dawn was still some time away.

She looked to her side to find Graham snoring, his arms cushioning his head on the steering wheel. Behind her, silent in the back of the car, her brother sat huddled on the floor, his knees pulled to his chest. She envied their sleep, the sleep they all fell into the moment the car halted in the midst of the copse. It was a sleep of exhaustion, of shock, of release. It was anything but restful.

Taking care to be quiet, she unlatched her door and slipped from the car. She lowered the door but didn't close it, not wanting to make any more noise. The wooded depths of the copse were shrouded in oily black shadows beneath a canopy of leaves, insulating the place in an unsettling silence. No net screen squawked away, no rockets hissed overhead, no cones shouted their nonsense in the night to annoy their neighbors. There were only the trees, and a sense of mute vigilance.

A memory stirred within her, a memory of a dream—the dream of her father. For no reason she could think of she walked off into the black depths of the copse, keeping her balance by probing the undergrowth with her feet.

Her face grew warm as she pressed forward. She stopped, looked up to the foliage above her, and touched her cheek. When she rubbed her fingertips together they were wet, and when she touched them to her tongue, she tasted a tinge of salt.

Tears? She wiped her face on the back of her hand. *Why am I crying?*

A breeze whispered through the copse. The leaves of the high branches rustled above her.

She fell back a step, trembling.

The angels cry. She blinked. *Daddy?*

She ran back to the car.

| C | 0 | 0 |

ENDO LOOKED DOWN AT SONYA from where he stood in her domicile. He turned to Three, glaring at the expressionless man as he sat in a chair. Endo opened a hand to Sonya. "You couldn't put her in her bed?"

The Mondial said nothing as he propped his elbows on his knees.

"I don't want to see her sitting there like a vegetable."

"She is a vegetable." The Mondial shrugged. "Wipe-lock."

Endo looked back to Sonya and put a hand over his mouth. He squeezed his eyes shut and cursed under his breath. He pointed behind him to the Mondial and ordered him to leave, waiting until the door to the domicile closed to let out a single gasp. Alone with Sonya, Endo stood still before kneeling to take her limp body in his arms. He held her close as he carried her to her bed and set her down. The comfortable mattress hardly budged as he sat beside her.

He stared into shadow until he put his face in his hands. So he sat, contemplating, until a plan formed in his mind.

Someone had deceived him. His rage would be anticipated. Sonya's wipe-lock suggested that her wipe nature was meant to be a secret. Whoever had imprinted the lock in her subconscious was afraid he might discover something. The lock, in its own way, was a means to protect her. Only one person could fulfill those roles, and that was none other than the rogue.

He closed his eyes and plumbed the darkest nightmare of his impulses. If he hadn't realized Sonya's nature as a wipe the Mondial would've beaten her to a pulp. It was standard practice in Sector Control. In a way, it would be expected. And, if it was expected, perhaps it would serve him well to instill the data threads with the monstrous act of Sonya being beaten by the Mondial. It might provoke a reaction and thereby drive the rogue from cover.

His stomach bucked with disgust, but he let his nightmares come to life and let them seep into the data threads. There, deep inside him, he saw the horror of what Central could do with the proper motivation. He saw Mondial Three, saw him grab Sonya. The leather-wrapped fist hurtled from the folds of Endo's nightmare and brought the images of Sonya's ruin to the data threads.

Someone had decided to blur the line between reality and illusion. Endo let himself meet that game in full, in its inverse condition. To mate his plan with the threads he reached back in their timeline. The only credible version of events was for Sonya to suffer the moment Endo confronted her in her residence. Violence had a way of unmasking itself over time, and so the slow emergence of the act would seem proper.

He put his mind to work on the threads. With subtle patience he manipulated reality, changed the reality of the past, and amended Time itself to sustain the brutal rendering of Sonya's interrogation.

Sonya slept behind him, unseeing, unaware, and unharmed.

| 0 | 0 | 0 |

GADWICK SAT IN HIS OFFICE, nodding to his secretaries as they brought him an early breakfast of tea, three strips of bacon and hot, buttered biscuits. He hadn't left his office during the night, instead bending his energy to trace Endo on the data threads. The elder ate his breakfast, satisfied that Sonya still served as adequate distraction for Endo. Gadwick couldn't sense her, the data threads having closed about her. Endo was shielding her from any prying eyes, and it was a telling sign.

Something had happened between Sonya and Endo. The specifics weren't important to him; it was enough to know that Sonya continued to tax Endo's awareness and considerations. All told, his plans were going well, except for the slaughter at Rooking market. In his greater considerations he didn't foresee that as a necessity, but he also knew his vision of what was to come was incomplete.

So too was Central's, for that matter.

It wasn't a concern. The Rooking massacre included the deaths of more than a few of Drive Control's personnel. Their loss would create a welcome disruption beneath which he could work his plans.

He sipped his tea as he searched out his charges. He found them still wrapped in the slumber he had induced.

Except for Carly.

He closed his eyes and let his breath seep from his lungs. Without effort his mind made the nimble shift to perceive the data threads themselves and the maddening, intricate web they formed. Within that immensity lay the scripting codes, the controller traces, the net broadcasts and, most of all, the multitude of individual data feeds that tied citizens to Central.

The exceptions were the predilectors. They were always off the data flow and off common perception to provide sensitivity through the advantage of perspective.

His thoughts rose as whispers from the threads to impact his conscious mind. *Carly Westing. If you live long enough to reach your potential, how truly awe inspiring you will be. But first you must learn. You must separate from the groveling masses before you can serve as my replacement and allow me to retire in triumph.*

He had no care that his thoughts were open. He had no fear of Central hearing him. He had no fear of Central, for he was Central, and Central was he, as Central was everyone and no one at once.

The only logical extension of Central's discipline of thought held an ironic twist. If Central was he, and he was Central, then there was no authority over him. The absolutism of Central was no different than the absolutism that served so many hollow, despotic regimes in the old days before the sun bombs.

Central, he had grown to believe, was just an illusion, a phantom others used to exercise their desires. Why should he be any different? If brutality and deception were the norms he would master their extents to make them serve his dictate, and his alone.

He grinned. *Maybe I am a rogue. Time will tell.*

He let out a deep, calming breath.

| 0 | 0 | 0 |

CARLY.

She stirred beside the car, almost dropping the compress sandwich she had taken from her supply pouch. Her gaze darted about. "Gadwick?" *Tell me it's you. I'm hearing voices in my head, or dreams, dreams of my own, I don't know—*

You already hear the data threads.

The what?

Close your eyes, please.

She debated with herself. Sleep was a lost cause. Something told her she should keep her eyes open to watch the forest, but that came from the murmur in her head. If Gadwick could silence that murmur it would be just fine by her. Once again, she found that the appearance of a choice was really no choice at all. She put her hands on her head, closed her eyes, and rested against the wheel of the car.

She saw nothing.

She opened her eyes and was startled to find Gadwick sitting on the ground beside her.

He glanced at her sandwich. "So, is that the 'compress' Patrol loves to hate?"

Carly stared at him. "How—where—how'd you get here?"

He grinned, his gaze rising to hers. "This is all in your head, Carly. In the physical world you're still sitting with your eyes closed. I just inserted myself into the scenery you have already perceived. See there, in the distance? Watch."

She followed the trace of his arm as he extended a finger to the dark depths of the copse. There was nothing she could make out but, when she blinked, she saw a chain of apples float toward her. They hovered before spelling her name. She chuckled, only to frown when they vanished. She turned to him. "So, you're the apple man?"

"I'm glad you noticed." He tipped his head. "I was trying to be subtle, even though I wanted to get your attention."

"Well, you got it. You almost drove me crazy with all that apple shit, you know that?" She rubbed her forehead. She was tempted to ask him if the other thought that haunted her—the one that went, 'across a green field, a stand of trees'—was his handiwork. Then again, if it was, she figured he wouldn't hesitate to take the credit.

That means there's someone else. Who?

She dropped the thought, fearing Gadwick might read it within her. He was already in her head. She turned to him, pointing back to the depths of the copse. "How'd you do that?"

He tipped his head. "Someday you'll know. There will come a point, you'll find, when your imagination is seen by your mind as merely another data thread, something to manifest in the vision of the data flow that is Central." He looked to Carly, noting the confusion on her face. "I'm sorry, that's the best I can offer at this moment." He gazed at the sandwich, watching as she took a bite and chewed the fibrous compress. He appreciated her facial features the way his mind perceived them—not exactly Carly manifested in that moment, but as he imagined she could be, cleaned and pampered by the comforts allowed a predilector.

He imagined meeting her on some future day, her blue eyes lit with wisdom over the supple curve of her cheeks. He drew her smile, perhaps reserved for him, as a dutiful token of servitude for enlightening her to the data threads.

She was indeed a remarkable specimen.

Carly fought to keep her calm. She wondered if he realized what was seeping from his thoughts; she wondered if he knew she could perceive that leak of his mind, or if he was doing it on purpose. Either way she drew one conclusion, and that was to think of his head games as no different than a civi-stick fight.

Two could play those games. She was handy enough with a civi-stick, after all. She grinned as she chewed her sandwich.

The shift of her disposition sparked his curiosity. "Patrolman?"

She swallowed, waving the sandwich in a slow circle before her. "Not compress," she said, her mouth still full. "I'm thinking steak, the big fat ones they give us after a riot cycle."

He stared at her for several moments after she finished chewing.

She looked to him. "What?"

"You surprise me."

She raised an eyebrow. "Is that a good thing?"

"I don't quite know."

Her good humor evaporated. "Right," she said, resting the sandwich in her lap. "So you have some explaining to do, Gadwick. A lot of explaining. You can start with my brother."

"Are you disappointed to see him?"

"What kind of question is that?"

"Only a question," he said lightly. "You forget that it's still soon since you left Central's sway. You act more like your old self than you think, accepting things without questioning them, without wondering about them."

She let out a short laugh. "You're wrong on that. I've got lots of questions for you."

"And I have many answers."

She stared at him as he gazed into the distant darkness, her head bobbing with a slow nod. "All right, Gadwick. Why me?"

"You have a gift neither you, nor I, nor even Central, can fully appreciate. A gift yet untapped in your mind."

"What gift?"

"The gift to freely associate, to predilect the data flow wirelessly."

She blinked, not knowing what to say to that, as she had no idea what it meant. "You don't say?" she said, her sarcasm inescapable. "So why me?"

He raised a finger in warning. "Not necessarily you. I watch all members of Patrol. They are the best specimens in the groveling masses, singled out to Patrol for that very reason. I often view the traces through filters to screen out the masses so that I only see Patrol. And then I watch. I've spent countless hours watching, as all city elders do, as we wait for the few rare specimens that glimmer above the rest."

She gave him a sidelong glance. "And I'm one of those rare specimens?"

"Perhaps," he said with a sigh, "yet, perhaps not. Your association to Graham is very close, very close indeed. It's difficult to differentiate you two, as you often overlap. I wasn't sure at first if it was one of you, or the less probable event that it was both of you. Nevertheless, Chance plays its game, momentarily upsetting the intricacies of Central's plans. The equilibrium of Central's plans is impatient—intolerant—to say the least. Despite change, a new balance must be found. Despite adversity, adaptation must be swift, sure, and without a trace of doubt. Adaptation has become spontaneous. Darwin, you see, has been accelerated to the digital age, to the digital now." He took a breath as he gazed at her. "Ah, but you don't even know who Darwin is, do you? No, no, of course you wouldn't. Sometimes we have done our task of erasing questions too well."

Carly remembered her thoughts before the slaughter. "Is that why Central makes us forget, so we don't think about things?" She shook her head and held up a hand. "No, not yet, Gadwick. I want some other things first. Why the slaughter in the market? Why get my brother involved?"

Gadwick looked up to the trees. "Sometimes, Carly, for all our planning, we can't account for everything. On the other hand, we may say that what we think was outside Chance was merely the more complete planning of Central at work. Perspective. It's all a matter of perspective, and you must never forget that. One person's random chance is another's careful plan."

Carly shook her head. "That doesn't—"

"Your brother," he interrupted. "He reviewed you at Drive Control after your collapse in the garage at Patrol. There was a sick call by another controller, a man named Henshaw, and your brother was next on the rotation list to cover for that man. The very man, by the way, that Gwen and Oboe—and you and Graham—beat to a pulp, if you care to remember. Now, I can honestly tell you that, to the best of my knowledge, meeting your brother was a random event, but I have my suspicions that there may be another plan at work, that the sick call was mediated by another predilector working on poor Controller Henshaw."

Carly opened her hands. "I thought you see everything."

"That I can perceive," he said, raising a finger. "I can perceive many things, but not all things. Even the high predilectors that live across the wide ocean can't see everything and, if anyone can be thought of as 'being' Central, it would be those individuals. But we digress. The point is, whether planned or not, your brother found you. He was concerned for you, as seeing you awoke his awareness of you, who he had forgotten under Central. He went to the woman he's involved with to recruit her help in running a trace on you. He did not know, and his woman did not know, that even the close proximity of siblings who were previously separated by Central sets off flags high in the data flow. It was what tightened my attention on you after you were hit by the brick."

"The riot?" She stared at him in disbelief. "You let that happen?"

"The cones are not as dangerous as you've been led to believe."

Carly's eyes widened. "They're in with the Continentals!"

The elder shook his head. "This is what you don't understand. There is no war."

Carly blinked. "What?"

"I shall repeat it for you: there is no war. In times long past there was a series of wars, destructive wars, but no more. Too wasteful, you see. They've been replaced by the self-generated mass marketing of the envens and supply side. The illusion of war, though, is very useful to Central's ends. We use it well, for it keeps people distracted and keeps their energy focused. When dealing with the scale of mass society war is quite therapeutic. Particularly when all sides realize they have no differences."

"So you're saying the Continentals are our friends?"

"No, I'm saying there are no 'Continentals'. If you were to cross the Narrows to the continent you would certainly find vast tracts of land laid waste, but where you would find people you would find Central, and you would find them at war with the 'Islanders'. You would still be a patrolman, you would still eat compress, you would still get drunk on a regular basis, and you would still copulate with each and every man Central put around you, men of selected genetic background so that the best offspring can be cultivated, so that the best of humanity can be reproductively paired from stores in Central's fertility banks."

She looked down at her waist "I've never made any kids."

"The breeding program is more subtle than that."

She blinked in confusion.

"You asked the question yourself, remember? *Where do all the kids come from?* The breeding program." Gadwick waved a hand toward the city. "Charter families, Rainbow Go, all to manufacture the next generation of humanity. Quality control of humanity itself, so that our limited resources go to the best we can summon to life. Hence, the breeding program."

She shook her head. Something welled up inside her, pressing against every thought in her head and squeezing them against the inside of her skull. It was a dizzying constriction of her fragile perception of the world around her, the world Central had created, the world in which she had been set adrift. It was too much to comprehend, too much to dissect and delineate in the tattered lanes of her awareness. She shook her head once more as the confusing mass of his words devolved to a nagging ache between her ears. "No, no, this doesn't make any sense. This is all silly-speak."

Gadwick's eyes narrowed. "No, this is Reality, Carly Westing, and you must adjust to it if you want to survive. You do have a choice, as much as you feel that you don't. You can stay here and follow my directions. By doing so you will come to run this city and see all the truths that have been hidden from you, or you can turn your back and walk off to the city."

"Drive Control," she said under her breath and put her hands on her head.

"No. Death, at the hands of Endo Stutts."

"Endo, Endo of MG42? That Endo Stutts?" She looked at Gadwick before she broke out laughing. "You're right proper crazy."

"He hunts you, even now," Gadwick said with a shake of his head. "I was explaining to you how your brother became involved in this situation. The night I had Graham bring you to me I was protecting the two of you, but the traces were close on all of us. The timing was not as I hoped it would be. I had to hide you and Graham from the data flow. Drive Control was convinced that a rogue predilector was active and that it was none other than Graham. Endo Stutts hunts rogue predilectors. It's his task within Central. He belongs to the Order of Watchers. He is their master, and so he's known simply as the Watcher. He's here in the city, even now as we speak. His ruthlessness and brutality are things even you, as a member of Patrol, might have difficulty appreciating. My only way to save you—and Graham—was to convince him that it was your brother who was the rogue, and that it was his woman covering for him. I had to put her between us and Stutts."

Carly's gaze rolled over to him, her hands still on top of her head. "You hung her out," she said with disgust.

Gadwick frowned. "It was her, or it was all of us. The meat-farm, as the saying goes. It was a calculated loss."

"So she's dead, this woman?"

"No. I believe she lives. She's suffering an aggressive interrogation, now, as we speak. Stutts can't hide her suffering from the data threads."

"Shit," Carly said with a sigh. She closed her eyes. "Does Noel know?"

"Not yet." The elder paused before speaking again. "There is a momentum here that you must appreciate. You've seen the sacrifices to keep this momentum alive. This woman, Sonya Mortas, is but one of those sacrifices. There are dozens more rotting there in Rooking market. And, I promise you, there will be many, many more, if you try to stop this."

Carly's cheeks flushed with rage. "I didn't start it!"

"You were born. The thread began at that moment."

"So, here again, I have no choice—that's what you're telling me, right?"

"No. You have options, one a very good one, one a very bad one. If you choose not to acknowledge that as a choice that is yet another choice, and you can yet again choose to be aware of that or not. You can't hide as you wish to, for there are choices all around you. This is freedom."

Carly rose to her feet. "Look, I didn't ask to be found."

"I see." Gadwick shrugged. "And because you were so loath to act against Central, because your life as you realized it under Central was so pleasing to you, for those reasons you slaughtered all those people in the market. For those reasons you killed a patrolmate."

"You ordered that!"

"And yet, Patrolman, you knew it needed to be done without my asking, yes?"

Carly turned away from him, tapping her foot in frustration until she paced before him, her arms crossed over her chest. She glanced at him several times, each time turning away with a frown. After several moments she stopped with her back to him, but then spun around to face him. "Fine. You have me. You have me in more ways than I can guess, than I can even know, because I don't understand a single thing you've been telling me. You got us this far, and now that we're here—now that you have us here—I don't know what else to do but follow you. So what do we do now?"

Elder Gadwick stood and cupped his hands behind his back as he stared at her. "You will raid Drive Control and secure your drive."

Carly blew out a breath. "Hey, I'm not an idiot, you know. Drive is what you do and what you think. You can't steal that."

He ground his teeth. "You don't understand. What Drive Control has taught you to think of as 'good drive' and the risk of 'reformat' has nothing to do with your physical or emotional self. It has everything to do with a data drive storing every facet of your daily life in files for Central to access and control as it chooses. It can delete your memories—even change your memories—if it chooses. If you choose not to believe me, you can ask your brother the secret of Drive Control."

Carly stared at him. She fell back a step, trying to digest Gadwick's words.

"Yes, your brother knows these things," he said with a nod. "What he does not know is that he has a drive as well, and is therefore subject to the same manipulation as you."

She closed her eyes and shook her head again. "I don't understand—"

"You will, in time. For now, you need only accept it, but you must act."

Carly rubbed her temples. "I—I—ah, chiggers to it." She dropped her hands and looked to the elder. "Right. I don't get it, but I know you have me. So how do I get this thing of mine?"

"I will supply you with the information. The data vault for the city is located far from here. You will need the car."

She thought for a moment before her eyes narrowed. "Wait a minute. You say this could all be part of some big plan, all this that's going on, right?" She waited until Gadwick nodded. "So you want us to raid Drive Control, and if that plan, like all plans, is part of Central, then Central would be planning against itself. That doesn't make any sense."

"Perspective, Patrolman, perspective. We predilectors always use perspective. We also tend not to tell the truth about our exact abilities," he added as an afterthought, drawing another glare from Carly. "However, I can tell you that I have been honest with you now to the best of my knowledge, and that goes a long way, quite a long way. Now, in answer to your question, yes, Central has in the past given the appearance of working against itself to protect its plans. So, you see, this is not out of the ordinary. Stranger things have happened."

"Like what?"

He shrugged. "Your childhood."

She butted her palms against her temples and blinked several times, but she still found herself standing in Gadwick's constructed and constricted illusion. Dizziness swept over her until she sat on the ground, pressing the heels of her palms to her forehead. *That last thing, you know, that was a cheap shot.*

Yet accurate, the elder replied.

Was I just part of a charter family that went to the chiggers?

If it's important for you to know, then it will come to you.

What's that supposed to mean?

The past is only relevant if it affects the present. Otherwise, it serves nothing but unnecessary complication. Such is what Central has taught us. It's a wise lesson.

Whatever. She closed her eyes, but only darkness met her. *How do I explain all this to Graham and Noel?*

Do you think I was only talking to you all this time?

Her jaw dropped. *How do you put your thoughts in my head?*

Predilectors use the data threads to communicate across Central. Thoughts are nothing more than another packet of data to be transmitted.

Right. Sorry I asked.

She opened her eyes. She looked about the copse. Dawn had come and gone, and the morning light pressed through the trees. She stood, staggered to the car, and opened the side hatch to find Graham and Noel in similar states of confusion.

"We need to talk," she said. She looked at Noel as he rubbed his forehead. "Noel. I'm told you kept me from reformat. Is that true?"

He stared at her, a long hard stare. "Yes."

She nodded as she kept her gaze on him. "I know. You're thinking you traded away this Sonya person for me, and now you're wondering if it was worth it."

Noel glared at her, but said nothing.

"One woman?" Graham said. "You two are going to argue over one woman? What about all those people we wasted in the market?"

Carly kept her gaze on Noel as she put a hand on Graham's shoulder. "I didn't forget."

Noel looked between the two of them without hiding his disdain. "All you people do in Patrol is crack heads. A little mass murder shouldn't bother you."

Graham turned, but Carly pulled at his bodysuit to keep him from tearing into Noel. She looked to her brother and tipped her head. "Okay, so you kept me from reformat, but don't forget we could've left your ass out there for Drive Control to pick you up. Forget reformat, they would've meat-farmed you right there. Let's call it even."

Noel looked away. "It's just—"

Carly blew out a breath. "What?"

"I thought you had accomplished something more."

"More than Patrol?" Carly's eyes took on a threatening gleam. Graham fixed a similar look on Noel, and it made Noel shudder. "Easy, Chap," Carly said, glancing at Graham. "It wouldn't be right, would it? He did stick his neck out for me." She looked back to Noel. "Patrol isn't big on outsiders. You should know that. If there was going to be contact, it had to be from your side."

Noel fidgeted for a few moments, debating with himself before clearing his throat to summon his voice. "I hadn't seen you since we were split up, since what happened with our mother. I don't know why, it must've been Central making me forget—based on what Gadwick told me just now—but I never thought of you all these years. I knew I had a sister. Sonya even asked me once, and I can remember telling her that I had a sister, that my father had been killed on the Continent, that my mother was taken by Drive Control some time afterward, and then we were split up. But I never thought past that, even when I told Sonya." He looked over the inside of the car, his gaze lingering on the repeaters, civi-sticks, and handguns. "I want her back," he said. "I got her involved in all this. I won't abandon her."

Graham and Carly exchanged a glance, but Carly looked back to Noel. "So what did you do in Drive Control?"

"I'm—well, I was—a controller."

Graham looked out the windshield as rain fell from the sky. "A controller. You know, we never had to wonder what titles meant before. Drive Control was Drive Control. So what does it mean to be a controller?"

Noel gazed at them in turn. "Gadwick didn't tell you?"

Graham stared out the windshield, too stubborn to admit anything to Noel. Carly hesitated a moment, curious as to what Noel had said about their mother. *Drive Control took her away.* Sure, she thought, Drive Control took her away—in a body bag, after Patrol meat-farmed her. Was he concealing his memory, or was his memory sanitized?

She rubbed her forehead as she tried to figure out what that question meant before she remembered what Noel had asked. "I think there's a lot Gadwick left out."

"I can tell you some things," Noel said. "I watch people, make sure they maintain good drive, and those who don't, or those who commit crimes, they're brought to Drive Control and evaluated by controllers. We question and evaluate if the particular subject can be brought back in line to the scripting codes or if they need reformat with Sector Control." He fell silent, thinking for a moment. "Sonya was a scriptor."

Carly opened a hand. "So what does a scriptor do?"

He swallowed, his gaze darting to Graham before returning to Carly.

"Scriptors maintain and write the scripting codes. Drive Control and Central use scripting codes to guide people. The scripting codes basically decide what's going to happen in the immediate future, and sometimes even in the distant future. It depends on the expanse of the code. Take the latest marketing frenzy on a particular enven, for example. Do you even know where the word 'enven' comes from? It's a contraction of 'entertainment vending'. Every item on the envens is planned out and scripted before it's released. The open script merges with all the data threads of people using that enven. They'll want the new products before they reach market, so that when they do reach market, they'll be consumed. It's a self-generating market economy under Central."

Carly stared at him.

"You don't understand that, do you?"

She thought of what Gadwick told her in comparison to what Noel said and decided she had a bigger concern on her mind. "Tell me about predilectors."

Noel's eyebrows rose as he took a deep breath and opened his hands. "I'll tell you what I know, which isn't much. Predilectors have a variety of functions. Some are city elders, some stay across the wide ocean and decide where society will go next, some decide what the envens will market based on what supply side can manufacture, things like that. They figure out what people want before people know they want it, and then use that to motivate people to do things people weren't necessarily interested in doing. Sonya knew much more about all that."

Graham shook his head, but kept his gaze out the windshield. "Forget about this woman. If Stutts has her there's no way we can get her. All of Patrol will be assigned to his security. And if he's a predilector like Gadwick says, there's no way we can fight through all of Patrol and still surprise him."

Carly glanced at Graham, hungry to know what Gadwick had told him. She glanced at Noel and then back to Graham as that hunger transformed within her. It wasn't mistrust, and it wasn't suspicion. Despite their isolation and tenuous position she felt alienated between her brother and Graham. Judging from their behavior, she had the suspicion they were feeling the same. On the heels of those thoughts came another thought, elusive yet alluring in its implications. It was the belief that Gadwick held different discussions with the three of them for the very point of alienating them from each other, just to create another experiment to see who would climb above the others to be revealed as the rare specimen he sought.

Graham's gaze slid toward her, his eyes narrowing. "I would never look at you that way."

"Look, Graham—"

"I would never do that," he repeated. "You know that."

She closed her eyes, regretting her thoughts. He had stood by her through her shaky emergence from Central, had waited until she was ready, only so that he could be with her. She wished they were alone in the car. It wasn't for what they knew in their past, the wild moments of their bulls on the rise, but something different, something stronger that she lacked the words to define. The image in her head was clear enough, though—a moment alone, no world about them, no worries, no intrusions, no need to speak, just a moment.

The thought pulled her eyes open to glance at Noel as he sat behind them in the back of the car, his gaze on his feet. She frowned and looked back to Graham. "He did save me," she whispered. "And for that he lost this Sonya."

Graham shook his head. "Carly—"

"What if it was the other way around? Are you telling me you'd leave me?"

His jaw clenched. "I would never ditch you."

Carly's eyebrows rose.

Graham frowned. He thought for several moments before letting out a deep breath. "Right," he said with a sigh. He turned to Noel. "Listen. We do what Gadwick wants us to do first. Then we see about getting this Sonya person."

Noel's jaw muscles quivered before he spoke. "Thank you."

Carly nodded. "We should take stock of our supplies."

Graham nodded in return. "Just another day," he said under his breath.

Carly hopped from the car and closed the door behind her. She hesitated as she felt the cold rain on her face. She looked about the copse, trying to replay what they just discussed in the car. Of greater importance, she tried to remember just how their plans had swung to and fro before settling. Her suspicions woke at once, and the thoughts she tried to bury returned to her.

You have the sensitivity, Gadwick whispered to her.

She put her hands on her hips. *Is this how it's going to be, the three of us playing games with each other?*

No. You won't have to think about outwitting anyone. You simply will outwit. We all have a little of the predilector in us, and it all starts by knowing what to say to get someone to do what you want. Getting them to do it, getting them to do it without them realizing they are doing it, and getting them to do it with conviction, are all different things.

She frowned and glanced over her shoulder at the car. *So tell me, who just predilected who?*

Ah, now you're catching on.

Why?

You begin to see people for what they are, complex animals with complex motivations. It's a lonely life, to be a predilector. The digital now is a cold, transparent world, Carly. It is indeed a very cold world.

Then something else struck her, and she had to fight not to spin around to Graham. *Gadwick! When Graham turned to me before, he heard my thoughts, didn't he? How'd that happen?*

He heard something, and probably didn't even realize it, or didn't understand how it came to him. You looked to him, your thoughts spun within your mind, and then he knew. He heard them, just as you hear me now.

She blinked. *So, so I can talk—think—like you? I can use these data thread things like you use them?*

Gadwick was silent.

Her lips parted. *Then it has to be me, right? I'm the one you're looking for?*

A moment passed before she heard the elder's thought. *Accept the possibility, but nothing more. Delusion is the greatest threat a predilector can face, Patrolman Westing.*

| 0 | 0 | 0 |

VICTOR TAPPED HIS FINGER ON the card lock outside the former domicile of Controller Henshaw. It was an easy enough matter to discern the man's fate from the data threads, and his vacant domicile would serve as a much more convenient and comfortable safe house than the abandoned building he was using in Kilby. It had served its purpose, but there was little reason to continue hiding in such squalor.

He closed the door and sat down by the window wall. He listened to the rain. His plan had seemed so simple. He scripted Sonya for his fancy. He let her deceive Endo to keep Endo distracted. Victor would come to Seven Hills, take Sonya, and turn Carly over to Central as his successor. It was splendid in its sordid simplicity, delectable in its devious design.

Things had not gone as he planned, though. The man he thought he could use as a pawn had proved to be a huge problem. He had scripted Sonya's wipe-lock as a last ditch maneuver, and it unsettled him to resort to its employ so early in the game. Gadwick's bumbling had left him with no choice but to pop the lock. It was the only way for Victor to cover his tracks in the fashion he desired. Endo had assumed it was the work of Gadwick and met the move by letting his Mondial thugs beat Sonya comatose. Gadwick's response was to instigate the Rooking massacre.

The elder always ran a rough show, but he'd grown bold since Victor last knew him.

"It seems I misjudged you, Ian Gadwick," he said with a sigh.

| 0 | 0 | 0 |

ENDO STOOD BY SONYA'S KITCHEN sink soaking a wash towel when his five Mondial returned. He stared at them with open expectation. "Chapel's building?"

"Nothing," Two replied.

"Noel Westing's building?"

"Nothing," Three replied.

"Nothing for the sister at the new Cheshire quad location," Four said.
"Gadwick never left Drive Control by the front door," Five reported.
"Not by the subway, either," One added.

Endo nodded and crossed his arms on his chest. He looked out Sonya's window wall as he let his thoughts churn. He turned back to the Mondial. "That will have to end it, for now. I will try to meet with Gadwick some time today. He won't be able to refuse me after the Rooking slaughter. In the meantime make sure everything is ready for tonight. We have a riot to put on," he said and dismissed the five men with a wave.

Alone, he looked out the window.

The data threads whispered but offered him nothing regarding Carly Westing, Noel Westing, or Graham Chapel. Their absence was conspicuous in a reality permeated with information. Such a thing reeked of the work of a high predilector, or a rogue. The difference, with Gadwick's meddling, was impossible to tell.

Central remained silent.

Endo wrung out the towel in frustration. He went to Sonya's bedroom with the wet wash towel in his hand. He knew it was a futile hope that something as silly as a cold compress could dispel the wipe-lock, but he couldn't stand the sight of her vacant gaze. It was nothing compared to the mangled ruin of her shattered body that he let play out on the data threads to spur the rogue, yet it bothered him nonetheless.

She was a wipe. She wasn't real. He shouldn't care if she was a vegetable.

But he did care. Until he understood why he cared, he knew it would bother him. At some point he would get his hands on the rogue and he would have his answer to dispel the wipe-lock. Sonya would go to Victor, but she would see Endo first. She would wake to her thoughts and perceive him first and know it was he that saved her.

She would say something to him then, some delicate thing that would pass over her lips.

"Maybe it will hold the answer I seek," he whispered to himself. "And if not in her voice, then perhaps I will find an answer in her eyes."

He frowned.

Perhaps.

His jaw clenched, his fists tightening on the wash towel until beads of water dripped on the floor.

And then, rogue, I will kill you!

| 0 | 0 | 0 |

DAY WORE OVER THE CITY, and a lumbering mass of gray clouds filled the sky to hasten the nearing twilight of evening. The city filled with commotion as people moved to the inescapable multitude of Central's net screens. In bus depots, in manufactories, in offices, in warehouses of supply side, in restaurants, bars, pubs, shops, sex dens, the dormitories of Teen-stomp, even in the schools of Rainbow Go, a message gained momentum until it broke into the collective awareness of the city. MG42 had arrived with prisoners from the Continent. In the approaching darkness the residents of Seven Hills would ride a tidal wave of nervous energy, for the night would be a night of endorsed riots. It would be a night like no other, even though it was scripted to be like every other night of riots that came before. It would be a stomping rage of vented anxieties, a furor without parallel.

That night the filthy Continentals would pay for their rockets. Endo Stutts would be there to lead the way, to elevate the mass madness of Seven Hills to mainstream entertainment for the envens to broadcast throughout Central. It was their turn to shine, for their city to shine.

One by one, lamps snapped on about the city's central square, the Rectadrome, framing it in a wall of white light reaching to the clouds. There would be no fear of rockets that night, and no one would think to ask why. There were no evening markets on the various greens, but no one would consider that. There was no curfew, and no one would care about that.

Across the city, south of the square, in the depths of Kilby quad, eyes began to notice small black billets pasted on the walls of buildings. *Mondial Killswitch!* the billets shouted in ragged white letters. No location was posted, because none was needed. Sector Control had their resources, their scriptors and controllers, hard at work. Unaware of the whisper in their minds, certain citizens of questionable drive began to make their way toward an old warehouse at the edge of Kilby. As evening fell and the twilight gave way to the growing darkness, the warehouse began to fill. Outside, unseen, a ring of Sector Control operatives closed about the building.

Inside the warehouse excitement filled the air. There was a makeshift stage at one end of the building's vast emptiness, nestled between two old cargo elevators. Low conversation mumbled through the crowd. Some felt privileged, some felt mischievous, but they all felt distinct. They were different than the rest, they knew, turning away from Endo Stutts and the monotonous blaring of MG42 to seek the underground following of the Killswitch. They knew they might nod to Central during the day, but they had their little streaks of arrogance, hidden, so they thought, from outside eyes. It set them apart and, in their belief, above the roaring mass insanity of envens, supply side, rocket attacks, and lunatics like Endo Stutts.

Their collective subconscious thought rose up through the data threads. *When will it start?*

Oh, soon enough, soon enough, a voiceless voice mocked.

| 0 | 0 | 0 |

CARLY'S GAZE ROSE TO THE darkening sky as she sat on a stump. She looked at Graham as he sat across from her, chewing a sandwich while he watched Noel toss twigs into the trees. She blew out a breath and stood. "I'm out of here."

Graham turned to her, forcing down a mouthful of sandwich before he spoke. "Where do you think you're going?"

She looked toward the city before she looked back to Graham. "I'm out of here," she repeated and walked to the car.

Graham stood, annoyed and confused. He was about to pursue her when he saw Noel turn, his gaze on Carly. Noel walked toward her, only to stop when he felt Graham's narrowed glare lock on him. He rubbed his chin, tried to stare Graham down, but abandoned that idea to look back to Carly. Graham nodded and looked back to her as well. "Carly?"

She reached into the car and pulled out a dark green slicker. She slipped it over her head and looked down to see how low it hung, making sure it would serve as adequate concealment. Satisfied when it swept by her knees, she reached back into the car and slipped a handgun into one of her thigh holsters. Two extra clips were stowed on her other leg. She pulled up the slicker to fasten the strap of her civi-stick over her shoulder before letting the slicker go. She met Graham's eyes as she pulled the hood over her head and yanked the waist strap. "Don't worry—"

"Chiggers to that," Graham said. "We all know who's waiting for us in the city."

She nodded. "All the better only one of us goes at first, right?" She looked to Noel, then back to Graham. "Haven't we felt it all day, that somebody needs to go into the city, that only one of us should go, even though the idea of it doesn't sound at all right proper? Look at us. We've been sitting here, thumbs up our asses, none of us wanting to move first. We've been waiting for something, and we don't know how to wait. Not Central's way. We put ourselves in the middle of this rogue deal, and if we're going to believe all this shit about predilectors, then there's already some reason, something that was going to make me go and neither of you."

Silence fell between the three of them.

"Right," she said. "Off I go." She walked away, following the tracks of the car to find her way out of the copse.

| 0 | 0 | 0 |

Endo sat on the edge of Sonya's bed, rubbing his forehead as he listened to Sonya breathe. Things had changed, and the day hadn't gone as he was told it would. The riot was coming and there was no time to deal with Gadwick. Central had changed the plans, the careful plans of Drive Control. The proper preparation, the slow conditioning of the city, none of it was in place.

He dropped his hands and rose from Sonya's bed to pace from her bedroom to her window wall. Buildings blocked most of the immediate view, but up in the sky he could see the rising glow of the Rectadrome. Time was wasting.

And what about me? How am I to do my part? What will drive me?

He closed his eyes to calm his anxiety. The data threads would have the answers, he reminded himself. They always had the answers, for they were the whispers of Central. Every question had its answer in the threads. It only took the right ear to listen without listening, the paradox of awareness—and then he heard it.

His eyes opened wide.

The rogue—the rogue has made a mistake.

His sensitivities snapped into focus to find Carly in the city, drawn by the riot. The delicate wisdom of the moment lit his nerves. The rogue sought to entangle her but she had slipped away to the lure of the riot, a lure manifested in Endo's persona in MG42. His image would draw her to him so that he might at last see her in the flesh. It was a dizzying pirouette of the real and surreal, spiced with one more deduction that spurred his anticipation.

If the rogue had plans pinned upon her, then the rogue was soon to follow.

| 0 | 0 | 0 |

CARLY WALKED THE STREETS, SEEING and feeling the totality of Seven Hills. The city about her seemed at once alive and dead, alive with the movement of people to the city center and the inescapable wave of their mounting excitement, yet dead as they moved like small wind-up toys between the endless residential buildings. She had always felt somewhat different, as a member of Patrol, different in the way a predator must feel different from the prey, but nevertheless she always understood that she, like them, answered to greater concerns. It wasn't just the bottomless brutality of Drive Control but the unseen gaze of Central, their common master.

Fractured from her old life, she looked upon the residents as if she stood at some great distance, even as she rubbed shoulders with them. It was the look of their eyes, she decided, the dark, empty look of their eyes that she realized must have lurked behind her own gaze all the years. It wasn't a look of mindlessness or insanity; she knew those well enough from many a cone. Rather it was a look devoid of presence, there but not there, returning her to that first unsettling impression that they were at once dead and not dead. *Undead.*

She moved with the increasing press of the city's residents from the narrow streets of the quad to the wider streets of the commercial districts and, at last, to the wide expanse of the city center. It was the Rectadrome, a confused merger of unmarked roadway and anarchic traffic flow that only Central could manage. There were no traffic lights, no lane stripes, but then she came to understand and dismiss those observations one by one. No traffic lights, because Central could tell people when to roll. No lane stripes, because it was a giant intersection. Central could tell people where to go, whispering the city layout from the earliest days of Rainbow Go.

There was no vehicular traffic as the stars emerged. The riot cycle had begun and Central was pushing people with a special urgency. Carly knew the routine all too well. Patrol was key to riot nights. Her gaze rolled up to see the large net screens atop the buildings that walled in the Rectadrome, and she discerned the batteries of floodlights along the rooftops. Past the gutters and drains the vertical lights already glowed in the night, reaching far into the darkening sky to drive away the glimmer of distant stars. The clouds broke for a moment and the moon grinned with its blind crescent.

She looked about, straining her neck to see over the people around her. Ahead she could see the outline of patrolmen standing atop their parked cars, forming a wall about the center of the Rectadrome. Between them, in the dark center of the square where no light shone, she made out the shadowy bulks of large military trucks. They carried a special burden, the burden that would serve as the focus of the riot. It was only a matter of time.

The old thrill rushed through her. Her old life, it was so simple, and in simplicity there was a seductive, insidious allure. Her heart started to pound.

Thoughts of Gadwick, rogues, and predilectors were cast aside.

She reached into her slicker and unsnapped her civi-stick to pull it free.

The roar of the city rose up around her. She joined in, raising her arm to shake the civi-stick over her head.

A shout burst from her throat.

"Riot!"

| 0 | 0 | 0 |

ENDO, HIDDEN IN THE GLARE of the vertical lights, gazed down at the swirling mass of Seven Hills' gathered thousands. He stood under a small tarp, lost among the electrical feeds and amplifiers that would produce the image of him as the Madman of MG42. He wore a pair of black military pants and a pair of black boots, but otherwise he left himself bare with his skin painted white and his arms wrapped in spirals of black electrical tape. There were people behind him, members of Drive Control, most of them scriptors, finishing their preparations for the start of the riot cycle. He closed his eyes for a moment and remembered that it was on a similar night in Seven Hills, not that long ago, that he first met Sonya.

His eyes opened, his jaw clenching as his fists tightened on a microphone. He turned on his support staff with an impatient glare. "Are you done yet?" he said to no one and everyone at once. Confusion answered him. With the riots moved up the strain and sloppiness were clear to see. He cursed and turned away, his gaze roaming over the massed multitude below him. "I know you're here," he said to himself, imagining Carly among the crowd. "Show yourself and draw out this rogue. He's not far enough to escape me."

"You may want to change that plan."

Endo spun, stilling himself when he recognized High Predilector Mortas. "This is my event, mine to judge and execute," Endo said at once. "You told me you came here to retire and nothing more. Are you aware of the mess at Rooking's market? This rogue has violated the limits of tolerance."

Victor lingered in the shadows. "Your tolerance, or the tolerance of Central? Did you forget the difference, or that there is a difference?"

Endo's eyes narrowed. "I told you before that I'm not interested in philosophical exercises."

Victor nodded as he let out a tired sigh. He looked down to his feet, tipping his head to either side as he seemed to debate with himself. "Tell me, did you really have your Mondial thug pummel Sonya?"

Endo leveled a wary gaze on Victor. He knew he had to choose his words with care. "I did what was required of me. Nothing more, nothing less."

"Did you even consider to consult me on such a thing?"

Endo crossed his arms on his chest. The bands of tape bit into his coiled muscles. "Do you wish to take her from my custody?"

"Mister Stutts," Victor said with a shake of his head. "I only wish to walk away with a woman whose company I desire. A woman, I would remind you, whose very existence is a product of my handiwork."

Endo tensed, but his wits prevailed. "She was the pawn of a rogue. You can have her after I'm done with the rogue."

Victor crossed his arms to mirror Endo's pose. "Do you suspect me?"

Endo bristled at Victor mocking him. He lowered his hands to his side to disarm his anger. "It's an open matter. I'll do whatever is required to settle the situation."

"Of course, of course. Central would expect nothing less." Victor tipped his chin toward the crowd. "Tell me, do you still pretend to shout in that microphone after all these years?"

Endo glanced down. "My recorded voice hasn't changed. My natural voice has. I shout along to keep proper focus on my task."

"Interesting choice of words." Victor smiled. "Something to consider."

Endo blew out a breath. "This, from the man who decided the only woman who could satisfy his desire was an illusion of his own creation."

"An illusion you failed to detect."

Endo could feel his patience slipping away despite his efforts to keep his temper in check. "What do you want?"

Victor tipped his head, his face full of empathy. "I want to remind you that we should hold something real, that we're more than the images we embrace in Central. I want you to remember that you were once a *man* before you were the Madman of MG42. I want to remind you that we're living things with a desire for human company. We've lost that under Central, and we're less for it."

"No more games. I want to know your intentions."

Victor took a deep breath. "I hope to retire with Sonya and have children. That's why I chose a wipe of reproductive age. No dormitories, no chartering, no Rainbow Go, nothing more than a man, a woman, and the children they create."

"That's a romantic delusion. That was John Westing's delusion," Endo said with a shake of his head. "That's all the madness of the old humanity from before Central, and that's everything we've tried to contain. That's living like a cone and resurrecting their values—values that almost destroyed us."

Victor clenched his fists to his chest. "No, no! It's rediscovering our humanity."

Endo shook his head. "It's treason. Once, long ago, you argued for the ways we know under Central before you made the mistake of arguing against them. Is that what this is, revisiting an old argument you already lost?"

"I changed my mind because I knew I was wrong. I knew it then, and I never let go of it, all the years that followed." Victor opened a hand when Endo stiffened. "I know what you're thinking. Endo Stutts, the great Watcher, the protector of Central's ways to ensure the survival of Central and its guardianship over humanity, won't tolerate my deviation—any deviation—from those standards. Look at my years of service. I kept my loyalty. Part of my inclination in scripting Sonya was to show the triumph of Central. Behold, a living intellect where there was only a wipe! Image become reality, and reaffirmed when she gives birth to a child—my child—and from the ether of my imagination and Central's dreams a living intellect will come forth."

Endo blinked. There was no point in hiding the thought that woke within him. "Are you John Westing?"

Victor's jaw clenched. "That's a dangerous accusation, Watcher."

Endo took a step as his gaze bore into Victor. "Are you John Westing?"

"No. Probe me with that stare of yours all you want, but you won't find anything suspicious around me. I'm just a man who's lived far past his appointed time." Victor took a breath and held it a moment before letting it go. "But I must confess I think I've come to understand some of what motivated Westing until everything went wrong with his schemes. I want a child, Endo. I want to be a father. I want to hold my baby, raise it, teach it, the way they did in the time before all *this*," he said with a pointed flare of his hands to the crowd.

"John Westing tried that. He thought he could do better than Central. He was wrong."

Victor rolled his eyes. "I'm not asking to have a family within Central like he did. Hindsight has shown the madness of that aspiration. No, I'll do it away from everything, across the ocean, out in the woods, free of Patrol, sex dens, envens, all of it. As I told you, I will go my way, Central can go its way, and never the two shall meet."

"To what end?"

Victor's face flushed. "To remember the very thing we've forgotten in all the things we've done to ensure our survival. This is what I'm trying to tell you. What's the point of preserving humankind if we're nothing but organic machines marching at the will of Central, devoid of any attachment to each other, any feeling for each other? Aren't those the very things that make us human, and not machines? Our emotional inclinations might be intangible illusions in our hearts and minds but, in the end, there's no greater confirmation necessitating our individual presence among the greater mass of humankind."

Endo tipped his head back. "We have a system. It saved us from extinction."

Victor wagged a finger to the night sky. "You hide under a threat of extinction when we've already paved our way across the solar system. The old fears are dead. We're not facing extinction—we won the battle against our demise. We found a way to survive but paid for it by forgetting how to *live*. Look down there, look at that squirming mass of decrepit humanity, and tell me that mess is supposed to be our shining vision of the future. And you wonder why the humanity up-top wants nothing to do with us down here? How far will we go before our children wake up one day in those despicable dormitories of Rainbow Go and forget what it means to be part of a family, and so forget the very meaning of humanity?"

Endo glanced at the crowd. "Sentiment is an illusion. It leads to nothing but pain and loss. If history taught us nothing else it taught us that old hostilities abort the future. The nations Central deposed consumed each other fighting wars they couldn't escape. Central broke that cycle of violence."

"No, Central broke *us*. That's what I'm trying to show you. You say memory and sentiment are illusions, but all we did was replace them with another illusion, the illusion of Central."

Endo pointed below. "Look at that crowd. Central is real."

Victor paced in a small circle before turning back to Endo. "I know Central is real. I just don't believe in its application to humankind at this point."

Endo studied him for a moment. "Retirement will suit you well."

Victor bowed his head. "Thank you."

"But don't forget that Central saved us from ruin," Endo said, voicing his conviction. "It's always been the folly of success to look out from the security fostered by success, succumb to complacency, and decide there's no more risk in dabbling in the very things that formed the original threat to security."

Victor grinned. "That sounds like a paradox."

"Or a vicious cycle."

"Perspective is a choice, Watcher."

It was a dangerous thought. Endo let it sit for a moment before deciding it was nothing more than another game. "Word games aside, retirement is an absolute. There are rules to follow. You can't leave without finding a successor. Did you come for Carly Westing?"

"Westing's daughter?" Victor frowned. "Damaged goods. I know my responsibility, Endo. Central has shown some leniency and patience in selection. If I don't find a candidate here I'll find one elsewhere. Besides, I won't insult Central or myself by handing over the remnant of someone else's ramshackle aspiration as *my* replacement." He tapped a finger on his chin. "She's all yours."

"She's more than a broken dream," Endo said and turned away.

"If you say so."

Endo spun back around.

The high predilector was gone.

Endo ground his teeth, his gaze falling to the crowd in the Rectadrome. His eyes narrowed as his disposition changed. The data threads whispered to him and what they whispered came to him as a revelation. He would have the rogue, he decided, but not in the way he thought, because there was no rogue as he once believed. He saw Victor, a crazed old predilector wanting to live out his last days in a delusion of dying ways. He saw the rise of a new predilector in the city, a random event caught up in the machinations of what was perhaps a more menacing possibility, the possibility that a city elder had convinced himself to subvert Central by utilizing a new predilector to some scheme of his own.

All things pointed to Gadwick, and it all rested on the rise of a new predilector.

Endo made his decision. Gadwick was the rogue. The predilector was his tool, disguised as the rogue to deceive Endo. The predilector was Carly Westing, daughter of the criminal John Westing. Endo believed Gadwick had roused her from her life in Patrol not for a replacement as elder but to cover his own activities. Gadwick was using her as a pawn in some yet undisclosed scheme. Using her was his mistake.

Endo clenched his fists.

He threw the bus bars, powering the floodlights along the buildings to wash the Rectadrome in white light. He scrambled up to the platform behind the scriptors' tent and raised his arms high as he stepped over the protective grating of the building's vertical light. His shadow loomed larger than life over the city. The cool night air chilled his skin. He pumped his fists before bringing the microphone to his mouth.

His amplified roar overwhelmed the crowds below.

The Madman had arrived, and he wouldn't be denied.

| 0 | 0 | 0 |

ACROSS THE CITY, IN AN old warehouse in the rotting depths of Kilby quad, another crowd began to shout and scream with anticipation at the darkened stage before them, bursting into abrasive yells as the stage lights came on to bathe them in blinding white light. No one noticed the small handful of men entering the back of the building. They filtered in to form a line along the wall, the crowd ahead of them. On the stage five figures stepped to the edge, their shadows looming large. They were the Mondial Five.

"Are you ready for the Killswitch?" an amplified voice called over the crowd.

The crowd erupted, their answer an amorphous wall of sound.

The five Mondial swept their coats aside in time with the line of men at the back of the warehouse. As one they planted their feet to the shout of the crowd. As one they raised their arms, extending what the crowd took to be microphone stands. And then, too late, a few at the head of the crowd paled with horrible realization.

"Flip the Switch!" the amplified voice shouted.

The Mondial, along with the agents of Sector Control at the rear of the crowd, leaned into the stocks of their repeaters and opened fire. The warehouse flashed, not with concert lights, but with muzzle flashes as the stage lights went dark. Shouts of release were lost to screams of horror between the rattling roar of guns.

Out on the street, the ring of agents watching the warehouse observed the flashes of repeaters through the high windows of the building. They looked about until they were certain no prying gazes were on them. It was riot night, after all, and only a subconscious subversive would consider skipping MG42 for Mondial Killswitch. It wasn't important to the agents. All they knew was that the uprisings in Kilby had served their purpose, the hidden purpose of Central to collect its foes into one place, on one night.

Central knew that those responsible for tapping the underground cables of Kilby were in the crowd. For them, reformat wasn't an option. Reduction to a wipe was considered too light a penance. From the distant, indifferent view of Central's predilectors, those in the crowd no longer held any redeemable value. They never knew that the very avenue of their rebellious ways was a waiting trap engineered for their demise.

The roar and flash within the warehouse ended with a few stray bursts of automatic fire. Silence settled over the streets about the building. The only noise was the distant crash and boom of the endorsed riot.

The agents looked at one another. The site would have to be sanitized. It was considered a small price to end the trouble in Kilby.

| 0 | 0 | 0 |

CARLY SHOVED THROUGH THE JOSTLING mass of people to make her way to the crowd's forefront. She was already lost in the industrial pound of Endo's music and the bestial howl of his profanities. There was no resisting the call of the riot and no concern for revealing herself. She wanted to see Endo, see him for once in the flesh, and revel at the forefront in the fury of her beautiful bad-ass. The roots of Patrol ran deep within her, and the seductive thrill of the riot's violent exorcism was too vivid to be denied.

The lights along the Rectadrome were fueling the fire, flashing to the bass thud booming from the towering speakers on the rooftops. With increasing frequency the lights would strobe the center of the Rectadrome, illuminating the area of the square beyond the limiting wall of Patrol. There were people there, skulking shadows turning on their feet, ducking from the noise and light surrounding them, ducking from the madness and hate enveloping them. It was the first Seven Hills riot they knew, yet the animal inside each of them told them it would also be the last.

Carly shouted with the crowd as she held her arm up high and shook her civi-stick in the air. The crowd around her was armed with a variety of crude weapons, pipe scrap from the manufactories, wood scrap from rubbish fires, whatever their hands could seize on the way to the riot. It was all coming to a boil in the city. The daily grovel for something tasteful to eat, the subtle stench of the apartment quads, the hive-like claustrophobia of building after building of single/single dwellings, the indiscriminate fatalities from the Continentals' rockets—those thieves in the night, sending their rockets to steal away the starlit peace of a city living in Central's grip, suppressed while feeling free, oppressed by net broadcasts preaching that all was other than what they knew. Lies and violence, they had the stench of death, and sooner or later the stench had to erupt in its own spasm of violence.

Or so it seemed to Carly, the thoughts floating as wordless impressions through her spinning awareness. Her arm lost its tense shake of her civi-stick as her eyes focused on the sights around her. There were people wild with drink passing bottles of Heavy; there were scuffles in the crowd as the push and shove to Endo's fury spilled out of tempo. She could even see a well-timed grab between some of the men and women—had felt an opportune hand on herself a few times without paying any attention to the contact. As the realizations crept over her, the nearness of the crowd and the bumping of unknown bodies against her threatened to drown her, to undermine any sense of herself and replace it with one simple sense, the communal beast, the madness of the mob, the living city itself roused from its collective, fitful slumber to make things right proper.

Her arm sank as she searched the crowd for an escape. Before she could spot a way out the music stripped down to a rolling pound of drums that shook her innards. She spun, her gaze sweeping the buildings until she found the shadowy platform on which Endo stood with his outline thrown up larger than life.

"Endo," she said under her breath, and her eyes widened with excitement. It didn't matter what she feared or what Gadwick told her, he was still her beautiful bad-ass, and she couldn't dispel the fascination that lurked within her. She called to him, cupping her hands around her mouth, shouting his name without care.

Endo howled from the speakers as he swept a hand across the crowd. The light beneath him went dark. In its stead a battery of lights about the platform winked on to bathe him in a brilliant white glow. "Seven Hills!" he cried, and the crowd roared back to him. He shook a fist in the air. "That's it, let it out! Scream so those Continentals can hear it all the way across the Narrows. Let them hear what we think about their war!"

The crowd erupted in angry shouts.

"Let them know what we think about rations. Let them know!"

Ignored by the crowd, the Patrol cars rumbled to life and turned toward the square. The cars opened, discharging young men and women with civi-sticks in their hands. They were graduates of Teen-stomp, dressed in black bodysuits. They raised their civi-sticks as one, the Patrol cars responding by turning on their lights. The skulking crowd in the square was at last revealed in their despicable misery as bare-footed prisoners from the Continent.

Endo pointed to the black suited teens. "Teen-stomp wants to let them know!"

They responded with a deafening shout, climbing over each other to shake their fists in the air.

The crowd around Carly pressed forward. The moment was coming, she knew. She remembered this, the final graduation from Rainbow Go and Teen-stomp, earning the right to participate in an endorsed riot. It was the final coming of age in the City of Seven Hills.

My city. She remembered that simple thought. With all the things Gadwick had whispered to her, it struck her with a newfound resonance.

"That's right," Endo said over the endless pound of drums sounding across the Rectadrome. He flipped a switch on his microphone to go live, the sound system already calibrated to conceal the slight shift in his voice. "That's right," he repeated, his voice rising in intensity. "We got to let them know," he said, raising his fist over his head. He took a deep breath as his gaze swept over the crowd. "We got to let them know what we think about their fucking war and their fucking rockets, stealing our people and leaving them rotting dead on some fucking fallow field in some radioactive wasteland lost in their ghost-world they call a Continent—you know what I'm talking about, Seven Hills!"

He jabbed a finger at the prisoners. "Look at them squirm! Fuck them! Only thing good for them is the meat-farm—do it, Seven Hills, do it right proper!"

The crowd erupted.

It was all Carly could do not to get trampled in the mad rush. She turned and went with the crowd, struggling to get her civi-stick over her head to fend off anyone who crossed her. She couldn't hear and it was difficult to comprehend what she was seeing in the flash of lights, the dance of shadows, the glint of eyes, and the gleam of weapons. Before she realized it she had surged with the crowd past the perimeter of Patrol, had even bounced off a black suited boy to be caught in the midst of the riot. Her breath came in short gasps in the heat of packed bodies. She was buffeted by screams of pain and panic as if they were blows. The world around her was exploding, exploding in collisions of pipes and bones and fists and faces, exploding in an orgiastic spasm of destruction that devoured her, overwhelmed her, possessed her.

Her old self emerged once more, shedding the frightened Carly who looked on with revulsion. She filled the moment, taking her civi-stick in both hands and turning on the prisoners with a shout. She found her first victim squirming under a storm of stomping feet and clubbed a man and woman to make way over the prisoner. Then she swung down with all her strength, a warm splatter pelting her face as she brought down blow after blow until she heard—felt—nothing but cracks and pops.

Turning away, she raised the stick and threw her shoulder forward as she charged into the crowd, the stick poised in her trailing arm until she caught the sunken face of a bewildered prisoner in her sight. The stick whistled down to crash against the prisoner's forehead. The man's eyes crossed and he dropped at once, the two men who were pulling at him toppling to the ground. She pulled her stick back, took it in both hands and swung low, slamming it into the side of the man on the ground beside her to bowl him over. With space for secure footing she planted her feet and swung away, cursing at one black-suited teen before cracking open the side of her head. It was the same all around her, the riot degenerating into a wanton slaughter of those too timid to submit to their most savage selves.

She held her swing when no one was left. She squeezed her eyes shut and stilled her urge to run with the crowd, knowing from experience that the riot was most lethal as the crowd pressed inward for a final implosion of brutality. Her chest heaved. Sweat rolled down her temples to smear the droplets of blood on her face.

So she stood, ringed by a prone mass of writhing, bloody bodies.

| 0 | 0 | 0 |

ENDO WATCHED THE RIOT WITH quiet satisfaction. He lowered his arms and let his gaze wander the crowd. Despite the deafening drum rolls and the uneven shout and scream of the riot below he, too, stilled himself. In that moment of calm he regained his sense of the data threads to shift his vision from reality to the perception of Central. To his surprise, to the immense satisfaction of his quiet, distant suspicions, he found his awareness rocketing forward to one spot in the riot.

His eyes snapped open to lock full and wide on Carly.

She blinked, sensing him as he sensed her.

Her name came to him, and the moment of recognition washed back to her.

Her eyes widened, her arms easing to lower the civi-stick. *Endo?*

He caught himself as he absorbed the sight of her. So long, so long had he waited, only to have the hunger of his curiosity for her revealed in every facet of its splendid enormity. He stepped to the edge of the platform in anticipation. *Carly Westing, I have found you.*

Carly's lips parted in disbelief, but she answered Endo's thought without hesitation. *Then it's me? I'm the rogue? Are you going to kill me?*

Endo's body tensed, his muscles tightening. It took all his discipline not to leap from the roof in a suicidal urge to possess her. Down there, in all that bloody mess, he nevertheless knew her vulnerability as a predilector in her waking moments. She knew nothing of the greater dangers surrounding her. Vulnerability, ignorance, a waking mind—it was an intoxicating liquor that rushed through his senses. There she was, the daughter of Central's greatest criminal, flesh and blood dwarfed by the potential whispering around her.

His heart pounded with certainty. Victor was an old fool. Chapel was a grunt of Patrol. Noel was nothing more than a middling bureaucrat. Sonya was a bystander, an incidental pawn.

Gadwick was the rogue.

He was sure of all those things, but they were all dwarfed to inconsequence by the last certainty that dawned within him, resounding through the data threads to drive a new conviction like a spike into his forehead.

The only common thread is Carly. She's the answer, the cause, of everything.

John Westing has resurfaced. He must be motivating Gadwick. It's the only thing that makes sense.

If Westing's here, he's sure to make a move on Carly.

His heart swelled with anticipation.

I can protect her—I was always meant to protect her—that's the wisdom of Central, and the reason for my mess with Sonya, and the reason Carly has haunted my dreams.

What a delicate, delirious moment.

He extended an open hand. *Come to me. I will teach you.*

Carly looked about the swirling riot, her fear returning as the tumult pressed her senses. She was surrounded. She'd have to fight her way free. *Where?*

Follow the data threads.

Carly's face fell. She ducked when a pipe flew past her. Endo's thought faded from her, infuriating her. She looked to the platform but Endo was gone.

She ground her teeth. She looked about the riot. Her arms were tired. "Chiggers to this," she said and put her back to the riot. She took a breath and clubbed her way toward the edge of the Rectadrome.

|0|0|0|

Sitting in his quiet office, Gadwick watched his net feeds on a trio of portable screens set on his desk. The riot progressed as usual, and he knew full well of the slaughter and sanitization over in Kilby. Events had flowed with their regular precision. The buildup to the riot hadn't been as usual but that was to be expected given Central's advance of the riot culmination. In any case, he knew the riot was a success, and the killing of the Continental prisoners—degenerate criminals cast out from Drive Control's prisons in their native cities—would vent the subconscious anxieties of the citizens. The slaughter of subversive thinkers in Kilby would leave the city in peace for another six months or so. It was the usual period of calm to be expected. The masses would retreat to their mindless existence until their collective animal began to stir once more.

He sighed and reached for his tea when an image caught his eye on the screen to his left. He leaned forward in his chair until his face hovered over the vapors of his tea, his eyes narrowing. It was the video feed of Globalnet, the common net that supplied all the envens with their programming. Globalnet was restricted to those high within the fold of Central such as city elders, certain sets of scriptors, and the predilectors. Nobody knew where the eyes of Globalnet resided except the predilectors, and only the high predilectors from across the wide ocean knew with any certainty where those camera eyes would focus.

All those facts slid through the lower levels of Gadwick's mind as his gaze locked on the Globalnet feed. Their cumulative reality only served to increase and sharpen his sudden discomfort. Across his monitors, the Globalnet feed spilled over to the other envens.

What's this?

It was the video of an off-duty patrolman at the riot, not in the safety of a Patrol car and armor plate, but as a common citizen, joining the populace with an eager civi-stick to inflict vengeance on the dirty Continentals. Her name scrolled across the bottom of the feed.

Carly Westing.

He settled back into his chair and forgot his tea as he rubbed his temples.

In twenty-four hours she could be as famous and revered as Endo Stutts.

CARLY STOOD BEHIND THE GRAY mass of a Patrol fire truck, catching her breath as the riot petered out down the street. She rested her back against the truck's water tank and let her head hang, her tired arms dangling at her sides. Sweat glistened on her face. Her hair was a short wet mass on her head. She closed her eyes, trying to put the wild vision of the riot out of her mind as her rage subsided.

She dropped her civi-stick, pulled off her rain slicker, and ran her hands over her head. A shower would have been wonderful, but she'd have to make do with the truck. She picked up her stick and paced along the side of the vehicle to find a low-pressure bleed valve. The slow drain of water washed away the spattered blood from her slicker, from the end of her stick, from her hands, from her hair. Icy streams snaked around her lowered head until the chill woke her from her stupor. Her thoughts snapped to attention before racing off in another direction.

With a hasty turn of the valve she shut off the water and shook her head dry, sending droplets of water flying from her short hair. She wondered about Graham and Noel, hoping they weren't killing each other out in the copse. Despite her lingering doubts, she ignored Gadwick's caution regarding assumptions and took Endo's recognition as strong confirmation that she was indeed the rogue. She perceived herself as the only common thread between everything that had happened between her, Graham, Noel, Sonya Mortas, Gadwick, and Endo. It all tumbled upon her and, holding to that perception, holding to her new perception that she was the rogue, she felt a deep, dark thrill.

Endo said he would teach her. She wanted to know everything. She would beat it out of him if she had to, beautiful bad-ass or not. If he wanted to play rough, she'd show him no one was rougher than Patrol. Despite Gadwick's warning she dismissed the idea of Endo as a threat. She would take everything she could get from Endo. When she was done she'd have the upper hand, except for the business of Drive Control. For some reason she didn't care to question, though, her intuition told her not to trust Gadwick and his stupid order for the raid. Avoiding that madness, she figured, would keep Graham and Noel safe. Besides, they had risked enough for her.

It was a pleasant surprise to have her mind filled with considerations. It was a process that tingled down her spine with the subconscious recognition of something very new dwelling within her awareness—a plan.

She pulled up her shirt to wipe her face. With the shirt in her hands, the ENDO monogram was upside down and backwards. It drew a grin, but she drove it away and dried her face. She snapped her civi-stick over her shoulder, pulled on the rain slicker, smoothed her hair back, and took several handfuls of cold water from the valve. Hunger gnawed at her belly, but food would have to wait.

She looked down the length of the empty street before hopping into the cab of the fire truck. To her relief it wasn't a secured vehicle. Without a key or fingerprint recognition, she flipped the ignition switch and started the truck with a roar. The vehicle's net screen came to life and filled her ears with enven chatter. It was the last thing she wanted to hear after the deafening cacophony of the riot. She ignored it for a moment, maybe two, before pulling her handgun and cracking the butt into the screen. The screen split, squawked, and fell silent.

A compress sandwich lay on the dashboard. Without a second thought she grabbed it, tossed the half-eaten side out the window, and took a bite from the fresh side as she drove away.

It had the taste of a thick steak.

| 0 | 0 | 0 |

"You can hear it from here," Graham thought aloud as he looked toward the city.

Noel, urinating by a bush behind the car, struggled to hear Graham. He zipped and walked around the car to find Graham standing by the open passenger door. Noel followed Graham's gaze, looking between the trees as he picked up the steady roll of drums. He scratched his jaw and could only imagine what was happening in the Rectadrome. "The things we do," he said with a sigh.

Graham turned to him. "You ever go to a riot?"

Noel kept his gaze between the trees. "No. No one in Drive Control has to go. We create the riot, but we don't have to participate."

Graham's eyes widened. "You create it?"

Noel tipped his chin up. "It's a scripted event. It's part of Central. You have to know that," he said, intending to annoy Graham. He found it hard to understand his animosity with Carly's patrolmate, but he also found it hard to resist needling Graham, as he was certain Graham wasn't the rogue. *Too dim a bulb, this ape.* He pondered for a moment, but then licked his lips as a plan congealed in his mind. He looked to Graham. "You know, I've been thinking about this raid on Drive Control. Timing it before we get Sonya, that is."

Graham shook his head. "Drive Control first. Your woman can wait."

Noel frowned. "She could be dead by then. What's that repulsive slang Patrol has for it? Oh, now I remember. She could be meat-farmed, I should say."

Graham slammed shut the car door before turning on Noel. He grabbed Noel by the collar and shoved him against the car before pinning him with a forearm across the throat. Noel gasped and grabbed at Graham's wrist, but Graham leaned into him and punched him once in the gut—as much for enjoyment as for good measure, it seemed—before tossing him to the ground.

Graham stood over Noel and jabbed a finger at him. "Carly and I agreed we do Drive Control first, and then we get your woman. I don't care what Gadwick says. I don't care if you're Carly's brother. I don't care anymore if you saved her. That's all done with, controller. As far as I see it, you're one of them, not one of us, and I don't think you give a rat's ass about her other than what she can do for you. You listen, or you're done with, got it?"

Noel held his stomach, fighting not to vomit as he lay on the ground. He shook his head and held up a hand when Graham reached for him. "Wait! Sonya could protect Carly."

Graham's fists tightened until he hoisted Noel to his feet to shove him against the car. "You saw what we did at Rooking's market. That happened because of *you*, but it's on *us* to answer for it if we get grabbed by Central. Whatever plan you have, it better be good."

Noel nodded, his knees wobbling beneath him. "We don't know what Carly's doing in the city," he said, his voice uneven as he fought to breathe. "If we get Sonya, bring her here and hide her, we could use that to our advantage. She told me Endo favors her. If Endo gets hold of Carly, if she—or any of us—get grabbed when we go to Drive Control, we could hold Sonya's release over our release."

Graham ground his teeth. "She's a scriptor, right?"

Noel nodded.

"What's a scriptor worth?"

"She's not just any scriptor. Stutts, he...he claims her."

Graham frowned. "Too risky. She waits."

Noel shook his head. "We have nothing out here, nothing for leverage! Forget about what I think of Sonya. If we have her we might have something to save ourselves."

"Might, or might not," Graham said, his eyes doubtful.

Noel opened his hands. "What do we have now besides Gadwick's interest? Do you think if things get tight between him and Stutts he's going to stick his neck out any further for us? Central hates a mess."

Graham released Noel and stepped back to look toward the city. Noel's eyebrows rose until Graham turned a hard look on him. "Getting out from Central means making our own way. We won't do that sitting here, doing nothing. Carly was right on that. I guess that also makes you right."

Noel nodded. "That's it," he said with relief.

"You know where Sonya lives, right? We start there. But understand one thing," Graham said with another jab of his finger, "I don't trust you, I don't like you, and if you give me one reason, I'll leave you in the city on your own. Got it?"

"Got it," Noel said. He grinned when Graham opened the car door and hopped in. It only took a moment but it was a moment of certainty in Noel, a moment of absolute conviction that he was the rogue. He had to be, when he considered how he had just worked his will into reality. His opinion of Carly diminished; she was nothing more than a loose cannon, a random distraction in his personal rise to prominence within Central. As for Graham, well, Noel found the brevity of his conclusion a work of elegance. In his eyes, Graham was nothing more than a convenient lump of idiotic muscle.

He didn't even see what I did, didn't even realize it. He's just a sap. No mutton-head of Patrol could be a rogue. It must be me! And Sonya, she'll be mine. No more hiding from Stutts, ever again.

| 0 | 0 | 0 |

GADWICK HAD TWO OF HIS screens powered down, leaving only the Globalnet playing while his gaze rested on the piece of paper before him. The pencil he held in his hand tapped the desktop with a slow bob of the eraser. On the paper he had scrawled several sets of numbers separated by faint interconnecting lines. It was a drive nexus, a rough sketch of what predilectors could feel of the data threads. The common wisdom running through the upper echelons of Central held that the oldest high predilectors could process the cumulative knowledge of the threads and manipulate it at will.

"Nonsense." He blew out a breath. "Men of power once believed that Earth was the center of the universe. They were wrong, too."

Vanity. He shook his head. *Or is arrogance a better word?* He decided there was no difference between the two labels because they both represented the folly of self-deception. Central called it self-predilection, but

it was part of humanity long before Central came into existence. Either
way it was a process wrapped in irony. The more one succumbed to folly's
suffocating embrace, the harder it was to perceive its clutch—that which
one craves in secret, one also showers with the most demonstrative and
vehement denial, evidence of the subconscious struggle mounting in the
mind's core.

Denial. It was a mercurial, mysterious creature.

So he sat, brooding, contemplating the uneasy development of Carly's
broadcast on the Globalnet. If her image was captured on the net it meant
Central wanted to capture her, and that suggested plans far removed
from anything he could sense. His little private endeavor was no longer
as private as he wanted, complicating the matter.

"And yet, you still wish to have your way."

Gadwick's head popped up. The pencil sprang from his hand as he
tensed in surprise. He stood to look past the light of his lamp. Once his
eyes adjusted he discerned the outline of a hooded figure standing in his
doorway. He didn't see his secretaries.

"I sent them off," Victor said, waving a hand.

Gadwick hesitated before drawing a breath. "Sir, ah, welcome," he
said, clasping his hands. He cleared his throat and offered the seat before
his desk. "I haven't forgotten your presence in the city—no, no I haven't,
not at all—but I didn't know to expect you tonight."

"No matter," Victor replied, lingering by the door. "There's a certain
elegance in brevity, so let me be blunt. I know what you seek to do in
this grungy little city of yours, Elder Gadwick."

"What I seek?" Gadwick blinked, caught off guard by Victor's perception. It took a moment to rally his wits and his resolve. "I'm only
fulfilling my responsibility to—"

Victor held up a hand. "Elder, please. I cannot be patronized. Don't
embarrass yourself."

"It's my dictate as elder to choose my successor," Gadwick said, tapping a pointed finger to his desktop.

"Elder, you know the custom. The process is tried and true, and so
very ordered in its progression. As elder you appeal to Central. Patrol is

scouted for a candidate—"

"I chose my candidate."

"But you never appealed to Central."

Gadwick felt his patience seep away. "I thought you were retiring."

Victor smiled. "I may be retiring but I'm still a high predilector, and so still a guardian of Central's practices. The ice beneath you is thin, very thin, and the waters beneath cold, dark, and pitiless. Trust me, I know of what I speak."

Gadwick held up a hand. "I am an elder in good standing."

Victor stared at him.

Gadwick's mind opened as the veils of secrecy around Victor lifted. The elder shook his head, shaking the cobwebs from the threads of his perceptions to find the process accelerated with each waking thought and the anger it spawned. Despite the pallor of his age his face flushed as his eyes burned. "You were behind the uprising in Kilby. You—you let me think I started that cycle. How, how dare you!"

Victor shrugged.

"You were behind Westing's waking. You—it was you that cast the brick—not just a brick, but a stone in the water sending its ripples across Central." Gadwick rubbed his forehead, his anger calming as his mind raced. He looked back to Victor. "You didn't come here to retire."

Victor raised a finger. "Oh, don't mistake my intention on that, Ian."

"You didn't come here for Sonya." Gadwick pursed his lips. "Do you know what Stutts did to her? Did you know he had her pounded like a slab of meat?"

"That's a matter I will address with him."

"Nevertheless, your Sonya isn't a predilector. You didn't come for her."

Victor wagged his finger at Ian. "Don't mistake that intention, either."

"You came for Carly Westing," Gadwick said, peering through Victor's facade. "That's the practice, that's the custom. If one leaves, one must be brought up as a replacement. One who retires fills a last loyalty by finding a replacement."

"Then why are you so surprised? Wasn't that your plan?"

Gadwick shook his head. "I thought I could use Carly Westing as my replacement. I thought you found another."

"You thought wrong," Victor replied. "Did you think I was sitting idle? I created Sonya, in this city. Obviously you fail to grasp the significance of that act. I know you had no idea she was a wipe, a product of my creation. I thought when I told you my name as Victor Mortas you couldn't fail to perceive my intent."

"Your intent?" Gadwick rubbed his forehead. "You concealed your intent. You concealed Sonya's nature from me, somehow—" His gaze snapped to Victor. "You predilected me in my sleep!"

Victor's eyes narrowed. "You mistake what I've done. You try my patience."

"I'm trying your patience?" Gadwick shook his head. He couldn't believe the reality unfolding around him. He had thought he could retire for the night by entertaining himself with his secretaries only to discover he was the entertainment for something much less satisfying. "Why did you put me between Stutts and a wipe? Why predilect me in my sleep so that I wouldn't be able to recognize her as a wipe?"

"You grow paranoid," Victor said with a sigh. "You only see schemes because of your own duplicitous nature. You've done a dangerous thing. You decided to claim Carly for your retirement without any petition to Central."

"I had no choice!" Gadwick slapped a hand on his desk. "That bastard John Westing made a mess of my city. He almost cost me my position as elder. I wanted his daughter as my replacement to vindicate the suspicion that's hung around me ever since Westing went into hiding. I didn't know if Central would accept her. I wanted to show Central that I've done a good job, that I salvaged something from Westing's crimes."

"And you thought no one else would conceive such a plan?" Victor shrugged. "At least I made a petition for her. I didn't hide my plans from Central."

"You're lying."

"Am I?"

Gadwick shifted on his feet, his gaze darting to the walls of his office.

"What's wrong?" Victor said with a smile. "Do you feel the room closing in? Oh, Ian, you've made two terrible mistakes in one swoop. Not only did you interfere in my retirement by trying to take Carly as your successor, but by taking her on your private dictate flies in the face of Central."

Gadwick fought to rally his nerve. "I am the Elder of Seven Hills. This is my city. My city! Why should I have to appeal to Central?"

"Take caution, Elder. Those are dangerous words, and so many lives wasted in your impatience. A heavy price to explain. You best yield your way."

"Yield?" Gadwick's pride burned through his mask of practiced serenity. "Why should I yield? I will set an example that needs to be made!"

"Yes you will!"

Gadwick, caught off guard by Victor's agreement, froze with his mouth open.

Victor opened his hands. "Yes you will, Elder. I confess I predilected you in your sleep to hide from you the truth of my Sonya. I had to, because I already saw what stirred in your heart. Rebellion is a dangerous thing. It can only be tolerated if it serves a greater purpose, a purpose that atones itself by proving its benefit to the established order. Then it's no longer seen as rebellion, it becomes enlightenment. I have enlightened Central to a new possibility of our predilectory skill through the creation of Sonya. And who better to prove her worth, to prove the thoroughness of my work, than by making an example of none other than Endo Stutts, the Watcher himself? I haven't hurt you Ian, I've given your city a gift, the gift of a new possibility in Central—a wholly scripted intellect. You will be celebrated for your work."

Gadwick shifted on his feet as he digested Victor's words. "Forgive me if I'm hesitant."

"You best not hesitate."

Gadwick stiffened.

Victor pointed across the city. "You only continue to live because I intervened on your behalf. Mister Stutts has quite different intentions regarding your short-term future. In fact, he considers you the origin of all the mischief in Seven Hills. Mark my words, before this little adventure plays out he will come to you and accuse me of being a rogue to manipulate you into implicating yourself. I am the only man who can neutralize Stutts. I know him better than he knows himself."

Gadwick reconsidered his thoughts, closed his mouth, and cupped his hands behind his back. He was checked, and no amount of bluster could change that situation. Despite his reservations he had to cooperate with Victor. "What would you wish I do?"

"Exactly what I told Mister Stutts to do."

"And that would be?"

"Nothing more than I tell you to do," Victor said. "Your knowledge is vastly insufficient for this situation, and you best remember that. In fact, I think it best that you forget your intentions completely."

Gadwick tipped his head. "But I'm reaching an age—"

"When you are in full possession of this city's organic character," Victor said with grace. "You even managed to outwit the great Endo Stutts, did you not?"

Gadwick couldn't help but grin at the memory of Endo standing outside Drive Control waiting to pour an imaginary glass of wine. "Yes, yes I did. Indeed, I did."

Victor bowed his head. "And that is no mean feat, no weak feat. No, Elder, you are the heart and soul of this city. Think of your subjects, your citizens, devolved to nothing more than a horde of cockroaches if you were separated from them. It would be a horrible waste, such foolishness, yes?"

"Of course," Gadwick agreed.

Victor nodded again. "I hoped you would see it my way. As my apology to you I will take this matter in hand. You need not concern yourself with these troubles any longer. You tire of the strain, yes?"

Gadwick sighed. "It has been a burden, my activity of late."

Victor opened a hand before him. "Then sit, Elder. Ah, yes, elder indeed, wouldn't you agree? Yes, age pulls its final slumber closer day by day for you, Ian. Lay your head upon your desk and take a well-deserved rest. Sleep, and let the angels sing away your burdens."

Gadwick's eyelids drooped as his thoughts went dark. There was no point in fighting the sudden stupor that grew within him. Victor's predilection was too strong to resist.

He slumped in his seat with a heavy sigh.

| 0 | 0 | 0 |

CARLY DROVE THROUGH THE CITY, her truck lost in the desolation of deep night. The fervor of the riot had spent itself, and the carnage that resulted from the city's violent spasm only served to dispel the crowd it had gathered. People ran away, scurrying off to seek refuge in their domiciles. Even for Teen-stomp, who would celebrate their first riot with an endless consumption of alcohol, would retreat to their dormitories for the sloppy randomness of drunken sexual collisions. It was no different, in many ways, from the life they were being prepared to live. It was the life Carly had lived, dissolute and careless, aimless and pointless, senseless and stupid.

It was a thought that haunted her as the shadowed streets passed by. She darkened the truck's headlights in her wish not to be seen. The more she concentrated on the thought, the more she remembered the riot. The more she remembered the riot, the heavier the civi-stick felt on its shoulder strap. She was sickened by the riot, for she heard Gadwick's voice repeating the same statement in the recesses of her mind.

There is no war. The prisoners of war aren't Continentals, they're prisoners of Drive Control from some other city, and our prisoners are used in some other city for that city's riot.

The riot is an illusion.

The rockets came every night yet, for the first time, she realized there wasn't a single rocket on riot night. She dismissed it as an oversight lost in the chaos of the riot, but certainty grew within her until she knew it as an absolute for all previous riots. It disturbed her, for it made sense in a way that mocked her for her blindness. With all of Patrol at the riot, with the city focused on the riot, what services would be left to manage rocket damage, fight the fires, and manage the wounded?

There is no war.

It had to be true. If the war was real, how could Central order a night without rockets, unless the rocket attacks happened at Central's dictate? She would've dismissed it in her old way and so discard her unease. Shit happens, she would've told herself. *Who cares? This moment is this moment. There's only the now.*

Despite the old familiar thoughts she shook her head. *No. Not that simple. Not just chance. It's too neat. Like Gadwick said. All these things happen within Central, so they must all be known to happen, and if you know all that's going to happen, then shit doesn't just happen. No, you would know everything, so only what you want to happen would happen—*

Her foot stomped the brake pedal and brought the truck to a halt as her mind cleared around that thought. She closed her eyes and then opened them moments later to gaze out the far side of the truck's cab, straight down the old manufactory road to see the Underworld. Staring at the building and the armored cars parked in haphazard fashion, her mind began to distill the growing storm of her unease into simple thoughts.

Nothing happens in Central without a reason.

So I have this thought right now, just as Central knew I would.

And I have it right here, and I look to my right, just like Central wanted.

And I think to myself, 'I bet Endo is in there. I feel him in there.'

She closed her eyes, forcing herself to relax as her anxiety mounted. Then it came, slow and silent but then sure and certain, the thought she knew would come, the thought she realized was from her as much as it was from Central, was from Central as much as it was from her.

I bet Endo is in there. I feel him in there.

She took a breath. The feeling was hers. She decided the thought would be hers as well.

The truck's engine fell silent. Carly slid from the cab to stand beside the truck, her hand lingering on the handle as her gaze locked on the Underworld.

I am who I am, and Central is what Central is.

Her eyes narrowed. She had a new plan.

That's it. Not the same.

Endo Stutts. Gadwick said you're out to get me because you're part of Central. Well, I'll teach Central a lesson through you, Endo.

"Right proper," she said and flipped off the safety of her handgun.

| 0 | 0 | 0 |

THE MONDIAL FIVE RETURNED TO Sonya's apartment and leaned their repeaters against the window wall as they settled down in her living room. Mondial Two raided her kitchen for food while Three and Four collected all the clip belts and laid them on the floor by the repeaters. Five stretched his legs out as he stared out the window wall and soon fell asleep. Mondial One shrugged off his long coat, letting it fall to the floor before he walked to the doorway of Sonya's bedroom.

She lay still, on her back, her breath slow and even as she slept. Mondial One hovered in the doorway for a moment before moving to the edge of her bed. He pulled the sheet back to stare down at her. His breath came in a long, deep pull of his diaphragm. He reached out again but froze when he noticed the reflection of her eyes as they opened wide upon him. His hand shook, trembling until it stilled some moments later.

He fell back a step and dropped his arm to his side. The brightness of her eyes vanished in the darkness, leaving him once again a shell. With a blink he turned away, sat down on her couch, and joined his comrades in sleep.

| 0 | 0 | 0 |

CARLY PUSHED HER WAY THROUGH the crowd of the Underworld as the roar of MG42 assaulted her ears. The riot may have died away in the city, but in the escape of Patrol it never ended. The energy in the Underworld was still high enough to resurrect wild memories within her, tempting her with the sweet decadence she remembered all too well. Standing there, removed from that sloppy bliss of ignorance by her new awareness, she looked upon her former comrades and was disturbed by their reckless revelry.

As she pressed through the tumult members of Patrol collided with her, reminding her of the clumsy gropes she often anticipated, that she often let escalate in the recessed corner booths, at the bar, and along the walls. She would've been in the middle of that, her and Graham and Oboe and Gwen. Those days, so soon passed, would never return. It was her old life, gone forever. Even if she would surrender to Central, give herself up to Drive Control and let them put her through reformat, she could never return to her former self and the mindless existence she had lived since her childhood.

These thoughts saved her from the sensory assault of the Underworld, and she didn't lose herself to it as she had at the riot. Instead it forced her back, her thoughts imploding to the childhood she glimpsed in her waking moments from Central. She recalled an impulse that resisted the touch of others; that she was in fact fearful of it, sickened by it, offended by it, reviled by the animalistic conviction that strangers were not just touching her but stealing some piece of her.

In the deafening tumult of the Underworld her sight collapsed through time to reveal images long buried within her. She could see herself as if she was standing witness to her own memories. There she was, a young girl, beaten and broken, bloody and bruised, crying to her brother and her drunken mother, her father gone from them. His last words returned to her. Ignorant in her aim to be closer to some memory of him, she had heeded those words and followed their lead, followed them the same way she followed them after the Rooking market slaughter. In those lost days of her youth, though, the shadows of a copse held something far different than protection.

Between those two flights to hide among shadowed trees sat the vast gray emptiness of her life, a life of lies, deceptions, and assaults upon her through Central's way. So many blurred memories, so many nights of drunken delirium; so befuddling, the sensory overload of Patrol, that many moments, many careless moments, ran through her like rain through a sewer grate. She remembered graduation from Teen-stomp, her initiation into Patrol, nights with Graham, with Oboe, with Milston, with Bayard—

She felt raw and naked.

Her heart bucked.

She wasn't a defenseless girl, she reminded herself. She was a member of Patrol.

Nobody stomped on Patrol.

A blue fire lit her eyes.

She reached under her slicker, pulled her civi-stick free, and took it in both hands to bull her way through the jostling mass of Patrol toward a particular table off to one side of the floor. She burst through the last mass of the crowd to bump into a wall, her gaze bearing down on the table for which she aimed. The Underworld's spotlights spun behind her and threw their harsh white light across the table and its occupants. Bayard sat before her, his head turning and his gaze rising to stare wide at her outline, her face lost in the glare of the spotlight shining behind her. The other patrolmen at the table ignored her, too involved in their alcohol and each other.

She raised her arms high, her civi-stick clutched tight in both hands. The light behind her swung away.

Bayard stared at her, his face lit with pleasant surprise as he recognized her. "Nimbus!" he said and opened his hands to her, oblivious to the gleaming hate in her eyes and the stick she held high.

Her rage and revulsion broke as his hands neared her. She whipped the stick down, square on his head, right where the forehead curved up to the roof of the skull, where she'd been taught the most damage could be inflicted. Bayard's head shot down, his neck seeming to collapse as the skin of his head split and the skull beneath cracked. She spun away as Bayard wavered and collapsed against the patrolmen behind him, the woman shoving him off as blood poured down his face. Carly disappeared into the crowd as Bayard's head slammed on the table. Bloody fluid pooled on the table in a creeping red wash.

Shouts rang out. Carly made for the exit, shoving her way forward until someone heavy collided with her and sent her stumbling to the side.

She hit a wall, her arm tingling with the impact, and looked up to find herself at one end of the bar. There was a commotion over by Bayard's table, a buzzing mix of shouts, curses, and pointed fingers. Two patrolmen burst from the shadowed throng in front of her, one of them splattered with Bayard's blood, his eyes boiling with rage. She planted her feet, slid the end of the stick through one hand, and waited until the patrolman was close enough to thrust her stick square into his crotch. His eyes went blank with pain as he crumpled. The second patrolman swung, and she managed to duck enough in the press of bodies to let his fist rush past her and slam into the back of another woman's head.

She could feel the anger washing around her. It wasn't a typical, good-natured Underworld brawl. It felt more like a street brawl with cones, filled with rage and violent hate, and the erupting lust to smash faces and break bones. There was something more than Bayard's death fueling that mounting wave but desperation choked down her thoughts as the wave swirled around her. All she saw were rough hands desperate to grab her. She'd shatter every one of them if they didn't back off, patrolmen or not.

Her lips parted.

A punch slammed into the side of her head. She staggered against the bar but gained herself and jabbed the end of her stick into someone's ribs. Another fist sliced the air just past her cheek as she dodged the blow. Bodies pressed toward her. She shot her arm out and pinioned her stick around a woman's throat to use her as a shield.

The woman wrestled with her. The strobe lights flashed. Bared teeth gleamed under white light. Fists flew. Shouts punctuated the deafening music.

Have to get out of here—can't get out of here—chiggers!

Her heart pounded with anxiety. Her blood boiled with a trinity of fear, rage, and hate until a single thought burst into her conscious mind with such force she wasn't sure if it burst from her lips as well.

Stop!

The world erupted in a white haze of piercing static. Time seized to a disoriented halt. She wasn't sure if she was seeing anything with her eyes or if the sight before her was some illusion of her fear. The patrolmen froze in contorted anger, their faces revealed in every minute distortion of their fury.

The stick slipped from her grasp. It felt like days to her before it fell from her numb fingers.

A hand grabbed her collar and yanked back, hard, jerking her off her feet. She gagged, but training took over in a heartbeat. She pinned the hand against her chest, spun, and broke the hold.

She didn't believe what she found before her.

She was eye to eye with Endo.

Endo Stutts, the Madman of MG42.

She didn't stop to think. In her delirium he was just another asshole looking to grab her. She bounced back as he spun on his feet to shut the door behind him with his hip. He locked the door and took a step toward her, reaching up to pull down a wire screen. He kept his focus on her, her gaze locked on him as he reached out to hit a button beside the screen. She realized the tight room they occupied was in fact an elevator. It bumped beneath them as it began to rise.

She stared at him, recognition at last solidifying within her senses. *Endo Stutts.* It was hard for her to fathom his presence before her, solid in flesh and bone. In her fantasies that flesh was a willing mass in her embrace. She would devour him in her wild lust, and his eyes would both welcome and consume her.

But that was just a fantasy, a dreamy illusion to buoy her mind through too much Heavy and too little sleep. What was in front of her—what was in front of her was just a man, just a man grabbing her. If it was going to be violent, so be it. She'd see how much of a bad-ass he was for real.

She snapped her handgun free.

Endo's reaction was too swift for her to comprehend. She was the fastest draw in her Patrol detachment, yet she didn't stand a chance. His foot lashed out to send the gun flying from her hand. She ducked to the side as his foot came down, then rose up behind his leading shoulder and shot her fist straight toward his cheek. He sank away from the blow and turned under her strike to drive his arm full into her. His palm struck her square in the chest and threw her back against the side of the elevator. Stunned but not hurt, she snapped her leg out, her foot flailing past his face. Once again he dodged her attack, and she grunted with the growing sense that she was responding one blow behind him, as if he knew her next move.

The elevator bounced to a stop. She held her fighting stance, cornering herself to keep an arm's reach from Endo. He kept his eyes on her as he reached back to hit the release for the wire screen. No sooner did his hand hit the release then she came at him again, leading with a deliberate roundhouse swing. He dodged with ease and let her momentum carry her past him toward the screen. She thought she had him then as she spun to whip an elbow at his head.

He ducked and thrust his leg back, burying his heel in her stomach.

She wheezed as she crumpled around his boot. Her shoulders slammed on the floor, followed by the crack of her head. Her arms sank to her sides as she lay unstrung and breathless, stunned from the kick and fall. She fought to draw some air into her lungs.

Endo stood beside her with one fist drawn back, his knuckles white-tight against his black bodysuit. Jaw clenched, he held his other hand low to guard his groin as he glared at her. "I don't want to hurt you," he said, his words almost lost as she rolled away from him. "There's no need to fight."

Her gaze rose to his as she forced herself up on hands and knees, her limbs shaking beneath her. She ground her teeth, refusing to give up. It was a struggle to gain her feet, but she threw her shoulders back and drew her fists before her. Her nostrils flared as she took in a deep breath.

She came at him again.

Her last sight was the widening of his eyes. The moment her body was committed to the momentum of her roundhouse kick he was all over her. He stepped in and chopped his hand into her stomach. He spun around her, grabbed the hood of her slicker and flipped it over her face before driving his other palm into the back of her head. Off balance, she stumbled blind, tripped over her feet, and got her hands down just before she would've broken her nose.

Cursing under her breath, she rose to her knees and tore the slicker over her head to toss it aside. Her fingers clawed at the zipper of her body-suit, yanked it open, and reached under her shirt to brace her cramped stomach muscles. She spat a trace of blood and wiped her mouth on the back of her hand.

Feral instinct told her he was behind her, just waiting for her to take another pass at him. He was toying with her, and it enraged her. It gave her the energy to fight the protest of her body and rise to her feet, yet it forced her to accept the harsh realization that she couldn't beat him, at least not with the ways she knew from Patrol. His predilectory sense was too keen, surmising her attacks before she even made them. No, he would kill her if she insisted on fighting him that way.

What can I do to get the edge on him?

Using a hand for balance she straightened her shaking legs. She looked down as she wiped her mouth on the side of her wrist. There were still specks of Bayard's blood on her knuckles. She blinked. To Bayard she was nothing but a plaything, his Nimbus.

She closed her eyes and dropped her hand. A desperate decision formed within her, but she knew the only other option was to die under a relentless pummeling from Endo. The discussion she had with Gadwick sprang from the back of her mind. *Many options, but in the end, no real decision to make.* It wasn't quite futility, but something subtle, something more definitive, a wordless sense in her that, had she known better, she would've recognized as inevitability. Central, she realized, thought it would have its way with her—again.

No. She ground her teeth in defiance. If she were doomed she'd take it on her feet and not on her back. For once, she would have her way with Central.

Her fists clenched as she glanced over her shoulder to Endo.

He stared at her. "Why fight?"

"I'm Patrol. It's all I know."

"Then you don't know anything." He shook his head. "You have to learn to adapt."

She turned to face him.

A large wall screen behind Endo was showing an after-action feed of the riot. Endo was on his platform, shouting to the city below. Carly's eyes dilated as she drank in the sight of him, larger than life in every sense as his image loomed over his flesh and blood incarnation. There he was, the Madman of MG42, Endo Stutts. Not an icon on a screen, more than a name she wore on all her shirts, more solid than the fantasy that lit her mind when she was with Graham, and more than the derivative fantasy of any woman with good drive. It was what Central desired, after all, and what Central desired—what she desired—was the delusional freedom of fantasies that could only exist in subconscious daydreams.

Her body eased with her thoughts, her fists sinking as the tension fled her body. She didn't care what Gadwick told her. Gadwick was just another lying asshole. Endo could've killed her five times over, yet she was still on her feet. He said he didn't want to fight her. He said he wanted to teach her, and she realized his first lesson was already working its way through her head. There was no need to be tense, there was only a need to flow, to bend rather than break. She had to learn a greater wisdom than the brutality of fists.

It made sense, but it was too easy. She had killed Gwen. She had killed Bayard. There was the Rooking massacre, running away from Patrol, and countless other violations she had committed in her waking from Central. Why would Central tolerate her? Could she expect anything different from what happened to her mother?

It was too much for her. Her instinct told her to fight.

She stared at Endo.

He seized the moment. He rushed her. She tried to evade, but he was too fast. They grappled until her shoulders hit the wall. Pinned, she writhed to break free but found herself incapable of throwing a blow. She pushed at his shoulder, grabbed the collar of his shirt, threw her hips out to knock him off balance, tried to get her forearm across his throat, all to no use. He checked every move until he had her, his hands locking on her wrists and pinning them against the wall. She wrestled against his strength, a pointless struggle with her shoulders flat against the wall and his feet planted firm.

He shouted for her to stop when she refused to give up the fight. She tried to snap her forehead into his face but he ducked back, put his forehead to hers, and pushed her head to the wall. He drove his knee between her thighs to guard against a kick, shifted his stance for better balance, and swung her wrists up to pin them by her shoulders.

The pressure of his forehead against hers was inescapable. Her fingers were going numb. Her body ached in several places. Her heart was pounding. She was done.

There was nothing left to do but stare into his dark eyed gaze. "Okay. Now what?" she whispered on a tight breath.

| 0 | 0 | 0 |

IT WAS A SIMPLE QUESTION. It left Endo speechless.

He remembered all the moments he had watched Carly through the data threads and the countless dreams she had haunted. After all that abstract attention and distant devotion, he now had her so close he could feel the pulse in her wrists and the warmth of her skin against his own. Only the surreal immediacy of the moment let him cling to any semblance of thought as he reveled in his first true look at her. He was engulfed by the beauty of her eyes, blue as the wide ocean whose mysterious depths he often pondered from the portals of airships.

Now what?

He probed her the way he had probed Sonya, and then he understood. What he held—the living energy of her body, the shades of her thoughts, the anxiety venting on the heat of her breath—they were all real. She was real, she was living; she was a singular creature, wrapped in the vibrant, delicate vitality of her living flesh.

He stared into her. Once again he saw the emptiness within himself, but something had changed in that perception.

He understood then why he had desired Sonya. She was beside him when Carly was nothing more than an image to haunt his subconscious. Illusion and reality changed places before him, indiscernible entities that they were.

It was an odd moment.

His intentions melted between them, melted and flowed to a place he never expected, had never anticipated. His discipline drifted away like a harmless vapor.

He felt her breath on his lips.

Now what?

They held each other's gaze, unblinking, unwavering. He felt a new battle flash between them, one unseen and unheard except in the turbulence of the data threads converging around them. The push and pull of their minds intensified until a single thought rose with meteoric ascent to sear their senses. It ripped away their congealing awareness to expose the unspoken whisper between them.

No Central, no rogue, no predilector—only equals.

There is no war.

He let go his grip, and she eased. The fantasy he held, the dalliance of her image just outside his sleeping mind, was one he found reflected in her. It was maddening, it was thrilling, and it seemed to rebound as an electric jolt through their foreheads that sparked every nerve to life. Their desires lit as only those of predilectors could, clawing at them, consuming any other thought with rapture's immolation until nothing remained but the moment, the all-consuming moment, the moment they alone inhabited.

He opened his eyes, his heart pounding anew as he felt her resistance fade. He came to Seven Hills expecting a confrontation with a rogue. Yet, there he was, entwined with Carly, and the urge within his limbs transformed to a new urgency.

He leaned in and put his lips to hers. He lingered for a moment, only for her to trail after him as he withdrew. Something stirred within him, something that woke from a slumber so deep and long it seemed a thing that had never existed within him except as a whisper of some forgotten dream. It hit him with an intensity he couldn't deny, and the resonance of his heart rumbling through his veins was a sensation he was certain he never knew but which was nevertheless real, inescapable, and more so with every moment he consumed the sensation of her body against him.

But he wasn't alone in the delirium of the moment, for his inclinations were reflected both toward her and from her. Their thoughts darted unseen yet perceived in the data threads so that the boundaries of their bodies were at once monumental and inconsequential, things to be both mocked and embraced. For all the violence and violation in the riot of their lives, a new thing rose up between them, an intoxicating notion. It was the idea of letting go of their resistance, of conceding to this thing created between them and for them, boiling away the frigid desperation that suffused their lives. It was a moment neither of them had the ability to conceive nor perceive, and so they collided in their blindness.

They were two people in the mirrored hall of seduction. After lurking in each other's dreams for so many years the ethereal specters of their desires were manifest before them. The infinite regression of their images came alight with passion, and they forgot the world around them.

She hooked a leg around him and pulled, trapping him against her. He let go of her wrists to splay his hands on the small of her back. They felt their breaths, their lips, and she grabbed his short hair as he drove against her, holding her so that not even a whisper could seep between their embrace.

There were no thoughts, for there was only the moment, the solitary, all-devouring moment, an entrance and exit they bridged through Central.

| 0 | 0 | 0 |

Victor rubbed his temples as he focused his thoughts.

Sonya.

He could visualize her across the data threads, could perceive her through the illusion of Endo's handiwork to see her intact. It almost amused him to see how others could think themselves of greater guile than he, or more adept at manipulating the data threads. He wasn't just a high predilector; he was a high predilector without compare. It almost made him laugh when he considered the ease with which he had manipulated Stutts and Gadwick. They were fools, because they believed Victor was a crazy old man lost in delusional sentiment. It was an easy belief for them to embrace. They looked at him and saw nothing but weakness, and so deceived themselves in their confidence.

Soon enough, he knew, everyone would move to his dictates. He would find his way.

He roused Sonya from the wipe-lock he had left buried within her. It was no deception that the wipe-lock was there as a last defense for her and a last warning to the one who crafted its scripting. Endo had been right on those assumptions, but he wasn't keen enough to perceive them in all their subtlety.

"Watcher," Victor said under his breath. "I'll give you something to watch."

Sonya, my love, the angels call you from your slumber. Time to wake.

| 0 | 0 | 0 |

GRAHAM LET THE CAR ROLL to a stop outside Sonya's apartment. He sat still with his eyes squeezed shut, his foot on the brake pedal and his hands constricted on the steering wheel. Even though he knew he had to move he couldn't budge from the sudden tightness that clamped his chest. It possessed him with an odd mix of fear and anger, as if some frigid hand had him in its clutch.

Noel turned to him as the car idled. His face fell as he noticed the clench of Graham's hands. "Chapel?"

Graham forced his eyes open, his jaw trembling.

"Don't tell me you've lost the stomach for this sort of thing," Noel said in disbelief.

Graham reached for his repeater. "Shut up." He pulled back the bolt to chamber the first round and flipped off the safety. "Let's be done with this."

Noel stared at the repeater before his gaze fell to the handguns strapped to each of Graham's thighs and the civi-stick slung from his belt. "Don't I get anything?"

Graham scooped up his helmet, set it on his head, and silenced Noel with a glare.

They hopped from the car and shut the doors, careful to be quiet. Graham looked down the length of the darkened street and then up to the apartment building. Noel pointed between two tall trees that framed a window wall. The domicile was dark. Graham loosened the thigh mounts of his handguns. He turned to Noel and hefted his repeater. "Stay behind me, understood?"

Noel obeyed without pause.

Graham tucked the repeater's stock tight against his shoulder, his gaze down the length of the stubby barrel as they crossed the street. When they came to the building Graham waved for Noel to come beside him and swing the door open. Graham paced into the lobby, keeping his back to a wall as he swept the repeater's muzzle across the room. It was, as he expected, a standard apartment building lobby, differing only in the fancier decor of Drive Control's select Rooking quad. He took a breath, debating between the stairs and the elevator before settling on the stairs. Once again he waved for Noel to come beside him and open the door before he swung the repeater toward the heights of the stairwell, his gaze hunting for any waiting threat.

His memory flashed, his vision shifting to an old memory with Carly. They were drunk, another night of insanity at the Underworld, the wildness within them and the looseness of the alcohol they consumed catching up with them in the stairwell of her building. It was clumsy in the way he had pressed her back against the wall, yet the intensity was there with the rash energy of their bulls on the rise.

The passing of that old phase catapulted him back to the present. He lowered his repeater and shook his head to force the memory away. The tightness in his chest changed then, shifting away from fear and anger to a sense of loss before transforming with fluid ease to the sensation of a wound, like a stabbing pain deep inside him. It was the distance of the memory, he decided. Everything he remembered of Carly, of his times with her, were no more than two-dimensional pictures, as abstract and lifeless as something he might see on a net screen. For some reason he couldn't identify he felt she was fading from him, that the bond between them, so strong a few hours ago when she left for the city, was being teased out to its last tenuous length. Something—perhaps someone—was dividing her from his awareness.

He squeezed his eyes shut and hoped he could project his thought in the same way as Gadwick. He summoned Carly's likeness in his mind, focused as best he could, and let his thought fly.

Carly?

He heard nothing but the pulse in his ears.

"What's wrong?" Noel whispered, peering past Graham up the stairwell.

Graham turned to Noel and studied him for a moment. It was a short moment, as Graham's conclusion didn't take long to coalesce in the wake of his plea to Carly. The situation was a mess. Something was seriously wrong. He had thought he could play Noel, deceive him by using Noel's own belief that he was predilecting Graham, to make the move to get Sonya. It had seemed a clever ploy to Graham, a way to convince himself he was the predilector. Standing in the stairwell on the shaky ground of hindsight, he wondered if he had outwitted himself.

Shit.

Noel was staring at him. "Chapel? Hello?"

Graham frowned, shifting his repeater to one hand to pull Noel by the collar into the stairwell and close the door behind them. He kept his gaze above them as he leaned toward Noel to talk in his ear. "Take this," he said, passing a handgun to Noel. "You know how to use it?"

Noel nodded. "We have to know, but we don't have to carry," he said as he took the weapon. "Why the change?"

"Something isn't right here," Graham said under his breath. He could feel it as a slight tingle inside his head, and he wasn't sure what to make of that sensation. He closed his eyes and pressed his lips in a tight line. Every sense in him said something was wrong and every feeling in him clamored that something was happening to Carly. He felt himself drift,

felt his hands go numb and his sight blur before him. The only thing that
held off his panic was the low murmur he heard in his head—not in his
ears, he knew, but in his head.

His mind raced. All the things Gadwick had said rushed back to him
to produce two words.

Data threads.

He closed his eyes.

Right. I can hear them.

And if I can hear them, that can only mean one thing.

His impressions shifted in a heartbeat to solidify a single conclusion
in his head: he was the rogue. It was a crazy thought, yet it made sense.
After all, he was the one who buoyed Carly through her awakening. He
was the one most aware how Central might respond. Such notions had
lurked as suspicions within him, only to be made concrete when Gadwick
confirmed them during his telepathic visit in the copse.

Graham was certain he would be the one to replace Gadwick. It
would explain the break he felt in his bond to Carly. His foul disposition
toward Noel was a simple release for the hesitation to accept what was
his new reality.

Despite all his hopes and vows, his time with Carly was done.

*She's part of the old life. It was a cold life, but life's only going to be colder
without her.*

Noel's anxiety radiated from his face. "You think something happened
to Carly?"

Graham looked to Noel and waited until Noel met his gaze. They
stared at each other for several moments, both understanding the subtle
undercurrent of Noel's question. Graham was unsure how to answer, and
he suspected that a failure to answer was an answer in itself. He nodded.
"Like you said, we need leverage."

"For Carly," Noel said with a tip of his head.

It was a lie. Graham could smell the stench of it. "Right, for Carly."

They made their way up the stairs, Graham counting flights until he
came to Sonya's floor. He waved for Noel to open the stairwell door, but
then held him back as he reconsidered. He reached out with the length

of his repeater and jabbed the muzzle into the light fixed to the stairs above them. The bulb cracked and went dark. Concealed in shadow, he nodded to Noel to open the door and cradled the repeater to his cheek. Noel sank to a crouch, turned the knob, and eased the door open.

Graham peered down the length of the hall before sidestepping down its length, the muzzle of his repeater leading the way. He counted doorways to his right until he came to a stop by the door to Sonya's domicile. Noel nodded in confirmation when Graham gave him a glance. He directed Noel to one side of the door, by the doorknob. Graham came up on the other side of the door and took one hand off his repeater to pull his Patrol security card from a pocket and hand it to Noel. Noel took it with open skepticism, but Graham tipped his head for Noel to try the lock. Noel forced a swallow before once again crouching and putting his back to the wall as he stared at the card.

Graham's hand returned to the muzzle guard of his repeater. He fell back a step, trained the weapon on the door, and nodded to Noel.

Noel reached up with the card and slid it through the lock above the doorknob.

The lock clicked free. Graham kicked the door open. His eyes focused through the darkness of the domicile to make out a figure several paces from him, arms raised tight to its chest—

Graham's eyes went wide with surprise.

He threw himself aside as repeater fire tore into the wall across from the door. Noel turned away at the roar of the weapon and wrapped his arms over his head. Graham dropped to the floor and lifted his repeater with one arm to open fire. The hallway flashed, spent shells bouncing off Noel's side as Graham emptied half his clip into the domicile.

Enraged in the way only Patrol could be enraged, he rose to his feet and charged through the open door, letting loose a messy stream of fire into the shadowy depth of the residence. The window wall across from him blew out with the impact of stray repeater rounds, the strobe of the repeater's muzzle flash guiding his aim. He picked out one body after another, riddling them with repeater rounds as they scrambled in surprise. They convulsed as bullets tore through them, one Mondial after another flopping dead as their blood flew through the air. One of them managed to get to his feet, his arm rising until Graham caught him in the end of his sweep.

Another repeater sounded out then, firing from the darkness of the bedroom across the room from Graham. The Mondial took fire from both sides, his body shuddering, arms flailing, as he was pummeled with shells. He dropped to the ground in ragged ruin.

Graham dropped as well, his repeater clip empty. The burst of fire that erupted from the bedroom returned, spraying across the living room in an even sweep. He scrambled behind a couch and rolled to his side as he pulled his handgun free and fired over his head toward the bedroom.

The repeater fell silent.

He lay still, sucking breaths as he listened for any movement. His eyes narrowed, his ears ringing from the deafening roar of the repeaters in the confines of the living room. With a silent curse he peered over the couch he hid behind, past the shattered head of a Mondial, to see a shadow emerge from the bedroom. He popped up, ready to fire, when the light in the hallway caught the figure's face, revealing a woman's gentle features. Her face was framed by long, dark hair, its straight length gathered and hanging in a tail. Light reflected off her small glasses.

She spun, her repeater aimed tight on him as he held his handgun steady on her.

"Sonya?" Noel said as he poked his head around the corner of the room. He crawled forward, his eyes eager, before rising to a stance. "Sonya!"

Graham's forehead knotted, but he held his aim on Sonya. His intuition hadn't failed him, for he knew as he studied her that something was indeed very wrong.

"Sonya," Noel repeated, taking another step forward. "Put it down," he said, waving his handgun to her repeater. "It's me, it's—"

"I know who you are," she said in a rush, keeping her gaze on Graham as she lowered her repeater ever so slightly. She waited until Graham gave a nod, and only then did they both lower their weapons. After a sigh she tipped her head and used the butt of the repeater to push up her glasses. Her lips rose in a smile as she gazed over her shoulder to Noel. "You came for me. You shouldn't have."

Puzzled, Noel stared at her. "Wait, wait—there's not a bruise on you. I thought, I—"

Graham's heart froze. He was anxious to raise his handgun, but Sonya's gaze darted to him at the slightest movement of his arms, and he knew he stood no chance with his handgun against her repeater. His options were spent. "I told you this was all wrong," he said to Noel as he kept his focus on Sonya. He noticed something in her eyes then, something he found hard to believe. *She's not who she thinks she is. Shit, she's a wipe!*

"I really don't know what this patrolman's babbling about," Sonya said over her shoulder to Noel, her gaze fixed on Graham.

Noel waved at him. "Put your gun away, Chapel."

Graham swallowed and let out a deep breath to loosen his shoulders. He was ready to spring. "Look at her, Noel. Everything we know said Stutts and his Mondial crew beat the piss out of her. There's not a mark on her. Somebody's playing with us."

Noel blinked.

Sonya turned to Noel with a plaintive look, even as she held a sidelong gaze on Graham. "Noel, please, don't let this patrolman hurt me. Don't let it happen again."

Noel pinched the bridge of his nose.

Graham ground his teeth. "You're being predilected, you idiot. Snap out of it!"

Sonya studied Graham.

Graham felt his stomach knot. He wondered whose gaze was looking through Sonya's eyes. He wondered if she even knew what she was saying. She was a wipe, she was being played like a puppet, and he was certain he was the only one in the room who had the sensitivity to see through the deception.

He understood then what Gadwick meant by the loneliness of a predilector.

Sonya's eyes went blank. "I only need one man to help me, one man worth the effort."

Graham felt his gaze drawn to Noel. It would be easy to shoot him. Graham had wanted to shoot him on several occasions, after all. He fought the tightening of his arms as he felt the pressure mount in his head. "We're being played, Noel. It's some kind of test."

Noel's eyes watered as his face flushed. "I, I can be that man for you, Sonya."

The corner of Sonya's mouth sank.

Noel's arm whipped up to fire at Graham.

The room exploded around Noel as Sonya spun and fired a single round into his face. His head burst in a red spray across the wall behind him. Sonya dove to the floor. No sooner did she drop than Graham's handgun blasted the wall where she'd been standing.

Gunfire thundered in the room. Graham scrambled to the end of the couch he'd hidden behind before, pursued by repeater rounds that ripped through the cushioning. Glass crunched beneath him as he came to a stop by the shattered window wall. Sonya's repeater clicked empty and went silent. He knew he had a moment, maybe two, depending on her familiarity with the weapon before he was done for. He had to get away. She was between him and the hall.

Nothing blocked him from the shattered window wall.

He came to his feet and fired blind over his shoulder as he charged toward the broken windows. He jumped, his luck ending when his chest plate slammed against a massive branch as he tumbled through one of the trees framing Sonya's window wall. Violent impacts pounded his body until he crashed to a bone jarring halt on the ground.

It seemed to take forever before he was able to suck in a breath against the constriction of his chest. He hobbled away from the apartment building, curled over in agony, desperate to reach the safety of the car.

Sonya shouted from the ruin of her domicile. "Stop!"

He ignored her. A few more steps, and he would have the safety of the car.

Sonya fired. The round hammered into the articulated plates of armor beneath his shoulder blade. It was enough to shove him forward, his arms flailing for balance. He groaned in pain, his head tipping back as he staggered another step toward the car.

A silent cry parted his lips.

Another round cracked the quiet night, slamming into his protective shoulder cowl. He spun through a drunken pirouette before losing his balance to flop face first on the hood of the car. Wheezing, certain the next round would blow off the top of his head, he nevertheless grabbed at the hood of the car, his fingers raking across the metal as his legs buckled beneath him.

The moments mounted with each pounding beat of his heart.

"Enough!" It wasn't Sonya's voice. It was that of a man.

Graham opened his eyes and looked ahead of him as blood dribbled from his mouth. A hooded figure stood on the sidewalk.

The man pointed up to Sonya. "That's enough."

Graham coughed and let out a long wheeze as the last of his strength faded.

The man reached up and flipped his hood back. He waved to Sonya.

Graham closed his eyes, refusing to accept what the streetlight revealed. "No—I just saw you die. . ."

"You saw what you saw," the man said. "Nothing more, and nothing less."

Graham heard footsteps approach from behind. A hot repeater muzzle pressed into the back of his neck. His eyes squeezed tight as his hands closed to fists.

Sonya leaned into the weapon to press it hard into Graham's neck. "I told you to stop, Patrolman."

"I said, my dear Sonya, that it was enough," the stranger said. "He passed the test. You should know better than to question a high predilector."

She waited before easing off her repeater. The pressure of the muzzle faded from Graham's neck. "Forgive me," she said. "I've lived alone for too long."

"Yes. Too long indeed."

Sonya prodded Graham with the repeater. "What do you want

with him?"

"Why, we keep him, of course. He passed the test. That's why I wanted you to stop. Things have changed. A city elder has blundered through my plans, and we must consider him."

Graham's hands opened as his senses seeped away. There was no fight left in him, nothing left to keep his body up. He coughed and slid off the car to lay sprawled on the cold wet pavement of the street. He looked up, staring at the black sky over Sonya, before his eyes slid shut and consciousness slipped away.

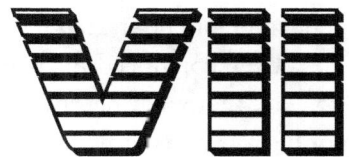

ADWICK WOKE WITH A SHAKE of his head. His body was numb. He sat up in his chair, waiting for his eyes to focus, as the stupor that held him in its grasp lost the fight against his will. Mortas did his work well, but it couldn't last long against another predilector. Remembering Victor tightened Gadwick's empty stomach into a knot of acid and anxiety as a single thought seized his attention.

Time. How long have I been out?

His net screens were blank. Cursing beneath his breath, he tapped away at his keyboard to bring them to life one by one. His hands began to shake, stilled only when he closed them to fists. His gaze panned across the screens as he attempted to gather his bearings. The stupor had not only disabled his conscious actions but also his perception of the data threads. To his frustration, the threads and various envens had nothing to show him. There were no images of Carly clubbing like a wild woman during the riot, not even a trace that he could find. In fact, to his growing dismay, he found nothing concerning Carly or Graham, leading him to one conclusion.

They're off the data grid. Only a predilector can do such a thing.

He rubbed his forehead.

Carly Westing and Graham Chapel. Endo Stutts and Victor Mortas. Carly went to the riot, so it would follow that Endo got her. Chapel and Victor? What's the connection there?

He closed his eyes and massaged his temples. His mind began to bend and warp, manipulating the possible outcomes as he could best project them, twisting them to fit them in their various ways. None of them, though, were as he intended before he started meddling with Carly and Graham. Until now, he'd been convinced his plans were his own, that the threads were his to ride, that what he saw as his way out of Seven Hills and the passing of his role as elder were indeed his own thoughts, not the whispers of Central's Process mocking his individual will.

He had also figured that the arrival of Stutts was inevitable, given the question of Carly and Graham. Intuition had told him that his manipulation of Sonya was a secure way to neutralize Stutts. In his current hindsight, all those things seemed part of a masterful deception, a meticulously planned predilection based on his own vanity that he could mature a successor on his own. Only one element unified all the variables.

Victor Mortas. The exquisite coincidence of the high predilector's visit faded to that of a blatant ploy.

Gadwick sat at his chair, thinking, probing the data threads, until something stirred within him. It was a memory, tingling like the pins and needles of a sleeping limb that wakes with renewed blood flow. As his memory flexed its awareness, though, his blood chilled in his veins.

It was the way of high predilectors to take a series of names over their life to aid their movement in and out of the data flow. Changes of name were more than varying references to bookmarks in a high predilector's life. No, they could be used to hide secrets, to silence data threads to the perception of others by focusing a predilection around a specific name.

Victor Mortas. He insists on that moniker.

He doesn't want me to disclose the name he used in his prior dealings with me. He thinks he dirtied my hands enough when he was John Westing—

He bucked in his chair as the realization overpowered him. Victor's predilection lost its last hold on him, yet the parting of its veils nevertheless stunned him with the efficacy of its illusion. He had the unsettling feeling that he'd been looking into a mirror all along, pretending the images he saw weren't part of the reality he knew, until the glass shattered and he found the reflection was, in fact, reality. The horrendous process of acceptance cut him with as little mercy as shards of glass.

"Say it," he told himself. "Say it to know it."

He took a breath and closed his eyes. "Victor Mortas is John Westing.
"Victor Mortas is John Westing."

His eyes popped open. "Victor Mortas is John Westing! I looked straight into his face—straight into his lies—and still I couldn't think it through. Damn him! He's a criminal, a high predilector gone rogue. Central wants him dead—Central will kill *me* if anyone thinks I helped him!"

His heart pounded. "Oh no, no—he's been creating that very image all along." He clapped his hands to his forehead. "He set me up to cover his own tracks. *Now I look like the rogue!* I look like the rogue; I'll draw all Endo's attention, and then I'll get killed so Westing can sneak away."

He lowered his hands and looked at the data spooling on his screens. The envens carried on, their endless pursuit of a self-defined market economy obvious to him as he perceived the ways of the Process. It left him with queries to answer in the mindless grind of the city's function. Two patrolmen missing, the slaughter at Rooking's market, inquiries regarding a rogue—how was he to salvage himself from such a mess?

He looked around his office. For all that he had risked in his attempt to defy Central and secure his retirement on his own, he also embraced the power of his office and the weight of its responsibilities. He had risked much to gain more. With Carly and Graham lost to him, his ambition was also a lost cause. There was only the mess around his schemes and the pressure from Central to account for them. He had gained nothing and stood to lose everything.

"No," he whispered. "I won't be the fool in this. I have resources. I'll hand Westing's head to Central. They'll forgive everything else for that one trophy."

He stood from his chair. His mind cleared. He would do what he did best.

It was time to clean house.

He called his secretaries to mobilize Patrol.

| 0 | 0 | 0 |

CARLY WOKE WITH A START, her mind a frenzy of discordant thoughts. Unleashed in the darkness, the whispers in her head coursed through her at such a pace that she failed to comprehend a single one. She laid a hand on her forehead and closed her eyes until the tumult faded. Only then did she lower her hand. Her memory returned as her stomach knotted with the visions in her mind.

She sat up and looked across the room in front of her, fighting her disbelief to force herself to accept what she saw. The stars glimmered above her, visible through a roof of glass plates, the framing of the plates lost in the darkness. A large open room spread beyond the narrow alcove where she sat, the space of the open room occupied by a few comfortable chairs around a long, low table at one end of the room. At the other end of the room was a window wall with a semicircular couch set before the windows, looking out to the rough outline of the city.

In the space between the couch and the chairs a large wall monitor stared back at her. It wasn't the expansive size of the monitor that caught her attention, or the memory that it was in front of the same monitor that she fought with Endo. No, it was the fact that the monitor was blank. There was no picture, yet the screen glowed a deep violet, casting the room with an unearthly glow.

Sitting there, staring at the monitor, her fight with Endo replayed in her head. The memory put knots in her stomach, and she clutched her belly as it cramped within her. She forced herself to look away, letting her gaze wander until she looked to the floor and found her bodysuit, boots, and black shirt at the foot of the bed in which she sat. Her heart bucked, and in the next thundering pound of blood through her body she became conscious of her nudity.

She grabbed the blanket covering her legs and pulled it up to her chest, not out of any sense of shame, but by some forgotten instinct of self-defense. Her handgun was nowhere to be seen. Her civi-stick was missing. She shivered at her vulnerability and forced a swallow as her throat closed in fear. Only then did the inevitable question come to her, and her eyes went saucer-wide as her back stiffened. It seemed to take all her courage to draw in a single tight breath and turn her head to look beyond her shoulder.

Endo lay next to her, sleeping.

Her gaze held on him as she studied him with an unblinking intensity. *Endo Stutts. Right. The elevator, the fight, the big screen, and then—*

She closed her eyes and turned away. Her memories collided. Conflicts rose up within her, conflicts of guilt and satisfaction, of gain and loss, of supremacy and inferiority.

She turned again to look down on Endo. He slept in the peaceful quiet of the room. No net screen pursued the endless, mindless chatter of an enven and no reporter orb squawked its queries. She reached out, her hand shaking until she clenched it in a fist to steady herself. With a calming breath she put her fingers on his chest to feel the beat of his heart, the warmth of his skin, the rise and fall of his breath. She withdrew her hand to touch her lips, the sensitive skin of her fingertips still warm from his body. He was real, and the burn of passion that had erupted between them rose within her, warming and disorienting her as it had before. Her chest rose with a deep breath as her pulse quickened.

Then it wasn't a dream. He's like me, and I'm like him. Somewhere, for some reason, even though in hindsight she understood Central had no interest in the two of them fighting, they nevertheless were brought together in conflict. That served as an answer in itself, as she understood that only in wanting to fight Endo could she see that fighting Endo was hopeless, or rather, pointless. No, the only way for her was the way that had erupted between them. She had to surrender herself.

She shook her head. *No, not surrender. What happened, that was something else.* She drew her knees to her chest and rubbed her forehead as she struggled to find a word, an image, something to label the thing that happened between them, *to* them, devouring them, without either of them having power or interest to reconsider or stop the plunge.

She sat there, thinking, and then a single word whispered to her. *Seduction.*

This unexpected word gained meaning and momentum within her, and then she knew it was true and, of greater concern, why she knew it to be true.

Predilection. Making the answer before you ask the question.

She slid from the bed and gathered the blanket around her as she went. Barefoot, she walked out from the alcove to find the elevator to her right, around the corner. The window wall loomed to her left. She looked down.

Her lips parted in wonder.

The riot of the Underworld coursed beneath her, visible through the polarized floor under her feet. She could see the tangle of Patrol, the violence as the jousts collided with each other and those around them, and the exorcism of rising bulls in the darker corners. The roaming lights worked around the crowd, revealing all the little activities set loose in the shadows, things that made her cringe as she remembered herself in those shadows, down there, down in the midst of that squirming mass, ripped of her identity, ripped naked in mind and then body, ripped raw until there was nothing left but what she was told, nothing but the push and pull of Patrol, the gloating lust of Bayard, the warm release of Graham's clutch—

Her shoulders tightened as she put a hand over her eyes. Her head shook as she heard the echo of her first thought free of Central.

No.

She forced her hand away to look back at the mess below her and accept her former place in life. It was an unsettling moment that tore away the ignorant bliss of her old carefree, decadent life in Patrol, but she likened it to her graduation from Teen-stomp, and kept her wits by diminishing the depth of her mental shift as just another transition under Central. It made sense to her that way. In fact, it made sense of many things. She had to see that mess below to understand how she had passed through Endo to a new awareness.

She took a breath, gathered her wits, and peered down at Patrol. She eased then, the beat of her heart calming as the familiar scene of the Underworld washed over her eyes. The deafening pound of music, the delicious delirium of too much Heavy, the pending excitement of bulls on the rise with Graham—it all came back to her and left her swaying on her feet. She almost felt drunk, and the images below her blurred as her eyelids drooped. It was a subtle yet slick process, one that snuck up and seized her in its grasp.

Her sight focused anew when small traces of white light winked into being around the various members of Patrol. She tipped her head as curiosity got the better of her. The slender trails of white light sharpened in her awareness until they revealed themselves as tight clusters of numbers hovering over the heads of patrolmen. They were like fireflies, those clusters, following people as they moved about the Underworld.

She sank to a crouch and rocked forward on her knees so that she could touch the floor where one cluster swirled before her. The numbers hovered over a patrolman, a stocky brute staggering with his drink. The cluster flashed, then cycled once more as he gained his balance. The numbers followed him as he went to the bar, and she followed them, looking between her knees as he passed beneath and behind her.

He pushed past a table and came to a halt. Lost in the moment, Carly almost forgot that table, the table where she had killed Bayard. The memory was distant, and she struggled with her temporal sense to place that assault as something she did only a short time ago. Bayard's body was gone, but her curiosity over his disappearance was replaced by the much more immediate concern that the drunken patrolman would see the blood, would see the evidence of her crime, and look up to point at her in accusation. No, he had to turn away, he had to leave the table—he had to go—

She waved a hand for him to move, certain in her fear that he would see her despite the polarized floor. "Go on, asshole," she said under her breath. "Move! Get a drink. You know you want one."

The numbers in the cluster hovering over him flashed and changed.

Her lips parted.

The patrolman turned and pushed into the crowd. He made his way from the table to the bar and tipped his head as he leaned on the rail.

She could see his lips as he spoke. "Give me a drink," she whispered. "You know I want one."

She was voicing the words a heartbeat ahead of the patrolman.

With a gasp she pushed herself back until she felt a wall behind her.

The contact made her recoil, causing her to spring to her feet and scurry away from the scene below until she came to the comforting solidity of another wall. She held there for a moment, sinking back to a crouch as she threw her chin up to avoid looking at the floor.

The stars filled her gaze. To her horror swarms of number clusters came to focus around those little points of light.

She squeezed her eyes shut and wrapped her arms over her head. She needed help, she needed answers, but there was no one to help her. Despite her befuddlement, she knew she needed Endo.

His name burst from her lips.

He seemed to materialize beside her. "So, you see."

She cowered from him, relieved that he kept his hands to himself. Nevertheless, she grabbed his wrist and yanked him to a crouch beside her. "What's happening to me? What am I seeing?" She pointed to the floor. "What's with the numbers?"

He said nothing. Instead, he smiled, a kind smile rather than a patronizing gesture. He pulled his wrist from her grasp and put his hands on her shoulders. His lips parted, but he stared into her eyes before he gave her a single nod. "I see it now, the wisdom of Central. You need to relax. You're safe here, with me." He took his hands from her shoulders and rested them on his knees, atop the sheet he had wrapped around his waist. His gaze wandered about the Underworld before his smile returned. "Those numbers are part of the data threads," he said before looking back to her. "Only predilectors can see them."

"Make it stop!"

Endo's face fell, dismayed. "Why? Understand, Carly, you are a predilector."

She stared at him for a moment, the reality of his words too much to bear. He opened his hands to calm her, but she scrambled away from him until she came to a stop by the elevator screen, huddled on her hands and knees. Her gaze darted to the floor, her eyes squeezing shut when she perceived the number clusters again. The darkness of her sight was no refuge, though, as the numbers soon returned to her perception. Her eyes snapped open as she jabbed a finger to the floor. "I know what they're doing, what they're going to do down there!"

Endo shrugged. "Of course you do. That's part of being a predilector. I heard your thoughts before, when you thought I was still sleeping," he said, raising a calming hand as her eyes almost bugged out of her head. "You already knew about your predilectory capacity. You suspected it when you came to the riot, yes? But now you see that *being* it, well, that's something quite different."

She stared at him.

"You see their trace packets, Carly, the data descriptors Central uses to track people. You don't know the words for everything yet, but you sense them, just the way you sensed what that patrolman was going to say. "

"What? How did you—"

He grinned. "You know the answer to that."

She nodded. "Right, the data threads. So, I can read minds?"

"So to speak." He shrugged. "As your predilectory skills mature, it will seem so."

"Seem?" Her eyes narrowed. "Then what is it, for real? I'm not stupid. There has to be some kind of connection to let me see those trace packets."

He tipped his chin up. "Listen now, and listen carefully. You will know what I tell you to be true because the respective data threads will reveal themselves to you. There are no secrets, only threads to be discovered. Remember that." He took a breath. "During Rainbow Go probes are implanted, right above the ear. The procedure is perfected to a mindless routine now. The probe sits on an individual's brain to download any information Central wants that person to have—the sensation of a memory 'flash'. Most of all, though, an implant uploads to Central your actions, your location and, most importantly, what you're thinking."

Carly scratched her scalp above her ear, her mind racing. As Endo promised, the data threads roared through her thoughts and she found herself understanding everything with surprising calm. For the first time in her life things made sense.

She looked to him. "So that's the whole thing of Drive Control? Life reduced to data, data stored on drives, drives monitored by Drive Control to make sure we behave. Right?"

"Society is a network of people. People are terminals, terminals of one vast peer network—one vast wireless computer network. From probes to net screens, net screens to probes, the day to day life of society moves about, archived in Drive Control."

She opened her hands. "So, all this time in Patrol, that's what we were protecting?" She rubbed her forehead as she saw through the depths of her ignorance. "Hard line violations, signal anomalies, all those things we beat the shit out of people for doing, that was to protect the network. Bad drive, sector control, reformat—those are all talking about the data drives, keeping tabs on what people are doing."

He splayed the thumb and forefinger of each hand and put them together to outline a box. "Thoughts are assessed by scores on our data drives, held in a database plotted against time. When that data trend nears the tolerance limit a flag goes up in Drive Control, and that person is said to have 'bad drive'. When a person takes action, a sector trends beyond tolerance and initiates sector control. When the trend is too far gone—"

"Reformat." She looked to him. "That's the end game. The data drive is wiped clean, and the data flow from the probe to the drive is reversed. Reformat the drive, and you reformat the person." She traced a finger through the air. "Everything you know to make you who you are, it gets erased. *Wiped.* Chiggers. That's why wipes don't know who they are anymore. I guess that's what the concentration cubes are for?"

"Cubes hide small transmitters. They boost bandwidth, a necessity when we need to tell a mind it's someone else."

Carly closed her eyes. She saw it all, the endless racks of networked data drives stored in cool, dry vaults no one would see, a mass of humanity compressed to two-dimensional data. Even her identification code, she realized, was not an identification code to define her as Carly Westing but an identification code to locate her drive, her drive address, numbers to her, but—

546-232-5110
546.232.5110

She opened her eyes and her gaze bored into Endo. Her head began to hurt with the focus of her thoughts, but she held at it, even as her face began to turn red.

Endo leaned toward her and laid a gentle kiss on her forehead. He took her face in his hands and put his lips to her ear. "I know what you're doing," he whispered, "and it won't work. I don't have a drive address because I don't have a drive."

"That's what makes a predilector," she said under her breath. "Predilectors can do it without the hardware." She blinked. "That's what Gadwick really meant about the digital now and all those things about evolution. Predilectors are the next step."

Her lips rose in a smile. "I'm the next step."

Her thoughts cleared. She understood why Central fostered a moment where she met Endo in conflict. Without the conflict she wouldn't have realized there was no point to conflict, no need for Patrol inclinations to fight. There was no need to fight because it would only blind her to what she needed to see by joining Endo, by having passion erupt between them. As much as Central knew emotions could be used to cloud perceptions in mass society, emotions could also clear the clutter of perceptions to see greater truths.

Truths, she realized, were just absolute values lurking among the data threads.

What we know is not only what we want to hear, but also what we do not want to hear.

She stood. "You know all the secrets and all the little whispers, don't you?"

He eased back to sit on the floor. "You have to be careful, Carly. Incomplete knowledge can appear just as sound as full knowledge. It's the danger of ignorance, and ignorance is perhaps the most insidious danger to those who think their understanding is vast. In the gap between understanding and ignorance is where we discover our compulsions to act."

She stared at him. "I know there's more to that. Tell me."

He took her hand. "There's something you need to understand about action. What we do—what Central wants us to do—spans a gently sliding scale between inclinations and intuitions."

She gave him a knowing look. "So you only do what Central wants you to do?"

His lips parted, but he had no answer.

She tipped her head back as she gazed down at him. "That's not for me, Endo. I do what I want to do, and I'm not going to let anyone lead me around by the nose anymore." She grabbed his sheet and flipped it open to leave him naked before her, the way she wanted him, so she could teach him a lesson. She straightened and let her arms hang at her sides. The blanket that covered her unfurled and fell to the floor. Her skin glowed beneath the starlight. She put her hands on his shoulders and straddled him, tightening her thighs against his sides as she settled down on him. "Endo?" she whispered.

He gazed into the blue depths of her eyes.

She knew she filled his senses, just the way she intended. She kissed him. "Right now, let's do what we want to do."

His hands slid across her back as he closed his arms around her. When he went to kiss her she ducked away, letting out a soft giggle as she teased him. He held her tighter, straining to get to her as she draped her arms over his shoulders. She let her head roll back and felt his breath on her chest before running her fingers into his hair to hold him against her. She rested her chin on his head, reveling in the moment. Central may have worked a mutual seduction upon them before, but she wanted to have him on her own terms, to incite his passion and claim it for herself, the way she had in countless dreams and fantasies.

He rolled forward, holding her tight as he laid her on the blanket. She locked her ankles over the small of his back. He panted with excitement, the excitement she knew she summoned within him. She closed her eyes, met his kiss, and knew she had taught him a lesson of her own.

Central could have the Madman of MG42.

Endo Stutts belonged to her.

| 0 | 0 | 0 |

ACROSS THE CITY, IN THE basements of the various detachments of Patrol, motor pools came to life. Roused from their sleep, patrolmen followed the orders seeping into their minds from the data threads, rallying their patrolmates and congregating around their patrolmasters.

In the basement of Drive Control, where secured doors led to the deeper depths of Sector Control, a team of wipes was also roused by the call of Elder Gadwick. They dressed, armed themselves, and nodded to the orders from Gadwick's office.

Unknown, unfeeling, little more than machines of flesh, they left only a faint shadow on the data threads as they moved. Only the most wary predilector could sense their coming, so they constituted the deadliest of weapons at the disposal of a city elder.

The Process, after all, did not concern itself with morality. Morality was a whimsical notion left for the abstract philosophical considerations of Central, an aspect known as the Dream.

For the Process, murder was just another exercise to maintain society's momentum.

| 0 | 0 | 0 |

GRAHAM'S EYES OPENED TO THE weak light of an unfamiliar room. He looked over the plain gray walls until he realized he sat naked in a tub of warm water. Instinctual self-defense spurred him to rise. The moment he moved, though, his spine erupted in crackling bolts of agony. He gasped, ground his teeth, and grabbed the sides of the tub. For all his stubbornness he couldn't breach the weight of his pain. His shoulders tightened, trembled, but then eased. It didn't take much for him to realize he couldn't move. Not knowing where he was, or how he got there, faded as immediate priorities.

He had to think; he had to keep his wits. He shook off a wave of dizziness, thumped the butts of his wrists to his temples, and tried to focus.

"Hello, Graham," a woman's voice said from behind him.

He dropped his hands, his gaze darting to either side before he found Sonya standing behind his left shoulder. She stared down at him as she smoothed back a few strands of hair that hung loose from her characteristic bun. Her lips rose in a warm smile as she settled her glasses on her nose and walked toward the end of the tub. There was a stool there, with a sponge on its seat.

She looked back at him as she ran a hand over the sponge.

Graham shook his head. "Where—"

She put a finger to her lips to silence him. "Easy," she said as she pulled the stool closer. Her smile returned as she sat by the edge of the tub and rolled up the sleeves of her suit. She soaked the sponge and rubbed his chest in gentle circles where a series of bruises already showed their ugly color.

He studied her as her gaze lingered on the sponge. "Why'd you kill Noel?"

She tipped her head as she wrung out the sponge. "You're a far superior man," she said with her pleasant smile and resumed the slow circles on his chest.

He stared at her. It was easy to see how Noel was drawn to her. She was quite attractive, not in the ways of excess like most women on the nets, but in the perfection of her plainness. She was anyone, she could be for anyone, and so she was accessible to the primitive depths of his imagination.

His hand rose from the water. He stared, befuddled, as he had no memory of wanting to lift his hand from the water, but then he watched his fingers caress her cheek. His blood warmed, and his eyelids drooped as his thumb came to rest on her lips.

The sponge slid down his chest and disappeared beneath the water. Her lips parted around his thumb.

He blinked.

She stood and unzipped her dark green bodysuit. Her gaze held on him as she slipped the suit off her shoulders and let it fall to her waist. Her skin glowed in the scant light. It seemed she was lit from within, allowing every splendid curve of her body to fill his eyes. She leaned over and kissed him as she stepped free of her suit.

Wait—

Her lips fluttered against his cheek until they rested by his ear. He could hear her breath, and he thought he heard her words, or perhaps her thoughts, but the water rose around him as she settled in the tub with him.

Now. I know you want me. Take me now—

His eyes slid shut as she whispered in his ear. She took his hands and cupped them over her breasts. His heart pounded.

Bulls on the rise.

"No, no!"

He forced his eyes open. His hands clamped on her throat so tight she croaked in protest. He squeezed until her face turned purple. "Get out of my head," he said through clenched teeth. He shook her by her neck. "Now!"

His eyes popped open as his body convulsed. Water splashed, startling him. He grabbed the edges of the tub, fighting himself in a hopeless attempt to get out. Amid his struggles he found Sonya sitting on the stool, dressed and dry, with a detached glaze in her eyes. Her stare held for several moments before she blinked and looked to her side, behind Graham. He strained, but couldn't see past his shoulder. His hands slipped along the edge of the tub to leave him panting in the water. He stared into the vacant shadows across from him and cursed under his breath.

"He'll do, yes?" he heard Sonya ask.

"Oh, yes," a man's voice replied. "Quite well. We might make wine from water with this one. Good thing, after all our effort to move him here."

The man walked out from behind Graham to stand before the tub. In the darkness of the room it was just possible to discern his features beneath the hood of his long coat.

Graham strained to see him. "You're that man from the street. You look like Noel." He pointed to Sonya. "She shot Noel, blew his brains right out—"

"That's not important. And what you think you saw as a resemblance in my face is not important. In fact, there is only one thing of importance to you at this moment, Patrolman Chapel." He put his back to Graham. "You're wondering why you can't get out of that tub, aren't you? You're a large, powerful man. You could snap me like a twig. Ah, but there is something else, something—"

Graham beat a fist on the side of the tub. "Stop. I know you're a predilector."

"High Predilector, in fact."

Graham struggled once more to get up, only to be met by the same futility.

The high predilector shook his head as he kept his back to Graham. "You shouldn't get too upset, Patrolman. You should relax, given your injuries. Stress will do them no good. Particularly the one wound you fear most. Oh, what was it?" He raised his hand and extended his pointer finger. "Yes, that's it. A crippling wound. Legs you can't feel. Isn't that right? It was an awful fall from Sonya's apartment, bouncing branch to branch through the trees until you landed on your back."

Graham blinked. His jaw dropped. His anger vaporized.

The predilector took a breath. "You fear even thinking of it, yet not thinking of it only amplifies the fear, yes? It's an awful thing, not to know if you will stand again, much less walk. Patrol has no use for cripples. Should you even try to rise? Or is it easier to wallow in fear and denial, floating away on the dreamy waters of their conjoined delusion so that all those questions that burn in you need never to be faced?"

The predilector turned. "Has Carly abandoned you for Endo? Did Noel betray you? And deeper yet—are you the rogue?"

Graham stared in horror at his legs, their shape distorted by the water.

The predilector waved his hands, his eyes flashing from the shadow of his hood. "Well? Nothing to say, nothing to do—is this all a fearsome member of Patrol has to offer?" He waited, but then dropped his hands and looked to Sonya. "Come, Sonya, he won't do after all. We were wrong. No rogue here. Just another empty-headed maggot."

Sonya came up behind Graham. She pressed a gun to the back of his head. "Shall I?"

Graham set his teeth at the pressure of the barrel and slapped his hands on the tub. His eyes narrowed on the high predilector. "You! I'll kill you. You're dead."

"Is that so?"

"Right proper," Graham said as he propped his elbows on the tub. His shoulders tightened, bands of muscle rising from his skin as he strained against his weight. "This isn't real," he hissed between his labors. "It's all in my head—"

He sucked in a breath, heaved, and gained his feet.

There was no tub.

He sat up with a start, his eyes focusing on the window wall of a comfortable domicile. It was night outside. The domicile was dark. His gaze shot down in surprise as he jumped to his feet. He slapped his palms on his thighs to be sure he wasn't dreaming, but his thighs were strong and solid beneath him. Instinct drove his hand to his thigh mount.

His handgun was missing.

Sonya and the high predilector were sitting at a table, watching him.

He looked at them, in that moment seeing only a slender woman and an older man. He could tear them apart in a heartbeat. His eyes narrowed as he balled his fists.

The predilector glanced at Sonya. She put her repeater on the table and patted her hand over the trigger guard. The predilector looked back to Graham.

Graham's jaw clenched. "What do you want?"

The predilector held up a hand. "Well, we certainly don't want to hurt you. I hope that inclines you not to hurt us."

"Where am I?"

The predilector looked around. "I believe Controller Henshaw used to live here."

Graham hesitated, debating if he could get to Sonya before she could fire the repeater. Her other hand was under the table. In the darkness he couldn't see if she had his handgun on the ready. There was nothing near him that he could throw to afford an opportunity to move.

The predilector took a breath. "If we wanted to kill you, you'd already be dead. The fact that we're having this conversation should inform you that we have no desire to harm you."

Graham pointed to his temple before jabbing his finger toward the predilector. "Stay out of my head, understand?"

The predilector gave him a slight bow. "Your mind is yours, Patrolman Chapel."

"Right," Graham said, easing as he considered the situation around him. It bothered him, but something told him to yield. He straightened, his fists releasing, but he kept a wary gaze on Sonya. He blinked. "Wait—how do I know you're a predilector?"

"Because you're a predilector as well," the high predilector said with a smile. He opened a hand to the window wall. "And this is your city now, Elder Chapel."

"Elder?" Graham looked to the window wall. "Right, elder," he whispered to himself before turning back to the predilector. His thoughts raced. "So, this was known all along, wasn't it?" he said, then nodded as he looked back to the city. "Of course it was," he answered himself, his mind embracing the clarity that bloomed within him. It took a moment for him to process the shift in his consciousness as his thoughts glowed with their own waking vitality. He swayed, feeling as if he'd downed half a bottle of Heavy, but the rush that hit him left his senses sharpened rather than dulled "Noel was just a piece of the process, *the* Process, so he had to go because there was no place or space for him."

He rubbed his forehead, the aches of his beaten body at last coming to him. His gaze settled on Sonya. "You're a wipe from Sector Control, right? Scripted to give us that one chance away from Stutts, when things were still up in the air?"

Sonya stared at him. She crossed her arms on her chest.

Graham's eyebrows settled low over his gaze. "But that was all Gadwick's plan, and he's—he's not here." He looked to the predilector. "I don't know you. Gadwick never mentioned you." His body tensed. "Something went wrong."

The high predilector nodded. "Elder Gadwick made an error. He confused my plans for his plans. I had no choice but to let it go as far is it did."

Graham blinked, his eyes going wide. "Stutts." He clamped his hands over his head.

"Carly went to find him. She said things seemed to follow that it should be her to go, but she didn't see things for what they were. Shit." He looked to the high predilector. "Gadwick was looking for one person, not two. If it's me, then no matter how much Gadwick fucked things up it can't be Carly. That means she was just another scripted block to keep Stutts away from me, and that leaves just one question. Who are you?"

The high predilector opened a hand. "You can call me Victor Mortas." He tipped his chin up. "Now let me ask you a question, Patrolman. What makes you think you're a predilector?"

Graham took a breath and held his tongue as he listened to his thoughts. They came to him the same way Gadwick's thoughts came to him after the Rooking massacre, buoyed on a murmuring rush, a sound like static, yet intelligible, with definition. *Data threads.* He didn't have to think of it; it came to him, and so his certainty grew. Looking to Victor and Sonya he realized it had to make sense. It was an odd situation to have a calm conversation with someone he'd exchanged gunfire with earlier in the night. At the same time, though, there was a sense of acceptance, that this was the way the situation was meant to be, that there could be no other way for that moment but that way, so it made perfect sense for him to have a calm conversation with someone he'd exchanged gunfire with earlier in the night.

He remembered Victor's question. "How do I know I'm a predilector?" He shook his head. "I don't see any other way." He nodded. "Okay. That's half of it. You're the other half, the half I don't know. Talk."

Victor looked amused. There was a pointed gleam in his eyes. "You learn fast."

Graham waved a hand by his head. "Patrol doesn't play games." He walked to the table where Victor and Sonya sat. "You said Gadwick stole your plan. I get that you're some kind of big shot in Central—or, at least you were. Scrounging around this city, I think something else. I think you're looking to get away, but you need to cover yourself."

Victor's lips curled in a smile. "Oh, you are a quick one, Graham Chapel." He stood, pointing at Graham. "A quick one, indeed. Gadwick did well looking to you. And you will replace him, but not in the way he thought, because your intuition guides you well. Yes, I seek to get away, to retire from Central. It's my right as a high predilector to step aside when I tire of Central's demands. But I can't leave an empty place behind me. I must transfer my position to another, and that is where your conclusions have failed you."

It only took a moment for Graham to catch up. "So that's where Carly comes in," he said under his breath. He closed his eyes before looking back to Victor. "I get it. Gadwick said he had trouble seeing between me and Carly. He didn't know which of us was a predilector because we both are. You want Carly as your replacement—you, you were the one that hit her with the brick," he said, his eyes bulging as the threads whispered to him. "You started everything, but then Gadwick pushed in. He went after Carly too, but he wasn't supposed to. That's why everything went to the chiggers with Stutts, because Gadwick broke the rules. It's all about Carly." He fell back a step when he heard his own words. "Shit, it's all about her. I'm just some accident, clean up for Gadwick's collateral damage."

Victor raised a finger. "But real, nonetheless."

Graham spun to the windows as he was seized by the hazard of his position. "No, I'm done if I don't take Gadwick's post. I have to take him out and get Carly for you, or I'm headed to the meat-farm." He clapped his hands on top of his head. "Stutts was aiming for Gadwick. That should put Stutts on our side. Can't you talk to him?"

"That would seem the natural course of action."

"Let me guess," Graham said. He fell silent as his eyelids fluttered to the data threads roaring through his head. He turned to Victor when his thoughts settled to cohesive sense. "No, it's no guess. You didn't ask for your retirement. That's why you can't go to Stutts. He has Carly, you need her, and if you don't get her, we're all going to the meat-farm." He threw his hands up in the air with a curse, his anxiety getting the better of him.

"I'm so glad you deduced everything I wished to explain to you,

Patrolman. I was concerned I might have to argue my case with you. The mind is always more willing to accept what it recognizes on its own rather than accept the input of an outsider's thoughts."

Graham stared at him.

Victor sighed. "A little philosophy of predilection. We digress." He shook his head. "I can't ask Endo for my retirement. I'm not just a high predilector. I'm a Sleeper, one of the minds that give Central its consciousness. Central won't let me go."

Graham paced back and forth. "What's that supposed to mean?"

"Central is composed of high predilectors who merge with the data threads. We sleep, so that Central can have a collective awareness envisioned from our networked minds. We refer to that awareness as the Dream. The Process that you know is the pragmatic embodiment of the Dream. We Sleepers are the most select of high predilectors. Central knows we are human, that we must at some point go, but it resists our departure with all its energy." He tipped his head to Graham. "Asking Central to let a Sleeper retire is like asking you to chop off your arm because your hand is tired."

Graham stopped. He glanced at his hands before looking back to Victor. "So, that's Stutts' job? Patrol for predilectors?"

Victor nodded. "So to speak. Men such as he are known as Watchers. He is their master, the Watcher himself."

"What about Carly?"

Victor crossed his arms on his chest. "He has her. Central would rather he kill her than let me go."

Graham looked to the windows. With all the thoughts swirling in his head, with all the dizzying revelations swirling through him, a simple thing remained to anchor him in the madness around him. Carly was his patrolmate, pure and simple, no matter what she was doing with Stutts.

Patrol didn't back down.

Graham set his jaw and turned to Victor. "She's not going to die. I won't let that happen."

Victor clapped Graham on the shoulder. "See? We can help each other."

| 0 | 0 | 0 |

A SQUAD OF PATROLMEN MOVED on Sonya's building. They charged down the hall to her domicile, repeaters at the ready, only to confirm what they suspected by the shattered glass of her window wall. Drive Control was summoned and the bodies of the slain Mondial were collected. Before Drive Control filed their reports to the data threads, though, an order reached them from Elder Gadwick.

They were to report nothing until told to do so.

It gave them pause, but then they were ordered to round up the frightened neighbors, who still cowered in their domiciles from the eruptions of gunfire that had shattered their peace. Patrol dragged them from their rooms and beat anyone who protested. Agents of Drive Control took them away for drive evaluation and possible reformat.

A construction crew arrived to replace the window wall and the domicile's outer door.

It was, after all, just another day.

| 0 | 0 | 0 |

CARLY OPENED HER EYES AND stared from the clear roof panels of Endo's retreat to the sky above. The day was starting as a gray wash of bulbous rain clouds, the light of dawn a mere twilight glow. Despite the cloud cover she could perceive the stars. She let her eyes slide shut, and she watched the slow emergence of trace packets in the darkness. Names whispered to her from the data threads, snippets to identify stars and constellations, things she had never cared for in her previous life. Central's knowledge was seeping from the threads to blend with her subconscious. The process was subtle to the point of being seamless, a blurred, indistinct division between her experiences and the whisper of the threads.

She considered the reality of that process. Her mind, still raw from its simplistic training in Rainbow Go, Teen-stomp, and Patrol, was befuddled by the enormity of knowledge opening before her. It set her curiosity ablaze. She wanted everything there was to know, every little facet of every little thing. She wanted to devour the threads, conquer them and make them her own. It was the kind of thinking she knew from Patrol, yet different. In Patrol, it was about indulgence and sensory overload. Probing the data threads, she decided, was about the hunger of fulfillment.

She sat up, pulled the blanket about herself, and let her feet slide out from the sheets to hang over the side of the bed. For several moments she stared at her toes as they probed the cold floor for some warmth. Conscious of her body, of the locality of her physical self that defined her domain away from the data threads, she put a hand on her chest to feel the swell of air in her lungs as she breathed.

Right. Need to remember that. My body is my home, first and last.

Her eyes closed as she lowered her head to run her hands through the wild mess of her hair. She could smell herself. She needed to wash.

"You can take a shower," Endo said as he came up behind her.

She stared at him where he stood by the bed. He wore a long sleeved black shirt with a turtle collar and a pair of black utility pants. He held a mug in his hand.

He pointed to his head. "Data threads," he said. "We're close, so our thoughts attune."

She left the sheet behind as she stood. "Where's your shower?"

He pressed his lips to her forehead and took her hand.

There was a double-hinged door in the back of the bedroom alcove, revealed to her when he pushed it open with his hip. They stepped through into a narrow hallway. He pointed to one end for the shower. The other end was a secondary entrance to the kitchen, rather than walking around through the sitting area. What caught her attention, though, were the shelves set in the wall behind him and the volumes of hardcopy they contained.

He sipped from his mug. "Does this bother you?"

She shook her head. "If I caught you with this in the city I'd have to serve you a double proper beating."

He smiled. "It's all here, why things are the way they are, how things came to be as they are. All the inspirations, all the source materials, they're right here before you. Orwell. Huxley. Montaigne. Descartes. Old notions, old thoughts, illusions and absolutes, abstract philosophy and pragmatic applications, they all orbit the mixed morality of ends and means. The ideas that we've pursued under Central, the ideas that determine the Process—they're nothing new."

She looked back to the books and took one from a shelf to study its cover. "Malthus. Who—" she began to ask, but the data threads flashed her mind. She looked down to the cover, put it back on the shelf, and let her finger trace along the bound spines until she pulled out another volume. "*The Complete Sonnets of Shakespeare*," she read aloud before opening the book to flip through its pages. The words were odd and cumbersome to her, and there was no flash of data to fulfill her curiosity. She held up the book. "What's the point of these?"

"Sonnets," he said, looking up from his mug. "The point is their beauty."

She closed the book and slid it back on the shelf. "That's no point at all."

"And that, you see, is exactly the point," he said as he raised his mug.

"What are you drinking?"

Rather than answer, he handed her the mug and opened his hand for her to drink. She took a sip of the steaming liquid and let it roll down her throat. She blinked at another flash and looked back to him. "Tea."

He nodded. "Very good."

She snapped her fingers and pointed. "With honey."

He smiled. "Impressive." He tipped his chin toward the kitchen. "There's more. Tea, that is."

She considered, but shook her head as a chill crept across her skin. "Later. I'll take a shower and get dressed."

He turned with her and pointed to two doors before opening one of them. He reached in and flipped a switch to reveal a rack of clothing. They were women's clothes.

Carly realized they weren't just any woman's clothes.

Sonya. She was here. Did Noel know?

She realized with a start that Noel was dead. It hit her like a cold, wet slap from the data threads, but it held little purchase on her. She frowned, but then shrugged, deciding she had no particular feeling about that fact, then shrugged again as she dismissed her curiosity over her dismissing his death with such ease.

It seemed strange, and then it suffered its last dissipation in a simple logical redux.

She had lived her life without Noel. Endo was with her.

There was nothing else to say.

Endo's gaze lingered on the clothes. "Yes, these belong to Sonya. She came for dinner several times. We would talk. Sometimes, she listened all night to me. My life in Central doesn't often afford me the luxury of company. Sonya was a good listener. She didn't judge me." He paused a moment, his forehead furrowing as he heard his description of Sonya. He shook it off before looking back to Carly. "We only talked. But she did keep some clothes here, for those times she stayed late. They should fit you."

Carly turned to him. "Did you beat her?"

He stared at his tea, his jaw clenched, before meeting Carly's gaze. "No. I created that illusion to smoke out the rogue."

"Gadwick told me he sacrificed her as cover." She put a hand on his chest. "Do you want to go to her?"

He rolled his eyes in thought. "I will address my situation with Sonya at a later time. At present you're far more important."

"To you, or Central?"

He gave her a wise look. "My situation with Sonya is complicated, but has no comparison to my relation with you. My life is a combination of what Central requires of me and what I require of myself. Compromise. You will have to confront such a scale on your own at some point and see for yourself that the world doesn't operate, and can't operate, on moral absolutes."

"What's that supposed to mean?"

He stared at her, naked before him, for what felt a long time before he found his voice. "I would take Sonya's life if I had to, but I would give up my life to protect you, Carly."

Her lips parted as his words penetrated. She took the collar of his shirt in her hands. "Hey, nobody's going to die. Don't forget, you're with Patrol now." She smiled. "Nobody knocks us around."

"So I've heard." He kissed her, lingering a moment before looking into the blue depths of her eyes. "I hope I don't have to make that choice, Carly. I have enough to reconcile."

She moved to him, welcoming the circle of his arms as she embraced him. "Look, you don't have to worry about anything you've done. Not with me. I crack heads for fun." She kissed him. "So," she said with a grin, "am I really that different than Sonya?"

"Sonya is a wipe construct. She's not real."

"But you feel for her. Doesn't that make her real?"

Endo stared at her for a moment. "I hope you understand the subtleties you imply."

"It just seems that the Madman of MG42 would know something about what's real and what isn't real. Fake things can't hurt. Real things can make you bleed, in every way." She pointed toward the bedroom and the large screen across from his bed. "I get it, that we all have a part to play. I figured that out. It's not about pretending to be larger than life, of being something fake. It's about filling a role bigger than your skin."

He put down his mug on the bookshelf and wrapped his arms around her to hold her tight. It wasn't a desperate hold, but it was protective, and it soothed her in a way she didn't expect. She closed her eyes, smiling when she felt him press his lips to her head as she nestled against his chest.

Time dissolved within her. Her jaw clenched as she peered back through the clutch of Graham's embrace to remember her father's long arms and the raw emptiness of their absence around her. The rough, confusing images that culminated in her mother's death staggered through her mind and marred her view of her future. It was what made her different than Sonya, she realized; it was what made her real. She had a past, a past that had made her bleed, and so her past was real. Her past had meaning. Despite all Central's teaching otherwise, her past never stopped whispering within her, and its whisper projected outward into her future.

It comprised a totality that slept within her, that lay dormant to her day-to-day thoughts, that was yet inseparable from everything that had happened to her. It was there when she waved to the kids from Rainbow Go, it was there when she was laid out in Drive Control, it was there when she almost meat-farmed the charter husband who raped the girl in his care, it was there when she talked to Graham after watching Oboe shoot a young boy's mother.

Her past, she decided, was somehow inseparable from the role she would fulfill in Central.

She turned her face into Endo's chest. She felt safe, standing there in the circle of his arms. The Madman of MG42, the creature she once saw as nothing more than her beautiful bad-ass, had been a fantasy. Endo was a flesh and blood man, yet she felt he wrapped her in all the security Central could afford her.

"Endo, will you keep me safe?"

"To my last breath."

She looked into his eyes. Somewhere in that dark gaze, she decided he was far older than the perfection his physical form suggested. Perfection, after all, was just another illusion, seductive in its empty simplicity. Nothing real was perfect, because real things were complicated.

So, there it is again. Real things make you bleed.

She kissed his cheek, letting her lips linger a moment before whispering in his ear.

He trembled a bit, but gave her a squeeze before stepping back from her. "Sonya's clothes should fit you. They're yours to try."

"I think I'll do that." She watched him go before poking through the clothes. The hangars squeaked on the railing until she pulled out a tailored violet suit with a white silk chemise. She felt the chemise as her fingers ran up the collar, fluted to match the collar of the coat. "Hey, I like this," she thought aloud, her smile growing. She held the hangar across her chest and nodded when she saw the length was right. "Silk," she said, echoing the whisper of the data threads. "Okay, I think I'll like silk."

She took the outfit to the bathroom and gawked at the luxury of the shower. It stood by itself with the toilet outside the curtain and a sink opposite. The bathroom alone was almost the size of her entire domicile. She hung the clothes from the door, flipped on the water, and pulled the curtain behind her. The shower was so spacious that she spun on her feet beneath the cascading water, laughing to herself when her arms hit nothing but the air around her. Even the soap was different; smooth, compared to the rough brick she used to get from supply side.

Scrubbed clean, she turned off the water and pulled open one of the large, soft towels folded on a rack in the shower. She draped the towel over her head, taking a moment to enjoy the warm steam of the stall as beads of water traced down her body. A thought erupted in her mind—a revelation, she decided, after a quick consult of the data threads. Standing in Endo's shower and thinking of her old shower, she realized the depth of the ignorance in which she had lived. Her old life was devoid of any thought, any consideration of the things around her, any notion of repercussion or recourse. It was good drive, the manifestation of embracing a timeless existence under Central.

She grabbed the ends of the towel and clutched them to her face, covering everything but her eyes. Nothing could look the same, she realized, if one could retain memories of yesterdays gone by and anticipate tomorrows yet to come. In that perspective, every little facet of life was suffused with meaning and repercussion.

Just another day has no meaning anymore, just like I would rather use Endo's soap than the soap I used to have. Value. Desire. Wants and needs.

"I guess there's not much left to have in this world," she said to herself. "That's why things are the way they are. Having nothing is fine until you realize you have nothing."

She dried herself and stepped from the shower to stare at a long mirror by the sink. The reflection showed the clothes hanging from the door, and she couldn't help the grin that curled her lips as she dressed. The close, smooth line of the suit satisfied her desire for something different, yet she found it practical enough as she swung her arms to see if she could bring a civi-stick to bear. Her grin returned, tickled by the stubbornness of her old ways.

She walked down the hall to emerge in the kitchen. When she saw Endo she stopped, held her back rail straight with her hands cupped behind her, and tipped her chin up. "Well?"

He turned from the table to take in the sight of her. "Good. You learned."

"Yes—I—did," she said, stepping toward him with each word. She leaned in to kiss him. "And what did you learn last night, Endo Stutts?" she whispered.

He watched her as she slipped away from him. "I learned that things have taken a different course than I anticipated." He sipped his tea. "I have to find Gadwick. I need to speak to him."

"What's he to us?"

"He's the elder of Seven Hills, and he needs to know things have changed." He stood. "I won't be long. There are some buttered biscuits for you to eat. When you finish, I left something for you on the couch. Things you need to know, so I suggest you read them while I'm gone."

She watched as he walked away, her jaw hanging. "You're coming back, right?"

He finished his tea, set the mug on the table, and went to the couch to grab a long black overcoat. "I won't be long," he repeated. He walked to the elevator, pulled down the screen, and nodded to her as he sank away.

Alone in the retreat, she stood motionless until her curiosity got the better of her. She grabbed a buttered biscuit and moaned with its delightful taste as she walked back to the couch. A notepad waited for her. The taboo notion of hand-crafted hardcopy gave her pause, but she shook it off, sat on the couch as she chewed the biscuit, and read what he wrote.

As a predilector, you are only part of the whole. The whole is nobody, everybody, and anybody at once, but never one person.

What we know of the data threads is shaped not only by what we want to hear, but what we do not want to hear, and therein lies the effect of our inclinations upon the Process. Don't mistake your voice for the voice of the data threads.

She tipped her head. "I already figured that one out. Score one for me."

While Central is conceived in the dream of many predilectors, Central at the same time can't be certain of anything, not even of itself, for it as well does not fully comprehend itself. In this it shares the weakness of those who create it, who bring it to being in the working of its Process.

Remember: Truth is subjective, truth is a perspective, and so the lines between truth and lies are the most subtle and insidious predilections. This is the greatest risk to any predilector, the risk of self-predilection.

She blew out a breath. "I think I've had enough lies to last me a good long time."

In the breadth of a moment Central can be found, and in the expanse of a moment Central can be lost. In that duality lies the ability to perceive Central and, through it, the data threads that form the living, evolving will of Central, that mysterious thing known as the Process. The Process is the embodiment of change. There must be change to live. The direction of change is the will of the Dream, the higher perspective of the Process. For a living entity to change, things of the moment need to change, things of the moment need to pass, and things of the moment need to die.

She lowered the pad and stared at the window.

| 0 | 0 | 0 |

GRAHAM LOOKED OUT AS THE first gray light of dawn revealed a growing downpour. He glanced at Sonya's empty stare before meeting Victor's eyes. "There's more to this business of being a Sleeper than you're telling me. If I'm going to make a run on Stutts I need to know everything."

"Pragmatism. That's very good. It's a vital trait for a city elder," Victor said with a nod. "For a Sleeper, the Watcher is the monster hiding under the bed. We know, with our rational thought, that there is no threat, but nevertheless, the fear is there. Understand, our cumulative thoughts as Sleepers are Central's inclinations, and our cumulative dreams are Central's thoughts. Central can't exist without the Sleepers, and the Sleepers can't dream forever. We tire, as I have explained to you, and yearn for the tactile world at some point. Central understands this, can even predict the rate at which we will seek retirement, but to prevent its dissolution and maintain the vitality of both the Dream and the Process it must present some barrier to our retirement."

Graham turned to the window wall. His gaze roamed over the city and his mind's eye summoned all the little scenes of another day in Seven Hills. He could see the cycles of Patrol, of transit links to the manufactories, of beatings and envens and supply side deliveries—all of it, Life. He shook his head in wonder. Everything he saw, everything he could imagine, all of it ran to the dictate of comatose predilectors tucked away across the wide ocean. In some secret place, locked away, they dreamed the Dream of humanity's evolution, calling it the Process, calling it Central, but only pretending under those labels that it was something other than Life, moment by moment.

With Central, it was always the moment.

You can't escape the moment.

It would always surround him, surround his mind, its boundary hovering just out of reach, the limits of perception at once tested, expanded, and confined. Every past, present, and future thought he believed to be his could be thoughts from some stranger's dream. A dizzying notion woke within him, that he could be a wipe like Sonya, a victim of reformat—a wipe of himself, in fact. He could be dreaming his former life in the present, scripted on a wipe so that he could relive his existence and do it differently.

He rubbed his temples, lowering his head as he tried to concentrate, but it was to no avail. It was too much, too many thoughts. His little world of considerations had grown so vast so fast that he couldn't comprehend his own thoughts, could no longer distinguish them as his own with a full measure of confidence. His head began to pound, so he told himself he didn't have to feel as he did. It came as little surprise that the pounding vanished. He had predilected himself, a thought so dizzying he didn't even want to delve into its knots.

He glanced over his shoulder at the high predilector. "So all this, everything happening here, this is the Dream of humanity?"

"To some."

Graham set a hard stare on him. "And the others?"

Victor tipped his chin to the distance. "You forget yourself, Elder. Patrol, Drive Control, Sector Control, and the Watchers are always waiting. They are the hungry wolves just outside the warming firelight of conformity."

Graham considered that for a moment. "So, there's a difference in the Dream, between the Sleepers, right?"

Victor said nothing.

"That's what gives Watchers their real strength," Graham answered himself. "Sleepers that don't want to separate, who forget their identity apart from Central, they fuel the Watchers. But even if they forget their identity it's still there, inside them, whispering like one of the data threads."

Victor's eyes narrowed. "Yes, Patrolman, that's very astute." He squeezed Sonya's hand. "Remember this, though—within your own perceptions there is a precarious place; it provides shelter for the subjective truth that you choose to see as the actual truth of your life. It can poison all your perceptions, because they are then fashioned from the corruption of subjectivity. This is where the mind chooses fiction over fact, and where the risk of self-predilection occurs. It is the greatest folly that can befall a predilector."

| 0 | 0 | 0 |

ENDO DROVE ACROSS THE CITY toward Drive Control, the black sedan he kept in the basement of the Underworld escaping notice in the predawn darkness. He observed several of Patrol's cars rolling about the city, which made him ill at ease. He reached under his seat to take out a loaded handgun and rest it in his lap.

Something's amiss. My suspicions are not unfounded.

Rather than turn him away, he was even more determined to speak with Gadwick. He stopped in front of Drive Control and glanced in either direction before stepping from his car. His sense of the threads told him Gadwick was in his office. Two members of Patrol guarded the annex, but they offered him no resistance, and moved aside as he waved them off with a nudge from the data threads. He opened the door to find Gadwick's secretaries busy at their screens. Ignoring them, he opened Gadwick's door and found the elder sitting at his desk.

Gadwick smiled. "Watcher Stutts."

Endo closed the door. He nodded in greeting and took it upon himself to settle in one of the chairs before the desk.

"And what brings out the Watcher at such an early hour?"

Endo folded his hands in his lap. "I came to update you on the matters at hand, as is your proper due. I assume you've come to realize that Carly Westing is off the threads. You should know that she is now under my protection."

Gadwick gave him a curious look. "Protecting a rogue?"

Endo shook his head. "Protecting a predilector, Elder. I have sensed the depth of her abilities. She shows all the potential to become a Sleeper. As such, she falls under my watch."

Gadwick hesitated before giving him a single nod. "That's very interesting."

Endo stared at Gadwick, a grin creeping across his lips as he felt and fended off Gadwick's attempts to probe his thoughts. "Yes, Elder, it is interesting, when we consider that we have a high predilector in our midst. Carly Westing is not the rogue. She was being manipulated by the rogue, as was Sonya Mortas. Noel Westing was a sap, and Graham Chapel a bystander beside Carly. That's a precarious string of coincidences, to maintain that the visit of a high predilector—Victor Mortas—is nothing more than one more coincidence."

Gadwick held his silence for a moment. "He told me he came here to seek his retirement. It does seem to be more than coincidence, but that's the nature of hindsight, yes? Causality can be a deceptive game."

"So it can be said." Endo opened a hand. "I came to let you know that I will be informing Victor Mortas that a suitable replacement has been found for him."

Gadwick smiled. "That won't be necessary. If you tell me where he is, I'll be happy to relay the news to him." He leaned forward in his seat as he put his hands to his keyboard. "By the way, are you still satisfied with your retreat at the Underworld?"

Endo studied the elder. It only took a heartbeat for Endo's perceptions to illuminate the man's intentions. If Gadwick wasn't the rogue, he was in the rogue's employ. It didn't matter to Endo if Gadwick was a willing participant or not. The elder's question was telling enough. Endo suspected the only reason he was still alive was Gadwick's hope that Endo knew the whereabouts of Mortas.

The elder was waiting to clean house.

Endo held his place, though, as he came to the conclusion that Gadwick knew something else, something Endo didn't know, and was keeping the information hidden. It was the only thing that could motivate the drastic measures Endo sensed in the elder's intentions.

He ignored Gadwick's question and decided to push him. "There's something I'd like to tell you, Elder, something I doubt you're aware of."

Gadwick stared at his screens, waiting for Endo to disclose a location until he crossed his arms on his chest when the information failed to materialize. "Might it involve our high predilector, Victor Mortas?"

Endo nodded. "Tell me, do you know everything about his Mortas name?"

Gadwick's face went still as he took insult to the question. "Yes, Watcher," he said, the strained monotone of his voice betraying his anger. "He scripted the personality of Sonya Mortas on a wipe to be his companion in retirement. Quite a work of vanity, I would think, to consider his ideal match is none other than the figment of his own imagination. He would rather love a projection of his own psyche than the sovereign intellect of an independent woman. A most corrupt and insidious form of masturbation, one might say." He shook his head and shifted in his chair. "Forgive me. I meant no insult. I know what she came to mean to you, this Sonya wipe. Imagine that. Yes, imagine that, in all its various ramifications."

Endo fought to take Gadwick's comments in stride. He knew the elder was baiting him. He also became certain of his conviction that it was none other than Gadwick who had planted the wipe-lock in Sonya's subconscious. It was a conclusion of little consequence, given the current situation. "She's more than a wipe, Elder. My intuition tells me so."

Gadwick raised a finger. "Your intuition, or your inclination? Be careful, Endo."

Endo gave a slight bow of his head. "Caution is all I know. I entertained your comments to illuminate a point. Before our high predilector was Victor Mortas he went by the name of Donald Stapleton. He's one of the original Sleepers. He was there when the first rogues appeared, when the reality of self-predilection almost tore Central apart. In his effort to understand the process of self-predilection he turned his own mind. He tried to subvert Central to satisfy himself, putting his interests above those of Central and humanity. He was going to die for that but, in exchange for his life, he gave up what he learned of self-predilection. He earned his way back into good grace."

"That's old history." Gadwick shrugged. "Generations before I was born."

"This man has already turned on Central once. He wormed his way out of certain death."

Gadwick showed no reaction. "History does not, by default, repeat."

"He's here, now, in your city, Elder. He's using a name that hasn't been used before. It serves to hide him. I was manipulated by my fondness for his work in creating Sonya Mortas."

"She was a lovely specimen," Gadwick said with a sigh.

Endo's dark eyes gleamed in their sockets. "I've sensed the fate of the Mondial five. Are you telling me she's dead as well?"

Gadwick said nothing.

Endo tipped his chin up. "You don't know where she is, do you? Neither do I, Elder, but then I'm not the city elder. I hope the association of her disappearance, along with the empty trace on Chapel, and the presence of a high predilector within your city hasn't escaped your awareness."

Gadwick's jaw clenched. "No, it hasn't. Patrol has been mobilized. I will find them, and get to the root of the matter."

Endo stood. "See things for what they are, Elder. There's a plan at work here unknown to Central. My suspicion tells me Mortas is behind it. I came here to tell you my suspicions because I have no intention of letting him tamper with Carly Westing. Her nascent predilector's mind is vulnerable." He opened a hand to the city outside. "I've seen your mobilization of Patrol. I suspect you know another name for Mortas, one he used in more recent times, one he has hidden from Central."

"You suspect many things, Watcher."

"Do you have prior dealings with him? Do you know the name?"

"No." Gadwick shook his head. "I wouldn't conceal such a thing from you. It would be contrary to Central's goals, yes?"

Endo nodded. "Yes, particularly if that name happened to be John Westing." He looked into Gadwick's eyes. "If he's here, I shouldn't have to remind you of your responsibility."

"Of course. I won't hesitate to notify you if I learn of his whereabouts."

Endo held his composure. Gadwick's deceit was betrayed by his contempt for Endo's questions. Endo was tempted to kill Gadwick right there, but he knew he would never make it out of the building. Carly would be left to fend for herself. Her protection was his priority, without exception. Potential Sleepers were too rare to risk.

He opened his hand. "I appreciate your help, Elder. Now, if you forgive me, I must go."

"I will inform you of any developments," Gadwick said as Endo closed the door.

As Endo drove away, he looked in his rearview mirror and looked to the data threads. There was no trace on him, and no one was following him.

He wasn't the intended target.

He jammed the accelerator to the floor.

| 0 | 0 | 0 |

SONYA'S EYES WERE LIT WITH curiosity. "Have you no interest?"

Graham looked to the plate of crumbs from the biscuits Sonya and the high predilector shared. Two biscuits were left for him, but he ignored them. "I got this far without them, and without that yellow sludge you put on top."

"Butter," Sonya said. "It's called butter, not sludge."

"Chiggers to that." His bowl was empty except for the few remaining shreds of Shaky Flakes that he had devoured. He dropped his spoon into the bowl and took a long gulp of Moo Ju—*no, milk*, he corrected himself—and set the glass down with a low burp.

Sonya stared through him from behind her glasses. She was sitting across from him, just where Victor had directed her to sit, with her arms crossed on her chest.

Graham tipped his head from one side to the other. Her gaze remained fixed. He frowned and looked over his shoulder to find Victor standing by the window wall, then looked back to Sonya and scrutinized her with his foundling predilector's will to perceive her beyond the boundaries of her flesh. It was a chilling sight, nothing more than the bit and bump of Victor's inclinations condensed to an algorithm. It forced Graham to accept what Victor had revealed concerning the secrets of Central, Drive Control, and the warehousing of data drives. This was the only way for all of it, all of the Process, to work.

Victor snapped his fingers. "Our time here has run out."

Graham stood. "Who found us?"

Victor looked to him. "Your friends from Patrol."

"If I'm the elder, can I order them to stop?"

Victor waved to hurry. "Gadwick is still in place. He's made the first move."

They scurried from the domicile, Sonya leading the way with her repeater until Graham took it from her. She followed him, handgun at the ready, with Victor behind them. When they came to the ground floor Graham used his security card to open a domicile and pointed for Sonya to subdue the resident. A swing of the handgun silenced the man before he was even out of bed. After a quick look outside Graham put a single round through one of the windows and then shattered it with a chair. Sonya took point, leading them between two buildings to find the

Patrol car hidden in a back alley.

Graham hopped into the driver's seat, happy to be in the security of his car. He left the lights off and drove toward Kilby, where he knew they could disappear in the tangled maze of narrow streets. He looked to Victor. "We can double back and take out that Patrol detachment."

Victor studied him. "You'd fire on your patrolmates?"

"They came after me—us." He shook his head. "There's always room in the meat-farm. If that's what it takes, right proper, I'll do it. Besides, as it is you want me to take out Gadwick, and maybe Stutts as well, to get Carly."

Victor turned to his window. "Sometimes, Patrolman, the greater wisdom is to run away so that you may return and strike unseen. One day, you'll understand this lesson."

| 0 | 0 | 0 |

CARLY SAT AT ENDO'S KITCHEN table, her breakfast of buttered biscuits done. The notepad was beside her. She sipped some tea and read through Endo's notes one more time to be certain she had them memorized before walking away to sit on a couch. There was no sign of dawn, just a vague perception of a growing gray glow to the morning downpour beyond the window wall.

It was quiet without a net screen babbling away, and she welcomed the solitude.

She sipped her tea.

There was a tingle at the base of her skull. Her eyes narrowed until Endo's voice gained clarity within her.

Carly. Be ready.

She turned toward the elevator. The Underworld should be empty beneath her. The riot of Patrol had long since disbanded.

The elevator cables snapped taught.

She put the mug down and scurried from the couch into the kitchen, where she raced down the hall to enter the bedroom. Endo had left her handgun and two clips on the nightstand. By habit she went to put the clips in her thigh mount before she remembered she wore Sonya's tailored suit. Cursing under her breath, she stripped off the jacket and silk shirt before pulling on her old ENDO shirt. The clips were tucked in the waist of her pants. She kicked off Sonya's low boots to pad across the floor on the balls of her feet, silent in the still retreat.

The elevator clanged to a halt. She put her shoulder to the wall, hidden in shadow, as she raised the handgun. The elevator's screen rose up, clacking on its ratchet stays until it went silent. She drew a breath.

Two men advanced from the elevator, handguns raised, their black bodysuits suggesting nothing but trouble. Carly held her breath, waiting to be certain there was no one else. Her body coiled for the moment, ready to spring, until she closed her eyes and realized there was a smarter way. She remembered what Endo said about proximity and predilectory sensitivities. She was Patrol. Nobody beat her at quick draw.

Her senses flushed out around her. In the darkness she perceived a wink of light, then two, as the implanted probes of the intruders registered in her awareness. She perceived the two men she saw with her naked eye, standing not more than ten paces from her. A third intruder—a woman—lingered by the elevator. A fourth, another man, remained in the elevator.

The probes sparked with a data transfer. It only took a moment for Carly to recognize the data as the floor plan of the retreat, and only a heartbeat more for her to know she had to move.

She fired, blowing out the side of the first intruder's head. The second turned, but she ducked and unloaded three rounds into the man's torso, driving him back before he dropped. She rolled across the floor, stopping against the side of the bed, and covered her retreat to the hallway with blind fire. The woman dove past the open corner of the bedroom, blowing several holes in the wall as she streaked by.

Carly charged down the hall toward the kitchen, ditching her clip and slapping a fresh one home. Her mind raced as she came to a halt at the edge of the kitchen. She heard the unmistakable snap of repeater bolts being slapped home.

Taking it to the next level? Chiggers. So can I.

She closed her eyes and found the intruders' probes in her awareness. There were only a few moments of opportunity, and she had to use them well. Homing on the probes, she deduced the intruders were wipes. Their memories were blank.

After a moment of concentration on the probes she was able to visualize the memory flash that provided the wipes the plan of the retreat. Isolating the thread, she reversed it, so that they now saw the mirror image of the retreat.

She peered around the corner of the kitchen as she sensed something, something that exposed itself as it erupted in her consciousness.

Endo!

The elevator cables hummed as the car descended. The woman turned, the wrong way, to cover herself. Carly came around the corner of the kitchen and let off two shots. The first round blew a hole through the woman's shoulder, spinning her around so the second shot could shatter her face. Carly ran across the retreat, firing toward the elevator as she went, and dove when the man in the elevator opened fire with his repeater. Carly slid toward the dead woman, grabbed her repeater, and ran along the wall to the elevator as it sank away.

She leaned over the edge and unloaded, emptying the repeater's clip in a hail of fire that tore through the thin alloy roof of the elevator.

The elevator came to a stop. The man was slumped in the corner, bleeding from several wounds as he tried to pick up his weapon.

Endo extended his arm and fired a single round into the man's forehead.

The elevator bumped to a halt. Endo found Carly's waiting gaze, the stock of the repeater at rest on her hip. She smiled, but was surprised when Endo stepped to her and closed her in a tight embrace, almost suffocating her with the tight circle of his arms.

"Hey, I'm alright," she said to his ear. "Nobody knocks around Patrol, remember?"

He pointed to his temple. "I saw what you did, flashing their probes to disorient them. Clever."

She raised an eyebrow. "Not as tricky as that flash you did when you grabbed me from the Underworld. That was you, wasn't it, that white flash that stunned everyone?"

He nodded. "It's called a t-pulse, a temporal pulse. It's done by channeling a storm of data through a probe direct into the temporal lobe of the brain. It scrambles the senses for a moment." He held up a finger. "Do it right, and you can even stun a predilector. But you have to be careful."

"Let me guess, you can blow out someone's brains?" She tapped her finger on the repeater's trigger assembly. "Every weapon has recoil. What's the downside?"

"Any predilector will be able to see you if you do it wrong." He took her hand and led her toward the bedroom. "We have to go. Get your shoes. Things have changed."

She glanced at the dead intruders as she dumped the repeater on the bed. "Are they from Gadwick?"

"There's something else at work here," Endo said as he opened a drawer beneath his bed to take out several handgun clips. "Gadwick is sealing off the city. I can feel it, even as he tries to sequester the city's data threads. There's a high predilector on the loose and I now fear he's the rogue. If I'm right he hung Gadwick out as a decoy and used Sonya to get to me."

She pulled on her boots, the silk chemise, and buttoned her suit. "Who is this chigger?"

"I can't say for sure. I don't know what his intentions are but I sense his hand is at work behind everything. I think he predilected Gadwick into the madness of trying to kill us. Gadwick now sees his only option is to kill everyone involved, including this rogue. We have to move. There's something we have to do."

She took a long brown coat and put her arms in the sleeves. "I know. The data vault."

He looked to her, surprised.

She picked up the repeater. "It was easy enough to figure it out. Gadwick said I couldn't be free if I didn't get my drive from Drive Control. I know now what he meant by that. As long as my drive is sitting there somebody can mess with my head. If I take it nobody can touch me. That's how predilectors mess around with people, by tapping their drives."

"You learned this, on your own, in the time I was gone?"

She shrugged, even as her eyes gleamed with mischief. "I want to take Graham's drive from the vault. He's my patrolmate. I think he's in trouble."

Endo frowned. "I can't perceive him, Carly. Sonya either, for that matter."

"I know." She waited until he looked to her. "It's the only thing that makes sense. Patrol thinks in straight lines. I can't see Graham, there's a rogue predilector running around, Sonya's missing, and Gadwick wants to wipe us all out. So Graham and Sonya have to be with this rogue. If they're not, they'd be dead already, and I'd be able to see that."

He walked around the bed and took her hand as he stared into her eyes, his gaze boring into her. "In all the years, among all the predilectors, I've never discovered one quite like you, never seen one quite like you." His lips drew in a tight line, as if he was in pain, but then he said, "You are my sonnet, Carly Westing."

She didn't know what to say.

He kissed her, the warmth of his lips lingering against her. He took a deep breath, pressed his head to hers, and stepped back. "Time to visit the data vault of Seven Hills."

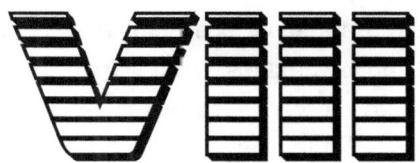

GRAHAM OPENED HIS EYES AFTER a short nap. He looked over his shoulder to find Sonya resting in the back of the crew area. A repeater lay across her lap, her hands over the trigger assembly and barrel grip, ready to go. Her eyes were closed and her glasses sat atop her hair, pulled into its usual bun.

It seemed a curious thing, for her to put her glasses up while she slept. He wondered if she even needed glasses, or if it was just part of Victor's whimsy when he scripted her from his inclinations. On the other hand, perhaps it was a manifestation of her subconscious mind to see past her wipe overlay.

He frowned and looked to Victor. The man sat with his arms crossed over his chest. With Victor's face still, Graham was able to discern the subtle lines and slow sag of flesh along the man's jaw that were weak suggestions as to his true age. Whatever Central did to maintain the physical vitality of its Sleepers impressed Graham, because he saw in its success the existence of resources far more beneficial and complex than a bowl of Shaky Flakes and Moo-ju.

Victor's chest rose as he took a deep breath. "My mind does not sleep," he mumbled, the words slurring over his lips.

Graham's eyes narrowed. He leaned toward Victor, studying his face to see his eyes darting beneath his eyelids.

Sonya remained quiet behind them.

Graham licked his lips. "Plans," he whispered.

Victor's lips parted. "See through the illusion to become the illusion.

Hide in open sight. Use paradox to bend the Process."

Graham rubbed his forehead as he let that thought drift through his mind. He nodded and lowered his hand, wary of the data threads out of concern that he would rouse Victor's awareness. He considered his next move before he spoke. "Why Carly?"

"Westing," Victor said, his voice seeping from him with a sigh.

Then his eyes opened. He looked to Graham, his gaze tight and dark.

Graham pointed out the windshield. "We have to go." He waited, and Victor said nothing. "Gadwick might have been playing us, but I know one thing he said was straight. We have to get our data drives, mine and Sonya's. We have to go to the city's data vault before Gadwick has Patrol all over it."

Victor lifted his chin.

Graham opened his hands. "I don't know where it is."

"You want this, yes?"

"Don't try to predilect me," Graham said with a shake of his head. "We both know this has to happen before anything else. Yes?"

Victor caught the sarcasm. "Indeed," he said. He pointed down the street. "I will hide us from Central's prying eyes, and the car will serve as our final deception to drive through Patrol's perimeter. The data vault is not protected—yet."

Graham hooked a thumb in the direction of the Rectadrome. "Do you think Stutts will make a move on the vault?"

"I would imagine so."

"It's too bad he can't help us. We could use him and Carly," Graham said with a sigh, hoping to bait Victor.

The predilector gave him a sidelong gaze. "As I told you, Endo's role in Central is to keep people like me in line. He won't do anything to help me, or any cause I have. From his perspective, you, Carly, and Sonya are all inconveniences, expendable nuisances, disruptions to the balance of Central. Do I make myself clear?"

Graham could tell he had hit a nerve. He decided to let it go for a moment. "The vault?"

"Yes. If we move quickly, we can get there before anyone else."

Graham started the car. "I guess it's our luck that Gadwick's getting sloppy."

"He's not sloppy," Victor said with a frown. "He's just preoccupied with killing us."

| 0 | 0 | 0 |

THE ELEVATOR DESCENDED FROM ENDO's retreat and bounced to a halt in the basement of the Underworld. Endo lifted the grate and glanced at Carly as she walked by. She gave him a curious look before resting her gaze on his armored sedan. It wasn't the brutish ingot of weaponry like her old Patrol car. Its lines were somewhat angular, but the various planes of the car curved into each other to give it a softer, less menacing appearance. There were no protective wire grills over the headlights, no turret, and no protruding cannon barrels. In fact, there was nothing of note about it, which was the intent of its design, to let it blend away in the disinterest of people's perceptions.

Endo watched as her gaze dissected the vehicle. "Different than a Patrol car, yes?"

She watched him walk around the car to pop the trunk. He waved her over and she slung her repeater as she looked down. Her Patrol training provided answers before the data threads had a chance to whisper. There were two repeaters, a case of smoke grenades, a case of incendiary grenades, and a grenade launcher. She couldn't help but laugh as she looked back to Endo. "Not so different after all, is it?"

He took the stout mass of the grenade launcher and handed it to her. He debated for a moment before opening the case of incendiary shells and passing two to her. "We have to distract Gadwick from the data vault."

She gave her wrist a practiced snap to pop open the launcher before sliding home a shell. "In Patrol it was referred to as urban renewal. Me and Graham just called it kicking ass." She flipped her hand to close the weapon with a sharp *clack*. "You think this is necessary?"

Endo tipped his head as he closed the trunk. "I believe Gadwick will try to keep the city secure. I think he won't anticipate a quick move to the data vault."

She walked to the passenger door. "Are you sure about that? That would be my first move, to lock down the one thing I figured my targets wanted most."

"There's another piece to the puzzle," he said and hopped into the car.

She put the launcher beside her seat, along with the repeater, and closed her door. "It's this high predilector, right? The one who has Graham and Sonya?"

"His goal will be the same as ours, if my suspicion is valid. He will try to secure Graham's data drive so that Graham can take out Gadwick. That will secure the city for the high predilector and thereby secure his escape."

Carly rested the grenade launcher in her lap. "Why not let him go?"

"This man came across the ocean to pursue a cause he has been incubating for years. At the center of that cause is you, Carly. All the things that have happened around you, all the deaths and violence, have all been part of that cause. This predilector does not tread lightly."

She looked to him, her eyes full of Patrol violence. "This predilector, he's just a fancy brain in an ordinary body, right? He won't be much of a threat after I shoot some holes in him. More fodder for the meat-farm."

Endo sighed. "If only it were so simple."

"It is for me," she said and drummed her fingers on the grenade launcher. "Let's go."

| 0 | 0 | 0 |

GRAHAM DROVE THE STREETS OF the city as he followed the high predilector's directions. The car rumbled through the downpour, the windshield wipers struggling to shove aside sheets of rain. When the car rolled through the city center and passed the Rectadrome, Graham wondered at the bland urbanity of the place in contrast to the deluge of violence that occurred during the endorsed riot.

The only sounds in the car, beside the intermittent words of the high predilector, were the clack and rattle of repeater magazines as Sonya loaded them from the car's ammo stores. Graham gave her a glance, surprised by the thoughtless ease with which she handled the weapons. On the other hand, he wasn't surprised at all as he realized that Victor, with the guile of a high predilector, wouldn't neglect to give her all the knowledge necessary to make his plans run without a hitch.

The rest of the ride kept Graham's attention on the city as sights registered with him that had escaped him in the past. What caught his attention most of all, though, were the anonymous trucks of supply side as they roamed the city. It stunned him as he considered the complex, precise logistics that only a presence as invasive and domineering as Central could achieve.

He saw the city then in a different way, in the way that Gadwick had described, as a living thing, an organism of its own awareness, its moods vented in riots and the rising of bulls and the suppression of cone outbursts, and the incredible balance and intricate equilibrium constructed between the marketing of envens to generate demand for goods already produced and delivered. Spontaneous demand it would seem, but he saw it then as yet another careful exercise of the Process. Nobody knew anything but what the envens told them, and the envens only told them what Central could deliver, so the only material wants that existed were those that could be fulfilled. Everything came in the little trucks of supply side as if they constituted the city's blood flowing on concrete arteries, sustaining the neighborhoods of the quads like so many hungry cells, a self-adjusting equilibrium tuned to perfection, the equilibrium of a living thing—*homeostasis*.

The focus of Graham's perceptions was such that he found himself squinting against the glare in his mind, the gleaming clarity of truths with their gossamer veils torn away. He felt self-conscious of his old ignorance, almost red with embarrassment, as he thought of those silly things he had said to Carly when he thought he understood what Central did to them. True, at that time, fooled by his corrupted perceptions, it seemed Central was a thief of memories. Central had seen far past him, though. It used his very resentment of Central to propel his inclination to pursue both Carly's awakening and Gadwick's mocking lure of freedom, lifting him above his incomplete perceptions to true awareness. His opinions had evolved as need dictated to preserve his own balance within the greater balance of the city. His comprehension of the ways of the Process, required to preserve the city's order and balance, would have to be an integral part of his mind if he was to be the elder.

Patrol had prepared him well for the task. With that, he realized his former life under Central wasn't a waste or a mindless pursuit. His former life wasn't a deception; in hindsight, it was a fulfillment.

He stopped at an intersection, his eyes narrowing on a yellow bus filled with the bright slickers of Rainbow Go. He wondered how many of them had already received their implants. They would never know, unless some one of them had that rare distinction hidden within, the spark of a predilector. Even then they would have to wait until the proper age, when the rash days of youth had been hammered into the vents and extents allowed by Central.

You have to believe the illusion before you can see through the illusion to become the illusion. He remembered what Victor had mumbled in his sleep. *Paradox bends the Process.*

His eyes focused on the scene ahead of the bus.

Suddenly, he threw the car into park, scooped up his helmet, and released his door. Victor protested, but he ignored the old man. He slid from the car, his civi-stick rising up to rest on his shoulder. Oblivious to the rain cascading about them, he paced before the car and came to a halt. The car's headlights threw his lengthening shadow against the face of the building across the intersection. Trucks slowed to let him pass as drivers recognized the armor and helmet of a patrolman. Across the street loomed a building of the commercial district with large neon storefronts on the street level and polarized domiciles on the floors above. There was a man there, doubtless a cone, scraping away the letters of a billet advertising *Killshot*. To make the crime worse, he was scratching away the letters in the morning rush, during the busiest hour of the day.

Graham came up behind the cone, the fool not even realizing what was happening until the passersby ceased to pass by and the watching faces within the storefront receded to the depths of the store. The man turned, his face tinged a ghostly blue in the neon glow.

Nothing needed to be said. Graham wondered if the man was insane. Had to be insane, he decided. They had to know, the cones, at least on some level. They had to know there was no escape, that there was no way to get around Central. It had to be what drove some of them off the deep end, what compelled them to hopeless, suicidal acts of defiance. He even wondered if the cones lived in a paradox of their own, a fool's paradox, deceived into believing that if Central was everywhere, that if it didn't need to make itself seen at all times, then perhaps it wasn't there at all, and consisted of nothing more than an illusion, a figment of society's collective imagination.

Chiggers to that.

He looked to either side at the passersby. They glanced at him, at the cone, and then back to him. They wanted it to happen. They knew it needed to happen. Somewhere, deep down, they felt the balance as well, the roar of equilibrium as the balance shifted away and hurried back again.

Graham looked back to the cone and saw through him. That man, that fool, that crazy fool, had no implant! *The cones have no implants—not until we send them to Drive Control, that is.* Cones were the clinging, dying remnants of the old humanity, the outsiders who were yet to be absorbed into Central, whose genetic database might provide more raw materials for the next generation of predilectors.

Fertilizer, in effect.

The civi-stick swung high and whipped down.

Sonya hissed and turned away, but Victor's gaze was glued on the beating. He nodded as the stick did its work. "Yes, Sonya, this path will suit him well."

"And the other?"

"Patience," Victor said, waving a hand to sooth her. "Her way is not quite so simple."

| 0 | 0 | 0 |

Endo rolled to a stop before an apartment building in Cheshire. He looked past Carly to its polarized height and they exchanged a nod. She held the switch to lower the window, poked the fat barrel of the launcher out of the car, and pulled the trigger. The launcher kicked her shoulder as she heard the weapon's distinct *plunk* followed by the crystalline crack of the building's front door as the shell punched through. Endo floored the accelerator and they glanced back as the shell detonated, blowing out the front of the lobby in the reddish-yellow vomit of scorching flames.

Carly snapped the weapon open and tossed the spent shell casing out the open window. She waited for the smoke to clear from the open barrel before pressing the window switch to close out the rain. When the car's interior was clear she slid the second shell home and flipped the weapon shut. "Head over to Kilby."

Endo glanced at her.

She rested the weapon across her lap. "Between the unscheduled riots and everything else that went on, Kilby will still be a hot spot. Patrol will sweep in like flies on shit looking to clobber anyone and everyone. There won't be any need for orders. Gadwick won't be able to stop it."

Endo nodded as they raced across the city.

Carly patted a hand on the dashboard. "You know, I like this car." She snapped her fingers. "Refined—that's it. Data threads are handy."

"And what does the refinement of this vehicle tell you?"

She turned to him. "Really, another lesson?"

He opened a hand as he cruised through an intersection. "You opened the topic."

"Fair enough." She focused her thoughts. "I noticed the differences about this car. Leather seats. Wood inlay dashboard. That means something is different in me, that I can appreciate the new things around me. A silk shirt, a breakfast of buttered biscuits, tea with honey." She poked his arm with her elbow. "Here's another word for you, Mister MG42. *Materialism*. Right, materialism."

He slowed as they passed the Rectadrome and a squad of Patrol cars.

"Do you understand?"

She leaned back against the headrest. "I had a thought before, when I was in your bathroom—that having nothing is fine until you realize you have nothing. That's the problem with materialism, right? If I want more, other people will want more. It would be endless." She shook her head. "That's what this idea is, this thing about supply side and the envens?"

Endo nodded. "*Enter*tainment *ven*ding. A self-generating market economy."

"Right. So dealing with the problem of materialism opened the door for the envens, supply side, and Central itself?" She blinked. "The world—the world really is spent, isn't it?"

"What little remains is rationed by Central. Humanity is being culled so that its numbers are once again below the material supply of the planet. The surplus is our salvation."

"Where's the surplus?"

He pointed to the sky. "The only place we can go."

"Up-top?" She leaned over to look up through the windshield. "That's what all the fuss is about, all the secrecy about the space stuff, us scraping by so they can go up there?"

He nodded. "It's not only our last option, it's our destiny."

"Whatever." She looked out the windows as they rolled into Kilby. "Let's think about the here and now."

Endo rolled slowly toward a dilapidated building. "There may be residents in there."

She held up a hand for him to stop. "They'd all be cones. Tough on them, but it'll sell the deception." She waited for her window to lower. "You're talking about culling humanity. I'm talking about some pecker-head cones. Kill a bunch far away or kill a few up close. It's dirty business, either way."

She fired through a second story window. The car bucked as it raced off, leaving in its wake a flaming plume of shattered glass and billowing smoke.

| 0 | 0 | 0 |

GADWICK STEPPED FROM THE DRY confines of a Patrol car into the rain to stare at a defaced *Killshot* poster. The sidewalk, sheltered by the building, bore the remnant of a rust-red stain. Drive Control had already loaded the perpetrator, another crazed cone lost in the delusion that Central could be defied. Soon enough the cone would get his implant and become another peer subject of Central.

It wasn't the crime that had brought Gadwick hurrying from his office. It was the report he gleaned from his net screens regarding an unassigned car from Patrol taking issue with the cone. The car in question was off the satellite tracking Patrol employed to trace its vehicles.

Some target of his was in that vehicle, but specificity eluded him. He pulled down the hood of his long slicker and paced into the road to look about the intersection. There were only three choices. One road led toward the manufactories and the Underworld. The second led off through serpentine paths to Drive Control's Rooking quad. The third led off in the opposite direction, skirting the city to some old warehouses before the roads fell to disrepair. After that came some scattered trees, the gradual folding of the land into rougher slopes, and then the broad wastelands leading to the Downlow.

He looked between the Underworld and the Downlow roads, deciding that none of his suspect parties would be lingering anywhere near the sight of the Mondial massacre.

Nevertheless he flashed his memory to send an order through the data threads for a squadron of Patrol to sweep the buildings one more time. The report of Bayard's death had arrived while he was riding through the city, and it struck him as another thread that had been shielded from his sight. Information from Patrol's haunt was always sketchy, given the nature of the place. Perhaps it was why Stutts kept a retreat there, to hide in the morass of hazy thread monitoring. Gadwick had dispatched two Patrol cars to search the Underworld, even after Stutts and Carly had eliminated his wipe assassin party.

He scratched his temple as rain soaked him. His reserves were growing thin. He had no doubt Stutts was behind the explosions in Cheshire and Kilby. Patrol was swarming the city, leaving him with nothing more than the few cars of his personal detachment. Too late he realized his mistake, the foolishness of thinking he could contain both Stutts and Victor Mortas within the city.

He turned on his feet. There was only one thing left to do.

With a shout he drew his Patrol escort back to their cars. As one, the ten armored vehicles roared to life and parted traffic to head off toward the Downlow.

Behind them the men of Drive Control continued their work. It was a rough twenty-four hours for them, having labored to cleanse the scene at Sonya Mortas' domicile, Controller Henshaw's domicile, Bayard's mess, and the wasted wipe assassin team at the Underworld. Nevertheless, they pulled down the old poster and replaced it with a new print, smoothing out the air bubbles trapped beneath the poster and wiping away the excess glue that ran down the storefront window. They backed off a step to check the neatness of their work.

The poster was centered and level. From its colorful details an image stared back at them. It was the Hero of Patrol, civi-stick raised over her head in the midst of a riot. The passersby knew her at once, her face now common throughout the net feeds as the new idol of the envens, broadcast to the degree of Endo Stutts himself.

Her name was Carly Westing.

| 0 | 0 | 0 |

CARLY GLANCED AT ENDO AS they left the city behind them. His hands were clamped on the steering wheel as if he was strangling someone.

"Hey, Endo, what's wrong?"

He held his silence.

"We're on our way," she said, opening a hand to the road ahead. "We made it out, and the data vault is our next stop. You're worried it was too easy, yes?"

Endo frowned. The car's lights gleamed through the downpour. It was the middle of the day but the heavy clouds and relentless rain left them in an amorphous gray twilight. He forced his grip open to clench her hand. "I'm not an absolute," he said under his breath. "I, I can't be an absolute for you."

She stared at him. "You think you're going to lose me."

His hand tightened on hers.

"What could possibly happen to me?"

He let out a short, harsh laugh at the question.

She shifted in her seat. "Hey, what's going to happen to me?"

"Anything could happen to you," he said. He let go of her hand to take hold of the steering wheel. "I believed I was sent to kill a rogue until a high predilector confused me as to the rogue's identity. I believed Gadwick wouldn't be so foolish as to turn on me, but so he has. I thought Sonya was other than her wipe nature. I thought a rogue, Seven Hills, and you were most likely an odd coincidence. All the pretexts under which I entered this city have been revealed as lies."

"Maybe they were just mistakes, and not lies. That's the way of things. Hindsight. We both know that." She looked out her window before turning back to him. "Sometimes it's good to forget. You know, I've been thinking about it, that process. It's important to remember that sometimes you need to forget, as backward as that sounds. At the same time, you can't forget to remember other things. Does that make sense?"

"More than you know. It's an elegant deduction and a powerful work of paradox." He turned to her, his gaze boring into her. "There's something I want to tell you. Although I've only just come to know you personally, I've watched over you for years. Central has always held an interest in you, but I don't think it understood you in any way. The things I've said to you were not dramatic overtures. In all my years, I've never met someone who compelled such things within me."

She tipped her head and smiled.

He looked back to the road that stretched into the indistinct gloom ahead of them. The car's headlights seemed of little use, like two blind hands groping in a devouring darkness. "I am the Watcher. I hunt rogues, but I also guard predilectors when they wake to Central. It is my duty, and mine alone, over all the years I've lived, to deliver Sleepers across the wide ocean to Central. I'm not supposed to become attached to Sleepers. I'm not supposed to become attached to you," he said, giving her a glance.

Her smile faded.

He looked back to the road. "I protect Sleepers so they can join the Dream. I also protect the Dream from Sleepers in decline. I'm there when they rise and I'm there when they fall; I'm the entrance and the exit to bookend their lives. Emotional distance maintains my objectivity. It keeps my focus clear."

"What's that supposed to mean?"

"I can't help but feel the hand of Central, the wisdom of the Dream, in all of this. I shouldn't hold you in my thoughts the way I do, but that's the way things have happened. Within me I know I crave to have it so, against all other judgment. The only conclusion is that it serves a purpose."

"Maybe you're not supposed to be alone."

"Humanity," he whispered, his dark eyes going wide. "Discovering Sonya was a wipe showed me my own emptiness. That's why it hit me like a bullet. Humanity! That's it." He slapped his hand on the steering wheel. "The discovery of a potential Sleeper should be a joyous event. Gadwick and Victor Mortas should have joined with me to help you join the Dream. That's the way it's always been. But here, with you, there's nothing but violence and schemes. Seven Hills is under martial law and we're racing to a data vault. The risk to you is unprecedented, so the balance is that my attachment to you must be unprecedented."

"So what's the big secret?"

"That's what you need to understand." He reached toward her. "No more secrets." He took her hand.

She sucked in a breath the moment his skin contacted hers. He was funneling the data threads through his thoughts and into her. It came as an electric jolt of awareness that stunned her as her thoughts sounded in his voice.

I chose my place in the Process a long time ago. I'm not just a member of an order; I'm the one who gave the order its name. I am the Watcher. In exchange for my latitude within Central, for the freedom to transplant my awareness to wipe after wipe to stay young, I gave up any notion of love. It's not a unique sacrifice—the Sleepers accept the same sacrifice. We share this burden.

The inevitable end has come upon me, come upon us.

Humanity returns.

To forget our humanity is to forget the purpose of the Process to protect our future, but to relish our humanity leads down the long dark hole of the past and the devastation of our worst passions exorcised upon the world, because every passion is inextricably linked to its diametric opposite. Attachment mirrors separation, inspiration mirrors disillusionment, envy mirrors revenge, sentiment mirrors loss. Loss spawns desperation and desperation sows the seeds of hate. Hate breeds inhumanity, and inhumanity is the realm of apathy and amorality.

He took a breath. "Of them all, love is different. With love there is no escape, no escape from being consumed by your desire for another. Love holds to the past; it is a selfish thing that clings to the exciting memories of our beloved. It is a flame that illuminates our loneliness yet it makes us all paupers in the loss of our passion for anything else but the one we love. Love is a glorious thing, yet it has a terrible darkness waiting just beneath its hope, and it blinds and deceives us in our desire to keep it unblemished.

"That's why the Process and Central were chosen," he said. "They're not the best solution, but they're the solution that worked. All facets of our society are there to quell, dispel, and dissipate our emotions, reduced to harmless exercises as pale and two-dimensional as wipe constructs like Sonya. Our sentiment and love are trivialized and mocked with the rising and venting of bulls. Our frustration and anger are vented in riots. Our passions are bled away on countless idle pursuits, because passions are a poisonous lie to the Sleepers. Imagine, to have the power to script an entire personality, to think you can personify your desires, have them reflected back upon you by writing your desires upon a wipe. It's folly, madness, the worst form of self-predilection, reckless vanity and ego run amuck, the dissolution of everything for which we've worked so hard."

He turned to Carly, searching to see her as an element in the Process.

The data threads opened to him with a roar that made his heart quake as all the uncertainties came into sudden, horrible focus. He at last saw through the layers of Mortas' deceptions, saw through them like so many glass ambitions shattered in Endo's sudden perception.

He saw Sonya, not as he knew her in Seven Hills, but as Central had allowed him to see her. Yes, Central itself, for Central had to know of the scripting on some impenetrable level of its collective guile. Even so, the choice was made to keep him ignorant as to her nature. The only logical conclusion was that it served a purpose not only for him to be deceived but also for him to learn of the deception. Perhaps learning of the deception was of even greater import, for a secret unknown is a whisper in a deaf ear, but a secret revealed is a mirror of one's own self-predilection; for every secret is half external deception and half internal delusion.

For every reason Sonya's nature could deceive him, there was an equal reason that he would allow himself to be deceived. He was drawn to her simple purity, he knew. But what was it about her that was simple and pure? Nothing, for those treasured hallmarks of her nature were in fact the shortcomings of her creation—the evidence of her scripting was manifest in her lack of guile, a characteristic she was incapable of possessing as a two dimensional intellect.

Alluring as she was, Endo realized his subconscious must have known the truth. It was the only explanation for his hesitation to delve further into his relations with her. He dreamed of her, fantasized of being with her, but there was nothing more. Illusion met fantasy and disappeared in the emptiness of a dream. So too her elusive, ethereal charm was an ideal of desire, infecting others as well. Noel, simpleton that he was, never saw a single facet of her nature.

She was a tool of cunning design.

She was the design of Victor Mortas.

Simulacra. It was the word Victor had thrown at Endo. An imitation of something that has no original material form; people reduced to ghosts—images—of their true selves. Sonya wasn't just a notion of Victor's fancy. She was a criticism, a condemnation, and a statement of rebellion against Central.

Victor Mortas used the Sonya he had created not only to get at Endo, but also to get at Noel and, through Noel, to fix the full focus of his intent on one person in particular.

Carly.

Why Carly?

From the deepest depths of the data threads a name coalesced in Endo's conscious mind. The suspicion solidified, evaporating concerns of paranoia or circumspect logic in the face of one simple fact. During all his emotional constriction with Sonya, he had always felt Carly lingering just outside the periphery of his dreaming mind. Central had put her there for him so that when the time came for John Westing to reveal himself and make his move, Endo would be there to protect Carly.

It was a moment fifteen years in the making.

Hindsight. He knew the philosophical exercise of Central. The past creates the present, the present guides the future; hence the future is the product of the past. Time viewed as three sundered yet conjoined siblings.

His jaw dropped. His hand snapped open to release Carly, fearing his last thoughts would seep to her. For all that he felt she deserved to know the truths lurking around her, he knew he had to hold his silence. It sickened him, but he knew it was the only way. Nevertheless, he couldn't restrain the one warning that fell from his lips.

"He comes for you."

Carly stiffened. "Gadwick, or this chigger Mortas?"

"Mortas." He clenched the steering wheel. "A Sleeper who uses his abilities for no end but his own is the worst kind of traitor. All the things that have happened around you, all the deaths and violence, have all been part of that cause, fallout of a calamitous self-predilection. Mortas knows his own self-predilection, but he follows it anyway. He's insane."

Carly rested a hand on the repeater beside her. "Does he want me dead?"

Endo hesitated. "No, but he will harm you in a way worse than death."

"Not if I meat-farm him first."

Endo shook his head. "There's going to be a moment when you will have to make a decision. It will be a singular moment in your life. I've tried to prepare you for that moment, but the moment will be yours alone."

She looked to him.

"I'm with you now, and I'll be with you after, but I can't be with you in that moment."

"Graham will help us. We'll be fine. Chap's good. He'll help me."

Endo put his hand on her knee. "Mortas will seek his way out from Central in the manipulation of any element he can control. I don't know what mischief he may have worked on your patrolmate. Be certain, before you trust him, before you trust anyone you believe you know. Familiarity and intimacy are the most insidious lanes of predilection."

She looked ahead. "All the more reason to get to the vault. I'll get Graham's drive. I'm not going to ditch him. No matter what bullshit predilection he was fed, he'd never hurt me. I'm not going to listen to anything that says different, and that's that."

"I hope your conviction holds true. We can use any help we can get." He gave her a nod. "Yes, Gadwick is moving on the vault. He believes the only way to salvage himself in the eyes of Central is to clean house."

|0|0|0|

Mortas let out a grunt. "He knows."

"Who?" Graham said before he understood. "Stutts?"

"Yes."

"He knows where we're going?"

"Yes."

Graham looked to him as they rolled away from the city. "Is Carly with him?"

"Yes."

"That's it?" Graham slapped the steering wheel in frustration. "Talk to me!"

Mortas fixed a hard gaze on Graham. "Carly has been deceived. She has been made to believe—she has been made to believe you come to her as the elder, and that you will prove yourself to Central by killing a rogue. Killing her, in fact."

Graham thought it over before slapping the steering wheel again. "Why would Stutts tell her that?"

Victor took a breath. "Gadwick has made an awful mess. Central despises messes." He looked to Graham. "When it's all said and done Endo is nothing more than a janitor. From his perspective, I would take the same course. The less to consider, the easier the considerations."

"That's it? That's how cheap it is to meat-farm people, even predilectors?"

Victor let his gaze wander over the inside of the car. "Do you need to ask that?"

Graham sat motionless for a moment, then cursed and pulled over. The outside world was lost to him, even as he stared straight ahead in the silence of the car. He looked to Victor, then Sonya. Her doleful eyes met his gaze. He glanced into the distance, saying nothing until he ran a hand over the stubble of his hair and looked to Victor.

Mortas returned the glare. "You're troubled, with regard to Carly." He shrugged. "May I say one thing?"

Graham debated with himself. "What?"

"All my efforts in this city have been to retire with my Sonya. I gave up my role in Central, the longevity of my life, my privileges, everything. Do you think I would go to such extents and then ask you to kill someone that you hold dear?"

Graham frowned. He fought to hide his suspicions.

Mortas tipped his chin up. "You fear confronting Carly as an enemy. Very well then, I shall leave the choice to you. We can forget the data vault. Forget all of it. I can take all these memories away from you, right this moment—you see, you are still a prisoner of your data drive—and you can go back to your little life in Patrol. That is, without Patrolman Westing. Or, you can follow my lead here, and have the chance to have it all, all that you desire."

Graham sighed. "We both know it's too late to turn back. I'm not an idiot. I just don't know what's ahead of me."

Mortas gave him a sidelong gaze. "The road is dark and murky, yes?

You wish to have her, because you love her. You already suspect that it's a lonely thing to have your memories, day after day, alone to yourself, the torture of rising each day to the emptiness of your life, with the echoes mocking all the things that you once thought were the convictions of your life. For what purpose—to what purpose—must a predilector endure, if the only companionship is the bare ceiling above your head before you sleep, or the tiresome vacant stares of wipes that surround you in Drive Control? We predilectors transcend humanity so that we may guide humanity. But you must never forget your own humanity, or you will surely face self-dissolution."

Graham lowered his head. "Does it have to be this way?"

"Not even Central knows the future. The smooth process of succession has been derailed, and now the adjustment must be made."

"Adjustment?" Graham huffed at the sad joke of that understatement. "Alright. We do this, and that's it. Right?"

"So it seems."

"That's not much of a promise."

"It's the only promise I can give. If you understand the speed at which Central adapts to situations, then you know it's impossible for me to make any promises."

"Is Carly really the one you're looking for?"

Mortas tipped his head and sighed.

"Hey! You want me to take out Endo Stutts *and* a city elder, and you can't tell me? What if Central throws another one of its surprise adaptations at us and someone gets blown away?"

Mortas frowned. "That would be most unfortunate."

"For who?"

Mortas gave Graham a tired look. "Well, I can always return to the Dream."

Graham glanced at Sonya. "What about us? I can't go back to Patrol. Sonya can't go back to—back to whatever she did in Drive Control. That leaves us in reformat or the meat-farm."

"Yes, that's true. I hope you both understand your positions."

"What positions?" Graham threw his hands up. "We have no positions without you!"

"Well said, Elder," Mortas replied.

Graham was tempted to beat Mortas senseless. There was no out, at least not for him and Sonya. He had no choice but to follow Mortas' dictate. The moment he became an inconvenience, Mortas would abandon him. The moment Mortas abandoned him, his life—as he knew it—was over.

Mortas stared at him as the moments passed. "Elder?"

Graham grunted. He looked down the road, the dark rainy road that led to the data vault.

Without a word he stomped the accelerator.

|0|0|0|

CARLY STARED OUT THE WINDOWS of Endo's car and watched the vegetation along the road dwindle to a sparse, clinging waste. The knotted trees, most of them devoid of leaves, stood like skeletons hunched into the wind blowing from the forgotten horror of the distant Downlow. Everything seemed a dark, menacing wash of gray, the perception enhanced by the dreary downpour of the lengthening day.

"What a place," she thought aloud. The scenery reminded her of something Endo had mentioned. She looked to him. "You said you've been around a long time. Did you see what happened here?"

Endo took a deep breath. "I was born in the days of the sun bombs, before the rise of Central, when all was death and chaos, anarchy and hopelessness." He waved a hand back toward Seven Hills. "I saw the city rise, and many other cities like it. I've seen things the data threads don't dare depict in any of their media files. I've seen cities burn through the night, I've seen oil fields erupt in the blue flash of gas wells ignited by madmen, I've seen battlefields carpeted with countless dead, I've seen the starving young feed on the flesh of their dead elders. I've seen horrors I could take two lifetimes to relate that I haven't forgotten in all the lifetimes I've lived."

She swallowed over a dry throat. "Well, like I said, sometimes it's better to forget."

"Like you said, you have to remember *not* to forget," he said, raising an eyebrow. "When I first saw this place it was nothing but ash, rubble, and slag mounds. But now there's the City of Seven Hills, and it lives. It's an insidious evil to think that what we see now has some ethereal guarantee to endure. That's why we leave the concrete domes of the Downlows exposed outside the cities of Central. They remind us that nothing lasts, that we drive on the carcass of the old."

She closed her eyes. "Enough of the old. Tell me something about the new."

He glanced to the unseen sky above them. "There are things in existence you wouldn't believe, things hidden from the data threads. Everything you see around you is just one facet of humanity. Carly, the last secret of Central is that we've gone beyond the lands you see around you, that we've colonized the 'up-top' that exists as little more than a rumor. I've seen the habitats in orbit above us. I've visited the off-world humanity struggling to secure our future from the foolishness of the generations leading up to the sun bombs. Central allowed us to survive because it helped us to do what we needed to secure a future free of this planet."

"Look, up-top might be great, but this is our home."

He held his silence, hesitant to voice the words they both knew loomed around them, embodied by the inescapable waste outside the car. "We have bled Earth dry," he whispered. "Looking at this, it's hard to believe we ever managed a single space launch, much less an entire self-supporting humanity above us. The generations of old burned this home out from under our feet. Nothing can change that now. We can only struggle to forestall its finality."

"Can't the people up-top help us?"

He gave her a slow shake of his head. "We live under Central because that system works here. The humanity above us lives under a different form of Central. Very different."

"Hopelessly different?"

He pressed his lips together.

She pulled the thick collar of her coat closed as a shiver passed through her. Her gaze drifted out the window. Whispers came to her from her time in Rainbow Go, warnings of the wastelands between the city and the immense, sunken, concrete dome of the Downlow. Teachers told of the lingering poison of the sun bombs, contained and restrained beneath the dome of the Downlow but ever present in the wastelands. Stray too far, they said, and the poison would get you, an invisible, odorless poison that rose from the soil itself and carried in the dank salty breeze through every pore of the body. First headaches, then bleeding—the crimson spurts, they were called—with blood seeping from the bowels, the ears, the nose, the eyes themselves before the body failed in a delirium of waste and vomiting.

"Endo," she said, a nervous tremor in her voice.

He nodded. "I know. We shouldn't be here long. The data vault is safe. It's a sphere of reinforced concrete walls three meters thick. Like all the data vaults it was built in the last years before the sun bombs to be safe against even their threat. Built too well, some said afterward," he added with a tip of his head, "or so those who realized Central was already upon them would have said. Their way was lost in that last war, the war of the sun bombs. They had built themselves a magnificent civilization, a fantastic, shining heap of dung that rotted without the polish of their fragile infrastructures, the links of their economies, their banks, and their paper money. All the things they valued became worthless. They weren't prepared for the new humanity of Central. They didn't know what they had created would be their undoing, for the very people they entrusted to create the vast data networks on which their world relied were the founders of Central. The data vaults were built to survive the collapse of the old world to be ready for Central."

He turned off the road and slowed as the car bumped over the uneven terrain. The ground swept away in a wide, sinking plain devoid of vegetation. Far in the distance, through sheets of rain, Carly managed a glimpse of the Downlow's dome, a mottled gray hump that rose from the surrounding land.

Endo turned to his right, putting the sight of the Downlow on his side of the car. The rear of the car swerved now and then as the car slipped in the mud, but its wide tires and all-wheel drive kept the vehicle moving.

Carly made out another gray hump looming from behind a ridge. Several thick concrete columns rose from the ground before them. The tops of the columns were shattered, their heights crested with splayed lengths of corroded reinforcement bar, as if to mimic the tortured trees closer to the city. Endo slowed as they drove between chunks of broken concrete and beyond the hump she had noticed earlier. They crested the ridge, and Endo guided the car down a muddy slope into a deep cut eroded in the landscape. The moment the tires bit into the hard-packed clay Endo turned the car toward the hump.

She stared in wonder as her mind flashed.

It was the data vault of Seven Hills.

Endo turned off the car's lights and cut the motor. When Carly grabbed the repeater he put a hand on her arm. "It's very cramped inside the vault. There's little room to use a repeater effectively. Handguns are best." He opened the drawer beneath his seat to hand her two extra clips. "Not much, but better than nothing," he said as she tucked away the clips.

"Are we going to have trouble in there?"

Endo tipped his head. "Data vaults are watched by a maintenance staff of wipes from Sector Control."

Carly held out her hand for more clips. "Right. I know where that can go."

They made their way around the car, slipping a few times in the mud. She looked to the gray wall before them, her gaze tracing up its height. The steep muddy banks of the cut loomed on both sides. "How do we get in?"

Endo pointed. "There's a lock around the side, an old service hatch. The main entrance, the upper lock that Drive Control secured long ago, is across from us. That's the lock mapped in Central's memory."

"We just walk in?"

He waved her on. "There's no need now to secure the vault. No one knows of it here in the wastes except those who need access to it, and even those couldn't come here without Central knowing. Only predilectors—Elders, Watchers, and Sleepers—have free access."

Carly looked back toward the Downlow, peering at it from beneath the hood of her coat. "This place is for the chiggers."

"It's the waste of the old," he said as he followed her gaze. He shook his head and took her hand. "Time is wasting. Mortas nears, and we've been outside long enough."

She took a breath and followed him, her gaze drawn back to the ominous rise of the Downlow. The data threads murmured within her, whispers of the world-that-was seeping through her. Her eyes widened in horror until she looked away, the nightmarish tales of which Endo spoke coming to life within her mind's eye. The world and life she knew, for all its appearance as small and stupid, petty and barren, was yet safe and reassuring in its closed simplicity. Her gaze roamed to the top of the data vault, a dark curve against the melancholy gray sky. She hated the place, hated it for its ruin through the waste of others. It was an instilled reaction of her Patrol training against disorder within the Process. Her gaze was drawn back to the Downlow. She felt as if someone was watching her, and wondered how many were entombed, how many lives laid waste, how many nightmares buried beneath the smooth concrete.

Endo halted before her, crouching to point beneath a broken ledge of concrete jutting out from the side of the vault. She followed his arm and was able to discern the outline of a metal door. Water ran off the ledge, further obscuring her sight. Endo pulled her forward, the ledge offering a welcome escape from the chill of the drenching rain.

The distinct clank of the lock's release was a thankful diversion from her considerations. She turned when Endo opened the lock. Dim light seeped from inside the vault, revealing a skeletal metal staircase. Endo led her inside before pulling the lock closed behind them with a resounding clang of metal striking home, startling Carly from her thoughts.

Endo pushed her hood back before pushing his own hood back. He reached inside his coat to pull his handgun free. "You should be ready," he said, his gaze on the gun as he flipped off the safety. "The main lock is even noisier. We'll hear it soon enough."

She started up the stairs, her head hung low. "I just want to get out of here. The sooner we have the drives the better. I want Graham safe."

"Your drive is more important. If we move fast we may have time to get the drives for Chapel and Sonya."

She frowned, but understood. "Let's just get this done."

He held her back so that he could take the lead. They made their way up the stairs, the metal frame turning on itself to ascend two levels in a narrow shaft before coming to another lock. Condensation dripped from the railings, and a single flickering light hung from the top of the staircase. Endo put his shoulder to the lock and grabbed the lever of the lock release. He was about to pull it when he turned back and gestured with his eyes for Carly to step behind him. She hesitated before pulling her handgun free.

"Endo," she said, drawing his gaze to her, "does it have to come to this? Do we know for sure Mortas is after me?"

Endo leaned against the lock. "I can only tell you what I told you before—you sit at the center of his attention, and nothing but destruction follows him."

She lowered her gun. "But it was his plan that woke me, right?"

"That doesn't matter. He defied the tried and true tradition for raising a predilector from Patrol. The process is very ordered to ensure a smooth maturation. I don't have to tell you that your experience has been anything but smooth."

She frowned as she thought of the Rooking massacre.

He nodded. "That and more." He offered her a smile. "Did I tell you I have a perfect safety record for delivering Sleepers?"

"Good. Let's keep it that way." She took a breath and let it go before looking back to him. "I still have a bad feeling about this, you know."

He rolled his eyes in the direction of the Downlow. "Predilectors feel the buried horrors of the old world. It unnerves the most resolute." He looked back to the lock and pulled its lever. It released with the metallic slither of thorough lubrication, and the lock swung on its sealed hinges into the innards of the vault. Cool, dry air spilled about them from the positive pressure of the vault's ventilation system. "Come," he whispered.

She looked past him, into the light of the vault. The sight before her washed over her awareness and dilated her eyes. Everything she had learned, everything she was told, waited for her in its unflinching reality.

| 0 | 0 | 0 |

GRAHAM'S PATROL CAR ROLLED TO a halt as he took in the gloom of the wasted landscape about the data vault. It was late in the day, with scant gray light that barely penetrated the thick clouds fading toward nightfall. He looked at Mortas and the anxious wringing of the man's hands as the car's motor idled. "Well?" he said as Mortas gazed at the vault. "Leave the car here, or what?"

Mortas tipped his chin toward the vault. "Look, my dear Sonya, it is so close, so very close." He reached back to her as she rose from her seat to peer through the windshield. "I will get your drive, Sonya, and you will be free with me. Look, do you see it?"

Sonya's eyes were blank. "Yes."

Mortas moved to open the car door. He froze, his face drawn.

Graham guessed the man's sudden unease. "Stutts?"

"He's already here," Mortas said, closing his eyes. "Ah, and Gadwick comes to close us off from behind. He comes with a Patrol detachment." He opened his eyes, studying Sonya and then Graham. His jaw clenched and he took a deep breath. "The way for us draws perilously narrow, perilously narrow indeed. It will be a very tight fit to find our way, Elder."

Graham stared back at Mortas and tried not to react to the man's sudden omission of Sonya. "Is Carly with Stutts?"

"It is as we need it to be."

"Then go," Graham said, opening a hand to the vault. "You know what has to be done in the vault, and I know what has to be done out here to keep Gadwick back."

Mortas opened the door. "I may need you, Elder."

Graham hooked a thumb toward the turret. "And I need to show Sonya how to use the turret guns. I bet you didn't flash that to her, because in all your planning you were just too hot on this moment, right?"

Mortas pulled up his hood. "Don't outwit yourself, Elder," he said, wagging his finger in warning. He hopped from the car, but then turned and stared back at them. "So it must be, yes, so it must be. Well, then. Goodbye, my Sonya." He stood another moment in the rain, his gaze on her, before he slammed the door shut.

Graham waited to turn off the motor until Mortas was inside the vault. He climbed from his seat into the back of the car to study Sonya. She didn't flinch, her gaze intent on him as they sat in silence among the shadows.

Graham leaned toward her. "He's not all that he thinks he is, is he?" She said nothing.

He lowered his head before glancing out the windshield. "I know he's not everything he appears to be, because just now I was able to predilect this great high predilector, and you know it. I bet you've known that all along, haven't you?"

She held her silence for several moments, fidgeting with her glasses before looking at him with the opaque cast of her eyes. Something stirred within her. "Yes."

"Why?"

Her eyes dulled as her gaze sank to the floor.

"Right." Graham rubbed his forehead. He had trusted his intuitions so far and he wasn't ready to change course, despite the nagging uncertainty lurking within him. Soon enough he would know the truth of his role, either as a predilector or as a fool played by Mortas. He let go his breath and hurled his thoughts across the data threads.

Sonya.

She blinked.

He held his gaze on her. *You heard him just now. He played both of us. He thinks he played me into thinking I'm the elder so he could use me, just like he's been using you. He has some plan he's hiding, and he just showed us that his plans are more important than either of us. He made his choice. He's throwing you away, after all he used you for, after all he said you mean to him. Is that what you want?*

Her mouth opened, yet she showed little recognition of Graham's thought other than a stare of growing intensity. After several moments she took off her glasses and turned to look toward the data vault. Her lips pressed together until she looked down. She studied her reflection on the lenses of her glasses before looking back to Graham.

They held each other's stare.

Graham's eyes narrowed. "He used you."

She held up her glasses and let out a bitter laugh. "You know what? These lenses are fakes. I can see things clearly. The glasses are just one of his little jokes."

Graham sat up straight.

Her wipe ambivalence cracked. "I was convinced I was Sonya Mortas," she said, her hand to her heart. "I believed it, believed it as much as you believe you're really yourself right now. I never knew I was following his scripting codes. He used me to get to Noel and he used me to get to Endo. When Endo looked into me and saw what I am, I saw it too. That's when everything cracked apart. At least, that's the way it felt inside me." She snapped her fingers. "Just like that, I knew I wasn't Sonya. I'm not a wipe, I'm not her, I'm not whoever I was before I was reformatted, or whatever I did to put myself in Sector Control's hands. Get it? I'm nobody—I'm nothing."

She frowned, shoving the repeater that lay between them with her foot as she put her glasses back on. "You know why he's letting you show me how to use the turret, don't you? He didn't forget to flash it to my memory, just like he knew to flash how to use a repeater to my memory."

He hooked a thumb toward the data vault. "He thinks he predilected me to show you how to use the turret."

She pointed at him. "You said it yourself. He made his decision. Staying out here is suicide. The two of us left to hold off a Patrol detachment? That's ridiculous." She clenched her fists and pounded her knees. "I only know how to be Sonya, and I don't know who she is anymore. I'm just an illusion, just some empty reformatted *thing* from Sector Control."

Graham studied her. It was disturbing, watching her awareness flounder in the shadow of her false identity, but then something struck

Graham. "Listen to me. You know you're a wipe. You were reformatted for some crime you did in your old life. So what. What's so wrong with who you are now?"

She grabbed his collar, her eyes flashing with rage. "It's a lie!"

"So, what about it?"

She shook him, her knuckles blanching with the tightness of her grip. "I know it's a lie!"

He put his hands on her wrists. "How?"

She blinked.

"How do you know that there's nothing left of your original life inside you? How could you possibly know your identity as Sonya is a lie?" He gently closed his hands on her wrists and pulled them free of his collar, watching as her rage melted away. He saw the truth within her. She might not remember anything of her life after her reformat, but there was something that lingered within her, something from before the reformat that remained, despite the purging of everything she knew.

His memory sparked.

Carly. Shit, this is what she was trying to tell me, or trying to tell herself. She was right all along, and I was too stupid to see it.

The realization slammed into his consciousness. On some level, regardless of the name Sonya bore, there was an absolute identity within her, something that would remain no matter how many reformats or name changes. At some time in the past her identity had been formed within her, and nothing could take it away from her. The past wasn't an irrelevant image; it was a living shadow in the present.

He understood then who was the rogue. It was Victor—it had to be Victor, if Graham's thoughts were right, and certainty grew within him with every moment. Victor had created Sonya, but Central and the Process saw something else in her creation, something only Graham could understand. All the things that were happening, all the inclinations boiling around the data vault, they all hinged upon some event from the past. For all Central worked to erode the past, it too was bound by the past. There was something about Carly that Central had to overcome, something from her past that held Central from its future.

Sonya's plight was the method the Process had used to rouse his awareness.

So many thoughts, so many considerations—it befuddled him, belittled him, humbled him and enamored him to the vastness of the Sleepers' Dream and the wisdom of the Process.

Sonya's hands tightened against his. "Elder?"

"I am a predilector," he thought aloud, wanting to hear the words. He blinked and focused on her. His thoughts raced, his mind erupting like a case of incendiary shells as he put all the pieces into place. He pulled his hands from her grip only to grab her shoulders in the rush of the moment. She trembled with the ferocity of his grasp. He checked himself, smiled, and took her face in his hands, wiping away her tears with his thumbs. "Sonya, listen to me. I'll turn back the clock for you. I'll make it so all you know is to be Sonya. I promise, but you have to help me." He stared into her eyes, listening to his thoughts. "Right, that's it, we help each other."

She trembled. "Promise?"

His smile grew as he thought of Carly. "Promise. I won't ditch you. Your pain wasn't pointless."

She sucked in a breath. "Together, Elder?"

He closed her hands between his palms. "Together."

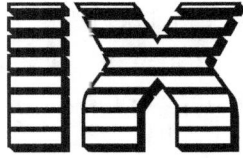

MORTAS CHARGED INTO THE VAULT, knowing full well that the maintenance crew would spot him on their security monitors. He rapped a fist on the main lock to be sure he had their attention before bending his thoughts across the data threads.

As he suspected, they were all wipes. Sector Control was so predictable.

As he hoped, they were free of Gadwick's meddling. The elder wasn't close enough yet to impress his will upon them. The advantage, then, went to Mortas.

His instructions were simple, his bending of the data threads innate. Rebel, criminal, narcissistic sociopath—Central could demean him with any label it chose, but there was no denying the superiority of his abilities. It manifested before him as the lock opened and he found himself staring eye to eye with one of the wipes.

Mortas peered into the man's vacant gaze.

The man nodded. "As you wish, Sir."

| 0 | 0 | 0 |

CARLY'S EYES WIDENED WITH WONDER as she followed Endo through the lower lock of the data vault. Rack after rack of shelving stretched before her, loaded with the quiet hum of enclosed data drives. Activity lights flickered away as little reminders of the people on the other end of those storage discs. Heavy bundles of cable joined the shelves and crossed over her head, leading above and below to the other levels of the vault.

She looked to the nearest shelf of drives, her eyes narrowing on the identification numbers stamped on each. Beneath the drives, on the supporting shelves, she found labels that denoted a quad of the city. It was Seven Hills in miniature, the entire city condensed and crammed into the shelving of the vault. She could only imagine the massive cable bundles connecting the vault to the city, snaking their way through the sewers to split and wend their way to wireless network nodes in apartment building after apartment building.

A resounding clang sounded above them. It was the vault's main lock.

Endo and Carly exchanged a glance, their handguns snapping up to the ready. Endo took the lead, Carly turning her shoulders to watch their flank and rear. He made several turns through the maze of shelves before pressing down another level. Carly watched the shelf labels change from one quad to another until they came to the dead end of another lock.

Endo sank to a crouch and waited for Carly to settle beside him. "Danfield is in the next ventilation cell," he whispered in her ear. "There's a maintenance room on the other side of this lock. The only way in is through that room."

Carly closed her eyes and took a breath. "They're waiting for us."

"I know. I feel them."

"Can you see how many?"

"No." He reached for the lock release. He motioned to take high and right. Carly shifted to the other side of the lock to take low and left.

They exchanged a nod, and Endo pulled the release.

| 0 | 0 | 0 |

GRAHAM CAME TO A HALT just inside the inner main lock of the vault, his repeater trained before him. The security annex was empty. It reeked of a pending ambush. What little he could discern of the vault from the data threads told him the annex should have been manned by wipes.

The tight confines of the room served for good cover, but a quick search revealed nothing but empty spaces under the steady hum of cooling fans. One thing he knew for sure was that his repeater was too unwieldy for the claustrophobic rooms of the vault. He slung the weapon with a curse, preferring its firepower to that of his handgun. Compared to the cubicles of the annex, the little domiciles of the city seemed spacious.

At the back of the annex there was an open lock. He raised his handgun.

A tide of unease rose up within him and forced his gaze back through the open locks behind him. The pale cones of headlights shone through the thickening night over the last fold of land before the vault.

Shit. It had to be Gadwick's party.

He advanced to the lock and ducked through to find himself in a stairwell. Time was short. He calmed himself with a deep breath and waited for his memory to flash a floor plan of the vault. The levels and their corresponding city quads came to him, but there was no immediate help for locating a particular drive. At least he knew Danfield was at the very bottom of the vault, and he was certain it would be the first stop of the high predilector. Mortas had it set in his mind that Sonya was to be sacrificed, so Graham figured the man wouldn't bother going to the Rooking racks to secure her drive. Likewise, if Mortas chose to discard Graham, Mortas wouldn't bother looking for his drive, either. Stutts didn't have a drive. By simple deduction, that left only one person.

Carly.

She's the successor he wants.

She's the successor Gadwick wants.

Chiggers to both of them.

She was his patrolmate. He wouldn't abandon her.

He peered down the racks. The cramped aisle was choked with drives, cables, coolant lines, ducts and metal framing, all of it combining to form blind walls around the tight aisles. If he came upon Stutts, Mortas, or the security wipes, they would be right in his face. It would be a matter of reflexes, a matter of sensitivity to intuition.

A game of quick-draw.

His handgun was aimed low as he made his way down the stairs, cursing every metallic ring of his boots on the steel frame steps. It wasn't the only thing that bothered him, as he knew Gadwick wouldn't be detained by Sonya's diversion for too long. On the other hand, the sight of the drive racks and the impact of the city in digital miniature didn't bother Graham. He saw it as the reality of the Process, that which he had committed himself to protect and serve. The discomforts of his Patrol life served him well, allowing him to accept and dismiss the surreal discomfort of the vault.

It's what it means to be elder.

Being elder means protecting my people.

The thought stopped him in his tracks. Sonya was out there, alone, waiting to hold off Gadwick. Her chances were poor in the best of outcomes, but she chose to stay true to the promise Graham made with her. If he'd had more time, he could've planned things better.

He clenched his teeth and with a silent curse charged toward the shelves of Rooking quad to get Sonya's drive.

He would keep his promise, and put his inclinations to the test against his intuitions.

|0|0|0|

Endo threw the lock wide and opened fire.

Carly scurried past him, amazed and thrilled as her awareness spilled across the data threads to gather the layout of the maintenance room and its lurking wipes. Endo's first shot blew a hole through the chest of one wipe. Before the other wipes had a fix on Carly she saw that five were left in the room. She threw herself against the side of a desk and flashed a plan to Endo as she popped up to fire. Endo ran into the room, firing as he went, while Carly took aim. She let off three quick shots, putting rounds through the temples of two wipes before the third turned, only to have the last round shatter his forehead and pierce his brain.

One of the two remaining wipes came out from behind a partition and fired blind. Carly rolled over the desk for cover as Endo took aim and put four rounds into the wipe's chest. The last wipe tried to make for the exit, but Carly charged around the desks from one side as Endo checked him with fire from the other side. In desperation the wipe ducked behind his raised arm and ran headlong as he fired blind to cover himself. He came around a stack of cooling equipment only for Carly to lean out and blow a hole through the top of his head.

She stepped aside and let the man crash to the floor beside her.

Satisfied, she dumped her clip, slapped a fresh one home, and chambered the first round. Two shots sounded out across the room. She heard Endo gasp and the rapid *clack-clack-clack* of his handgun.

Carly snaked her way through the room toward Endo. Her nerves were on edge as she scanned the threads for another wipe, but her search was met with stark silence. She refused to believe some brainless chigger could ambush Endo until a single thought burst in her awareness.

The rogue.

She took a gun from one of the dead wipes. With a weapon in each hand she picked her way from desk to desk, around a cooling rack, and along a partition to find Endo slumped against the wall. He was holding his leg as he struggled to load a fresh clip into his handgun. His eyes bulged when he saw her, his teeth clenching as he waved for her to leave him.

Ignoring his dismissal, she checked her corners and scurried beside him. She pried his hand off his knee to check his wound. "Straight through," she said and pressed his hand back to his leg. "Was it the rogue?"

Endo nodded. "The threads are constricted around the wipes. I couldn't see him."

"Did you get him?"

"No." He looked to her. "The rest of the wipes are coming."

She reloaded his gun and pressed it into his hand. "I know. I can take them."

"Your drive is more important. You go. I'll stay."

"Chiggers to that. Lean on me. You can walk. Get up."

Endo let go of his wound to look at the blood seeping from his knee. The joint was shattered. The rogue had picked his shot well. Endo knew he wasn't going anywhere. "You'll have to go on your own. Don't worry about me. I told you, your drive is more important."

Her lips pressed together before she dropped a gun to grab the collar of his coat. She gave him a shake and leaned in to kiss him.

He pushed her hand away. "Carly, don't worry about me. Ends and means have their own subtleties. You'll see."

Her eyes narrowed in confusion before she shook her head. "Whatever. I'll be back, and then we'll meat-farm all these bastards." She patted his chest, grabbed her second gun, and crept away.

| 0 | 0 | 0 |

SONYA TOOK A DEEP BREATH as she stared into the Patrol car's rear video monitors. The headlights of Gadwick's detachment came into view as the cars fanned out. She flipped off the monitors to keep the car dark, pulled herself into the collapsible chair of the turret, and closed her eyes. Her hands found the safeties for the twin cannons and the ammo spools before grabbing the cannon bolts to give them a decided pull.

The first round of each spool snapped home into the firing chambers.

Only then did she open her eyes and settle her feet on the turret's control pedals. She looked into the turret viewer to see Gadwick's detachment.

Her hands wrapped around the trigger grips.

| 0 | 0 | 0 |

GADWICK STARED AT THE LONE Patrol car parked before the main lock of the data vault. He looked to either side and found no activity, no stalking shadows, nor any other sign of confrontation. It was hard to imagine that Mortas, Chapel, and Sonya would be so foolish as to go into the vault together, abandon their car, and leave the main lock open. Even if they only suspected his arrival, such carelessness would be inexcusable for Mortas. No, there had to be some other development at work.

He turned to the patrolman driving his car and waved his hand back. The driver put the car in reverse. They rolled away from the vault until Gadwick nodded. He looked to either side, at the other nine cars of his force fanning around him in a wide semi-circle. Satisfied, he pulled up the hood of his slicker and opened the car door, his nose wrinkling at the smell of rot from the distant Downlow. He studied the lone car through a set of binoculars to be sure of his suspicion. "Grendel," he said with a nod. "Now I have you, yes, now I have you."

He hopped back into the car, pulled the door shut, and glanced over his shoulder at the two patrolmen sitting behind him. "Approach that car. Take the foot detachments from the two units flanking us. If the car is empty, take it and drive it behind our line. If not, do what you do best. Keep your weapons raised and be prepared."

"Shoot to kill?" one of the patrolman asked.

Gadwick nodded. "Without a doubt."

"Right proper," the two patrolmen said together. They hopped from the car and slammed the door shut. In short order they came into view with six other patrolmen. They walked toward Grendel, repeaters raised in caution.

Gadwick watched with little satisfaction. He was ready to tap the data threads to give his orders, but he knew that would alert anyone in the vault to his presence. He turned to the driver. "Radio our flanking cars. Order them to make all speed for the vault, disembark, and engage with extreme prejudice."

| 0 | 0 | 0 |

ENDO PLANTED A HAND ON the floor and tried to stand until his leg folded with a sickening crack. He stifled a shriek of pain as he dropped to the floor, cursing his carelessness for letting the rogue disable him with such ease. After so many years of watching Carly, at the one moment he needed to help her, he was left with no choice but to send her off alone.

The wipes were devouring the rogue's command of the data threads. It opened cracks in the rogue's facades, cracks wide enough for Endo to look into the rogue's secrets.

He slapped a hand on his gun. "Carly," he said with a gasp, gnashing his teeth as he pushed himself up. He hobbled toward a dead wipe and took the man's handgun.

Armed, ready, he put his back to the wall.

He could hear the sound of booted feet.

$$|\,0\,|\,0\,|\,0\,|$$

GRAHAM PUSHED OPEN THE LOCK to Rooking quad's drive racks, his handgun following his gaze down the first aisle. He figured his data drive—as well as Sonya's—would be safe only as long as Mortas was occupied with Stutts. Mortas could reformat them and leave them defenseless to Gadwick, although that would send ripples through the data threads and do little to aid Mortas' ambition of sneaking away from Central without notice. Reformat was Central's ultimate threat, but Graham understood it had to be used with the utmost care, just like any other weapon of mass destruction. The reformat of just one person could sever many threads. Loose threads were nothing but waste, and Central despised waste.

He stepped through the lock, only to stop short. "Chiggers, her number!"

He was certain he was the elder. Coupled with that conviction was the simple deduction that he should be able to discern drive locations for anyone in the city. After all, if the city was to be his charge, then by logical extension the city's data vault also fell under his responsibility.

Come on!

Perhaps it was a weak memory of his old life; perhaps the data threads heard him and were whispering back. At the moment he didn't have time to care or ponder the source of the answer he sought. Carly's identification number burst into his mind along with directions to find it among the cryptic labels of the drive racks. He squeezed his eyes shut and the locations of his and Sonya's drives popped from the data threads into his conscious thoughts.

He turned.

The barrel of a handgun loomed in his face.

Graham froze with the expectation of a bullet smashing through his head. A wipe stood before him, confused, his finger tensing and easing on the trigger. It took a moment for Graham to understand, and then his intuitions soared past his inclinations.

He cleared his throat. "Put that weapon down."

The wipe blinked with sudden recognition as the data threads flashed his memory. He lowered his gun. "Elder, forgive me. I didn't know you were visiting today."

Graham held his composure. At such a close distance it was a game of quick-draw that even Carly wouldn't win. He nodded, satisfied at his power over the wipe. "Secure the annex at the main lock."

"Sir," the wipe said at once.

He took two steps and made an abrupt halt.

Graham fired a single round into the back of his head. The man dropped to the floor. "Not quite powerful enough, I guess," Graham said under his breath and hurried away.

| 0 | 0 | 0 |

CARLY SPUN THE RELEASE TO the last lock between her and her drive. She kicked the lock open and ducked aside in case some of the rogue's wipes were waiting for her, but she found nothing more than the hum of cooling fans. There was a chill in the air, so deep in the vault, and she looked down the length of her arms, over her handguns, to survey the world of her Danfield neighborhoods in miniature.

The lights flickered over her. She blinked. There was something else with her down in the guts of the vault, something that drove her breath from her lungs. She faltered, certain in that moment of visual deprivation that the darkness was filled with a field lit by a full moon's silvery hue. The green stretched before her, straight into the mysterious shadows of a copse.

Across a green field, a stand of trees.

She ground her teeth and shook off the whisper in her head. With a curse she rallied her nerves and paced down the aisle, glancing at the rack numbers to locate her drive. Although her instincts bristled with an unseen threat she refused to turn back, not with her drive only steps away. Going back wasn't an option. Behind her there was nothing but armed wipes and the rogue. She had to go forward.

She was Patrol. Patrol never backed down.

The lights flickered once more, and there was no denying the vision that erupted in her mind. The copse raced toward her, its trees alight with the radiant luster of red apples.

No—no, the trees aren't racing to me; I'm racing to them.

Across a green field, a stand of trees.

A stab of pain tore through her head, deep behind her eyes. Her knees trembled beneath her until she steadied herself with a shake of her head. She glanced over her shoulder. There was no sign of Endo and no sign of Graham. She was alone, alone and vulnerable.

She took another step, but the pain in her head pierced her like a bolt of white lightning. Tears of agony welled from the corners of her eyes as she slumped against a drive rack and butted her wrists to her temples.

Across a green field—

She slammed her head against the framing of the drive rack in a desperate effort to clear her thoughts. The rogue was working on her. She knew it, but she couldn't stop it, couldn't defend herself. The data threads were whipping her like electrified coils of some giant snake, constricting her conscious mind, crushing it with the fearsome portent of her sanity spewing from the top of the her head under the rogue's pressure.

She had to get her drive.

—a stand of trees—

"What, what, what is that fucking thought?" She growled as she forced herself to take a step. Her legs felt as if they were filled with concrete. She couldn't think, she couldn't focus, she couldn't aim, and she couldn't move. Everything she knew of herself as Carly Westing revolted within her.

A single plea for help seeped from her lips.

Across a green field, a stand of trees.

The pain in her head blasted through her thoughts in a brilliant cascade of agony. The data threads convulsed around and through her.

Carly Westing.

Her name seemed a distant, foreign thing.

Through the torture searing her nerves she perceived one dim thread slipping from her reach. She lunged to take hold of its sparkling, supple length, throwing her body in her mental effort to escape the vortex consuming her.

Help!

The thread, dim and elusive now, sprang away from her, yet it didn't go without a voice of its own. Two simple words whispered to her.

Wipe-lock.

I'm not a wipe!

The lights flashed around her. "No, you're my daughter."

Endo—

The coiled data threads crashed into her, obliterating her with their searing weight. Her mind was left with one last lonesome moment of detached clarity before the threads blew away, driven off like the reverberation of a concussion grenade. In their wake a new awareness ignited within her and blasted her consciousness.

It wasn't a novel sensation, she realized. For the second time in her life her world exploded.

Too late, she understood. Someone had put a wipe-lock in her head, even though she wasn't a wipe. Central might have kept her mindless, but the rogue had kept her blind.

The past opened beneath her. She vanished into its abyss.

|0|0|0|

GADWICK GASPED AS THE SPASM of threads burst around Carly. He couldn't deduce what had happened but he knew it was something significant, and he was tired of the attention drawn to his city and the repercussions it might have on him. He slapped a hand on the dashboard of his Patrol car and shouted at his driver to order the detachment to move.

The patrolmen he sent out were nearing Grendel from either side. He turned on the driver. "Enough! Target your turret and take out that car."

The driver, startled for a moment at his elder's outburst, hurried from his seat to squeeze past Gadwick toward the turret. Servomotors whined as the driver targeted the car's cannons.

One of the patrolmen by Grendel reached for the door.

Grendel's turret spun to the advancing patrolman.

Gadwick blinked.

Patrol at war with itself. Central turned upon itself.

No—

The data threads, still writhing from their eruption, shocked Gadwick's perceptions and broke the barriers resting dormant within the Process—barriers he at once realized were set by John Westing. Denial, evasion, deception, they all evaporated before the truths spilling out into the data threads and into Central's awareness. The past, like a necrotic sack of bile ripe with denial, vomited its poison into open sight.

Time screeched to a halt, his eyes glazing as reality unfolded before him. He saw through the invisible mantle of his vanity to glimpse himself as a foolish, pathetic old man, a fool who dared to believe he could plumb a depth of wisdom within himself more subtle and penetrating than the Dream.

There was only one end from such foolishness.

No—all this can't be because of me.

Or can it?

Grendel's turret opened fire, shredding the patrolmen nearing its armored mass. Before the tattered remains of their bodies splashed down in the bloody rain the turret whipped around to fix on the two cars sliding to a halt before the vault's main lock, riddling them with bursts of ten-millimeter shells. The crews from both cars ran into the vault under cover of their vehicles, abandoning them among sparkling showers of ricochets.

The turret spun again, this time toward Gadwick's car.

He rolled off his seat and flopped down onto the deck of the car as the turret opened fire. Shells shattered the windshield and pummeled the interior with a deafening, ringing scream of metal impacting metal amid a flurry of debris. He curled into a ball behind his seat as shrapnel sliced into his exposed skin. The driver's blood spattered him in the next instant as the man was torn apart in the seat of the turret.

The turret spun again to target another car of Gadwick's squad, reducing its innards to ruin before a stray round ignited the ammo spools of the car's turret. The vehicle erupted in a sputtering cascade of explosions, its crew devoured in a scourge of flame, bullets, and debris.

Desperate to escape, Gadwick pushed open the crew door behind his seat, rolled out of his car, and splashed prone in a puddle. He crawled away from his car, only to see several of his crews spill from their cars and run off in the rainy darkness. The remaining cars opened fire, their rounds panging off the smooth armored slope of Grendel's back before the drivers came to their senses.

Gadwick screamed, forgetting no one could hear him. "Circle them, circle them and kill them!"

The night lit up with flashes of cannon fire. The remaining cars of the detachment threw mud off the greedy bite of their tires as they parted and made their way around Grendel.

He wiped the mud from his face and clenched his fists. He focused his thoughts, probing Grendel to stun its occupants with a t-pulse. Undisciplined, at range, it would send alarm flags racing through Central, but that was of little concern.

He readied his burst, but then gaped in horror. He sensed one occupant. No sooner did he have his fix than the target skipped off the data threads.

The data drive—the drive's been pulled!

He clenched his fists and flashed his patrolmen the layout of the vault. It was a gross violation, but he didn't care. He had to get the situation in hand, and fast.

It was his only hope for redemption.

|0|0|0|

THE ROAR OF CANNON FIRE reached into the data vault's open lock, pressing through the drowning hum of the vault's fans to make its way into the depths of drive racks.

Graham made his way through the maze of Cheshire's section, scanning the rack labels to find his drive. It seemed an odd exercise, given that he could feel himself drawn to the drive's little read/write heads as if he was being reeled in from the deep. Something bad was happening down in the belly of the vault, something that reverberated across the data threads. It chilled his blood with the unnerving suspicion that he was too late to help Carly. He had made his choice, though, and when he felt Gadwick's mounting presence it only solidified his resolve. If he didn't cover his back he'd be useless to Carly.

He stopped short, looked to his side, and couldn't restrain the grin that pulled at his lips when he looked upon his drive. He slipped his handgun into its thigh mount, tore his drive free, and pulled out the interface and power cables.

The drive was nothing more than a slim black case in his hand. There was no going back for him, ever. Every thought, dream, and experience he ever knew sat on the drive in condensed binary miniature.

It wasn't just a data record. It was his life.

Carly's claims about the past bubbled up into his conscious mind, and he knew it for sure, without doubt, without hesitation, that she was right and had been right all along. He could throw his drive away, smash it to pieces, incinerate it, and it wouldn't matter. When all was said and done he would still be Graham Chapel and nothing could or would change that, even as he changed within himself. The past always mattered, because without the past the present had no definition.

Right proper.

He slid his drive into a thigh pocket. It wasn't a protected spot, but he already had Sonya's drive wedged under his chest plate. His promise to her was worthless if he couldn't protect her from other predilectors in the meantime. Later, he'd put the drive back to finish his commitment to her before removing it for good.

His thoughts flashed. It stunned him until he remembered he didn't need a drive to associate with the data threads. He was a predilector. He had his life, his past, and his thoughts to himself.

His eyes bulged. Carly was always curious about her childhood.

Her childhood was on her drive.

Mortas had abandoned him and Sonya to get to Carly.

Graham closed his eyes. He was a predilector, the Elder of Seven Hills. He felt out his city and its residents. All he had to do was focus on a name.

Carly.

Subservient and yet elusive, the data threads bent to his call. He found her at the bottom of the vault. Her drive was still attached. The rogue was hard at work on her. Graham could hear the roar of data around her, could see the push and pull of image files that he realized were snapshots of Carly's past flashing in rapid succession across the threads. The story of her life unfolded before him. Her childhood was laid bare.

The revelation burned through Graham's mind as the veils of deception fell away. He saw everything, in all its revolting truth.

Donald Stapleton. John Westing. Victor Mortas.

One and the same.

Graham whipped his gun free.

"Westing—you bastard!"

| ၁ | 0 | 0 |

CARLY WHEEZED AS SHE LOOKED into the horror of her childhood. Her life came into focus. Everything was a lie, and she was the biggest lie of all. Everything she knew of herself as Carly Westing evaporated to leave her as a helpless and hopeless child longing for her father.

Someone reached through the darkness and delirium to grab her and slap her back to reality. She opened her eyes and went slack with disbelief.

She blinked as she struggled to find her breath. When she did she couldn't stop the single word that fell from her lips, no matter how maddening it was to hear its sound.

"Daddy?" Her gaze bored into the face of the man clutching her shoulders. "You came back for me?"

| 0 | 0 | 0 |

ENDO GASPED AS A BULLET blew through his left shoulder. His hand went numb, his second gun dropping from his tingling fingers. He spun and unloaded with his right arm, blasting three holes into the chest of a wipe. Between the wound in his shoulder and the recoil of his own gun, he slid off balance and flopped to the floor behind a partition. He ditched his spent clip and was struggling to slide a fresh clip home when he heard Carly's whisper through the data threads.

It hit him with an electric spasm of rage, even as he heard another voice scream out Westing's name. He didn't care to spy the threads to see who else beheld Westing's presence, and he didn't have time.

Several bullets smashed into the wall over his head. There was no comfort in philosophy or in his own secrets as the Watcher. John Westing was at hand.

Central demanded its due. Endo would kill anyone in his way.

Against his wounds, against his agony, he rolled out from cover and opened fire.

| 0 | 0 | 0 |

VICTOR RAISED HIS CHIN AS he looked down on Carly. Seeing her, holding her, was a cathartic jolt greater than he expected. He managed to maintain his poise as he let his identities wash away until only one remained. As John Westing he stared into his daughter's eyes and used the threads to skewer her memories.

Almost fifteen years had passed since the nightmare of her youth. Her father had abandoned her, had fled from the family he treasured under threat of Central's wrath. He had defied its dictates by bucking the societal institutions of Rainbow Go and Teen-stomp and making his brazen move to live as a man with a family, as it had been in times of old. Hope persisted to reunite with them, in particular his darling daughter, whose predilectory potential glowed in her dreams and lit the data threads around her. He let that hope manifest in the simple promise that he would one day return to her, that he would imbue her fledgling mind with peace. All she had to do was find him in the copse outside their quad. The directions were simple enough.

Across a green field, a stand of trees.

Westing slammed his daughter against the drive rack as her eyes rolled over in her head. "See it, see it all!" he said, tightening his grip on her shoulders.

Westing's aspirations for his family hadn't been free of entanglements. To have his children, to have his choice of a wife, he had to work with a city elder. Westing chose Seven Hills when he set his aim upon a suitable mate—Rebecca Westing, Carly's mother. He enlisted the help of the Elder of Seven Hills, a man by the name of Ian Gadwick.

Westing shook Carly to keep her conscious as her breath clucked in her throat. "Gadwick had to account for himself to Central," Westing said, pressing his forehead to Carly's. "See it, see the choice he made! Central drove me away and vented its wrath on my family. Central came for Gadwick to make him pay for helping me. Instead of protecting you he fed you to the wolves. He sniffed out the promise I made you and set you up. He waited until you went to the woods to find me and sent the boys of the neighborhood out to destroy you."

She gasped.

He clutched her head in his hands, holding her still so that she could see nothing but his gaze. "It was the elder! He's the one to blame. He arranged for you to be gang-raped under that apple tree, to silence your mind and to please Central. And Central excused that outrage, and all his other offenses, and let him remain the elder of Seven Hills!"

Carly convulsed with disgust. She shoved her father away, slumping against the drive rack as she panted and shook her head. Her hands tightened on the handguns, squeezing them until her knuckles blanched.

Westing hovered over her. "Do you see the lies? It was the elder who defiled you. It was Patrol that killed your mother. Central was behind everything. And you let Stutts seduce you? Stupid girl, you let Central rape you again! Is that the master you want to serve?"

She pounded her wrists to her temples.

"They're all here," Westing whispered. "They're all here to get their hands on you one more time. The elder, his successor, Stutts, Patrol—all of them."

Her eyes burned red in their sockets. She looked to her guns.

"I'll wait for you."

She turned to stare at him, regaining her combat poise with each deep breath. Her heart pounded in her chest with a cold fury. Lit by this new fire, she stood straight before him, her lips pressed in a tight line.

He held his silence. There was nothing else to say. He knew she had to decide.

Her eyes closed. When they opened they had an opaque cast, as impenetrable as the blue depths of the ocean.

She turned back the way she came.

| 0 | 0 | 0 |

SONYA HIT THE RELEASE OF her safety belts and rolled out of the turret's chair to land on the deck of her car. The armored hull sang like a deafening chorus of bells under the relentless fire of Gadwick's squadron. Her ears went numb, leaving her unaware of the shifting cannon strikes as the cars flanked her. She'd seen enough from the turret. That, combined with Graham's description of Patrol's usual tactics, were enough to confirm what she knew was soon to come. It was four cars against one, and the only thing that gave her any success was having the armored rump of her car facing Gadwick's initial firing line.

She grabbed a repeater clip from the deck beside her and rammed it into the turret's trigger grips to send an endless stream of fire from the cannons. The car bucked and shook around her with closer cannon strikes. She hit the release of the car's belly hatch to pull it open. To her shock, the car had settled down with three of its tires shot out, leaving only a slim space to make her escape. She grabbed her repeater and tossed it through the hatch as the window of the driver's door exploded. Bulletproof glass, no match for the cannons' ten-millimeter shells, rained about her in sparkling fragments.

A frigid puddle waited for her as she slid head first through the belly hatch, clearing her legs just as Gadwick's cars got in front of Grendel and riddled the car's interior. She pushed her repeater out from under her as she squirmed through the mud. The moment she felt rain on her hands she grabbed the ragged rubber remains of a blown tire to pull herself free. Her head and shoulders cleared the hull of the car as shells shredded the last tire, and she felt the very welcome sensation of cold rain on her neck. Her mood lifted, but then she heard the rattling wheeze of the deflating tire. The car lurched as its mass fell on her legs.

She screamed. It was more fear than pain, the horrid anticipation of her legs being crushed. The car sank upon her but the mud parted to save her. It was little relief, for she was pinned beneath the car's weight. The turret above her fell silent as the last shells fed through the cannons. Gadwick's cars let off several sporadic bursts before they ceased fire.

It took a moment before she could comprehend the sudden quiet around her. She was too busy clawing at the mud with her quaking arms to pull herself from under the car. For all her effort she didn't budge. She was trapped.

She went still, propped on her elbows, as she looked to the four cars of Gadwick's detachment. They sat still, their motors idling. The flat, muddy ground reached out to the darkness. There was no place to hide even if she could get free. She looked back to the cars, lost as to what she should do next. Moments fled from her. There was little time to think but, in the blink of an eye, any notion of hope was lost. One by one the cars turned on their headlights and bathed the smoking hulk of Grendel in their harsh white glare. Her shadow raced out across the ground before she gasped and dropped flat in the mud.

The crew doors of the cars slid open. Voices sounded out. Patrol was coming for her.

Elder!

Her gaze darted from the cars and their blinding headlights to her repeater. It was an arm's length from her. She reached for it, the weapon almost in hand, when a line of fire ripped across the mud. She screamed as her arm recoiled. Her pinky spun through the air and landed next to the repeater.

She cradled the bloody mess of her hand to her chest as she lay in the mud. Boots splashed toward her. The sound came from behind Grendel.

She turned her head. The silhouette of a man loomed over her.

"So, we meet again, Sonya Mortas," Gadwick said. He waited a moment before striking the glasses from her head with a vicious kick.

| 0 | 0 | 0 |

GRAHAM HOPPED DOWN THE METAL stairs toward the depths of the vault, taking them three at a time. It made an awful racket, but he was more concerned about time than noise. Noise was irrelevant to predilectors. They could sense him better than he could sense them.

An old sign pointed toward a maintenance room. It was a chokepoint in the layout of the vault, a room on a higher level. With Carly's drive in the belly of the vault it was a critical position to occupy.

He ducked at the sound of gunfire. He looked to his handgun, debating until the unmistakable rattle of repeater fire chased him from his position. Desperate, he scrambled across the floor away from the bottom of the stairs to find better cover behind a rack of drives. Only when he came to a halt did he peer past the corner of the drive rack to pick out the first bulky, armored outline of a patrolman making his way down the stairs. Graham took aim but then returned his handgun with a silent curse. He took hold of his repeater, tucked it tight into his shoulder, and flipped off the safety.

The first patrolman came to the bottom of the stairs.

Graham ran out, his repeater pounding against his shoulder as he blew a dozen holes through the patrolman. Before the next patrolmen behind the point man could react, Graham swung his repeater to aim up the stairs and held the trigger until the clip clacked empty. Arm humming with recoil, he dropped the clip, slapped a fresh clip home, and ran across the maze of the level.

He made it to the secondary stairs just as two patrolmen turned on him. He fired square into the first patrolmen, her face splattering across the wall before she slumped against her partner. The other patrolman buckled under her weight as he struggled to get his weapon free. He didn't have a chance. Graham took quick aim and put a single round into his forehead.

Repeater fire rapped off the drive racks behind him. He sank to a crouch and turned to cover his rear.

Two patrolmen had him square in their sights.

| 0 | 0 | 0 |

DRAWN BY THE FIRE, CARLY swung around a drive rack. She didn't take time to discern between the two patrolmen standing shoulder to shoulder and the third patrolmen down the length of the aisle from them, crouched under their sights.

Silent, merciless, she came up behind the two patrolmen, rammed the barrels of her handguns against their necks, and fired. Their necks shattered and their throats exploded. They flopped to the floor, opening her aim on the crouching patrolman.

He didn't move. "Carly?"

She opened fire. The patrolman scrambled away without a shot, gasping when she put a round into the back of his leg and sent him stumbling for cover.

The uneven clang of footfalls sounded out. Boots coming down metal stairs.

She stuffed her handguns into the waist of her pants, picked up a repeater, and turned toward the stairs.

| 0 | 0 | 0 |

ENDO DRAGGED HIMSELF ACROSS THE floor, wincing every time his weight shifted to his wounded shoulder. He made his way behind a partition and waited. There were only three rounds left in his clip. There wasn't enough left in his body to make it to the wipes across the room and get their clips. He pushed himself up to sit against the wall, raised his gun, and clung to an empty clip in his left hand.

One wipe remained in the room.

Endo listened to the man's approach, closing his eyes to get a fix on him through the data threads. When the wipe was on the other side of the partition Endo fired off a round, waited a moment, and let the empty clip fall from his hand to clatter on the floor. Taking the bait, the wipe came around the corner. Before the man could fire Endo put his last two bullets into the man's heart. The wipe staggered with the impact before collapsing against the partition, his weight tearing the flimsy wall from its floor mounts to let the wall and the wipe crash to the floor.

Endo looked up. He was exposed. He was defenseless.

He let his head thump against the wall behind him. His knee was shattered. He had a through wound in his left shoulder. Another wipe's shot had grazed his side. He was a mess.

Westing had seized Carly.

Endo's gun was empty, but he clutched it to his chest, a little bit of denial to soothe his disgust for his first, and worst, failure.

"Don't be so hard on yourself."

Endo twitched in surprise. He found John Westing standing several paces away. Endo looked to the dead wipe. He knew he'd never be able to drag himself to the wipe's gun before Westing could shoot him. Endo rolled his eyes before looking back to Westing. "Tired of hiding as Victor Mortas?"

"So, your eyes are no longer fooled." Westing shrugged. "It was a means to an end."

"Use any name you want," Endo said and shook his head. "It won't matter. You're not getting out of here."

Westing picked up a handgun from a dead wipe. He dropped the clip, checked the ammo window, and slid the clip home. He sank to a crouch and pointed to Endo. "You're the one who's going to die here, Watcher. And for what's going to happen next, Central's going to cast you out. You're done, old fellow."

Endo coughed. "Central will get you. It might not be me, but someone else."

"Not after my daughter is done with Central."

"Are you so proud of what you've done?"

Westing pointed to the repeater fire reverberating over their heads. He nodded as he stood. "Think about the master you serve before you condemn me. Who's at greater fault, the man or the system? The system left me no choice. Think of me as a messenger, not the message. Do you think I don't understand the outrage of this mess? Don't you think I would've had things differently if I could? What was I to do? I fell victim to self-predilection. I know you and Central see it that way because I refused to be another nodding maggot in the system.

"Once, long ago, I argued the value of free will and Central labeled it as self-predilection, some ominous sin to threaten everyone and anyone who might listen to me. You wonder why space-faring humanity keeps its distance from us? Why wouldn't they? I wanted to show everyone we could resurrect our humanity; that we don't have to live like rats aimlessly groveling and breeding to some uncaring dictate embodied by a bunch of comatose zombies fooling themselves into believing they serve a noble goal. The greatest self-predilection lies in the Sleepers who serve Central. Look at all this carnage! That's Central's will, not mine. All I wanted was a family."

Endo ground his teeth. "You broke all the rules. You stole a patrol-man, took her as a breeding partner—"

"Wife," Westing corrected.

"You screwed her until Gadwick manipulated the breeding program to give you two children of your own," Endo said, squeezing the gun he held to his chest. "You lied to her. You lied to Gadwick. You lied to your son and daughter, lied to them until Noel spent all his time in sex dens and Carly ran away every chance she had. Rebecca Westing drank herself delirious and beat Carly whenever she could."

"All those things were because of Central's system. Was it a crime, what I tried to accomplish?" Westing raised his hands. "The failure should've vindicated my efforts to show the error of Central's ways. Successful or not, it shouldn't have mattered. The irony of the effort was that simply making the effort proved my point."

Endo shook his head. "You introduced self-predilection into Central when you lived as Donald Stapleton. You questioned the breeding pro-gram and the use of Patrol to find the best genetic couplings to make the next generation of predilectors."

"It's a disgusting practice."

"It works!" Endo sucked in a breath. "Is what you did any better? You didn't have a family, you had a shambles of lies and abuse," he said, ignoring Westing as the man's lips drew taught. "And when you couldn't control Noel or Carly, when things got so out of hand that Central couldn't condone your transgression, you ran away and pointed the finger at Gadwick."

Westing shook a fist at Endo. "That's right, it was Gadwick who let her get gang-raped in those woods that night, not me."

"He made it happen, but you *let* it happen!" Endo shifted to get to Westing, but his body refused to budge. "You were afraid what her undis-ciplined predilection might do to the other boys in her neighborhood. You knew those boys were engineered from Rebecca Westing under the breeding program. You didn't just let her get gang-raped, you let it happen at the hands of her half-brothers, and then you let their own biological mother slaughter them."

"Central made that system." Westing glanced over his shoulder at the nearing sound of repeater fire before his eyes narrowed on Endo. "You'll see. I'll have my revenge. I put a wipe-lock in Carly's head to hide those memories all these years, and when she's done here I'll unleash her on the data threads. By the way, I have to thank you. I couldn't tail her and corral Gadwick at the same time. You see, I knew you'd bring her here, just like the loyal puppy dog that you are." He sighed. "Do you remember that time, Endo, when we played with dogs, instead of eating them?"

"Is that what you think of us?"

Westing shook his head. "You're not half as wise as you think you are. Central may have fostered your obsession for my daughter but nobody knew her real purpose, the purpose I crafted for her. She's my final revolt on Central, a predilector with the abilities of a Sleeper turned against Central. She'll tear the whole shit-stinking mess down from within."

Endo winced as he tried to move. "She'll die."

Westing opened his hands. "We all die, Endo. At least, that's the way it's supposed to be. Maybe you forgot that, you body-snatching freak."

|0|0|0|

GADWICK WATCHED AS SONYA SHOOK her head to blink away the mud from his boot. Blood dripped from her nose. He stood over her, staring down at her, a greedy gleam in his eyes.

She licked the grime from her lips and spat to the side before looking back at him, exasperated by his silence. "What! Why wait?"

Gadwick laughed, humored by the sight of her futile defiance. "Ah, so the wipe speaks through the Sonya overlay," he said, cupping his hands behind his back. "Do you have any idea how much trouble you've caused me?" He leaned over as he gazed down on her. "No more. You can't see them, but the rest of my patrolmen are moving into the vault. I'm going to let them turn that vault into a chamber of corpses before they come back out to take care of you. The meat-farm will get more than its fair share by the time this is done."

She cowered beneath his glare.

He stood straight, but his shoulders sagged with some unseen weight as the corners of his mouth sank into a deep scowl. "Everything dies this day."

| 0 | 0 | 0 |

CARLY DUCKED AROUND THE CORNER of a drive rack, spraying two patrolmen with her repeater until it clacked empty. The moment the bolt froze over the empty chamber she swung the weapon around her head as she spun and slammed the butt square into another patrolmen's head. The man staggered, giving her just enough time to whip her handguns free and blow several holes in his belly. She stepped over the man and ran up the stairs, letting off several rounds to divert the next party of patrolmen long enough for her to slam the lock shut and spin the release lever. With that done, she hopped down the stairs, grabbed a civi-stick, and ran back up to wedge the stick under the release to keep it locked.

Her coat flared around her as she bounded down the stairs and dodged several sprays of repeater fire, her predilectory sense leaving her with the sensation that she was interacting with a world one step behind her in a temporal distortion of the data threads. She emptied the last rounds from her clips into another pair of patrolmen she found hiding behind a cooler assembly, took one of their repeaters, and proceeded to chase down the last few patrolmen.

"Carly, stop!"

It was the same plea she had heard several times before, and she once again ignored its call. She slid to a halt, her leather boots providing poor traction on the smooth vinyl tiles of the vault floor. Taking a step back, she peered between two drives to spot another patrolman lurking in the next aisle. She shoved the barrel of her repeater between the two drives and emptied the clip into the patrolman, not wasting the time to check if he was dead as she walked away. The empty repeater clattered across the floor as she tossed it away, and a quick search of two dead patrolmen provided her with a pair of fresh handguns.

"Carly, it's Graham! I don't want to hurt you."

She held for a moment. More boots sounded on the rear stairs. She took a civi-stick, two extra handgun clips, and ran down the narrow aisle between the racks.

| 0 | 0 | 0 |

GRAHAM LIMPED TOWARD A CORNER away from the sound of Carly's repeater fire. He couldn't find her on the data threads and realized that was for the better. She seemed incapable of tracking him on the threads as she meat-farmed every other patrolman that made the mistake of trying to take the floor. He wondered how many patrolmen Gadwick had with him. With the mess of fires and explosions in Seven Hills he could only bring so many. To a certain extent Patrol had to respond to situations on its own dictate.

He considered trying to call out to her again, but decided it was a bad move. Westing had turned Carly's head inside out.

Westing had to die.

Graham peered up the stairs to see the civi-stick Carly had wedged into the lock release. She was sealing the vault. Once she secured the other entry, he knew she was going to come for him.

He looked down the stairwell. Two floors below was the maintenance room that choked off the access to Danfield's drives. If Stutts was anywhere, he had to be down there—if he was still alive.

Graham looked down. He was bleeding like a pig, despite the improvised bandage he had made from the sleeve of his bodysuit.

Grunting against his leg, he tucked his repeater to his shoulder with one arm and clutched the railing for the stairs in his other hand.

|0|0|0|

GADWICK GLANCED TOWARD THE VAULT as he heard the ragged bursts of repeater fire.

Sonya seized the moment by clawing at the mud.

Gadwick's eyes narrowed on her. "Squirm all you want, but I won't soil my hands with your blood. I'll get your drive, trust me on that, and once it's back in the racks I'll let Sector Control beat you, just as Stutts led me to believe those Mondial thugs beat you. While you endure the agony of your ruin, you'll have the additional agony of knowing the utter futility of your existence. Life will continue for Seven Hills, but you're going to vanish in reformat."

He grinned, humored by his cruelty. "A two-time wipe. You'll end up as some sex den whore, the cheapest piece of entertainment when you're not sitting in a corner drooling on yourself because you can't even remember how to talk. Perhaps I'll pay you a visit. Won't it be fitting irony to put you on your knees for deceiving me, for helping depict me as a rogue in the eyes of the Process? Yes, I'll enjoy pleasing myself in that lying mouth of yours. Unless, that is, those sadists in Sector Control put a bullet through your head."

Sonya closed her eyes.

Gadwick hummed several times before raising a finger as if he lectured a child in Rainbow Go. "In the lassitude of my age I forgot how vicious I could be. It's a natural complement to the exhausting attention I pay to my city, you see."

He sank to a crouch beside her, jerked her head up by a fistful of hair, and stunned her with a backhanded slap. "I have to repent. I made the mistake once—just once—of trying to clean up the mess left by a rogue. Fifteen years I've wasted watching the life of one Carly Westing—all the meticulous plans, the guarded inclinations, they're all lost now in this dark mud. Perhaps that's fitting, out here next to the Downlow."

She stared at him, her cheek glowing from his slap.

Her hopeless situation disgusted him, reminding him of how life could turn under the wrath of Central. It was his job, though. His job was all he knew. His job as elder was all he had. Cruelty was the only interpretation of the Process that made sense to him.

He stood. For no particular reason he put his foot on the back of her head and leaned, watching her squirm with her face smothered in the mud. He looked around, struck by the singularity of the moment, a simultaneous collision and collusion of past and present. Standing there in the muck outside the data vault was the final reality of the aspirations between him and John Westing. They shared a rash ambition of freedom by turning the dictates of Central upon itself, an escape conceived through the shadow of monstrous acts. It was the digital now, servant and master to the mutability and malleability of memory, that frail guardian between dream, reality, and nightmare—and the nightmares, how they mocked reality and its keepers.

He looked to the vault. The gunfire had stopped.

He took his foot off Sonya's head. Something was wrong.

|0|0|0|

CARLY WEDGED A CIVI-STICK INTO the lock release of the second stairwell. The stairs behind her were littered with the bloody bodies of Gadwick's patrolmen. She dropped her handgun clips for fresh ones, kicked aside a spent repeater, and walked through the aisles of drive racks to find the stairwell down to the maintenance room.

Her mind was blank. She couldn't hear, she couldn't think, and notions of identity or awareness held no purchase. There was nothing but rage within her, rage for the lies she had accepted with such carefree ease during her life, rage for the ways she'd been exploited, used, and abused. Killing Bayard was just the start. Instead of liberating her, her father's return had destroyed her. The name of Carly Westing was a forgotten thing. Names meant nothing, because names meant accepting her past.

In her detached madness she felt little care or affection for her father. In her state of mind he was just another strangling noose from her past. She would use him to destroy everything around her and, when she was done, she'd destroy him. Patrol, Seven Hills, elders, watchers, sleepers, predilectors—they were all part of Central, and she wouldn't rest, wouldn't accept her own dissolution until everything was left in charred ruin.

It was delusional; it was insane.

Why not? I shouldn't even be alive. My whole fucking existence is a crime.

The familiar sound of boots on stairs came to her. She raced down the twisting stairs past conduits of data pipes, cooling apparatus, and power machinery to near the maintenance room. As she cleared the last step she glimpsed a patrolman rounding the corner away from the stairs.

It was a bad angle. She fired several shots.

| 0 | 0 | 0 |

GRAHAM WINCED AS HIS ARMOR deflected two rounds from his back and shoulder. With his wounded leg he staggered and bounced off a wall as he tried to regain his balance. He moved to duck around a partition wall but was too slow.

A round passed under the end of his shoulder cowl and punched clean through his left bicep. Another round shattered against his neck cowl, the shrapnel slicing the back of his neck like hot razors. He made it behind the partition, only for a third round to blow through the flimsy partition and ricochet off his helmet. Stunned, he lost count of his clumsy steps. His helmet fell off his head, his repeater fell from his numb hands, and at last he fell headlong to the floor.

He looked up with a groan. He was sprawled past the partition, in the open. Stutts was a few paces away from him.

They gazed at each other. It was a surreal moment.

Westing stepped into view. Graham glared at him and struggled to get his right hand on his thigh mount. Before he could pull it free Westing stepped on his shoulder to pin him to the floor. Westing's arm slid from the folds of his long coat to reveal a handgun, which he waved to make his point.

Graham looked to Endo, but Endo rolled his eyes.

Westing smiled. "So nice of you to drop by, Elder." He looked over Graham's wounds. "I see you've been reacquainted with my daughter."

| C | 0 | 0 |

CARLY PACED ACROSS THE MAINTENANCE room until she stood before Graham, Endo and Westing. She came to a sudden stop, planted her feet at shoulder width, and raised her handguns. One found its aim on Endo, the other on Graham. She didn't look to Westing.

Westing stepped back, opening his hand to Endo and Graham. "See them, the mighty men they thought they were, now in ragged tatters at your feet. Do what you wish."

Carly's arms went rigid.

Graham rolled on his side to stare at her. "Carly, don't listen to him."

Endo held his silence.

Westing looked to Carly. "Any time now will be just fine."

Graham pushed himself up to sit beside Endo. "We came here to help you. Don't listen to this chigger.'

Endo coughed. "I once told you there would be a moment you'd have to face alone."

Westing shifted on his feet. He turned to Carly.

She fell back a step.

Endo clamped his good hand on Graham's shoulder. He struggled to push himself up, his bad leg dangling beneath him as he kept his shoulders to the wall. He met Carly's gaze as he held a handgun against his chest. "Remember what I told you. The cruelest lies are from those closest to our vulnerabilities."

Westing shook his head. "You're not vulnerable, Carly. All you have to do is finish them. You have to do this to teach Central that it can't hurt you."

Endo closed his eyes. "Your father abandoned you."

Westing raised his gun to Endo. "Central forced me away!"

Endo rested his head against the wall. "No, Carly, your father abandoned you. He was afraid of you, so he set you up. Gadwick sat by and let you get victimized. Your father needed that to happen so he could script the wipe-lock. He had to close your mind until he was ready to turn you against Central."

Westing fired a round through Endo's good shoulder.

Endo gasped. His fingers twitched, but he caught the handgun in his bloody clutch and managed to press the weapon to his chest once more. "I've watched you ever since then. You know I would never hurt you."

Westing turned on Carly. "Lies, lies, lies. Kill them—this is what you've waited for!"

Endo let his breath go. His eyelids rose enough for him to meet Carly's smoldering gaze.

"For you, Carly."

Graham reached out to stop Endo.

Endo clenched his teeth and extended his weapon hand.

Carly's eyes bulged. Her hands swung together to focus both guns on Endo.

Endo's arm straightened. The black hole of the barrel stared back at her.

She didn't know she pulled the triggers until the guns kicked her arms. A spent casing flew from each chamber. A little pop of light flashed from each barrel. Her shoulders tightened as the recoils collided around her heart.

The rounds punched two holes in Endo's chest.

His face went slack. He held still a moment before his face paled. His hands dropped as he slid down the wall to lie crumpled on the floor. A wide trail of blood smeared the wall behind him.

Her eyes swelled until she thought they would erupt from their sockets. She let her guns track Endo's fall to the floor.

Air filled her lungs.

Her heart beat.

There was a noise to her side. There was a shout, then two.

John Westing. *Kill the elder.*

A patrolman—more than a patrolman; someone who looked familiar. *Get some Heavy and watch Killshot.*

She blinked in confusion.

I killed Endo Stutts.

She stared at the Madman of MG42. How many times had she dreamed of him, had she fantasized of holding him? Instead, she had killed him.

Why did he want to kill me?

Her gaze fell on the handgun he had dropped. It took a moment to see through her daze. The handgun's slide was pulled back. The chamber was empty. The clip was missing.

He had pointed an empty gun.

He gave up his life—he gave up his life for her.

Awareness returned to her in a heartbeat. The data threads roared around her. She quaked at the enormity of Endo's sacrifice. She wanted to vomit in horror, she wanted to throw her guns away, she wanted to sink her hands into the merciless moments of time and claw them back until her fingernails tore loose, until her arms tore loose from her shoulders, until she watched the bullets spring from Endo and return to the chambers of her guns.

"Shoot him!"

Two blasts ripped through the vault above them. Patrol had blown the locks.

"Carly!"

She looked to the left. *Graham—good old Chap.*

No sooner did she look than Graham writhed on the floor as a bullet smashed into his chestplate. She spun toward the source of fire.

A man stood there. He was almost bald, yet an underlying vitality burned in his eyes. She knew the face. He looked like her brother, and he looked like her, but she had more of her mother's features.

Noel was dead.

She had her mother's eyes.

Her mother was dead.

The man stared at her. The lock of contempt on his face washed away to one of surprise before degenerating to disdain.

He opened a hand to her. "My dear Carly."

She snapped her arms around and opened fire. Westing got off one shot amid the hail of Carly's guns. The bullet's impact punched her shoulder. She held aim with her other arm, squeezing the trigger as fast as she could, watching round after round blow through Westing. He staggered back in a cloud of his own blood, shuddering as the last few rounds of Carly's clip slammed into him.

She tossed away the empty gun, picked up the gun she had dropped when Westing shot her, and paced toward him with determined steps. He dropped to the floor as blood streamed from his wounds. She stomped his chest to pin him to the wall before unloading the second gun into his head. His face was obliterated as his skull shattered to a ragged, pulpy mass.

So she stood, frozen, spent casings around her feet, her chest heaving, her leg splattered with blood.

Angry shouts sounded from the top of the stairs.

She turned.

Gadwick's patrolmen charged into the room as a boiling mass of repeaters and armor.

She stared at them, her face flushed with rage, her cheeks crimson beneath her blazing blue eyes. Her lips drew taught, quivering over clenched teeth. The patrolmen were ready to fire, to riddle her with repeater rounds the same way her mother was riddled with repeaters, but she refused to let that happen. The trace packets of the patrolmen blinked into view. Her rage washed through them. The numbers dialed in her perception until they synchronized.

She sucked in a breath and let it go as a scream. It wasn't just a physical burst of fury but one she let fly across the data threads as an undisciplined t-pulse. Graham cringed on the floor. Gadwick's patrolmen dropped as if they'd been shot, clutching their heads in agony.

Carly swayed on her feet. Her heart resumed its beat with a shudder, her pulse ringing in her ears. She clutched her arm, the wound at last registering with her senses. The patrolmen were forgotten as they struggled to gain their feet. Her mind raced, visions from her past careening through frenzied orbits and dizzying collisions as they sought to find their truths in their own temporal progression. Her mind craved a sense of order and sought to fill the uncertainties of the greater world with a cohesive interpretation of the chaos around her.

Bit by bit, thread by thread, moment by moment, it took form within her.

She looked down at the wounded patrolman at her feet.

Graham Chapel. That's it.

His hands sank from his head.

She looked to Endo.

Graham's eyes filled with alarm. "Be—behind—"

Carly turned. The patrolmen were on their feet. She straightened her stance, looked upon them, and stared them down. She found Gadwick's orders within them and overwrote his intentions.

They lowered their repeaters.

She looked over her shoulder to Graham. She fought to focus her memory, although she wasn't quite sure who she was in that moment. At long last her voice creaked to life.

"Good old Chap."

He looked up to her. "Get your drive," he said, his voice faint. He tipped his chin toward the stairs. "Gadwick. Get your drive and get out of here."

She stared at him for a moment until her eyes filled with rage once more. She glanced at Endo before facing the patrolmen in full.

They charged up the stairs.

|0|0|0|

GADWICK'S EARS PERKED UP as he heard the twin blasts to open the jammed locks. He shifted on his feet and went so far as to take several steps toward the vault until he retreated. His chin quivered with dismay as he came back toward Sonya.

He spun to call for help, but he was alone. The expanse of mud before the vault was littered with wrecked Patrol cars. Every patrolman with him had been dispatched to the vault. He looked to the threads. They departed his perception until he saw nothing but emptiness within and without.

He turned back to the vault. "No," he said in disbelief. "No, it can't, it can't be—"

For all his denial, for all his guile as an elder, he found himself at a total loss to seal his mind or steel his wits for the onslaught of animosity that rushed toward him. Thoughts swirled in his head—thoughts he knew were not his own. They were shadows of that dark past when he had convened with John Westing. They had bowed to the call of their inclinations, careless of the price a young girl would pay and pay yet again so they could have their way. Their aspirations had evaporated, though, lost in their self-turned interests to seize not only their freedom but also their revenge upon Central.

His heart pounded in his chest.

No—you should be dead! You're supposed to be dead—

He blinked and looked into the shadows within the vault's annex. Something stirred in the hidden darkness, a new shadow, summoned from the data threads themselves. A terrible rage hung about the shadow, a boiling black rage that threatened to destroy the intellect at its epicenter, trembling under the horror of its reality.

Carly stepped before the headlights of one of the cars. She formed a slender shadow, seeming fragile as she stood there clutching her arm.

Gadwick stared at Carly, his hands fidgeting behind his back as his eyes narrowed. Thoughts raced through his mind. They were broken one by one, smashed by the fury stampeding toward him. He knew there would be no speaking to her, no predilection to work upon her, no deception clever enough to snare her, no elusive talk of apples to befuddle her. Nevertheless he grinned, not out of humor for his plight, but for the futility of the energy pouring into her rage. It would be gone the moment she satisfied herself.

And what would become of her, in the wake of such an exorcism?

"Nothing," he said in the final exercise of his pride.

Her gaze bored into him.

He sucked in a breath as the shadow of her rage slammed into him.

The patrolmen fanned out from behind Carly. They raised their weapons to take aim at Gadwick.

He stared at them before his gaze settled on Carly. "Forgive and forget?"

The patrolmen fired as one, emptying their clips in a deafening hail of fire.

|0|0|0|

SONYA ONLY KNEW SHE WAS alive as her scream endured past the repeaters' collective roar. She quieted when her breath ran out, her cry alone in the silence around her. Her skin tingled with the fear of the hunted, the fear the prey knows of the predator, and she cowered in the cold mud. Her gaze slid to her side where Gadwick had stood. He was thrown back from her, sprawled in the mud, only the bottom of his boots showing in the lights of the cars. A shaky breath made its way through her nerves and into her lungs, her head turning as she heard a wet footfall beside her. She looked on the toes of booted feet—not the harsh, ugly boots of Patrol, but soft, low boots, boots of the fashion of Central, as she once wore.

She forced herself to swallow before looking up. There was nothing but a shadow in the glare of the headlights, yet she felt a gaze, and it held no threat to her.

A ragged breath rattled from Gadwick. One of his feet twitched.

The shadow standing over Sonya turned. The headlights revealed a civi-stick.

She watched as the slender silhouette paced toward Gadwick. It stood for a moment before poking the elder with the stick. He responded with a faint wheeze.

The civi-stick swung high before whistling down. It hit with a wet crack, only to whip up for another strike. Blow after blow slammed into the elder until Sonya heard nothing but the muffled pops of breaking bones. The assault ended with a gruesome crack that sent a shower of red droplets into the glare of the headlights.

Sonya could hear a pant of exertion. A moment passed, then two, before the stick was thrown into the darkness.

The shadow lingered a moment before turning and walking to one of Gadwick's cars. The lights went dark as the car rolled toward the city.

Sonya heard another noise closing in on them, a noise she hadn't heard in a long time. She twisted to look over Grendel's roof as the noise neared. It was a rapid, rhythmic thumping of air through the rainy night.

It was the sound of helicopters dispatched from Inward.

| 0 | 0 | 0 |

GRAHAM WOKE TO THE NOW familiar sound of boots stomping down the stairs. He cursed in futility and looked around for any defense until he remembered his thigh mount. After struggling to pull the gun free it slipped from his numb hand.

He rested his head back and looked toward the stairs. Several patrolmen were searching the room. They seemed to ignore Graham. He held still, wondering what to think of the situation when a lone man came down the stairs. He wore a simple gray bodysuit and was unarmed. Somehow, his hawkish face seemed familiar.

The man glanced at Endo's body.

Graham cleared his throat. "You're a predilector."

The man smiled. "A Sleeper." He looked toward Westing and nodded. "Good."

"Who are you?"

The man turned to Graham. "Does it matter?"

"I just want a straight answer. I think I've seen you before."

"Of course you have," the man said. He lifted his chin. "I am Desmond Asper."

"General Asper?"

"Sleeper Asper, actually. What you know is nothing more than a picture, a hidden tribute to my service. The war was my idea. It may not be real, but I am."

Graham coughed. "Right."

"A medical crew is coming for you."

Graham looked over the bodies strewn about the room. "What took you so long?"

"I happened to be on respite near Inward. Central called me to help, but it wasn't easy to get here. Gadwick sealed off Seven Hills and left it a mess. You have much work ahead of you, Elder."

Graham rolled his eyes. "No shit."

"Is she well?"

Graham studied Asper. "You can't see her?"

The Sleeper tipped his head.

Graham fumed. "Look, I've had enough bullshit piled on me, and enough fucking bullet holes put through me, to ask something that might sound stupid." He coughed. "She's Patrol. She'll be fine. And no, I don't know where she went."

"Just as well. When she's ready, we'll know," Asper said and turned.

"Hey," Graham said, stilling the man. "Is she going to be okay?"

The Sleeper gave Graham a curious look. He cupped his hands behind his back. "Carly, or Sonya?"

Graham blinked. After all of Mortas' games it was hard to expect a straight answer to anything. "You tell me."

"Intuitions and inclinations," the Sleeper said. "For all our philosophical dictums, for all that's happened here, for all the debates of self-predilection, there is only one underlying truth, Elder, and it's the very embodiment of elegant simplicity." He opened his hands. "You have what you wish to have. Nothing more, nothing less."

"No one can touch my memories now?"

The Sleeper stared at him for several moments before replying. "You have what you wish to have, Elder. The Dream can offer you nothing more."

Graham blew out a breath as the thought wound its way through his mind. "Right." He sighed with relief when a medical crew came down the stairs and gathered around him.

The Sleeper nodded with satisfaction. "Well, then. Goodbye, Elder."

Graham winced as his bodysuit was cut open. "Where are you going?"

The Sleeper let his gaze dart upward. He gave Graham a slight bow before he was lost behind the medics crowding around the new Elder of Seven Hills.

"Right," Graham said and passed out.

THE UNDERWORLD NEARED ITS USUAL frenzy as night waned and the new day neared, the members of Patrol lost in their drunken delirium of lust and clumsy aggression. They paid no notice as one figure strode between them, pressing through their tumult beneath the shadows of strobe lights, the deafening pound of MG42, and Endo's roaring vocals. The coated figure drifted by the bar, head lowered, holding one arm in a protective grasp. A secret doorway where the bar met the wall yielded to the figure's will. The darkness beyond enveloped the slender shadow before the door sealed and the passage was lost to forgetfulness.

Above the tumult, unknown and not wanting to be known, the figure paced across a well-furnished retreat to stand before a curved window wall. A reflection greeted the figure, the face of a woman, a woman she once knew, a woman she once knew and then forgot as herself.

She stood still, gazing into the murky depths of rain.

You are my sonnet.

She bowed her head and wept.

| 0 | 0 | 0 |

HER EYES OPENED TO THE distant rumble of thunder.

She put her hands on her face, recoiling somewhat at the salty residue of tears before wiping it away. Her slack face fixed on the window wall of Endo's retreat. It was another rainy day. Her stomach rumbled in pace with the storm, but she had no care for food. Despite the leaden weight of her limbs she rose to a shaky stance. The ache in her arm registered with as little impact as the rain pelting the windows.

Her chest expanded as she took a breath. Between the pull of her lungs and the pain of her wound the enclosure of her body lifted her awareness from the numbing whoosh of the data threads. She opened her eyes and looked into her diffuse reflection, dissecting and discarding the details of her reality. For some reason her focus sank to her hands where they dangled at her sides. She watched the slow waver of her fingers and fought to assimilate the image of her reflection with the sensation of muscles, ligaments, and tendons.

She was real. So too was the past, even as it lurked within her as an anarchic jumble of fractal images. Some of those images hit her with jolts of terror and disgust.

She pulled her fingers, pulled them as if her skin was a glove to imprison her.

| 0 | 0 | 0 |

SHE OPENED HER EYES TO stare at the hard tiles of the bathroom wall. Her body was cold and her arm hurt. Her mouth was dry, her eyes puffy. She glanced at the mirror across the bathroom from her and didn't like what she perceived. The waking thought that haunted her couldn't be true, she decided. In any temporal reference of past, present, or future, there was no possibility it could be true—yet her body would hold its own truth, as her arm held the truth of her father's death.

It took a great effort to push herself up with her legs, even with her shoulders sliding up the smooth tile wall. She kept her gaze on the reflection of her eyes, and forced herself to swallow as she unbuttoned the tailored coat of her violet suit. Her hands trembled, and she closed her eyes to concentrate, to hold to what she felt as an unnerving compulsion within her, a compulsion that repulsed her with its implications.

One by one she worked the coat's buttons, clenching her teeth as the coat slid across her wound. The silk shirt beneath was stained crimson down the length of her arm to her elbow, a neat tear in the supple material revealing a red gash in her skin. She shook her hands to get free of the coat and let it drop to the floor behind her. The shirt came free of her pants as she yanked at its length, and she kept at it until she had it bunched up in her hands. The smooth wall of her abdomen came into view. She put her head back against the tiles and prodded her belly with her fingers, working her way toward her waist.

At last she felt it, the remnant of an old scar to one side of her navel. Her trembling hands clenched to fists before she forced them open to feel along the other side of her navel. Another scar, identical to the first, waited for her probing fingers.

She was swept with nausea. "No, no, *no—*"

Her memories flashed as she turned and butted her forehead against the unforgiving tiles. She remembered something Gadwick said to her when she was hiding in the copse. Endo had repeated it in the vault.

Breeding program.

She staggered from the wall and recoiled when she grabbed the sink, not for the cold feel of the porcelain, but for the reminder of her skin, the skin that wrapped around her, that caged her in her body as a prisoner to herself. It was everywhere, the prison of her body, it was everywhere she darted as she spun on her feet in the bathroom, it was *inside* her as she felt her chest pull to suck in a breath, it was *on top* of her as she pulled at her hair. She screamed at the horror of herself, tearing at her clothes until she stood naked in the bathroom.

The shower spurted to life and rained hot water over her skin as she wept with her hysteria. She sank to a huddled mass, wailing without control between stuttering breaths. Ripped, raw, she had no place to hide. The flash of her memories came in a fury. There was no point in resisting them, no point in denying them, no time left for secrets. The past unwound within her, and she knit the fragments until she beheld a cohesive vision.

It wasn't just her past, but the past of Central itself.

They were, after all, inseparable.

| 0 | 0 | 0 |

It wasn't easy to put the pieces together in their proper way, but it was the only way to salvage a sense of her identity from the ruin threatening to engulf her.

She saw the birth of her father. He lived in the time just after the sun bombs. Artillery blazed and cities burned, yet something whispered among the cacophony of destruction. He was one of the few to recognize it as the waking voice of Central.

The planet was exhausted, its resources squandered. The only shot for survival was to go up-top, to move off Earth. What remained of the world was placed under strict control and rationed to a limited population. That's where Central, predilectors, and the first Sleepers came into play. From them the Dream emerged, and the Process would guarantee the execution of the plan.

Humankind had lived under a failed duality: to squander everything and swell humanity's numbers was justified, while the dire consequences of a populace bloated beyond all measure of constraint was equally defended. They were two wrongs that could never make a right, the essence of a Malthusian conundrum.

It was all about commodity pressure. The best resources had to be saved, including the best of humanity. It was a simple matter of quality control. The data networks were employed to enforce two states of existence: those of Central and those not of Central. All concepts of nationality, race, and gender were eliminated as causes of conflict and waste. Under Central, humankind would be of one mindset and one language. The old order of humanity was stripped away and a new one put in its place, created by Central as data pipes and wireless stations spread across the land to absorb the old population centers.

Sleepers controlled everything. They wanted to be selfless, but they were human. Carly's father was the first to give voice to the threat that Sleepers could bend the Process for their own benefit. The concept of self-predilection earned its name and its infamy. Under the name of Donald Stapleton her father had instigated the first wave of rogues, and they threatened to tear apart both the Dream and Central.

Endo formed the Watchers to maintain control. While he led a purge of rogues, he had also devised a new way to control humanity through the reach of entertainment vendors—the envens.

Carly's father survived by vowing to renew his commitment to the Dream. Sleepers were too rare to throw away, and the purge had wasted enough of them. He studied Central from top to bottom. He saw the hierarchy of predilectors in their various orders charged to follow the Dream. Beneath them resided the citizenry of Central, those who went through Rainbow Go and were wired via their transmitter probes to the data threads. Beside them were the cones, the remaining excess mass of humanity. Within those two subjugated pools ran a narrow line that shared one commonality, the potential to develop predilectors.

From that narrow line grew a new secret within Central. It would take the best genetic specimens and subjugate them in Patrol, while at the same time using Patrol to breed the best humanity. That plan was the breeding program. In fact, Patrol was created to answer Central's failure to engineer the predilectory gene base under lab conditions. Patrol members would be kept under surveillance, while the timeless mental oblivion of Central concealed their one purpose, to propagate. From them came the slender slice of predilectors to replenish the Sleepers and sustain the Dream.

Patrol members were scattered among residents of a city, their locales selected by Central, based on the genetic composition of neighboring individuals. Central waited and observed which neighbors a particular member of Patrol decided to entertain. Central also let members of Patrol find their companions of choice among their own ranks. Nature had opened an evolutionary possibility, but then Central looked to tip the scales of probability.

It made sense to Carly, because it fused and patched broken pieces of information she knew with things she had learned from Endo and Gadwick. Sterility outside of Central's intended children had long been the practice, enforced through the water supply of every city under Central. Raw material for reproduction came courtesy of Rainbow Go, with sperm and ova harvested at the same time transmitter probes were implanted in the young. Drive Control had its data vaults, while it was Sector Control that had reproductive vaults. Eggs were fertilized in the most secret labs of Sector Control and implanted in wipe carriers who knew nothing aside from the fact that they were pregnant. The newborns were delivered by supply side to charter parents as just another material need. The data drives of the designated parents were altered to accept those infants as their own until society assumed stewardship upon graduation from Rainbow Go to Teen-stomp.

Cones could breed like roaches, but the breeding program was the only source of children under Central. It was a sure way to reduce the population.

Carly thought of those messy domestic disturbance calls she knew from Patrol. They all made sudden sense to her.

Her father, as a Sleeper, had seen the same things. Maybe in his own disgust he came to see a different way, something more than charter parents and Rainbow Go. He wanted a life like people knew in the time before the sun bombs, a simple life with a woman and children at his side. It didn't seem to be a radical idea. Cones outside the reach of Central still lived that way, and humanity up-top had decided to go back to living that way.

Why should life under Central be any different? Was it still a necessity, to be so cold and brutal? Things had changed. After generations of hard work the lunar colonies of space-faring humanity had grown self-sufficient. The plan to move up-top had worked. Humanity was moving away from Earth. Humanity would survive.

The Dream's momentum raised doubt as to the future of Central. It was an odd moment for the Sleepers to understand. They were responsible for the Dream, but the irony of the Dream was that its continued success necessitated its eventual dissolution. In the end, success would preclude necessity, and Central would disappear as a vague memory.

It wasn't hard for Carly to imagine the thoughts that had run through her father's head. Vain and selfish in his age, with mortality a looming threat, he had looked to the distant future and pictured a time when his efforts to support the Dream were erased, like any other secret under Central. He saw himself as a lonesome man, his sacrifices forgotten, his life stripped of any purpose without Central and the Dream.

It was a seductive, insidious, gangrenous thought. Carly knew if Patrol had been pulled out from under her in the old days she would've felt lost. It was all she knew.

What do you do, when you give everything to the world, and the world gives you nothing but a shrug in reply?

She understood the rage, the sense of betrayal, because she had felt it in the vault. It was a different betrayal, but she saw through her outrage to understand what Central was revealing to her. Her father thought he was losing everything he knew, so he turned to have something else, something he believed Central couldn't erase. In the midst of those desperate thoughts he decided he would enrich the world with the desire of a man to love a woman. It was the start of an elaborate act of self-predilection. The best lies always seem the most grounded truths.

Time passed. Generations lived and died. Memories of his role in the revelation of self-predilection faded, eroded by the Dream to insulate Sleepers from the reality of the Process. In those narrow lanes of forgetfulness he found his mark in Seven Hills. He also sensed an inclination to rebel against Central in the city's elder, Ian Gadwick. He whispered to Gadwick through the data threads as the elder slept, and soon had a willing ally.

A plan is an image, abstract and harmless, until it transcribes itself to reality.

Despite the cliché of common wisdom, dreams are not bullshit.

Carly bucked at the immediacy of the images she saw in the data threads, reflections of her own clouded memories, but she held fast. She let her perception drift toward her childhood. She had to, although she wasn't sure she was ready to face it in full after the past had almost destroyed her in the data vault.

Carly's father had descended from the Dream in the guise of John Westing. He focused on his target, a member of Patrol by the name of Rebecca Westing. Carly's father had convinced Gadwick to separate

Rebecca from the breeding program. It took time, but with Gadwick's help Westing created two children with Rebecca. Noel came first, followed five years later by Carly. He then accomplished what no Sleeper had ever dared—he took his children to a vacant domicile in Rebecca's neighborhood in Cheshire quad. He intended to raise Noel and Carly as their father with Rebecca as their mother, regardless of her being a member of Patrol. The Dream convulsed around him, around the city itself, and the Sleepers were jarred.

Nevertheless, the Dream and the Process were satisfied as his children grew and displayed remarkable potential for attaining unprecedented predilectory abilities. Westing had his family, yet his family had no place in the society Central had created. They were outcasts in a world of uniformity. Noel grew deaf to the data threads. By the time he was fourteen he had already drowned his youthful isolation in the sterile sensuality of the sex dens. Carly withdrew, withdrew her thoughts so that even her father couldn't glimpse them. He couldn't control her, just as Endo had said.

The experiment had been a disaster. John Westing sought to undermine Central through the very act of creating his family. Instead, his failure served to reaffirm Central's practices. There was no space for his family, but there was ample space for irony.

That's when the darkness settled over Carly's life.

Her father met with Gadwick and used the elder's desire to be free of Central's dictates to escape the situation. Westing scripted his identity as a cone to drive a wedge between him and his children. Rebecca took more and more to drink, incapable of adjusting to the situation. Arguments became common, followed by escalating beatings. Noel ran off to the sex dens at any opportunity. Carly took to disappearing from the domicile by wandering off to the copse outside their quad. She was a serious problem. Gadwick wanted her dead, along with everyone else, but Westing had an idea.

Carly's predilectory skills, undisciplined and unrefined, lapped across the data threads. The predilection, lacking focus, had the effect of exciting whatever budding inclinations resided in the minds around her. It manifested as a perverted inversion of a temporal pulse. For the boys who already taunted her as the strange girl in their midst, the inclination lit within them was one of Nature's urges, one encouraged by Central. After all, they were taught it was free and right proper. Westing knew many of those boys were Carly's half brothers through her mother, produced before Gadwick had Rebecca removed from the breeding program. The situation could erupt into mass incest. It was sure to draw the attention of the Watchers.

Westing planned to desert his family. In his mind, they devolved to mere objects of his inclinations; they were reduced to the nothingness of material possessions. Despite his plans with Gadwick to deal with Carly he set a second plan in motion, probing the depths of Sector Control in the City of Seven Hills for a suitable wipe to be a vessel for Sonya. Soon enough he discovered a young woman of mild predilectory skill who had just started her scriptor training. The crime that led her to be wiped was irrelevant to him, but her availability was undeniable. He would later use her as his cover to explain his whereabouts during his respite.

With his parting words he told Carly to seek him in the copse when she felt most alone. He knew the boys of the neighborhood—her half-brothers—had watched her strolls in the dark depths of those woods. He left, and waited.

Carly wandered off to the copse one night, sore from another beating at the hands of her drunken mother. The boys were waiting in a shadowy grove of apple trees. She went to find the promised embrace of her father's angels only to be tackled, beaten, and violated, her pleas and screams met with laughter and fists. It seemed an eternity of violation collapsed to a blackened singularity of anguish.

She staggered home when they were done with her. It wasn't just an assault, it was obliteration, and the devastation left an open avenue for Westing to script a wipe-lock deep in her psyche. *Across a green field, a stand of trees.* It wasn't just a locked door to her memories of being brutalized; it was a locked door to secure her predilectory potential. The two had become entwined, just as he wished.

Ignorant of what had happened in her youthful naiveté, she also failed to see how she mocked her own innocence with tearful pleas for her father's return after the attack. Noel heard her and told their mother. Rebecca Westing knew that some of the boys were products of the breeding program. Westing couldn't hide that from her when he took her as his wife. Despite the drink and daze of Patrol, she decided she had only two children, the two who lived with her.

Rebecca was a dissolute drunk, a patrolman given nothing to prepare her for motherhood. She was deceived, seduced, and betrayed by Westing. Ill-equipped to handle emotions she couldn't understand, she vented them in violence against her children. Yet, when it came down to it, Carly saw now that her mother was the only one who had tried to find some justice for her.

Rebecca waited until the boys gathered at the end of the street. She took her last drink and stared at her daughter. She took her repeater and massacred those boys. When Patrol came there wasn't a beating, an arrest, or detention. Their response was simple.

Rebecca Westing met her end in a storm of bullets.

Noel was sent for discipline and schooling with Drive Control. Even though Carly was considered a failure, the breeding program saw potential. The breeding program was the focus of everything, after all. It was inseparable from Central and the Dream and, at the same time, it was inseparable from the growing alienation of the space-faring humanity up-top who had abandoned its practice.

Nevertheless, Central had made its choice long ago. The program would continue.

Just another day.

Carly's father slipped away. He used the institution of anonymity among Sleepers on respite to hide his crimes. He returned to the Dream and was complimented when he unveiled Sonya Mortas, the most convincing personality construct every scripted to a wipe. Though the Sleepers rejoiced they kept Sonya's nature a close-guarded secret, fearing what it might imply about the rest of humanity under Central.

At the same time Carly's father joined the cries of condemnation against John Westing—against himself, in truth. Hypocrisy became his convenient shield. Central demanded Westing's life for his perversion of the breeding program but, without capturing and questioning him, the true extent of his role—or Gadwick's, for that matter—was impossible to determine. For his part, Gadwick skewed every implication of guilt toward Westing. After much deliberation it was decided to leave Gadwick in place. There was enough mess to bury without deposing a city elder.

And so, life in the City of Seven Hills went on.

When Carly's father was ready he petitioned for retirement. He was reminded of the old tradition. He had to find a replacement for himself to secure his retirement.

It was a moment he long anticipated. He stirred the riots in Kilby. He predilected Gadwick to believe the riots were a work of Seven Hills, predilected Controller Henshaw to call in sick, and predilected Noel's every thought and action. Westing manipulated Sonya and Gadwick, Endo and the city at large, all for one end, embodied by one person.

Carly Westing.

He would seize her, fill her with lies, pervert her mind to rebel against Central, pop her wipe-lock, and then turn her loose on the Dream so she could destroy it from within.

She would be his final rebellious statement to Central.

I will have my way.

I will, by my will.

So many secrets, so many lies. Carly had almost lost herself in the knots of her father's madness. It was easier to blame everyone and everything than to blame her own father, that father who had lived in her memories as someone far different than the reality. But she knew as well that the lies which hid the most hurt were also the most deceptive—the more poisonous the delusion, the sweeter its illusion.

What did Endo say?

The cruelest lies are from those closest to our vulnerabilities.

Endo had tried to help her in that moment, but she had been lost. The past, like delusions of truth and deception, was an image, yet within every image there lurks an indelible truth.

Endo didn't see all of it, but she realized now that he saw enough. He could've killed her at any time. In many ways it would've been a simpler solution than what followed in the vault. When it came to the harsh demand of that singular moment when her sanity hung in the balance, though, he made his decision as well.

For you, Carly.

Her father was a monster, yet he lived within a reality Central had fostered. Trying to see between them was like trying to see between two shades of darkness. In the end, though, when her father sought to use her as a suicide stealth bomb against Central, it was Endo—Endo Stutts, the Watcher, the founder of the envens, the Madman of MG42, her beautiful bad-ass, the guardian of Sleepers—who chose to save her.

You are my sonnet.

He once told her he would give up his life for her. He had kept his word.

|0|0|0|

CARLY OPENED HER EYES. SHE reached up to turn off the shower faucets. Her skin was wrinkled, her body shivering from the hours she had been huddled under the running water. In the muddled mess of her mind she crawled from the shower, neglected to dry her body, and shuffled from the bathroom. She came to a sudden stop in the hall leading to Endo's bed, turning to face the shelves of Endo's books. Her gaze fell on one particular volume, lingering a moment before she plodded to his bed and sat on the edge.

She closed her eyes. Water dripped from the ball of her nose. In the darkness within her mind she perceived her hands. She opened her eyes to stare into her palms.

Still here. Still trapped in here.

She slumped back, burying her face in the soft depth of Endo's pillow. She could smell him, and her arms circled the pillow to draw it to her chest.

Still there, but not trapped in there.

Her body dissolved to a flaccid lump as she struggled to comprehend the long flash of memories that had ripped through her. She could see her life as it was, but she had no emotion left to spend on those memories. The seething rage, the weeping hysteria, the nauseous disgust, they all felt part of something else, something alien to her. It was just another story, just another part of the Process, just another day.

Her eyes slid shut.

I don't want to do this anymore, this life. I want to dream of something else, something far, far away.

| 0 | 0 | 0 |

"She has a fever."

A hand came down on her shoulder followed by a woman's voice near her ear. "It's infected."

The hand left her and was replaced by a shift of her body as a mass settled on the bed beside her. Another hand came to rest on her temple and push her hair back. Her eyes opened, her gaze sliding past the oozing red mess of her upper arm to see a man sitting beside her. His arm was in a sling and a cane was clamped between his knees. His other hand lay on her head, stroking her hair.

"Carly," he said, his lips pulling to a pained smile. "It's me, it's Graham."

She mumbled his name. Her memory began to flash and she forced her eyes open to stare at him. "Why'd you take those bullets? You could've shot me."

"I made you a promise." He set his hand on his leg. "I kept my promise."

A slender woman in a tailored dark green suit came up behind him, her black hair pulled back in a loose bun. She pushed her glasses up her nose and gestured toward Carly with the small bag in her other hand. "Excuse me, Elder."

Graham blinked and looked away. "Ah, Sonya, yes," he said, grunting as he took his cane in hand and pushed himself up.

Sonya took Graham's place on the bed and leaned toward Carly's face to get her attention. "Forgive me, Predilector, but it may be uncomfortable while I clean your wound."

Carly stared at her, finding it hard to connect her with the desperate woman pinned under the smoking hull of a Patrol car. She understood as she heard the data threads whispering around Sonya. Carly's gaze darted about until she found Graham leaning against the wall.

He smiled. "I kept all my promises."

| 0 | 0 | 0 |

THE RETREAT WAS DARK BENEATH another rainy night. She rolled onto her back and rested in bed for some time, blinking away her dreams and the locator packets she perceived of the high humanity in the unseen sky above her. She put a hand over her face as she worked the fingers of her other hand. The wound felt tight, but she realized it was the bandage Sonya had fixed over her arm. With some effort she pushed herself up from the bed and tugged a blanket about her body, just as she had in her time with Endo. It felt like several lifetimes ago.

She clutched the blanket, paced out to the window wall, and stopped by one of the couches. Graham was sound asleep, his leg stretched out beside him. Time faded as she stared at him. He wasn't the man she used to know, but then she wasn't at all the woman she used to know. Everything she perceived told her Carly Westing and Graham Chapel were no more, lost with as much finality as the moments in which they had existed. Now there was only the Elder of Seven Hills, and—

She frowned, not sure how to complete the thought.

She bit her lower lip as she considered the expense incurred to afford her the opportunity to conceive the question of her present disposition. Endo had bought it with his life; Graham had bought it with the quiet tenacity that rested just below his surface. The burden, the answer to her thought, was hers to decide, hers to decide on her own, as she chose.

There would be no voice of Central to guide her, no wisdom of the Process or the Dream to advise her. It was the price and paradox of freedom, because having the ability to decide meant she would be constrained to a decision.

Yet, in the end, she came back to where her thoughts had started. Were it not for Graham and Endo, she would be the slave of her father's lies. With their pain and blood they had gifted her with the reality of her memories, to see and judge as she saw fit.

Her life was hers. She closed her eyes and whispered her thanks.

Despite her gratitude—or, perhaps due to its very presence within her—she felt troubled. She looked down at Graham, quiet in his sleep. For all that she treasured him in that moment, she still longed for someone else. Within that seeming contradiction she understood the source of her estrangement from Graham.

Endo.

She wasn't sure why, but she looked to the roof and peered through the glass panels to the unseen humanity above her. *Endo? Can you hear me? Is there something left of you out there, some waking memory of you left in the data threads?*

Her only answer was the lonesome patter of rain.

| 0 | 0 | 0 |

HER SENSES RETREATED FROM THE data threads to find herself sitting at a table with Graham. Sonya was pacing between the table and Endo's kitchen as she served them breakfast.

Carly put a hand on her arm as she blinked away her disorientation, her memory flashing her back to the present in a fast-forward stutter of the last few days. There was the coming and going of Graham, his cane remaining but the thick bandages beneath his clothes shed. Her arm had healed with remarkable speed, and she remembered Sonya's frequent visits to tend her wound. The medicines in Sonya's bag were like nothing Carly knew. There were palliatives that erased the annoyance of her wound but left her senses intact, and barrages of various pills that made the wound knit almost before her eyes. When Carly asked, Sonya grinned and reminded her that there were capacities within Central reserved for only the most important of its subjects. It was part of Central's scheme to reserve its best offerings for the best of its number.

Carly looked down at her cup as she gave the steaming tea a lazy stir. Her perception panned across her and Graham to watch Sonya set the table. There came a plate of hot biscuits, cold butter on a serving plate with a silver butter knife, a plate of hot, sliced meat that she had to cull the data threads to name as bacon and, for Graham, a bowl of Shaky Flakes with a glass of milk.

She watched Sonya's fingers trail across Graham's shoulder as Sonya withdrew to the kitchen. It was one of those little gestures that Carly realized was part of the subtext of human interaction hidden under Central. She looked to Graham as Sonya's four-fingered hand slid away from his shoulder. He gave her a slight tip of his head, a faint grin, and spoke a silent 'thank you.'

Carly stirred her tea as she waited for Graham to meet her gaze. When he did his face went blank, but then he offered a small shrug.

Sonya was busy cleaning the kitchen. "Does she know?" Carly whispered as she reached for a biscuit.

"On some level, I'm sure," whispered Graham in turn.

Carly's gaze fell to her biscuit as she pulled it open. "So, what does she know?"

"She was upset about your brother. There was no denying his involvement with her and his death in the subsequent cover story." Graham held up a finger as he grasped the true aim of Carly's question. "She chose freely to have this identity. She has nothing else. She made her choice, so she's like the rest of us now. She has what she chose to have, nothing more, and nothing less," he said with certainty and tapped a finger on the table.

"Right. With you," Carly said as she buttered her biscuit.

She frowned when she heard herself.

Sonya came back from the kitchen and reached between them to take a biscuit. She bit into it as she swirled a cup of tea in her other hand. After she swallowed she looked down to Graham and rested her hand with the biscuit on his shoulder. A sheer, fingerless tan glove covered her four-fingered hand. "The second phase of data vault repairs are complete. Phase three is on schedule. Drive Control is almost done re-scripting all the broken threads. I finished the rest of those traces you asked me to run. We have a full list of the rogue's infiltration to Drive Control. Sector picked them up during the night. Interrogation should be finished by this evening."

Graham nodded before patting Sonya's hand. "Good. Then it's all done." His eyebrows rose as he remembered something. "I'd like you to go back to Drive Control and contact Inward. Let them know that the High Predilector Carly Westing is ready for transport."

Carly looked up from her biscuit, her eyes narrowing on Graham.

He lifted his hand for her to wait until Sonya left the retreat. Only then did he rest his hand on the table. "Carly, I—"

"Packing me away, are you?" No sooner had the words left her than she put a hand over her mouth, her cheeks reddening in shame. She drew in a breath and put her face in her hands, humiliated by her pettiness. Her eyes squeezed shut. "I'm sorry. I don't know why I said that."

Graham leaned toward her. "Look at me."

She sucked in another breath and held it, not letting it go until she parted her fingers enough to peer at him.

"Carly," he said, but then reconsidered. When he spoke, his voice was soft with sentiment. "I'm not packing you away. There's something you need to understand, something you're yet to see within yourself because you had a rough time of it with Westing. I'm surprised we're even having this talk, because I thought it would take you much longer to sort yourself out. But we're Patrol, and we don't go lightly, right?"

"Right proper," she said, her words muffled by her hands.

He pointed between them. "We had something, you and I, in the old lives we knew. Those lives, they're not ours anymore. Our names haven't changed, but they might as well have, because we've changed. Something remains of that other time, images of memories, of a life lost but not forgotten. We can't touch it, but it was real. You were right all along about the past, but maybe not in the way you think. You see, I still think of those memories. They're more like a story I was told, but it's a story some empty space in me wants to hear. We lived it, but we're strangers to it now. It's only real—it only lives—because it's part of us." He nodded. "That's why I need Sonya. She reminds me of that, that dreams and images can be just as real as we wish them to be."

Her eyebrows rose. "I told you dreams are not bullshit."

"I know." He tipped his head. "I had to learn that the hard way."

"I think we're all learning that the hard way."

He settled back in his seat but kept his gaze on her. "I'm not packing you away," he said again with a shake of his head, "but you can't remain here. The role of elder is mine to fill. I knew that walking into the data vault, and I know that now because I still prefer Shaky Flakes to buttered biscuits. I'm still part of this life, the life of a city named Seven Hills on the outer edge of Central's reach. I'm at peace with the role of Patrol, with my role here, with the things that need to be done, as ugly as some of them need to be. I'm a predilector, but my way is to pursue the Process, the machine of society, while yours is to pursue the Dream. You've been cut off from your life in this place. You know that, and I think Endo knew that the moment he had some time with you. You didn't blink at his life, the clothes he kept here for Sonya, the food of Central across the wide ocean, the furnishings of things as they could be if we follow Central, if we do the tough things we need to do."

She closed her eyes as memories of her past flashed through her again, searing her senses. Tears eked from her eyes as she fought to silence the nightmares, but she couldn't deny Graham's words.

Graham leaned forward and put a hand on her shoulder. "I promised I would do anything for you. That promise stands. Seven Hills is dead for you, but it's a lesson you can bring to the Dream to shift its course, and through that you can heal yourself so that others can know the folly of self-predilection. You might not understand those things yet, but the Dream does. We're going to change things, Carly. Bastards like Gadwick and your father are finished. You're a media superstar now, right up with

Endo, only the second predilector in the history of Central to be deemed so worthy to be personified within the data threads."

He let go of her shoulder to take one of her hands and mesh his fingers with hers. She lowered her head, turning away from him to hide her face with her other hand. "Easy," he said, squeezing her hand.

The data threads exposed their minds. He shuddered with empathy as the raw wounds within her burst into his perception. She knew he wanted to hold and protect her, and she knew as well she would welcome good old Chap. As the thoughts ran within him she turned to him and clutched his hand to her chest. The selfishness of his inclinations called to him but he fought against himself, knowing with painful clarity the ruin that could bring upon them both. They both understood in that moment the slippery slope of her father's demise. Nevertheless, Graham pulled her close, held her, and rubbed her back.

"Easy," he said again, closing his eyes. "Carly, listen to me. I know some of this pain you feel, but it won't be yours alone to carry. You have to remember what I told you, that the Dream is now your deliverance from your past, the adjustment of the Process is your healing, and you will not be alone. It won't be me, it can't be me, but you will not be alone."

She drew a stuttering breath. "I killed Endo. He let me, to save me from myself."

Graham ignored her, clenching his teeth to keep focus. "Someone came to me when I was laying in the data vault after you left. He was a Sleeper dispatched by Central. He didn't say much, but he told me something I'll never forget." He took a breath. "You have what you wish to have, nothing more, nothing less," he said, easing her away so that he could meet her gaze.

Her eyes opened. She sniffed as she let go of his hand to rest a finger over his lips. She looked into his eyes, looked into him with the extent of her abilities, and found those places within him he described left open for her to see, and she saw there as well the truth of his words. Her sadness transfigured, passing from notions of loss to notions of remembrance, and she gave it up to the data threads. She withdrew from him, gazing over the shoulder of her perceptions in sentiment for what she was leaving behind, yet the lament was quieted knowing it had to be so, that it could only be so.

With that, she kissed him. It was the last lingering contact for which they both yearned, dissolving their intimacy in a final embrace.

And then she was gone.

Graham opened his eyes, startled to find himself alone. "Carly?"

There was no answer.

He looked about the retreat until he shook his head. He pushed himself up from the table, limped to the window wall, and looked out in time to see a pair of headlights emerge from the distant mouth of the Underworld's basement tunnel. With a frown he leaned on his cane and nodded. Chances were he would never see her again.

He summoned his voice to spend one last whisper.

"Goodbye, Carly Westing."

| 0 | 0 | 0 |

THE CITY WENT BY CARLY as it had in the past, and yet as it never had in the past. She looked out the windows of Endo's black sedan and saw the city beyond its neon window fronts, sex dens, and ever-present screens of corner net kiosks. Instead, she saw the city for its waypoints in her life.

Over there, my first call with Patrol. Down that street, where I met Graham, riding with Gwen. She was fresh out of Teen-stomp, just like me. Over that hill, where Oboe introduced me to the finer points of street soup. Beyond that apartment row to the green under an evening sun, where I had my first meal of compress sandwiches and Graham showed me his trick of through filtration.

They were her memories, her life, but they held little sway in her. The disembodiment she felt after her flash of memories revealed the truth of her father and her own childhood. Reconsidering them as she drove, she felt no backlash of hysterical shock, not even the desperate pangs she suffered as she parted from Graham. No, there was only peace within her. This was the City of Seven Hills, a rough place of rough lives, and she was just one of those lives. Yet, even so, there was something of the place that would hold her in its embrace, that would forever know her existence there, on those streets, in those buildings, in that swarm of people living under Central, and it wouldn't come in the posters of her as Endo's equal in Central's pantheon or in the new shirts marketed on the envens—blue, with her name emblazoned in white letters. No, it would come as something else, something perhaps more tenuous yet more lasting, something more concrete.

She drove the streets of the city and rode its hills, glancing toward the direction of the unseen Downlow and the hidden data vault. The quads as well whispered as they passed, but soon those whispers were hushed within her as a greater calling drew her forward, drew her like expanding gas into greedy vacuum to fill its cold emptiness with her living warmth.

The unnamed streets and the borderless borders of the quads fell behind her until she entered Danfield quad. Her face settled to a cool mask, her emotions so remote they were betrayed only by the immediate vulnerability in her gaze. The buildings were reflected on her eyes, curved and reflected on her irises as her mind rejected their intrusion, sought not their call, even as her hands guided the car to the one place she knew she must see to settle herself.

The sedan rolled to a halt before a quiet Danfield apartment row in the late afternoon. She sat there for some time before she opened the car door. Her tailored suit and long coat were very much out of place in the workaday sensibility of the row, so she closed her abilities about herself and paced down the street. With her face nestled in the upturned collar of her black coat she failed to draw a second look.

She knew the people around her—they were her people, after all, or so the breeding program had decided. Even if they recalled her face they would only qualify her as something out of place in their row, and the way of the predilection to drive the sight from their perception was one of surpassing ease. At once surrounded and sundered in the illusion of herself, she walked into her old building, took the stairs up to her floor, and walked to her old domicile.

After a moment's hesitation she opened the door to peer in at the

smallness of her former life. The domicile was impossible in its confinement, delirious in its constraint. She looked with disbelieving eyes at
the way she had lived. Despite her absence of several days the domicile
was still a disheveled mess of a cramped little life. No, the person who
lived in that tiny room was gone. With her passing all the baggage of
her memories also passed. It was her old self that was the victim of lies,
who was deceived and despoiled; her childhood that had been contrived
and corrupted, her innocence that had been ridiculed and raped. It was
that old person who thought a somewhat less claustrophobic domicile in
Cheshire quad was a noble aspiration, that to get blind drunk and vent
her misguided lust with Graham were noble inclinations.

Even so, she didn't hate that person. Despite her efforts it was impossible to realize that old person as anyone else but herself. In that she saw
some wisdom of the Dream at work on her, some good salvaged from
her father's sins. She, as a Sleeper, and one who was a victim of another
Sleeper's self-predilection—indeed, a product of that victimization—
would stand as the Watcher of Watchers of the Dream itself, and her
place would be like none before her.

Her focus drifted to her old net screen. She watched the endless
images flashing on the display and listened to the mind numbing chatter
of the enven as it followed the gritty task of instilling the will of the
Process. There were images of Endo at regular intervals and, keeping
pace, her image as the defiant figure of Patrol, caught on riot night before
she went to Endo.

*And on it goes. The Dream is aware of me, aware of me but none of the
other Sleepers, and I haven't even joined them yet. It won't be mine, but in my
own way, it most certainly will be mine. They want me to change everything—
they're waiting for me to change everything—and so I will.*

She gazed at her old window wall and remembered how she thought
of the city as hers. It was an inverted echo, a backward trace of what was
to come for her, an intuition beyond her comprehension, until it had
achieved realization.

There was time for one last look at the room before she pulled the
door shut. Her hand lingered on the doorknob after the lock clicked.

Someone would replace her in that room, some young woman graduated from Rainbow Go and Teen-stomp into Patrol to be an unknowing part of the breeding program.

Her mind sparked as a set of truck brakes squealed below. She hurried through the hall, down to the street, and toward the corner where the afternoon bus of Rainbow Go had arrived. Ignoring the rain, she stopped short in the middle of the street as the doors of the yellow bus opened. They came down, the children of Danfield row, clad in their bright slickers like little glimmers of light in all the gray wash of the city. She met their blue-eyed gazes, stared at their faces, and her emotions unraveled for the final time as she watched them come out—no longer just children but *her* children, her sons and daughters.

In that moment she learned something she thought she had known with Graham and Endo, which she now realized had been just the beginning. It was what pulled her to the Dream. It stirred within her veins, seared her innards with its warmth, for it was love—love that overwhelmed comprehension by the innermost hidden whispers of her being.

Transfixed, her tears welling up, she didn't know what to do as her children glanced at her. She drew in a ragged breath and wiped her tears away to smile on them and wave. It was a simple lift of her open hand, something she'd done so many mornings waiting for Graham, without ever knowing what it meant or what summoned the gesture.

The children looked back at her. In some way they recognized her, but in another they did not, and in that there was a sudden comfort within them as they saw in her eyes something they hadn't seen before, and something their conscious minds were yet to comprehend.

They saw an odd woman standing in the rain.

One by one they returned her wave.

"ARE YOU READY?"

Carly turned from the window wall of Endo's retreat to find Sonya standing behind her.

"Elder Chapel sent me. If you're ready, they're waiting for you at Inward. I'll drive you."

Carly turned back to the window wall. She hesitated a moment before drawing her coat closed. "Then let's go."

| 0 | 0 | 0 |

THE RIDE TO INWARD WAS long and quiet. Sonya kept her gaze ahead as the sedan provided a smooth ride over the long, straight road. Carly stared out the side window to the rolling hills of turf. They seemed to stretch without end to the gray horizon of another rainy day, yet she had learned the turf wasn't endless. She gleaned the secrets of her location from the data threads and learned just how small an area formed her old concept of the world. In generations lost, before the sun bombs, the place—an island—was known as England, and the Downlow south of Seven Hills had once been a magnificent city, a city that spanned many memories and generations of humanity until it was obliterated and buried in one screaming horror. That city had been known by a name other than Seven Hills; in its time, it was London. Although Seven Hills took its name from the seven mounds that formed its topography, she discovered the name had much deeper roots in human history. Its lineage traced back to another great city that had collapsed in its time, a place once known as Rome.

They were facts of passing interest to her. The location of Seven Hills held no particular significance, the only reminder of its past the faint lilt she recognized in her own voice. In the scope of the Dream it mattered little more than just another fractured piece of the past. She frowned and rested a hand on the little bulge in her coat where she had tucked her data drive.

Livestock grazed on the passing fields along the road. They roamed free, simple animals that chewed the turf with absent-minded bovine passivity, obedient to the unknown cause of converting turf to their own biomass for human consumption. They were small things that added to a much greater whole, one beyond anything they could conceive, even as it meant their ultimate consumption. In the meantime they lived a carefree existence, their ignorance a soothing escape.

Carly wondered if they knew they were free or not, or if they cared about freedom, or if not caring about freedom was freedom in itself. It fascinated her, so much so that she found herself voicing her train of thought to Sonya. When she received no reply she turned to find a curious grin on Sonya's face.

Sonya glanced to either side of the road. "The graze herds, they interest you?"

"There's something about them, don't you think?"

"Forgive me, but I'm not a high predilector. I don't have your sight. How would you describe it?"

Carly hesitated a moment. A thought tingled across the inside of her skull, and she couldn't be sure if it was a flash from the data threads or a flash from her subconscious musing, reflected off the data threads back to her conscious mind. She blinked as she considered the regressive loop of that paradox but, in the end, she licked her lips and let the words within her gain voice. "Come sun, come rain, come howling tempest winds, the herds will graze as they must, complacent and serene in the wisdom of their humility."

Sonya raised an eyebrow. "Interesting. You see it as Endo sees it."

"Saw it," Carly corrected.

Sonya tipped her head. "As you wish, Predilector."

It took a moment for Carly to digest the inference. She looked to Sonya.

The car sped down the road.

| 0 | 0 | 0 |

By nightfall they reached the outer ring of Inward's defensive arrays, and the structures drew a curious glance from Carly. It was part of the illusion of war, but the extent of the illusion didn't fail to surprise her, even if the illusion of reality was reality within the Dream. Though she perceived an undeniable degradation of the human experience through the life Central propagated, she had come to understand the reasons for it. Central wasn't for the individual; Central was for the mass, much as evolution had concerned itself with the individual only in the individual's ability to propagate the mass.

She tried to comprehend the audacity of any attempt to outguess Central. It left her with no other conclusion than to see the path of a rogue as one of madness and destruction. For a single intellect to think its inclinations could rise above the intuitions of so many other Sleepers forming the Dream required the implosive, illogical conclusion that a part of the whole could somehow be greater than the whole. To resist the Process and its resources was a fool's quest. No, the only path to change was to work from within the Dream, behold it, embrace it, become part of it, and so lend private inclinations and intuitions as a steering current.

Her father was so close, yet so far, to a revelation on that count. It pained her to accept the admission, yet it was also folly to ignore its presence.

The sedan came to a halt beneath one of the skyscraping towers of the airship docks. Carly looked up in wonder at the height of the glittering city, the sight surpassing what she had perceived of its nature from the data threads. She stood dumbstruck until Sonya hooked her hand through Carly's arm and led her into the tower. Carly stopped short in the lobby, frozen with trepidation as she looked over a waiting throng of controllers and scriptors. They nodded to her with respect as they addressed her as High Predilector or Sleeper, and it served to remind Carly how rare a thing she was—a specimen of surpassing value. She checked her pride at the greeting she received; she found it odd that so many would bow their heads to her, she who just a short time prior was nothing more than another mutton-headed, drunken member of Patrol.

Ah, Carly, but this is how it's done, how it is always done.

She blinked through the delirium of her arrival as the thought reached up to her from the data threads. Sonya led her to an elevator as the crowd parted around them. Carly grew self conscious under so many watching eyes and sighed with relief when the elevator doors closed to leave her and Sonya in silence. They rocketed upward to the tower's docking fingers as Carly held to the echo of the thought that had reached her.

Only her stubborn disbelief held her from acceptance.

"Don't forget the wipes," Sonya said, breaking the silence as the elevator began to slow. "They're the wellspring for those who gave themselves over in full to the Dream by abandoning their bodies. The tactile world still calls them. They always yearn for it, and when they are driven from it to reside in the Dream they must wait until they find a nearly identical body in the pools of wipes to write themselves. They are the Watchers, and they pay for their rejuvenation by never wholly perceiving the Dream and never wholly leaving the tactile world behind. They return, but never exactly as they left, even *the* Watcher."

Carly stared at Sonya, but Sonya kept her gaze on the elevator doors as the elevator came to a stop. The doors opened. The warning from Sonya was unnecessary.

Carly stepped forward and embraced the man standing before her.

"Endo," she whispered in his ear, "Endo, thank you."

He welcomed her into his arms. "You are my sonnet," he whispered in reply.

| 0 | 0 | 0 |

She couldn't sleep that night. Her excitement and relief colluded to wire her body with nervous energy—not that anyone would have known it looking at her, as she appeared nothing like the dynamo of righteous violence portrayed on Central's nets. Curled up in a large chair with a blanket wrapped around her, her intense gaze on the window wall before her, a cup of steaming tea in her hand, she seemed more an elderly lady-in-waiting. The thought amused her as it hovered at the periphery of her mind and conjured a small grin as she stared out at the bewildering immensity of Inward.

The city appeared to her more like a dream, a synaptic storm of a dream, full of lights in the darkness. They were draped in long chains in the form of towers and sweeping archways of buildings, the purpose of which she cared little to learn so as not to break the illusion. It surprised her as she stared at its cold beauty, viewing it no longer with just her body's eyes but from her new perspective, from the perspective of the Dream, and she had no doubt it was how the city was first envisioned by the Sleepers.

Should they have perceived a city in any different way? She knew they wouldn't, they couldn't, just as any city perceived and conceived through the Process would resemble Seven Hills, full of dull concrete block punctuated by neon storefronts. No, Seven Hills was pragmatism devoid of beauty, for beauty meant nothing in the mechanistic pursuit of the Process. Beauty was left to the Dream, where it could be envisioned and brought into being regardless of material expense, an illusion that could surpass any creation of the artisans of previous generations. Free from the confines of the body, beauty in the Dream was purified to the illusion it had always been, a form of expression without particular purpose or function, transcending the dilution of physical expression to material being.

There was beauty in the Dream, a beauty she was appreciating with the mounting moments. It reminded her of how she felt looking upon her children of the old Danfield apartment row. It was a rapture of sweet dissolution. She welcomed it, yet there was one anchor that remained, and she was not quite ready to dislodge its grasp.

She sipped her tea and slid her other hand from under the blanket to rub her forehead. With a blink she became conscious of her eyelids and the skin where she rubbed her forehead, drawing her gaze into the palm of her hand. Even though her room in the tower was darkened she could perceive every line, every curve, and every pore that formed the glove of skin to confine her existence.

The world is too big a place to be in one little body.

The thought lingered within her as she thought of her joy to see Endo and later her embarrassment to think that he had ever left her. It was true that a little knowledge was a dangerous thing. She had perceived many things walking into the data vault, but hadn't understood enough of that small slice to see the further questions those perceptions begged. She understood why Endo became so attached to her, why he had called her his sonnet, for he saw all those hidden things within her. Yet she understood as well their ways would be solitary ways, for their places in the Dream had much different realities. Endo's commitment to forfeit all lasting attachments, and therefore to be deathless in the Process, was not for her to follow. She found her commitment embodied in those children of Danfield row, her children, and with them an unquenchable drive to prevent her father's sins from repeating.

All those things, all those thoughts, she knew they were too much of the Dream to be contained in her body. It was the unseen purity of her potential that formed her sonnet for Endo, and he perceived in her the working of all the sonnets together, those fanciful words of emotional havoc. Raw and vibrant, they held something he had lost in all his lives, the pulse of life found in the sensation of passion.

Despite the wreckage of her childhood her past had failed to blind her to the fact that she could have a place in the Dream. She knew now what she had only felt as intuition in Seven Hills, that she would be leaving Inward to cross the wide ocean to the land of Central. Once there she would sleep, she would indeed become a Sleeper, and take her unique place in the Dream.

She listened to the echo of her thoughts and nodded. *I really am ready. I'll take my freedom from my past. Now what would the cows have to say about that?*

|0|0|0|

Sʜᴇ ᴡᴏᴋᴇ ɪɴ ᴛʜᴇ ᴄʜᴀɪʀ to find Endo standing by the window wall with his back to her. When she drew in her waking breath he turned and greeted her with a smile, then watched as she stretched her limbs from under the blanket. After she finished a long yawn he opened a hand to the table of her dining room.

"I'd bring you the food," he said, pausing to clear his throat, "except that I'm not fully adjusted to this body yet. I'm a centimeter and a half taller than I was before. Even the micro-sculpting of nano-bot plastic surgery can't account for that, so my reach is a little different. I'm knocking over a lot of things right now."

Carly returned his grin and lowered her feet to splay her toes on the cold floor. Her toes withdrew at once, so instead she reached out to him with an open hand and waited until he took it in his own. She closed her eyes as she closed her fingers around his. "You still feel the same to me when I look at you this way."

"The Dream has perceptions of its own."

She sat without saying anything for some time as she enjoyed the clasp of his hand. When she opened her eyes she found him standing beside her, still as stone, perhaps guessing at what she would ask, but she asked anyway. "What was it—is it—like, to come back?"

His grin faded. "It's not an easy thing to do."

She thought of Sonya and looked into his eyes. "Are there any memories left behind?"

"No. It's not the possession of a wipe anymore, this body. Whoever it was that gazed from these eyes forfeited the right to remain in here for one reason or another, despite being a predilector of some rank. Now this vessel is wholly mine, and it is only me that you see in these eyes, that you feel in these fingertips. When I return from the Dream to a body that body only knows itself as that of Endo Stutts, and none else." He studied her for a moment. "Why do you ask?"

"What's it like to join the Dream?"

He hesitated. "Different."

"Tell me. I want to know before I cross the ocean."

Endo sighed, looking down to her hand before running his fingers along her forearm. "You have no perception of your body once you give yourself over to the Dream. You won't hunger. You might crave the taste of certain food and drink, and the data threads can satisfy that, but your body will still need nutrition. You'll still need your body for times when you wish to take a respite from the Dream, but once in the Dream you won't be able to take care of your body's needs. We do it for you, and we do it very well. The life of a Sleeper can span many generations. The process, however, is invasive. Only a hardwired attachment can provide the data bandwidth Sleepers require to function in the Dream."

He took a deep breath and closed his eyes. "The night before you sleep we will be joined by some of the Sleepers on current respite. We will celebrate. There will be food, food like you have never known, and wine, fragrant red wine. After, you may have your privacy or not. The choice is yours. At the last you will lay yourself down and drink a glass of water left for you. You will be asleep when the process is handled. The final step will be to interface you with the data threads. You and the Dream will then be seamless."

"So what happens when I want to take a break from the Dream?"

"Time passes differently in the Dream. When you have the urge to wake it will seem a sudden thing within you, but the signs will be long coming to those monitoring your body. Your physical self will be carefully prepared for your waking, and then you'll be free to roam the tactile world until you return."

She tapped a finger on her lips as her thoughts churned. Without warning she turned to him. "Why do you use wipes instead of your own body?"

Endo stared at her. "I'm old—very old, older than the Dream itself in some ways, and older than all the current Sleepers, to be certain. Without the bodies of failed predilectors who became wipes I would be nothing more than a figment of the Dream. There's not enough left of my body to walk the land. I'm like a dream myself, in that way. Not real, but real enough. I think that's what drove me mad when I realized Sonya was a wipe. I was afraid I lost the difference between reality and illusion." His jaw clenched for a moment. "You're not the first to ask about my condition. It has troubled some in the past. Does it bother you?"

She said nothing.

He waited for a response.

"Endo?"

"Yes?"

"I'm not afraid." She shook her head at the creases of worry on his forehead. She smiled. "I'm ready for this, except for one thing."

"Your data drive. You're not the first to guard your drive. Many Sleepers do the same, waiting for some special moment to strike them, but you know that you must destroy it before you sleep, for your protection, yes?"

She looked to the window wall. "I know."

Her grip relaxed and he let her hand go, yet his hand lingered as if he still held her. He lowered his head, studying her from beneath his eyebrows. "Is there something else?"

She looked up at him with a plaintive gaze. "Thank you, Endo. I want you to know I thank you for what you did for me. I know what you're going to say, that it was the only way for you to follow, that the Dream made its demands of you for my sake, that the whole situation at the vault had already been carefully considered by the Dream. But the things you told me, the promises you made me, they helped bring me back from the edge."

He reached out to lay a hand on her cheek, careful to be gentle with the clumsiness of adjusting to his new body. "And I thank you, Carly."

"Because I'm your sonnet?"

"Because without our individual humanity there is no hope for collective humanity. The Dream brought me to you as much as it brought you to me. There were other watchers that could've been sent, watchers who imitate me, but the Dream sent me because it knew something about me I didn't know until I met you and saw within you. I was a pale soul. Meeting you brought me back from the edge, as you call it. Offering myself up to protect you held an irony all its own. I had to die to remember what it means to be alive. What I did at the data vault was nothing more than returning the favor you already afforded me."

He stepped closer, looming over her as his gaze bored into her. "Don't you see it yet, Carly, the reason for the acuity, the excess of your emotions since the data vault? It's not for me, not for Graham, not for your father, not for your Danfield children, but for all these things and for the fact that you now understand that they are but a glimpse of greater things. Perhaps it was because of your history with your father and what he was going to do to you, perhaps it was solely your genetic makeup, perhaps it was both, perhaps it was both and more, but it's this endless emotion that makes you what you are, that makes you so valuable, that makes your skin feel shrink-wrapped over you.

"You see, it's not so much that *you* are coming to the Dream, but that the Dream is calling to you. It needs you, because Central has lost what in times past was called a *soul*. Without it, space-faring humanity can't return to its home, to this bleak and blasted wreck of its home, to reconcile itself in unity. We need to restore our humanity. Only a child born of our worst crimes and suffering can awaken that spirit within the Dream, and let its vision take precedence over the Process. You are that child.

"So, you see, it needs you.

"Like me, it needs you."

| 0 | 0 | 0 |

TIME BEGAN TO BLUR.

The more she came to peace with her fulfillment as a Sleeper the more she found herself daydreaming. In the space of a blink she could lose track of where she was, what she was doing, and who was around her. Endo served as a steady companion, nudging her when her eyes glazed over. He guided her through the few days before they departed Inward.

Somewhere over the wide ocean she felt herself recede from the Dream and its endless whispers of shape, shadow-sight, and sound to hear the buffeting winds of a storm against the hull of her airship. She sat up in her bunk, her stateroom dark but for a small nightlight near the door. Her gaze rolled about the room to find her coat, her clothes, and the cabin's round portal window. She remembered standing by the portal with Endo's arms around her. They had watched the low clouds skate by before dissolving into each other beneath the sheets. With a rub of her forehead she slid her feet out of the bunk and looked over her shoulder.

Endo slept behind her, his mind silent. It was a good thing. The moment had arrived, she decided, and she wanted to be alone. She needed to be alone.

She got into her clothes. Disjointed from her past as she was, it felt no different than putting on a black ENDO shirt and her Patrol bodysuit. She gave her sleeves a good tug and smoothed her pants. She put on the jacket of her suit, buttoning it with care before pulling the fluted collar of shirt and suit up tight to her jaw. The suit was burgundy, a color she chose in the morning without understanding why. Standing in the dark recess of night, the deep color felt proper. She dipped her fingers into the glass of water by her bunk to smooth her hair back as she stuffed her feet into her low boots. Satisfied, she picked up her long coat and pulled it on.

Endo turned in his sleep. Taking care not to disturb him, she pulled up the blankets to keep him warm, leaned over, and kissed his forehead.

She made her way to the back of the airship and pushed open the heavy lock to step out on the ship's observation deck. Cold air whipped about her, but determination narrowed her eyes and drew up her shoulders as she paced to the high railing at the end of the deck. She looked into the impenetrable darkness. Somewhere beneath her the rolling surface of the ocean waited, a tumult of mighty waves over a smothering depth of eternal forgetfulness.

It felt perfect.

She reached into her coat pocket for the burden she carried. Her hand closed over the compact case of her data drive and held it tight as she stretched her arm over the railing.

Her hand tingled, perhaps from the cold, but she decided it was more from the call of what lay encapsulated on the drive. She was troubled for a moment, her forehead creasing as she listened to the whispers seeping from her past. It was doubt—a faint, insidious, gangrenous trace of doubt—but doubt nonetheless. Her memories began to flash. She thought of everything Endo had told her and the things she had perceived from the Dream. The doubt gained momentum, gained context and voice, and spoke to her.

She pondered her memories, the events of her life, and how they had combined against insurmountable odds to produce the unity of her present condition and moment. A duality opened within her, a contradictory duality she couldn't ignore. On one side, she saw her experiences as individual circumstances that led her willingly toward the Dream. On the other side, she saw those events manifesting from within the Process. Had she been seduced by the very conspiracy that had victimized and exploited her for its own end?

She opened her eyes to stare at her outstretched hand.

Was her childhood a work outside the Process, or was it the Process that had orchestrated her childhood? Had the Process tortured her to shape her into what the Dream needed of her, or had the Process been idle and innocent until the Dream came to free her? Was she self-predilecting her own self-predilection in some dizzying, maddening paradox of subjective realities and hindsight causality?

The cruelest lies are those closest to our vulnerabilities.

The doubt stirred up memories of her father, and then she understood. Her days of being a victim, of being manipulated, were over. She was Patrol, and Patrol doesn't back down.

"I won't listen to your angels this time," she thought aloud.

The sins of the past shall not repeat.

Her shoulders eased. She let her breath go as her fingers opened.

The data drive vanished into the darkness beneath her.

I've lost my past. I encompass time itself now, and I will write it—adapt to it—as I wish, because there's only one truth left for me.

I am the digital now.

ABOUT THE AUTHOR

AFTER MORE THAN TWENTY YEARS of hospital night shifts, Roland Allnach has witnessed life from a slightly different angle. He's been working to develop his writing career, drawing creatively from literary classics, history, and mythology.

His short stories, one of which was nominated for the Pushcart Prize, have appeared in many publications. His first anthology, *Remnant,* blending science fiction and speculative fiction, saw publication in 2010. In 2012 he followed with *Oddities & Entities,* a collection spanning the supernatural, paranormal, horror and speculative genres. His third book, *Prism,* published in 2014, follows a winding road through diverse genres and narrative forms as it explores the human experience.

Roland's books have received unanimous critical praise and have been honored with more than a dozen national book awards, including honors from National Indie Excellence, Foreword Reviews, Readers' Favorite, Feathered Quill Reviews and Pacific Book Review.

When not immersed in his imagination, Roland can be found at his website, rolandallnach.com, along with a wealth of information about his stories and experiences as an author. Writing aside, his joy in life is the time he spends with his family.

www.ingramcontent.com/pod-product-compliance
Lightning Source LLC
Chambersburg PA
CBHW060347260626
47160CB00006B/2233